IGNITE: LIGHTING OF DREAMS

VIEN CHAU

IGNITE

LIGHTING OF DREAMS

BOOK ONE

To my precious boy, Leonardo, my miracle Kayla,
&
My brave Nicholas.
Daddy loves you all, and you can be whatever you want in life.
Put your mind to it, push your undefeated heart and undying will. Work smart.

Thank you to my beautiful wife, Jamie,
My world and love for giving me the opportunity to write Ignite. Love you!

TABLE OF CONTENT

Ourania World Map

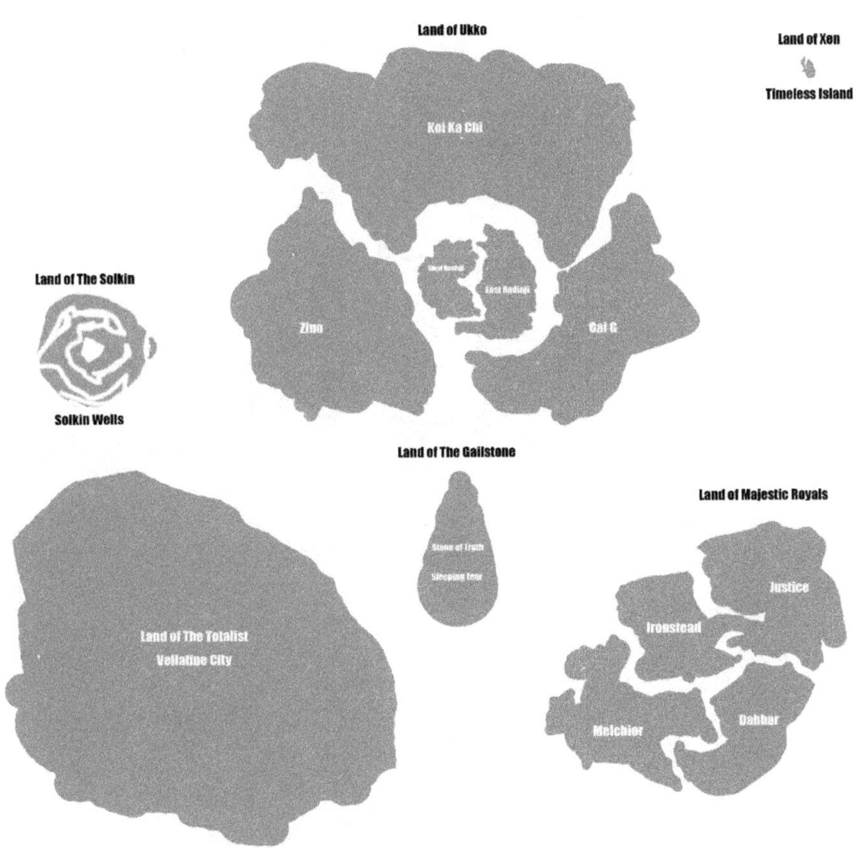

Vellatine City Top View

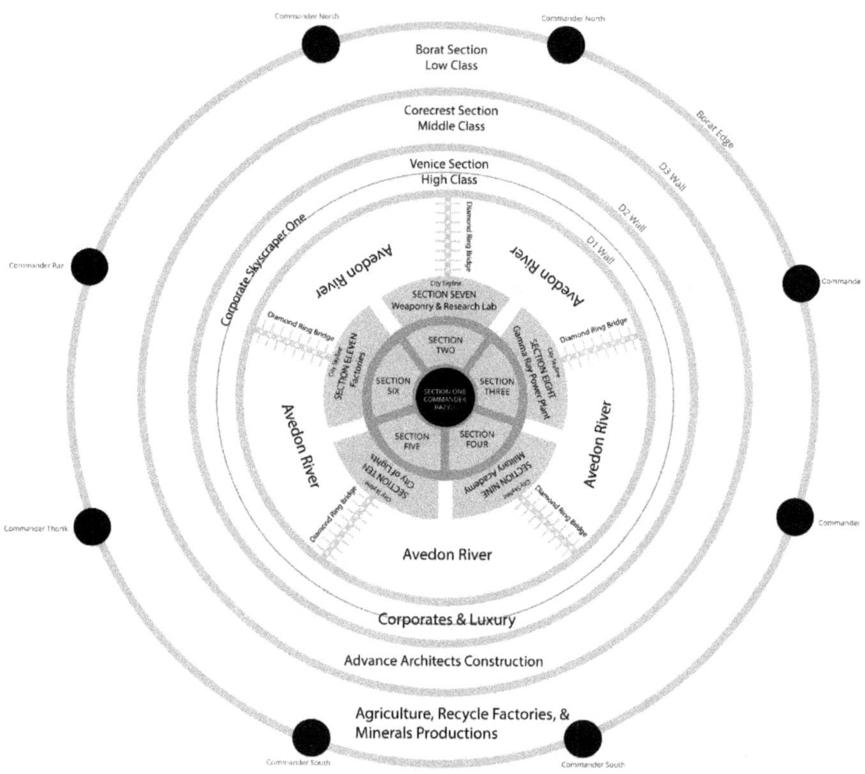

Chapter One
Viggo Van Hunt

Viggo's back rested painfully against the hard dirt ground. He stared at the black smoke rising across the sky, the result of destruction and deaths around him as bullets zipped over him. He could feel his blood throbbing vigorously in his heart. The beats of life dance rhythmically, skip, stumble, and started to fade within him. A deafening cry rang through his ringing ears.

"Viggo!"

It sounded like Rain, the love of his life. She threw herself over him and shielded him from the explosion beside them. She clung onto him tightly as they rolled off into the ditch. Dirt and debris hail down on her. The ditch provided a moment of cover from the bullets and fighting above. Rain tilted her head with unbearable pain; her right side took the most hit from the blast, but the adrenaline pumping through her body blocked the pain and provided a moment of focus.

She lifted Viggo's head and gazed at his soaked bloody clothing. Her voice cracked on her trembling lips.

"Vi...ggo..."

He opened his eyes as breathing became harder and harder through his mouth, and he instinctively grabbed her hand. Her warmth felt nice against his cold hands as he confessed his love to her, but the only sound was blood bubbling and spewing out.

"No, no, no!" cried Rain as tears streamed uncontrollably.

Her hand quickly wiped the blood off his mouth. He could feel her teardrops landing on his cheeks. Rain cried and screamed with a frantic looks, which saddened him as he watched her in slow motion, and her voice faded away. He held her bloody hand tightly, but his strength slipped from him. The pain numbed, drowsiness flooded his mind, and his body felt light as though it floated upward. It felt like a dream, and his hand fell to the ground. He lay lifeless in her arms.

"Viggo!"

Sewage water splashed apart from the leather boots racing across, echoing through the dimmed sewer tunnels of Vellatine City. Two skinny teenage boys, Viggo Van Hunt and Leaf Hunt, hurried along the familiar path. Their light brown eyes gleamed with joy. Viggo, seventeen years old, with a half-up ponytail, his hair matched the color of his brown and dirty leather boots. His waterproof fanny pack hung sideways around his empty stomach, partially concealed under his scruffy black hooded cloak. Following Viggo was Leaf, eleven years old with shoulder-length dirty blond hair. His loose clothing were handed down from Viggo and were ripped to fit his scrawny body. His black hooded cloak reached down to his boots, a generous fit that offered extra room for stolen goods and protection against the cold winds of the impending winter night.

"How many shins do you think we'll get this time, brother?" Leaf questioned.

Viggo leaped over the sewer rats and shouted, "Enough for us to eat good today!"

Leaf's eyes light up, "Even half of an apple?"

"A whole fresh apple this time and more!" Viggo replied, laughing.

"Really?!" His eyes widen.

Their faces lit up brighter and brighter as they reached the end of the sewer tunnel. Small brown birds flew over the cluttered tin can buildings of Section 12 below. Smelly, greenish-brown water rushed off the edge and plummeted 3,000 feet into the river, slithering through the heart of the rusty small town. Children played by the river's edge while women washed their clothes and dishes further downstream. A broken-down slum lay at the foothill of a massive, round, flattop mountain—a perfect, solid foundation for the glorious Vellatine City above.

Viggo and Leaf breathed in the crisp, cold morning air. The scent didn't bother Leaf; he giggled and laughed at the white smoke as he exhaled it from his warm breath.

Viggo looked at Leaf with a gentle smile.

His smile faded away as Section 12 crept into view below. Black smoke crawled out of old, rusted, cracked pipes. Rundown tin buildings piled on top of each other and stood side by side. The trash-filled alleyways were carved crookedly like a stick ran through the mud.

There was one main street, the Street Market, at the center of Section 12, where every nation's criminals found refuge in this false haven. From the exiled Majestic Royals warriors to the Gailstone giant Gargoyles, the ruthless Ukko Ninja, and the Totalist criminal of Vellatine City. Like any unwanted beings, they were welcomed and could ease themselves into this chaotic realm of unlawfulness. The usual morning hustle for goods before the dead of night arrived was a daily ritual. Even the most vicious knew to tread with caution when nightfall arrived.

A majestic royal shopkeeper proudly showcases colorful hand-sewn clothing, rugs, and any fabrics wanderers might need. At the back of the shop, an unclaimed child labored away with needle and thread. Many abandon youths would join the low-ranking gang known as the Good-Looking Boys or GLB, who seek a sense of family or protection. However, very few managed to make it pass their fourth birthday.

A hefty gargoyle butcher stood at the meat stand, chopping away at some lean, bony meat with his massive, rusty cleaver. The sheer size of the cleaver reflected the morning sun's rays. Viggo glanced away from its reflection and looked up toward the sky. The deep orange glow seamlessly merged with the morning daylight. Cotton candy clouds drifted above the semi-transparent Dome Shield of the Totalist, enveloping the entire country.

The Dome Shield was engineered using water from the surrounding Grand Ocean. The water could be manipulated, solidifying into an impenetrable barrier by infusing electrically charged particles with intense compression. The shield could be rendered dense enough to withstand external assaults and repaired by reinforcing it with additional water to solidify its structure.

The Dome Shield liquefied, opening a circular exit for the large Totalist Mothership fleet and Hell Raptor helicopters. These Motherships, the second largest in the air fleet, are equipped with electromagnetic pulse defense, electric force shields, lasers, and missile cannons. They carried a variety of fighter jets, Totalist marines, and tanks.

The Hell Raptor boasted four foldable arms, each equipped with a triple-blade rotor, rendering it virtually unrivaled in maneuverability and speed. Its midsection was fortified with detachable iron armor and housed heavy stationary machine guns on both sides. During battle mode, the interior side chairs automatically rotated, moved outward, and positioned themselves in front of the machine guns, ready for combat.

Viggo observed as the Totalist Air Fleets flew passed the Vellatine Forest and out of the protective Dome Shield and remarked, "Over the past three days, they've been increasingly sending them out."

"What do you think they are doing, brother?"

"Who knows? Those Totalist snakes are likely scheming again. Their Hell Raptor crashed in the Vellatine Forest years ago; it might still be rusting away. We should worry about ourselves and find a way out of this hellish pit-hole."

Leaf looked at Viggo, "I don't mind where we are, brother, as long as we're together. I like smelling the fresh air and seeing the Vellatine Forest every morning like this. It makes me happy."

Viggo made a stinky face and said, "I don't know about the fresh part."

He pulled a cracked, old, tarnished silver platter from his undershirt and added, "We've put in a lot of effort over these past few nights. This should get us something good to eat and maybe even a little extra for savings!"

"I'm fine with sharing an apple with you, brother."

Viggo tucked the silver platter away, disregarded his comment, and surveyed the Street Market. He spotted Rain's golden blond hair, tied up like a chicken tail, browsing through items with her distinctive brown teddy bear backpack at the store. She sported a petite, faded, snug blue shirt adorned with colors sprayed across 'No Rules!' graffiti just above her belly button. A thick black metal belt encircled her edgy black pants, and she wore pink punk combat boots with silver metal trim.

Viggo sighed, smiled naturally, and asked, "Ready?"

Leaf focused on a black wire attached to the tunnel's side, trailing down to the tin rooftop, and responded with determination, "I'm going to beat you this time, brother."

Viggo laughed, "We'll see, baby turtle."

Leaf pulled a cloth from his back pocket, hoisted his pants, and swung it over the wire before jumping off.

Below, Viggo gazed at the colossal, antiquated sewerage pipes embedded in the cliff wall—some shattered, others jutting from the rocks. He observed Leaf sliding down, a smirk playing on his lips. With a swift motion, Viggo launched himself off the tunnel ledge, effortlessly gliding sideways down the protruding pipes. He leaped from rock to rock, descending rapidly along the pipelines. Leaf lagged as Viggo surged passed him, jumping to a graceful landing atop a tin roof, while maintaining his momentum and darted towards the opposite side at an angle. Reaching the ledge, he scanned the area in search of Rain.

She was in the mechanical shop arguing with the owner. Viggo shifted his attention to the metalware store across the street, and Leaf landed beside him.

"How is it possible? Every time!" Leaf exclaimed; his voice tinged with disbelief.

"It's called skill," Viggo replied, a twinkle of amusement in his eye.

"Right now, you're as light as a feather. But once you've packed on some fat and muscle, you'll be speeding through like never before."

Leaf patted his skinny stomach.

Viggo leaped off the tin roof, seized the rope spanning the two buildings, and skillfully traversed his way to the opposite side of the street.

"I'm gonna be strong like brother one day," Leaf said confidently.

Viggo released the rope and landed beside an old Majestic Royal woman, who held a basket filled with red roses adorned with yellow pistils. Unaware of Viggo's presence, she inspected some antique metalware plates and bowls. Meanwhile, Leaf alighted on the tin roof, flattening himself against its surface, and peered over the edge to observe from above.

Viggo shouted, "Hey, old man! How much for this?"

Viggo pulled out the cracked silver platter, tossed it onto the table, and leaned on a metal pole.

Mr. Sill, with short gray hair, put on his eyeglasses and adjusted them slowly, "Oh, hello, boys..."

Viggo interrupted Mr. Sill, "It's not boys, old man; it's Viggo Van Hunt and Leaf!"

Mr. Sill avoided eye contact with him, "It's not old man, boy."

"Alright, pops. How many shins are you offering?"

Mr. Sill examined the platter, "I'm not your pops," and banged it against the table.

"Woah! Woah! Woah! Gentle with that old man! It's priceless; it exudes a sense of royalty! Can't you see?"

"Two shins," Mr. Sill said.

"Two shins? Pops, you should be donning another pair of glasses."

Viggo walked over to Mr. Sill and put his arm around his shoulder, "You're not looking at it the right way!"

Mr. Sill pushed Viggo's arm off his shoulder.

Viggo removed his eyeglasses, blew hot breath onto the lenses, and vigorously cleaned them against his dirty brown shirt. Then, he pointed at the dents on the platter with the glasses. "You have to pay attention to the intricate details. It's essential, examining the craftsmanship, the quality of the silver metal, and even the minutiae of dents resulting from scuffles by the royal family during dinners!"

Mr. Sill scrutinized it closely, squinting as he turned it around to inspect other areas.

"This enduring legacy of a silver platter has been passed down by the Royal Family for many generations." Viggo pointed at the cracks on the platter with the glasses. "Notice here, the fracture along the side? It was Prince Jaden Knight, scion of the Royal Family and destined heir to the throne, who inadvertently caused it during his infancy!"

The old Majestic Royal woman leaned in closer to examine it.

"I'm endeavoring to assist you, Mr. Sill, by offering rare, pristine, high-quality products—this item is akin to a cherished heirloom within a royal family, its value immeasurable," Viggo said confidently, handed Mr. Sill's eyeglasses back, and leaned toward the old Majestic Royal woman. "Crafting for your esteemed clientele, filled with admiration and appreciation!"

The old lady grew bashful and let out a giggle.

Mr. Sill squinted as he examined the crack.

Viggo turned to the old lady and whispered, "It's worth at least ten shins, my lady! However, considering the exquisite nature of your beauty...." Viggo gazed at her aged, round face, filled with wrinkles, warts, and freckles. Her mouth stretched into a broad smile, revealing her sparse, yellowed teeth.

Viggo quickly glanced down and noticed her slippers. "Wearing slippers that match your silver hair, my lady, would elevate your appearance to that of the Queen of Section 12!"

The old lady winked at Viggo as he noticed a large black wart on her earlobe, adorned with a couple of long, white, curly hairs.

"Gegegee... You strike me as an earnest young lad. Would you consider three shins for it?"

Viggo scratched his head, "Your adept negotiation skills, honed over centuries, make you an exceptionally formidable bargainer."

The old lady grew increasingly bashful, "Gegege... oh stop. You're such a smooth talker." She leaned toward Viggo and squeezed his arm, "And what a strong young man!"

Chills ran down Viggo's and Mr. Sill's spines as Leaf came crashing down next to them.

Viggo quickly pointed at a bunch of roses, "Uhhh... What variety of roses are those?"

"These are Rose Du Pare, which means Rose of Unity, encapsulates the essence of their beauty." The old lady reached into her purse, took out three shins, and added, "What if I added half of them to my three shins?"

Viggo's hand grabbed the three shins and took half of Rose Du Pare.

"Your negotiating prowess surpasses any I've encountered, my young lady, sealing the deal!"

Leaf pulled a ripped and tattered newspaper from his pocket, "Mr. Sill, here's the Venice Glam Newspaper you wanted."

"Thank you, Leaf. If only Viggo were more like you, simple and sweet, instead of using all these big words. He probably don't even know what they mean."

Viggo laughed and placed the roses in his fanny pack.

"What are you talking about, old man? I'm already too sweet! I will give you a toothache if I'm any sweeter! When we leave this hell pit one day, you'll miss us! So, remember the name. Viggo Van Hunt!"

Leaf pulled his pants a bit and called out loudly, "Yeah! And Leaf too... please."

They sprinted down the muddy street, shouting, "Thank you, Lady!"

❖

Leaf ran to the front of the pet shop and pointed at the three hamsters in the cage, "Brother, look at those furries!"

A hamster was racing on a loose, rusty metal wheel, making a constant squeaky noise. Another hamster sat at the food bowl, painfully squeezing a giant seed into its stuffed mouth. The last hamster had its tongue in the water bowl, drinking lazily.

"Can I have one, brother!" Leaf asked excitedly.

Viggo leaned down and examined them briefly before glancing at the price sign.

'Three Shins for One Happy Hamster.'

Viggo sighed, "I don't know. Their life sure looked better than ours. Free home, daily meals, exercise, and no worries."

Leaf softly said, "I can use the three shins I saved in my tin box. Can I have one brother?"

"Since when you have had three shins saved?"

"Whenever you give me an extra shin, I put it in my secret hiding spot."

Viggo turned to Leaf, "You have a secret hiding spot? Where?"

"It won't be a secret if I told you, brother. Can I have one, please?" Leaf eyes begged.

Viggo laughed and stood up, "Sorry, Leaf. Save your shins. We would only make its life worse."

Leaf gazed sadly at the hamsters, acknowledging the truth in Viggo's words.

They trudged along the muddy street and paused at the fat Gargoyle Butcher stand.

A short, slender, hunchbacked old man named Slitter Clyde, a low scammer Totalist criminal. His long, crooked nose and saggy chin glared at the lean meat as the Gargoyle Butcher chopped at it. "A small piece of meat is perfect for a light meal for someone like me."

The Gargoyle Butcher paused, casting a glance at him.

"I will be acquiring some shins next week." Slitter Clyde said, his dentures sliding side to side as he attempted to smile.

"No! You owe three silver shins four months ago!" Gargoyle Butcher bellowed as his massive cleaver cleaved through the bone.

"I'll pay you back. I promise! The Lighting of Dreams is coming! Won't you allow this elderly gentleman to savor a small portion of succulent meat during the welcoming ceremony and witness the four great nations fighting for the title of Ourania World Champion?"

"No."

"You should seize the opportunity, as such events occur only once a century, and your being will be there."

"Any nonsense, you'll be on a meat rack!" Gargoyle Butcher exclaimed as he crushed the bone with his hefty cleaver.

Slitter Clyde was startled, causing his fake, crooked smile to droop. He snarled at Gargoyle Butcher, "Curse you! You rotund old meat!" and shoved Viggo and Leaf aside as he strode away.

"Brother, have you heard about the Lighting of Dreams? I wonder if we can make it to the Welcome Ceremony?" Leaf asked.

"Hence the word dreams—I wouldn't hold my breath for it." Viggo's gaze fixated on the tender, lean meat, eliciting a low rumble from his stomach.

'Exclusive Offer: Get Three Ounces of Meat for Just Fifteen Shins.' Written on a sign.

"Excuse me, mister Gargoyle, could you please provide the price for one ounce?" Viggo asked.

"Eight."

Viggo gripped the three shins and looked at the meat.

Leaf tugged on Viggo's arm and smiled at him. Viggo let out a deep breath, and they continued their way. They stopped at the corner of an alley near the Bun Maker cart.

"Are those rose pu par for Rain?" Leaf asked.

Viggo cleared his throat, "It's Rose Du Pare, but of course!" and smiled.

He opened his palm, counted the shins with his finger, and

distributed them, "One for you and one for me."

He elevated the final one, "And this will be for us. Come on!"

They hurried up to the Bun Maker cart, which featured a digital rotating image of fresh fruits alongside a hot, steamy, plain white bun.

"Hey, Pops! How much for one of your finest apples?" Viggo asked.

"Half shin," Bun Maker said with a stone-cold monotone.

Viggo glanced around the cart and observed the rotating white bun hologram. Leaf peered through the glass of the cart and took a deep breath. Viggo noticed the Bun Maker glaring at Leaf, who had pressed his face and mouth against the cart's glass.

Viggo cleared his throat. "How about including one of your most famous steamed buns in our order, sir? Can you give us a good deal?"

The Bun Maker glanced briefly at Viggo before speaking, "Bun two shins."

Viggo put one shin on the cart, withdrawing the other from his fanny pack, and stared at his final hard-earned shin.

Leaf looked at Viggo, "Brother, we don't have to..."

"Both for two shins," The Bun Maker suddenly interrupted.

Viggo placed it on the cart.

The Bun Maker grabbed an apple from the basket and placed it on the cart. A fly was crawling around it.

"Hey, pops. It doesn't look fresh."

The Bun Maker slammed his hand on the cart, and the fly flew away. "Fresh."

Leaf reached for the apple, his fingers closed around it, feeling its weight before he rubbed it against his shirt, "Thank you, Mister!"

He ignored Leaf, opened the lid, and steam rushed out. The Bun Maker handed one steaming bun to Viggo. Leaf's eyes widened, and he gave a big smile.

Viggo handed the steaming bun to Leaf and grabbed his apple.

"We can share this, brother!"

"Remember, you need to fatten up to surpass my speed?" Viggo ruffled his hair.

Leaf waved goodbye to the Bun Maker and hastily pulled up his pants as they dashed to the end of the street. The Bun Maker showed no appreciation or emotion. They settled on the ground in a less muddy area and leaned against the wall. Leaf tore the bun in half and passed it to Viggo. Steam rose from the plain white bun; its sweet aroma made their mouths water.

"I said, it's for you. If you don't want it, I will eat it all!" Viggo bit into his apple and added with a mouthful, "Fruit good for ya, you know? It makes you good-looking like me."

He took another sizable bite, attempting to disregard the enticing sweet aroma.

Leaf held both halves of the torn buns in his hands, a smile playing on his lips as he carefully placed one half on his left leg. He retrieved an old rag from his back pocket, gently wrapping the remaining half before tucking it away.

With both hands, he raised the other half to his nose.

He took a deep breath, "It's hot and smells so..."

Two mud balls splattered onto Leaf's face, and a third landed near his feet. The dirty bun flew out of his hand and fell onto the ground. Leaf was frozen in shock as the mud slid off his face.

Three GLB gangs pointed and laughed at him from the street. Viggo looked up fiercely and recognized the teen called Loose Tooth, who was thin and tall with a loose tooth hanging on for dear life. Dusty was short and chubby, with his belly jiggling as he laughed. Crick, the oldest of the three, was blind in one eye and possessed less intelligence than the apple in Viggo's hand. They all wore tattered and ripped clothing without a shin to their name.

"Hahaha! Mud Face!" Loose Tooth yelled from the street as his tooth swayed back and forth.

Viggo leaped up in fury and gave chase. They sprinted down the street, shoving objects and people aside, causing chaos. Viggo placed his half-eaten apple in his fanny pack and retrieved a small red package as he pursued them. They abruptly veered right, disappearing into the dimly lit alleyway at the back.

Leaf slowly looked up to where Viggo sat, and his lips trembled.

The shady, filthy alleyway was hidden from the bustling Street Market. Overfilled trash bins lined the wall, and giant rats scavenged around them. The GLB gang halted at the alley's end, turning to face Viggo.

Loose Tooth spit on the ground, "Look who just crawled in, Vrat."

The three GLB gang members laughed as Viggo approached them, his fist clenched.

"Where's your mud face frien…"

Viggo leaped forward and rubbed red pepper powder all over Loose Tooth's face.

Loose Tooth fell to the ground, clutching his face, and screamed, "It burns!"

Dusty grabbed Viggo from behind as Crick sprinted toward him. Viggo thrust his arm out, two fingers spread, aiming to poke his assailant's eyes. However, Crick halted just inches from his outstretched hand and bit down on his fingers.

"Aaahhhh!" Screamed Viggo as he struggled to pull his fingers out with all his might.

Dusty laughed upon hearing Viggo scream in pain. Crick's face reddened as sweat rolled down the side of his face, and he opened his mouth with his tongue sticking out, "Hot! Hot!! Hot!!!"

Viggo's arm retracted with great force, elbowing Dusty in the face and knocking him to the ground. Viggo stumbled back slightly, feeling his fingers throb with pain.

"If you do that again to Leaf, I will make sure none of you ever stand up again! Tell Big B to leave us alone, or he will get what's coming for him!"

The three GLB gangs were on the ground, visibly frightened.

Viggo turned around; a wooden board shattered against the left side of his face before clattering to the ground. Four imposing GLB members loomed over him.

Big B, the leader of the GLB gang, was slightly older than Viggo. His large, round face, reminiscent of a bulldog, featured a stubby nose, long droopy cheeks, and round brown eyes, all of which bore down on Viggo.

Big B dropped the half-broken board, "You like to play dirty, huh? Now, what do you want to tell me? What's coming?"

Viggo attempted to look up as his left squinty eye quickly swelled. He could scarcely discern the four blurry figures amidst the blood trickling down the side of his head.

"What are you looking at, Vrat? I ruled Section 12! Know your place before you lose your face!"

Big B wore a frayed black denim jacket and pants, spiky gloves, and a brown chain necklace around his thick neck. His rugged boot stomped straight down onto Viggo's bloody nose, pushing it deep into the mud. Viggo violently shook his head, gasping for air as he coughed out bloody mud.

"You don't mess with the Good-Looking Boys!" Big B gave a stern warning.

Guth took Viggo's fanny pack, removed the roses, and examined it with a puzzled expression. Big B took the fanny pack from him and emptied its contents. Random items, powders, small traps, and a half-eaten apple spilled out.

"All useless junk! Not even one shin?!" Big B questioned angrily.

Guth ripped the red rose petals off the stem one by one, crumbling them onto Viggo's muddy, bloodied face. Viggo painfully reached for them.

"Oh look, he has a soft side." Guth teased.

Big B viciously kicked Viggo's stomach with his boot. "Let's see how soft he is!"

They laughed and continued kicking his head and body until he blacked out.

The bustling chaos of the Street Market gradually subsided, and people dispersed and crawled back to their so-called homes, where it all started.

The wearying two suns descended swiftly after their arduous journey across the sky. Shop owners disposed of their trash in the muddy streets, providing sustenance for the nocturnal scavengers, who feasted and hunted for feasible treasures.

Leaf went down the Street Market, pausing at each establishment to inquire about Viggo's whereabouts. However, he was met with dismissive gestures as darkness began to burn away the horizon. Half of Zephaniah's colossal world, the largest of all nine planets, loomed in the sky, signaling the onset of nightfall. Wooden doors were promptly shut and secured with multiple locks. Wealthier vendors reinforced their shops with the clatter of rusty gates and additional locks for added protection.

Despite his fatigue and sense of helplessness, Leaf continued, persistently knocking on door after door in search of Viggo.

The street emptied, and the market finally closed. Leaf pulled up his pants and walked into the middle of the road. A hand grabbed his shoulder, and he turned around, excitement coursing through him, "Brother!"

Rain leaned forward, twisting his ear.

"Ooowww!! Ooowww!"

She leaned over, one hand on her hip, and stared at him with stunning blue eyes that captivated the breath of those who gazed into them for too long. Her dirty, greasy blond hair obscured some of the smudges on her face. Her small, pointy nose and light pink lips added to her charm. Upon closer inspection, her natural beauty surpassed even the highest standards, reminiscent of the legendary Queen Glory of Vellatine City in the Totalist Federation.

"Why are you still out on the street? Do you not notice the suns setting? Have you forgotten that the dangerous bogeyman comes out at night? Where's your brother?"

Leaf pressed his hands to his ear and pushed her grip away. Numerous questions swirled in his mind, yet none seemed to penetrate his thoughts; all he could focus on was Viggo.

"Have you seen Viggo?"

"Why isn't he here to keep an eye on you? He's being incredibly irresponsible. I can sense it just from how he looks at me," Rain stood up, her gaze sweeping the area in search of Viggo.

"I think he likes you."

An image of Viggo with big, wet, kissy, plush lips entered Rain's thoughts, and instant chills ran down her back, "Eewww! You mean VGOOO?"

Leaf laughed.

"Not in a million years!" Rain shouted.

She noticed a couple of shady figures lurking in the corner, watching them.

"It's getting dark. Let's get out of here."

Rain grabbed his hand and started walking while Leaf pulled up his pants with one hand.

"But I have to look for brother!"

"He will know where to find you."

Chapter Two
Roldin The Dark Solkin

A yellow light bulb hung above the two wooden tables cluttered with tools, parts, and half-built objects. Mr. Hairo wore a dirty, brownish-white lab coat, hunched over the table, asleep. He often grew tired from working late into the night on small mechanical parts. In his hand rested a metering tool while a magnifying glass headband adorned his snow-white, oily hair. His once plump, rosy, red cheeks had grown pale and saggy, framing his unmaintained white beard. He snored softly through his long, pointy nose.

The rusty metal front door swung wide open, banging against the tin can wall.

Rain burst in and screamed, "I'm home, Daddy!"

She ran to Mr. Hairo and wrapped her arms around his shoulders as he jolted awake, trying to figure out what had happened suddenly.

He choked a bit and gently patted her arm as he sat up, "Oh, hello, dear," and calmly asked, "Rain, do you know why I gave you that name?"

Rain hugged Mr. Hairo tightly and softly said, "It signifies tranquility and elegance."

"Yes... Yes, you got half of it right." Mr. Hairo chuckled.

Rain glanced at the objects on the table, "Are you linking the ion exchange to the reverse photon receptor?"

"After completion, you can attach it to your new pet."

Rain reached into her teddy bear backpack and said, "Here's the level five hydro accelerator you wanted, Daddy. Mr. Tumber refused to offer any discounts and spent most of the day arguing with me."

Rain placed the hydro accelerator on her table.

"He's simply trying to earn a living, Rain, just like everyone else. Please ensure the accelerator is stored safely away."

Rain leaped onto her chair and spun around, "Yeah, but we've already made so many purchases from him."

"If someone offers you a discount, it's a gesture of kindness from their heart, not an obligation. It's best not to take it if they were forced to be given," Mr. Hairo calmly explained.

"I know!" Rain turned her chair to Leaf, "Daddy, remember Leaf? He's one of the kids I mentioned before."

Leaf stood timidly in the corner and spoke, "Hello, sir."

Mr. Hairo turned and glanced at him, "Leaf? Such a unique name."

Leaf softly said, "I picked it myself."

"It's a very simple name." Mr. Hairo added.

Leaf nodded and replied, "Yeah! It means simple and free."

"Free... Ah, yes, now I understand why it's such a fantastic name."

Mr. Hairo noticed Leaf's slender face as he smiled, "Have you eaten anything yet?"

Leaf's stomach emitted a low growl.

"Did you buy any groceries from the market, Rain?"

Rain spun around in her chair, "No, I didn't have enough shins or time, but there should be some leftovers from yesterday. I'll reheat them."

She rose and made her way toward the kitchen in the back.

"Thank you, dear." Mr. Hairo turned back to Leaf and inquired, "How old are you, Leaf?"

"I'm eleven, sir."

"Eleven? Well, you're nearly grown up."

"My brother, Viggo is seventeen and he's much bigger than me."

"Yes! I remember the name Viggo. Rain talked a bit about him. How come he's not with you?"

Leaf paused briefly, then responded with a tinge of sorrow, "All I remember... He was next to me, and I was looking at the bun... and when I looked up, he was gone."

"Don't worry, Leaf. He might already be on his way right now. You're welcome to stay as long as you want." Mr. Hairo said warmly, brightening the mood.

Leaf looked up, shocked by his kindness and the gentleness in his voice. "Thank you, sir."

Mr. Hairo rose from his half-torn, cushioned chair and wiped down the mechanical parts. "How did you find yourself in Section 12? Are your parents around?"

"My brother has always cared for me ever since I can remember."

"He appears to be an extraordinary individual."

"Yeah! I want to be just like him when I grow up!"

"There aren't many men out here who would stand up for individuals like us anymore and strive to rectify injustices. I am hopeful the next generation of young men can shape Ourania World into a more equitable society," Mr. Hairo reflected, pausing to direct his gaze toward Leaf. "There will come a moment when your brother needs you most. When that time arrives, stand by his side. Take care of each other and extend your watchfulness to those in your midst."

"Umm... yes, sir," Leaf said, but he was unsure what Mr. Hairo had said.

"You may address me as Mr. Hairo."

"Yes, Mr. Hairo, sir," Leaf said uncomfortably.

"Food ready!" Rain shouted from the kitchen.

"Mmm... That sounds good. Hopefully, it still taste good," Mr. Hairo winked as he carefully placed the parts down. "I believe you have the potential to become a remarkable individual, Leaf."

A newfound sense of elation, unfamiliar yet invigorating, enveloped him. Curious about his potential for greatness, he smiled and hoisted his pants, following Mr. Hairo into the kitchen.

A third of Zephaniah's world magnificently shone in the night sky beside its two moons. The chilled fog blanketed Section 12, its frosted blue rays illuminating the silent, eerie streets and alleyways. The semi-romantic rays painted the alleyway beautifully, gently touching the overfilled trash bins infested with giant rats. In the darkness, a soft sob could be faintly heard.

Rats crawled over Viggo's body, sniffing, biting into his black cloak, and licking the moist blood off his head. Multiple rats hastily fought over the half-eaten apple, a rare delight. A faint sob echoed again, a bit louder and closer. Viggo slowly awakens, groaning from the pain stretching from his head down to his legs. Unafraid, he grabbed the rat, which clung tight to his cloak, and tossed it away as it squealed loudly like a piglet. Pushing himself up from the cold, muddy ground, he found his left eye swollen shut and blood on the side of his mouth. He wiped it off with the back of his hand, a great pain stunned the whole side of his head, reminiscent of the common physical pains of his childhood. It was nothing new but a nuisance. Ignoring it, he swept his arms around, fanning the fog and rats away, then picked up his fanny pack to check inside.

Empty.

He sat silently under the frosted blue rays, illuminated by their glow, surrounded by his broken traps, scattered pepper powders, a small remaining piece of his apple core, and the crushed rose petals for Rain. His fingers moved along the ripped, muddy red petal, feeling the weight of everything he had worked so hard for.

Ruin.

A familiar thought of failure echoed in his mind, and overwhelming sadness filled his heart.

Angered, he brushed it off, determined to push through. He clenched his mouth, attempting to hold back the tears, yet they streaked down his cheeks unabated. With a quick swipe, he cleared them away, fastened his fanny pack securely, and retrieved the still-functional traps and unopened powder bags, stashing them back into his pockets and fanny pack. A faint sob echoed from behind, perking his ears up. He pivoted, peering into the darkness, his senses heightened.

A blue translucent child emerged into view. A lost soul of the dead stood before him, softly weeping.

This can't be real, Viggo thought.

He had heard scary tales about souls that roamed at night but had never seen one. Slowly, he rose from his spot and cautiously retreated toward the alleyway entrance. Two heavy metal chains, each adorned with sharp scythes, plummeted into the mud, their clang resonating through the alleyway entrance as they struck the hard ground.

Viggo halted, pivoting to face the alley once more as a gust of fog swept his path and dispersed. The scythes scraped against the ground with sluggish reluctance. Before him stood a dark, mystical figure clad in black armor plates and a billowing cloak, exuding an eerie blue aura. Proudly, the figure stood, face obscured, eyes ablaze with flaming blue intensity.

A deep sound resonated, "After a long search, I've finally found you, little soul! I believe you possess something I've seek."

The little soul trembled in fear, retreating a few cautious steps.

"Now, fetch me that rare Stone Rune you possess, or must I resort to more forceful means? Slicing you apart?" The Dark Mystic Figure voiced below his breath.

"Are you another lost soul from the beyond?" Viggo inquired, curiosity evident in his tone.

"What do we have here? A Totalist scrub venturing out past dusk?"

Viggo remained silent.

"Many inquisitive souls like yours, along with countless others, have mysteriously disappeared in the dead of night, never to be seen again. If you're not cautious, the specter of the bogeyman might just devour your very soul!" The Dark Mystic Figure laughed.

"I'm not scared of the bogeyman," Viggo declared.

"You should always be scared."

His chains extended, swirling in a circular pattern as he swung them. The impact tore through the ground, igniting sparks and flames that burst onto the scythes.

"Fear can serve as a valuable companion, keeping one alert, and a slither chance of survival."

"I cannot afford the luxury of fear." Viggo fearlessly declared.

The Dark Mystic Figure became excited, and the blue energy intensified, "Ah, it appears tonight holds promise, a fortuitous alignment of two souls for our shared pursuit. Approach me now and deliver unto me that Stone Rune!"

Little Soul backed into the trash bin with nowhere to go or hide.

Viggo whispered from the side, "When you spot an opening. Run."

Little Soul looked up at Viggo, surprised by what he heard.

Viggo stepped forward, positioning himself before Little Soul, and shouted, "Why don't you pick on someone your size, ten times bigger and less ugly!"

"Quite the proclamation from one who resides in the depths of Section 12. For your audacious yet perhaps misguided courage, I shall consume you to merge with me, becoming one with the most esteemed Solkin to emerge from the depths of the Solkin Well!"

"And who might you be?" Viggo inquired.

"Roldin of the Dark Solkin." Roldin lifted his head.

"Pssh, more like rolling in the dirt. Why do big, ugly ones always pick on the small and defenseless? This is why our struggles are never-ending."

Viggo dashed towards Roldin, extracting large rats from each pocket before hurling them in his direction. The scythes deftly cleaved the rodents in two, rupturing the accompanying bag of hot pepper powder, which detonated across Roldin's visage. He gagged, shielding his face with his hands.

"What sorcery is this?"

Viggo exclaimed. "10,000 searing hot peppers of agony! Run!"

Little Soul dashed pass Roldin towards the alley entrance, with Viggo swiftly trailing behind. Roldin unleashed a blue energy wave, dispersing the hot pepper powder away from him.

"A scrub mocking me? How absurd!"

Roldin violently spun his long chain scythe, sending it hurtling toward Viggo. It pierced through his chest, unleashing a burst of bright light.

"AH!" Viggo fell to his knees in agony.

Little Soul turned around and stopped. "No!"

Viggo looked down at the sharp, bloody scythe piercing through his chest.

Roldin tugged on the chain.

"AH!!" Viggo screamed.

"It's never too late to realize that bringing toys to a deadly fight isn't the wisest choice."

Roldin yanked his chain scythe back forcefully, causing Viggo's body to fly towards him. With a swift motion, Roldin seized the back of Viggo's head, extracting the scythe along with Viggo's soul still attached. He then discarded Viggo's lifeless body onto the muddy ground.

With Viggo's soul suspended in midair, held firmly by Roldin's left hand, he withdrew the scythe completely. "Now, you have the opportunity to depart from this sad world and embrace a path toward greatness."

Little Soul rushed towards Roldin, delivering a flurry of punches to his left arm in a desperate attempt to liberate Viggo's soul.

"Is that supposed to sting, boy?" Roldin said with a smirk.

Roldin clenched his right fist, rammed it into Little Soul's stomach, rendering him unconscious. Roldin lifted him into the air and roared with laughter.

A blue translucent ninja soul adorned with a half-face mask and spiked gray hair appeared before Roldin.

"This will."

The blue soul swiftly struck multiple pressure points on Roldin's arms, rendering them limp. Roldin cringed in agony as he dropped both souls. With relentless force, the blue ninja soul hammered his palms into Roldin's black armor chest plate, sending shock waves that shattered the armor's backside as Roldin was propelled backward, but a death grip clawed into Roldin's neck and yanked him back to face the blue ninja soul.

In agonized tones, Roldin muttered through his bloody mouth, "Who are you!"

"Kinori of Koi Ka Chi. A father!" Kinori amassed an immense surge of energy within his grasp.

"A Ukko?" Roldin winced in pain.

Kinori's face contorted with anger as he thrust his left elbow into Roldin's black armor chest plate, followed by a trifecta palm strikes that cracked the front of the plate. The force left large palm prints into the tin wall behind Roldin as he propelled back, crashing into the trash bins.

Viggo's soul and Little Soul lay motionless on the muddy ground. Kinori knelt, gently lifting Little Soul into his arms.

"Ninso, at last, I've found you, my son," Kinori reminisced about the days they were alive.

❖

Venice Section is the third-most inner section of Vellatine City, where the high-class Totalist reside in corporate skyscrapers towering into the clouds. It overlooks the Avedon River and the beautiful Vellatine City skylines on the other side. Late in the after-hours at a corporate skyscraper office, a guard patrolled the quiet hallway.

Ninso, you deserved a place to run and play without fears or worries, murmured Kinori.

The guard turned around the corner. Kinori thrust a small dagger into the guard's neck and hung him on the wall before he could react.

An opportunity to push your limits as far as you can and dream as high as you can, Kinori muttered.

He walked toward the two guards who stood beside the double doors. They raised their submachine guns and fired at him.

We left Koi Ka Chi to escape Emperor Razen's death grips, hoping to find a better life here. Still, this cruel society treated us no differently, Kinori reflected bitterly.

Bullets shredded the walls and the ground as Kinori zigzagged toward them. A bullet grazed his left arm as he threw ninja stars to deflect some of the bullets. A sticky bomb splattered onto the double doors; the explosion blew the doors wide open and killed the two guards.

You are the heartbeat that breathes strength into me, he uttered.

He walked into the room, the smoke settling around him. A Boss sat behind a big desk, with five imposing bodyguards close by. He kicked the half-broken door behind him shut.

"Ah, quite the explosive entrance, isn't it?" the Boss remarked, his tone lacking amusement. "It's best you crawl back to your Totalist master with your tail between your legs before I cut..."

Kinori appeared silently from behind the Boss's oversized chair. The five imposing bodyguards slumped to the ground while the Boss's agonized expression contorted further as Kinori's blade sliced through his neck.

Gazing through the towering glass windows, Kinori beheld the radiant lights of Vellatine City Skyline twinkling across the Avedon River.

I am merely a tool to them, and I have no choice but to be the blade of their sinister judgments.

He wiped the blood off his sword with a cloth.

In the dim recesses of an undisclosed location, a corpulent Totalist flung a silver shin toward Kinori, who caught it in his bloodstained hand.

Laughter erupted from the Totalist and his cohorts as they mocked the bloodied bounty bag laid on the table.

I had hoped to whisk you away to the far corners of Ourania World to show you the beauty beyond our grim existence. My greatest regret is that I could not use my earnings to make our dreams a reality. I am sorry.

He opened the door, entering his rusty tin home. Blood dripped from his left arm as he moved inside. Placing a small bag of buns on the table beside the wooden bed where Ninso lay asleep, he sat on the floor next to the bed, carefully bandaging his wound. His gaze softened as he looked at Ninso, gently running his fingers through the child's soft hair.

Morning rays illuminated the room as Ninso awoke and surveyed the space. Only two buns sat on the table. Meanwhile, in Vellatine Forest, Kinori darted through the undergrowth, leaping over boulders and darted between trees, with the Totalist Military following close behind. Ninso rose from bed, stepping outside into the embrace of the morning light.

The table held only two remaining buns.

In the forest, the Totalist Military and Wing Destroyer Airship surrounded Kinori, sealing his fate with execution.

The trash bins exploded outward. Roldin, in pain, struggled to rise and kicked the debris aside. The blue energy surged, and rats hovered around Roldin, their bodies contorted tightly.

The rats then ripped apart.

Little red life orbs emerged from their bodies, swirling around before entering Roldin's mouth.

Kinori gently laid his son down. "I've been observing you closely for some time now, Dark Solkin."

He stood up, "You are who they called Roldin, the infamous Dark Solkin known for your ruthless killing. I've witnessed the aftermath of your actions on countless souls, torn asunder and transformed into life and power orbs. Your sustenance is derived from consuming the crimson orbs for life and the azure orbs for their power. You have been searching for my son and Stone Rune for a long time."

"I never sensed your presence, not even once, and yet you seem to know so much of me and my actions."

"Every intel was taken from the last breath of your dying peers."

"The hunter becomes the hunted," Roldin laughed.

Roldin felt better and took a step forward. "This just got more interesting. Very few had seen what we've done, and none had lived to tell a soul."

He spun his scythes and dashed towards Kinori.

Kinori instantly hurled five ninja stars at Roldin. With his sword drawn from his back, Kinori appeared behind Roldin, repeatedly launching it toward Roldin's body. The spinning scythes created a moving shield, sparks flying as they blocked both the sword and ninja star attacks from both sides.

Roldin then turned to face Kinori.

Kinori jammed his sword between the two chains and twisted his blade, knotting them together. He pulled his sword inward, forcing Roldin to lean towards him, and thrust his blade into the ground, securing the two heavy metal chain scythes in place. Kinori leaped onto his sword handle and delivered a spinning kick to Roldin's face, causing him to spiral through the air before crashing.

Kinori balanced atop his sword handle, "Depart from us, and you will find peace in your passing."

Roldin slowly ascended from the ground to meet Kinori's level, cracking his neck as he did so. "Finding immense joy in the knowledge of your impending demise, I cannot wait to consume your soul along with the formidable power it holds."

Roldin winced in pain, his face contorting.

He gingerly touched the corner of his mouth, finding blood on the tip of his finger. Roldin clenched his left fist; he observed the long, heavy metal chain scythes pulsating with power as they shook and tightened around the sword, ultimately shattering it. With its cracked blade, the broken sword handle spun upward toward Kinori's face. Reacting swiftly, he somersaulted backward and kicked the fractured blade, sending it hurtling toward Roldin. Kinori appeared in front of Roldin, seizing the incoming handle of the fractured sword and driving it straight through

Roldin's cracked chest plate, piercing his heart.

"Now, who's killing whom, Roldin?"

Roldin clutched Kinori's hands tightly, his mouth seeping blood.

"Now die!"

He twisted the broken sword. Roldin screamed in pain!

"Dad?" Ninso said softly.

Kinori kicked Roldin away and appeared before Ninso.

"I'm here! You're safe now, my son!" He hugged Ninso.

Ninso thrust his hand into Kinori's chest, six blades spiking out from the back. Kinori screamed in agony, pushing Ninso away, confusion clouding his gaze. Slowly, Ninso transformed into the scythe. Kinori collapsed to the ground, his eyes catching sight of his son lying unconscious in the distance. Roldin approached Ninso.

"Seems like everyone falls for my Charms of Death. Many are captivated by my allure of mortality." Roldin pulled out the broken sword handle. "This strike at the heart is fatal to any ordinary human, but we, Dark Solkin, lack such vulnerability."

Roldin tossed the sword aside.

Kinori reached his hand out to Ninso, who lay unconscious.

"Even in the afterlife, your care for your son endures. Thus, I bestow upon you the gift of eternal togetherness." Roldin picked up Ninso as Kinori watched, filled with pain and anger.

Roldin emanated power as he whispered, "Separate."

Blue energy flared up on Roldin's hand. Ninso screamed in pain! Roldin grinned, his eyes widening as the Stone Rune floated out of Ninso's mouth before him. He lit up, shredded apart, then burst into energy flames. The flames dissipated, leaving behind a red life orb and a blue power orb floating around Roldin's hand.

Roldin seized the Stone Rune, which floated before him, "At last! The Stone Rune is in my possession!"

Roldin grabbed Kinori's face, lifting him into the air, one of his eyes visible between the fingers. "The depth of pain reflected in your eye stirs something deep within me."

Kinori clenched his teeth, enduring the pain.

Roldin emanated power, glowing with intensity.

"After absorbing your essence, my power will exponentially increase!"

Roldin pulled him closer, drawing their faces together until they were inches apart. He locked eyes with him, his gaze unwavering and intense. "It's time for you to… se… par… ate!"

Kinori's eye widened as he screamed in great pain. Roldin's hand lit up with energy, causing Kinori to shred and burst into flames of energy, which soon dissipated. In the aftermath, a red life orb and a blue power orb floated around Roldin's hand as he laughed mercilessly.

Roldin landed beside Viggo's soul, his fingers puncturing into his neck and raising him into the air. He held Viggo's soul aloft, his hand glowing with power.

"SE… PARA…"

Great pain tore into Roldin as his fingers dug deeper into Viggo's soul neck. Despite Viggo's soul unconscious state, his face contorted in agony. The surging blue energy abruptly halted. Black palm prints materialized on Roldin's back, prompting him to cough up blood. The black imprints morphed into a deep red hue, and blood seeped through.

"What is happening?!"

Roldin gripped Viggo's soul tightly and roared, "Waarrgghhhh!"

The palm prints light up white. Roldin grabbed his chest, his body cracked, and pure white energy blasted out of his body from different areas, creating a whirlwind of power around Roldin and Viggo's soul. The energy pierced through Roldin's fingers and flowed into Viggo's soul neck. Roldin's fingers disintegrated with his two heavy metal chain scythes and the broken blades on the ground. The red and blue orbs cracked and mixed with Roldin's white energy, absorbing into Viggo's soul. The red and yellow rose petals swirled around Viggo's soul as it glowed in pure light. The alleyway lights up in white. Viggo's body lay lifeless on the ground with the fog surrounding it, and his soul descended back into his body. All the wounds and swelling on his body healed. The energy dimmed out on his back. The red and yellow rose petals settled around his body. The Stone Rune fell next to him. The alleyway glowed in cool, frosted blue rays once again.

All calm, silent, and eerie, but beautifully painted.

Chapter 3
Family

Multi-colored light beams scanned over the cluttered trash and trash bins as two drones flew in slowly. Automatic assault rifle barrels were aimed in multiple directions, with Totalist soldier following back-to-back. Two spotlights shone onto Viggo's body, while the third illuminated the Stone Rune.

A soldier read the scanner, "General Crocrovich, the intense power source had vanished."

General Crocrovich strode in, sporting gold-rimmed black sunglasses perched on his broad nose, surveying the area with a keen gaze. His wavy brown hair was meticulously slicked back, and he carried himself with an air of authority—a heavy black cloak draped effortlessly over his broad shoulders. Beneath the cloak, he donned a crisply tailored black military suit adorned with an array of gleaming gold medals and chains, signifying his esteemed rank and decorated service.

"The scan revealed a palm print on the wall's surface, yet no corresponding match found within the databases." Continued the soldier.

General Crocrovich knelt and observed the deep slash in the ground.

"There's a Stone Rune beside the boy, General Crocrovich!" Alerted another soldier.

"Bring it to me."

The soldier handed him the Stone Rune. He held it up, rotating it—a square black rock with a gray calligraphy symbol inscribed with the word "疼痛" (pain).

All the resources for an old stone? Hmph. General Crocrovich thought as he rubbed his neatly trimmed garibaldi beard.

General Crocrovich ordered, "Place it within the Aerial Chamber Drone and dispatch it to the Weaponry and Research Lab."

"Yes, sir."

Two soldiers approached Viggo's lifeless body, one using his boot to nudge him over. He scanned his face with a device.

"Viggo Van Hunt. Age seventeen. Orphan. No match." The female voice scanner reported.

"General Crocrovich, there was no match or power source on his body. He's merely a sewer rat." The soldier said.

A muscular soldier carried a hefty gold throne on his shoulder and placed it beside General Crocrovich. He ascended the throne and took a seat. His sunglasses split in half and slid back into his temples. "What time was the power surge registered?"

"19:26 hours, precisely 22 minutes ago, sir," the soldier answered.

"Secure all exit points out of Section 12. I want every road, bridge, tiny crack, and loophole to be thoroughly locked down. Deploy our Totalist soldiers and drones to search the Vellatine Forest up to the Forest Edge thoroughly. Additionally, enhance security measures at the entrances of D-One through D-Three Walls."

"Yes, sir!" shouted the soldiers and exited the alleyway.

Four soldiers remained behind with General Crocrovich.

"Wake him up," General Crocrovich ordered.

A soldier brandished a steel baton, swiped it to its full length, then pressed it against Viggo's arm. An electric surge coursed through Viggo's body but elicited no response; his form remained inert. Adjusting the settings, the soldier increased the amperage and administered another shock. This time, Viggo's body convulsed slightly. Another soldier approached and adjusted his to maximum power. In unison, they delivered another jolt. Viggo's eyes flew open in shock, his muscles contracting violently, and his chest popped up as the electricity surged through him.

Viggo's screams pierced the air as he wrestled free from the current, blindly lashing out at the indistinct shape before him. Shielding his eyes from the blinding light, he struggled to discern the dark figures amidst the chaos.

"What happened here, boy?" General Crocrovich questioned.

"Who are you?" Viggo shifted his head, attempting to get a clearer view, but the overwhelming brightness and blurriness obscured everything.

"I am General Crocrovich, representing the Totalist Military of Vellatine…"

"Totalist snakes! What's the reason behind…" Viggo interrupted.

The soldiers knocked Viggo down, pressing their assault rifles against his head.

"We stand as guardians of peace and justice in our beloved Vellatine City, dedicated to safeguarding the Royal Families. Let's not overlook the significance of our noble actions. Vocalizing such sentiments might inadvertently align you with the SKA Rebels, a grave offense in our Totalist Federation, punishable by death. It's unwise for someone of your youth to risk being thrown into a cage full of ruthless and unlawful men. Your prospects are far brighter here, washing the back of this society's trash. Viggo, is it? Why don't you tell me what happened here, and in return, I can offer you a reward—a gold shin, perhaps?" General Crocrovich gestured, prompting the soldier to retrieve a gold shin from his pocket and hand it to him.

"How can I be certain it's not fake? Let me see it first."

"You are talking to a high-ranking General of the land. My words are as good as my bullets that pierced through innocent little girls and boys like you. You will never earn such a fine gold shin doing what you do. Consider this a rare chance for advancement. The gold shin is as real as the chilling rifle pressed against your temple." General Crocrovich snapped his fingers. The assault rifles withdrew, and the two soldiers backed off.

"Give me the gold shin first, and then I'll tell you what I know," Viggo demanded.

"It appears you may not fully grasp the complexities of the situation. A person entrenched in a particular environment often finds it challenging to escape its confines."

"Talk normal!"

"A sewer rat will always die as a sewer rat."

"I am not a sewer rat, and I'm not afraid of bullies like you! Once I tell you what I know, will you hand over that gold shin?"

"Go on."

"I was pursuing the GLB gangs into this alley, and we got into a fight… and then… something hit me." Viggo gently rubbed his head, though it didn't ache. "That's the last thing I can remember." He rose to his feet and extended his hand.

"Is that all you can remember?" General Crocrovich inquired.

Viggo nodded.

He stepped off his throne, "Recently, some peculiar events unfolded at this site, and you seem to be the sole witness remaining. Could you please shed light on what transpired and also enlighten me on where you got the Stone Rune?"

"Stone Rune? I've told you what I already know. I do not know what the GLB gangs did afterward. They are the ones you should be looking for."

"A tier-one petty thief isn't responsible for this level of damage. So, let's get to the truth one final time. What really happened?"

"I already told you everything I know."

"Once you remember everything, you can locate me, and I will reward you with the gold shin." General Crocrovich said as he walked toward the alleyway's exit.

General Crocrovich tossed a red shin by Viggo's feet.

He picked it up and examined it. Two letters, "GC," were inscribed on its surface.

"You connive Totalist snake!" Viggo shouted.

A soldier swung the rifle butt and knocked Viggo to the ground.

"I didn't deceive you. The information you provided was of little value, hardly worth a gold shin, let alone my time."

"General Crocrovich, should we apprehend him?"

"No. We have more important things to rot in our jail cells than rats. This place is a perfect sentence already. Consider yourself fortunate tonight, boy. There won't be any forewarning of your fate next time."

General Crocrovich emerged from the alleyway, trailed by his soldiers. Climbing into his war vehicle, he rolled away, accompanied by a convoy of more vehicles. Meanwhile, Viggo cautiously stepped out of the alley, observing the soldiers' march. His gaze shifted upwards as seven Wing Destroyers streaked across the sky.

Something terrible must have happened for those Totalist snakes to be here. Leaf! Viggo realized and ran on the sidewalk in the opposite direction of the Totalist Military.

❖

Viggo struggled to catch his breath as he hammered his fist on the old, rusty metal door. Rain swung it open, and he was breathless. Her beauty, accentuated by her piercing blue eyes, hypnotized him as the soft, frosted-blue light danced upon her.

"Rain…" Viggo stammered, his eyelids growing heavy as they closed, his heart melting.

A gentle, sweet voice reached his ears.

"Viggo… Where have you been?"

Viggo opened his eyes to a colorful heart-shaped soap bubble before him, and it popped! All around them were pink clouds and floating soap bubbles the size of their heads. Rain wore a captivating long blue corset dress with a slit at the side. She walked toward him slowly, slightly swaying her hips from side to side.

"I found myself dreaming of you every aching second. Every minute spent apart from you pulled at my heartstrings with increasing intensity. Your good looks send my thoughts spiraling on this roller coaster journey of our love." She reached out and touched his hand. Her fingers trailed slowly, inching up his arm until they gently brushed against his lips. Viggo's face relaxed, and a smile graced his lips.

"The gentle sensation of your soft, plump, luscious, wet lips ignite an irresistible flutter within my heart!"

Viggo drooled, exhaling drunkenly as his hot breath lingered in the air.

"The sweet smell of your aroma tingled my body. I can't fathom existence in this wondrous world without you by my side. Embrace me now! Kiss me the ardor you've always longed for! Let's elevate our passion to the stars and beyond!"

Rain puckered her lips and leaned in, prompting him to do the same. As their lips neared, the soft skin of Rain's palm slapped across Viggo's face.

Startled, Viggo opened his eyes, his left cheek flushing red as he rubbed the painful sting, "Ouch! Why did you slap me?"

"Why do you always have that perverted face?!" Rain exclaimed.

"I don't have a perverted face!" Viggo retorted.

"Yes! You do!"

"No, I don't! I have a very great-looking face!"

"HA! No, you don't!"

"Yes, I do!"

Mr. Hairo approached the door, concern evident in his expression. "Is everything alright, dear?"

"Yes, Daddy." Rain replied, sticking her tongue out at Viggo.

Mr. Hairo turned his attention to Viggo, "You must be…"

"Brother!" Leaf interrupted excitedly, rushing over to Viggo and embracing him tightly.

"Why did you leave Leaf alone in the street?" Rain questioned Viggo.

"I was chasing some bullies!" Viggo explained. Turning to Leaf, he added, "Leaf, we must be extra careful. The Totalist Military are everywhere."

Leaf nodded solemnly.

"Why are the Totalist Military out this late and in Section 12?" Mr. Hairo inquired.

"I don't know," Viggo admitted, furrowing his brow in thought.

"It must be because of you!" Rain accused.

"No!"

"Yes! You are always causing trouble!"

"No!"

Mr. Hairo looked up in the night sky and saw several Wing Destroyers zips by. "Viggo is right."

"See!" Viggo grimaced at her, eliciting a swift reaction from Rain, whose cheeks flushed crimson. Rain retaliated with a scowl directed at Viggo.

"Now, now, Rain. The Totalist Military is out tonight. Viggo, Leaf, it might be safer for you boys to stay with us until this situation calms down."

"Daddy!" Rain protested with a whine.

"Rain, remember the lesson I've always emphasized? We never abandon those in need and must extend a helping hand whenever possible."

Rain paused, inhaling deeply before releasing a sigh.

"Thank you, but we don't need to stay. We have a place of our own," Viggo asserted.

"Where would you boys go?" inquired Mr. Hairo.

"We have a vast place! We can go wherever we want," Leaf chimed in.

Mr. Hairo turned to Leaf and said, "That sounded wonderful. Would you like to finish your meal before heading out, Leaf?"

"Yeah, Leaf, let's finish our meal." Rain seized Leaf's hand, drawing him swiftly into the house as Leaf clung to his pants with a tight grip.

"Why don't you join us, Viggo? We still have some extra food," Mr. Hairo offered warmly, widening the door as he spoke.

"Thank you, sir."

"Please, call me Mr. Hairo."

"Thank you, Mr. Hairo," Viggo replied politely, stepping into the tin can house.

Rain sat next to Leaf at the table, enjoying a meal. A large pot of soup occupied the center, surrounded by plates of bread around the table. Mr. Hairo wheeled his chair to the opposite side of Rain. Viggo entered the room.

"Take a seat and make yourself comfortable," Mr. Hairo said and smiled.

Viggo sat down, already stuffed a piece of bread into his mouth before pouring soup into his bowl and grabbing a few more slices. Rain scrutinized each item Viggo seized, observing as he hastily shoved another into his mouth.

Mr. Hairo laughed, "Having such a youthful spirit is truly a blessing."

Viggo smiled with food in his mouth.

"It's not a blessing when a pig eats all our food, Daddy," Rain remarked.

"Rain, let's be kind. Remember what I always said, sweetheart?" Mr. Hairo interjected.

"Sharing is caring," Rain and her dad said simultaneously.

"I know, Daddy. I'm okay with sharing with Leaf," Rain affirmed

"I can't help it when it tastes so good," Viggo admitted, a piece of bread flopped out of his mouth.

Mr. Hairo chuckled, "You see, Rain? He enjoyed your cooking from yesterday."

"I don't cook for skinny piggies!" Rain retorted.

"Does that mean I'm a chubby piggy?" Leaf inquired innocently.

The room filled with laughter, yet Leaf remained silent. He busied himself by stuffing his mouth with a piece of bread.

Viggo smirked as he ruffled Leaf's hair. "I wish that were the case. Then, I wouldn't have to worry about you constantly."

"What is your occupation, Viggo?" Mr. Hairo asked.

Viggo paused, sat straight, and proudly exclaimed, "I work as a merchandise distributor."

"Wow, that sounds like important work." Mr. Hairo said, amazed.

"Indeed. We help..."

"He's a thief, Daddy."

"Now, Rain, we remain from making accusations..."

"We do what we can to put food in our stomachs. One day, we will get out of Section 12 and achieve my dream," Viggo declared.

"Dream. One doesn't hear much about those anymore. What dream might that be, Viggo?" Mr. Hairo inquired.

Viggo met Mr. Hairo's gaze squarely. "I think your daughter is lovely, sir..."

Rain choked while sipping her soup.

Viggo declared with conviction, "One day, I'll seek your blessing to marry her!"

Soup erupted from Rain's mouth in surprise.

"Oh, that's a fresh one!" Mr. Hairo laughed.

"Daddy!"

"But that is a very, very hard goal to accomplish," Mr. Hairo teased.

"DADDY! Don't give him any hope!" Rain protested.

Mr. Hairo cleared his throat. "Caring for someone is an enormous responsibility and a grand feat. I believe that prioritizing your well-being, as well as that of Leaf, should be paramount. Shin is a fundamental aspect of our basic needs and holds great importance, particularly when caring for a loved one. However, have you considered what might be even more crucial and valuable than shins?"

The room fell silent.

Leaf glanced at Rain and Viggo; their brows furrowed in concentration.

Leaf turned to Mr. Hairo and inquired, "Is it love, sir?"

Mr. Hairo smiled at Leaf.

Viggo turned to Leaf, "Love? HA! Love does not make our stomachs full. Love does not shelter us from the blazing sun or the bone-chilling sewage water in the winter. Love does not protect us from bullies!"

Leaf felt disappointed by his response.

"Viggo, you're correct. Love doesn't shield you from life's challenges. However, Leaf, your point is equally valid. In the end, what you have left is the one that loved you for who you are, enduring both the toughest and the rare moments of joy."

Leaf glanced upward at Mr. Hairo, attentively absorbing his words.

"In our loneliest, darkest moments, it's often not shin that could help you, but rather the light of love that offers a glimmer of hope amidst the shadow. Without the love of those closest to you, life can feel as desolate as a cold, empty chamber. Let your heart learn and lead you to feel the warmth of love. As time grows, you will be rich in more ways than you can imagine. Remember to stand by each other, offering unwavering support through all of life's twists and turns."

Rain embraced Mr. Hairo warmly, whispering, "I love you, Daddy."

"Sweetheart, I love you too. Leaf, what dreams are stirring in your heart?"

Leaf rotated his chair from side to side, "I don't have one, sir. As long as I am with brother, I'm happy."

Mr. Hairo nodded.

Rain looked at Leaf and Viggo curiously, "Are you two genuinely brothers? You both have nothing in common and don't even look alike!"

The room fell into an awkward silence. Viggo and Leaf exchanged uneasy glances.

"The bonds they share are undeniable. Blood ties don't solely define family; it's about the connections we forge." Mr. Hairo said.

Leaf's ears perked up, and he glanced upward at Mr. Hairo, "Does this mean we can all become a family?"

Mr. Hairo laughed, "Why, yes! Of course, we can all be a great, big family!"

Leaf's eyes lit up as he whispered, "Family."

"I don't want to be family with Vgooo, Daddy!" Rain shouted.

Mr. Hairo laughed again.

"You'll be so lucky if you are with me," Viggo smirked.

Rain kicked Viggo's leg beneath the table, prompting a pained expression from him. With satisfaction, Rain tilted her sharp nose upward and tightened her lips.

"What a delightful meal! It's been too long since I've shared such hearty laughter. You boys are always welcome back," Mr. Hairo said.

Leaf and Viggo smiled happily, "Thank you, Mr. Hairo!"

"Don't forget about me! I did all the cooking!" Rain shouted.

Mr. Hairo laughed, "Thank you, Rain, for being such a caring and thoughtful young lady."

Viggo and Leaf shouted, "Thank you, Rain!"

Rain gave a big smile, and everyone laughed. The room felt warm and comfy. Viggo filled his bowl again and took more bread. Leaf's belly poked out over the table from overeating. Viggo and Rain giggled, pointing at Leaf's belly.

The pot and plates were empty.

Mr. Hairo was fast asleep, snoring loudly. Leaf could hardly move with his big belly. Viggo lay face down on the table, exhausted.

Rain surveyed the empty pot and plates, "Now, who's ready to clean the kitchen?"

Mr. Hairo snored, choked a bit, and then opened one eye, scanning his surroundings. Viggo, barely awake, lifted his head from the table with a piece of bread dangling from his mouth. Leaf swiftly jumped up, hastily pulling his pants up a bit. The trio exchanged glances before darting out of the kitchen.

"Hey!" Rain yelled, seized a rock cannon from the table's edge, and fired it at them.

KA-BOOM!

Mr. Hairo and Leaf flew into the living room. Viggo hit the floor, and a large rock rolled off his back. Viggo was dragged back into the kitchen while Mr. Hairo and Leaf crawled toward the desks.

Mr. Hairo settled into his chair, "O, that was a close one."

"What was that!?" Leaf asked.

"That Rain's rock cannon. She crafted that when she was ten."

"A rock cannon?"

"Those stones can really pack a punch."

"Poor brother."

"We should be safe now. I noticed you're adjusting your pants a few times. Are they loose?"

"Yeah, they used to fit me perfectly," replied Leaf, frowning.

Mr. Hairo reached into his drawer and pulled out a bag. He took some black liquid magnets and linked them together on the table.

Leaf looked at them closely, "What is that?"

"It's a unique liquid magnet. When you connect it, it adjusts to the shape of your body, expanding and contracting."

"Adjust? Will it control my body?" Leaf asked nervously.

Mr. Hairo laughed as he looped it around Leaf's pants, "This should keep it in place. If you need to remove it, simply fold the magnets opposite end together, and they will repel each other, making it easy to separate." The magnet belt contoured to Leaf's waist, securely holding his pants in place.

"Wow. This is so cool!" He paused and then shyly asked, "Would one shin be enough, Mr. Hairo?"

"Hmm... Let me see," Mr. Hairo mused, his gaze thoughtful. "Since I like your name, I will make it the same as its meaning."

Leaf shook his head, his expression hesitant. "Oh no. I can't just take it even though my name is cool."

"I understand," Mr. Hairo nodded. "Then, here is the payment I am willing to accept. When you become a young man, be someone who will stand up for others, especially those who need help."

Leaf's eyes lit up with determination. "Yes, sir! I will do my best."

Leaf glanced at the table, noticing the variety of tools and gadgets on it. "Mr. Hairo, what do you do with all these parts on the table?"

"This stuff is how I make my shins."

"You make old stuff?"

"I make them work again."

Mr. Hairo moved the tools and other items, removed a small metal box and a big metal ball, and placed them in the middle of the desk.

"This one is still a work in progress."

Mr. Hairo pressed a small button on the metal box. Its sides slid up, colorful lights blinked, and a rapid flapping sound reeled loudly. Out flew a tiny robotic dragonfly, buzzing around Leaf. It landed on his hand, lights dimming. Leaf's eyes lit up. Mr. Hairo pressed the button again, and the dragonfly glowed, its wings changing colors. It tried to take flight, wobbled in midair, and bumped into Leaf's forehead, but he stayed fascinated. It returned to the box, which closed.

"Wow." Leaf finally said.

Mr. Hairo picked up a big metal ball that glowed red and green under his fingerprints. The ball opened, showing a lifelike statue of Mr. Hairo, beardless, with his arms around his wife, Helen, who held baby Rain in her arms. A slow, off-key piano played a calm melody.

"This was a gift from Helen, my wife. She wanted to capture this moment of us when Rain was only a month old. It's one of the few things I have left of her."

"It's... it's beautiful," Leaf replied softly.

He looked at Mr. Hairo and saw the gentle smile on his face.

"This was the second-best gift she had given me."

"What was the first?"

Mr. Hairo looked at Rain in the kitchen and smiled.

Rain wiped the table, the dishes were in the sink, and Viggo swept the floor with a broom. "I heard there's going to be a fantastic welcome ceremony in just a few days."

Rain was washing the dishes, and Viggo glanced at her to see if she heard it or cared.

"You get to make a wish, and it will come true."

Rain chuckled, "Really?"

"Yeah! It's called Lighting of Dreams. It sounds pretty cool, uh?" Viggo glanced at Rain with a spark of excitement in his eyes. "Do you have a wish you want to make?"

Rain paused as the water ran over the plate.

"You don't have to tell me if you don't want to."

Rain continued to wash the plate, "Do you actually believe in that stuff?"

"If there's even a sliver of opportunity to turn my dream into reality, I'll seize it in a heartbeat, no matter how slim the odds are."

"Where is it at?" Rain inquired with curiosity.

"It's at the Venice Defense One wall!" Viggo responded instantly.

"The Venice D-One wall? Where the high-class Totalist live?" Rain asked.

"That's it."

"We can't even get past the Low-Class Borat D-Three wall or Middle-Class Corecrest D-Two wall, let alone the Venice D-One wall."

"But I will be able to get us in."

"Well, I can't afford any expenses related to Vellatine City's sectors."

"You don't have to pay... I mean, you won't have to worry about that... but..."

"But what?"

"It's mainly for couples' events."

Rain paused from washing the dishes and turned to look at Viggo. "What do you mean couples? Are you referring to going on a date?"

Viggo cleaned the floor quickly and answered nervously. "If that's what you want to call it... Do you..."

Viggo tripped over the chair leg. The broomstick smacked Rain on her head.

"Ooowww! Vgooo!"

Viggo quickly picked up the broomstick, blocking a hefty, soapy metal soup spoon.

"Is that a yes?" Viggo asked nervously as he darted around the table while Rain swung a large, soapy metal spoon at him.

The choppy, sharp, low-key piano melody came to an end.

Mr. Hairo chuckled, "She is one of a kind, and I don't think I have to worry about her. I understand the predicament we're in, especially here in Section 12. Everyone is too preoccupied with their concerns, constantly wondering if there will be food on the table in the days ahead or even a shelter to call home. But they seem to have forgotten the importance of caring for and assisting those around them. That's why I found your earlier statement surprising, Leaf. You possess an old heart."

"Does that mean I'm old?" Leaf questioned.

"It seems your heart is deeply imbued with kindness and love. You harbor genuine intentions toward people; hopefully, their hearts will be good to you in return. Throughout our great Totalist history, many have held leadership positions, but very few have truly won the hearts of the people, especially here in Section 12, where Vellatine City lacks such compassion. Just remember, by showing genuine love to those around you, you will unlock the true power within yourself."

Leaf looked a bit puzzled, "I don't get it."

Mr. Hairo smiled, "I didn't know at first. But one day, you will."

Mr. Hairo gazed at his wife and the miniature statue of Rain.

Mr. Hairo and Rain stood outside their tin-can home, waving goodbye to Viggo and Leaf as they walked down the muddy road. Leaf turned around and waved back. Viggo stopped and knelt, allowing Leaf to jump on for a piggyback ride.

"Brother, is this what it feels like to be part of a family?"

Viggo walked on, carrying Leaf.

"It feels wonderful, doesn't it? Do you think someday we can all be a great big family and live happily together like tonight?"

"Ourania World is so vast; anything can happen," Viggo said.

"Are we meeting Arison tonight?" Leaf asked.

"Yes, tonight's the night we set our big plans into motion, but let's remember to be extra careful," Viggo reminded him.

Leaf rested his head on Viggo's back.

Fireflies glowed and faded away as they lazily flew around the trees and bushes near Mr. Hairo's home under the giant Zephaniah World and its two moons.

"What are your thoughts on Viggo and Leaf?" Mr. Hairo asked.

"Leaf seems nice, but Viggo always gives me these weird looks and feelings."

Mr. Hairo gazed at the night sky, "That seems about right."

"What is, Daddy?"

"Your mom was an extraordinary lady."

Rain grasped Mr. Hairo's arm and rested her head on his shoulder.

Mr. Hairo patted her hand, "She always seems to know. Most of the time, I was clueless. She had this undeniably vibrant about her, a life force that radiated from within. Everyone she touched seemed to flourish in her presence. The one thing that struck me most was her contagious laughter. It will make you smile even when you're having a bad day. You would forget about it and enjoy being with her at that moment. She was the warm brightness of my world."

"I loved how you talked about Mommy. I missed her so much, Daddy. I hope she is happy in heaven."

"I think she is, honey."

"Mommy's death anniversary is in nine days. We should go visit her by the Forest Edge."

Mr. Hairo nodded.

Multiple shooting stars streaked across the night sky.

Chapter 4
Dream Bracelets

Outside of the Venice D-One wall, a figure cloaked in black stood on a large rock by the Avedon River, barely noticeable to passersby. From this vantage point, the dark figure surveyed the Diamond Ring Bridge and the skyline of Vellatine City. The reflection of yellow, red, and green city lights danced on the water, imparting a sense of transcendent peace and contemplation on the magnificence of the Totalist accomplishment.

Five Diamond Ring Bridges span the Avedon River; each bridge runs through eight diamond rings. Adorning the apex of each ring was the most exquisite high-clarity diamond in all of Ourania World. A six-lane acrylic bridge traversed through the center of these rings, connecting the Venice D-One Wall to the Vellatine City Sections. Throughout the day, the acrylic bridge was illuminated with a color-coded system to signal Mega Trucks regarding its accessibility. When the Diamond Ring Bridge displayed a green hue, indicating it was open for transportation. Yellow signified ongoing maintenance, while red indicated restricted access. Currently, the Diamond Ring Bridges is displaying a green signal.

"Is that Arison?" Leaf inquired.

Viggo nodded as they made their way down to him.

Arison's dark brown eyes stared at the Vellatine Skyline, pondering his future. Born and raised in the Borat Section—the outermost and low-class section of The Totalist Federation. He had been immersed in the intricacies of recycling businesses since childhood. This was why he served as the right-hand man to White String, the leader of their group, the Huntsman, operating as low-level, tier-two thieves within the underground network. White String has ears everywhere in the Borat, Corecrest, and a few in Venice. Once in a while, there's news about valuable transportation, and the Huntsman will make the most out of the opportunity to steal it. An important string that had been vibrating intensely was the 'Dream Bracelets.' It's been in the works for months, and if they score this hit, White String will be elevated to a higher level of respect from all the low-level criminals and could deal with bigger heists with bigger rewards. Viggo and Leaf haven't met White String; they've only dealt with Arison, who's like a big brother, always watching out for them.

"I plan to climb out of my low-social status and become Commander of The Totalist," Arison said as Viggo and Leaf approached.

"Just cause you have a military buzz cut doesn't mean you can sign up with them. I always thought you needed to be part of middle-class society or shell out a gold shin just to get on their list to be tested for their Military Academy." Viggo questioned.

Arison turned around and faced Viggo. His robust jawline and square face suited him perfectly, "You do, and I will be the first from the Borat Section to do it!"

"Not to rain on your parade, but I reckon our odds for pulling off tonight's heist are higher than yours for reaching your goal," Viggo said.

"You're most likely right," Arison laughed, "If this mission succeeds, anything is possible."

"Could this be our tickets out of here?" Viggo asked.

"Maybe," Arison remarked.

"Now we're talking! What's the plan?" Viggo asked.

"Tonight's mission holds significant risk; it's high-profile, attracting the attention of Venice's elite who are willing to pay from their deep pockets. That means it will be extra dangerous, and I recommend that Leaf stay out of this."

"No!" Leaf shouted, "Wherever brother goes, I go too!"

Leaf and Arison looked at Viggo.

"No matter what, we always stick together," Viggo said.

Leaf smiled and nodded in agreement.

"Don't say I didn't warn you. White String mentioned that high-level, tier ten thieves also have their eyes on this shipment."

"Did he specify which group?" Viggo asked.

"SKA Rebels," Arison said.

Leaf tugged Viggo's arm, "Umm, who's SKA Rebels?"

"The Super Kick Ass Rebels—they're the Totalist Military's worst nightmare. Their unwavering dedication is to thwart the Totalist Military in every conceivable way and help the well-being of the Lower Class and below," Arison answered.

"It sounded like they're on our side. Shouldn't we help them?" Leaf asked.

"That is not our goal. We're trying to make a little shins and move on," Arison said.

"It's common knowledge that getting caught as one of them means instant death. Let's think about ourselves first. Then we will save the world later." Viggo smiled.

Leaf nodded.

"What is the good?" Viggo asked.

"Dream Bracelets." Arison turned around and gazed at the Vellatine City skyline.

"Dream Bracelets?" Leaf repeated.

Arison pointed to Vellatine City. "In Vellatine City, specifically in Section 10, known as The City of Lights, the prestigious Lighting of Dreams Ball Gala is set to take place the day following the Welcome Ceremony. This extravagant event is reserved exclusively for royal families, high-ranking military officials, and distinguished international VIPs possessing the coveted Dream Bracelet."

"That is precisely why every tier of thieves is after it," Viggo added.

"Exactly. With heightened security, the goods will be difficult to get."

"They already started on that earlier. General Crocrovich has deployed his Totalist Military snakes to scour Section 12 and fortify every access point."

Surprised by this revelation, Arison turned to Viggo and inquired, "How do you know that?"

"I was there when he questioned me."

"Questioning you about what?"

"About my fight with the GLB gang."

"That doesn't add up. The Totalist Military wouldn't mobilize over a mere fight, especially in Section 12. There must be more to it. I'll inform White String about this. For now, our primary focus is the Dream Bracelets."

"Do you know what this Lighting of Dream Ball Gala is about?" Viggo asked.

"Nope, and I don't care. It's probably selfish rich fools kissing each other's wealth and power. That's why the upper class is willing to pay a premium, even offering gems, for it," Arison replied.

"Gems? I'd never even heard of it, let alone seen one," Viggo said.

"Is that worth more than gold shins?" Leaf asked.

"That's right, Leaf," Arison answered.

Leaf was in awe.

"I thought you said shin?" Viggo asked.

"If it's a Military official or a member of the royal family's Dream Bracelet, it would be gems."

"Is there a specific marking on it?"

"Yes, a double crown—the symbol of the royal family."

"If we have extra, can we keep one of those bracelets for ourselves?" Viggo asked.

Arison shot Viggo a stern glance, "Remember, never bite the hands that feed you!"

"It doesn't hurt to ask," Viggo said.

"Sometimes it does," Arison said, "Now, the strategy is to let the SKA Rebels take on the brunt of the effort while we coordinate a two-person team to intercept each SKA carrier. I will leave it to you and Leaf to handle the one near Borat Edge while the rest of us will handle the remaining targets."

"How do we know who our guy is?" Viggo asked.

"According to White String, you won't miss your guy; he will be routed your way. Don't get yourself killed. Stay safe. We will rendezvous at Huntsman hideout in Section 12."

Viggo and Leaf nodded.

Borat Edge constitutes the outermost circular defense perimeter of Vellatine City. It stands at a towering 300 feet in height, comprised of a circular wall constructed from twenty-four-inch thick armor steel reinforced with solid concrete. Positioned atop this formidable structure are barracks for Totalist soldiers, laser turrets, missile artillery, and Air Totalist equipped with jetpacks. Eight massive statues of past Commanders stood around the wall, serving as a warning to potential invaders. Each stood at a towering height of 100 feet and bore the Totalist banner on their backs, engraved with their beliefs. Two statues were positioned in the North, two in the East, two in the South, and two in the West. At the center of Vellatine City, a colossal 1,000-foot-tall statue depicted the current Commander of The Totalist Federation, Commander Bazyli. It soared high into the clouds. His left hand extended outward with palm open, displaying a floating hologram of Ourania World. The hologram rotated at the same speed as the real world, showcasing live activity updates.

Within the wall lay the Borat Section, renowned for its agricultural farming, recycling factories, and mineral production. The buildings, constructed of concrete and bricks, were spaced out more accordingly, with commercial establishments occupying the ground floors and housing above. The streets were clear of mud, and only Mega Trucks were permitted for vehicular movement. Telegates were the preferred mode of transportation for residents traveling within the Borat Section. Most Totalist cannot travel outside their class without the credentials to cross the circular Defense Walls. The Borat D-Three Wall grants access to the Middle-Class Corecrest Section, the Corecrest D-Two Wall provides entry to the High-Class Venice Section, and the Venice D-One Wall permits access to the Diamond Ring Bridges leading to the Vellatine City Sections. Each D Wall entrance is heavily guarded with advanced monitoring systems from top to bottom. Totalist military soldiers, sentry machine gun barriers, and heavy artillery were constantly on alert at the top of the wall. However, the SKA Rebels were adept at creating counterfeit credentials and selling them on the forbidden markets, enabling access to each sector of the D Wall. If caught, death was guaranteed.

Borat's nightlife remained vibrant and bustling, unlike Section 12 during the late-night hours. Factory workers, farmers, and street hustlers filled the bars, food cafes, and nightclubs, seeking respite and enjoyment after their long days of labor. Near the center of the Borat Section, the Boogie Boogie nightclub reverberated with loud and energetic music. Every week, the young men would dress in the same stylish two-piece shirt and vest paired with loose, flowing pants, perfect for showcasing their dance skills and catching the eyes of the young ladies. Their shoes were crucial, adorned with lights that would flare and leave light trails following their dance movements.

Meanwhile, the young ladies opted for high heels and colorful knee-length dresses, often featuring a side split. They would gather closely, playing hard to get and protecting each other from unwanted advances. Every so often, a young woman would showcase her dance prowess in search of her soulmate.

The lively beats of Boogie Boogie music reverberated through the streets, energizing the crowd of young men and women as they danced and competed with their latest and smoothest kicks. Young Totalist cheered and applauded along the roadside, their feet stomping, sliding, and swaying to the infectious rhythm. At times, two or three ladies emerged simultaneously, each exuding their captivating allure as they spun their dresses midair. Their graceful movements synced with the beat, twirling and bending their dress colors harmoniously. Meanwhile, the young men, hypnotized by the scene, swayed and wiggled to the music, their arms swaying from side to side. The night was youthful, and the ambiance promised nothing but fun!

Viggo and Leaf perched on the flat rooftop, their feet dangling over the ledge. Below, the music and the excitement thrived, but their attention remained fixed on tonight's mission.

"Do you think it's him, brother?" Leaf pointed at a shady, petite guy who stood in a corner.

"Nay. He's just like us, on the hunt for his prey."

"How do we... oooh..." Leaf pointed at a tall, muscular man with a buzz cut striding down the street toward them. He wore a pink tank top paired with green and brown military pants and a large combat knife hanging from his side on a metal chain belt. He strolled by to the rhythm of the music and pushed aside the young Totalist.

"Heavy Caterpillar, he's the notorious SKA Rebels. He sticks out like a sore thumb with a yellow drawstring bag. That's our guy!" Viggo said.

"Isn't he worried about the Totalist Military catching him?" Leaf asked.

"He's renowned for his brute force, capable of effortlessly taking down a dozen Totalist snakes and demolishing a building in the process. He thrives on attention, yet his intellect is as dense as his muscles. That's why he's our target, and our odds improve significantly if we outsmart him. If anything goes wrong, break for it and regroup at our safe nest."

Leaf nodded.

Viggo hopped onto the loose pipe on the side of the building and slid down.

Leaf followed.

Viggo glanced at Leaf with concern, though they both understood that this wasn't the moment for apprehension. It's go time!

Viggo lowered his head, pivoted around the corner, and collided into Heavy Caterpillar.

"Oowww! Sorry, mister!" Viggo said, giving his rock-hard abs a hard pat.

Leaf walked past Viggo.

"I didn't mean to bump..."

"Move, kid! I don't have time to chit-chat," Heavy Caterpillar boomed in a deep voice.

"OK..." Viggo opened his fanny pack. "Well, let me offer you a gift as an apology."

Heavy Caterpillar grasped Leaf's hand from behind and turned around, "What a scrawny, sticky little hand thinks you're doin'?"

"Oouch! Mister, you've got toilet paper stuck to your pants!"

Heavy Caterpillar lifted Leaf by his arm, with toilet paper in his hand, as a crowd gathered around them.

Leaf said tearfully, "You're hurting me, mister!"

The group murmured and pointed at Heavy Caterpillar.

"You're hurting the little kid, you big blockhead," a young lady shouted.

"Just cuz you think you're big doesn't mean you can pick on us, little Totalist!" called a short man behind the group.

Heavy Caterpillar glanced around as Totalist pointed and shouted at him, the booming music echoing in the background.

Heavy Caterpillar roared, "Shut Up!"

"Hey! Mister!" Viggo shouted.

Heavy Caterpillar turned, and a flurry of chilly peppers flew into his eyes.

"Aaahhh!!" Heavy Caterpillar let out a scream.

Viggo kicked him in the shin, causing him to release Leaf. The crowd cheered!

"You little piece of pu pu!" Heavy Caterpillar swung his arms wide open and spun in a circle, his burning eyes closed. Viggo and Leaf darted into the crowd.

"Brother, I couldn't get it! He caught me too fast!" Leaf said.

"Don't worry, I'd cut his bag and got TWO Dream Bracelets! And..." Viggo said excitedly, quickly stashing them in his fanny pack, then passed three tickets to Leaf, "You keep these tickets safe, and I'll deliver the bracelets to Arison for the grand rewards!"

"Alright! But what are these three tickets, brother?" Leaf asked.

"HA! These tickets are my golden key to Rain's heart. They're for the Lighting of Dream Welcome Ceremony!"

I'll be showered with hugs and kisses all day, Viggo thought dreamily.

"Brother, are you thinking of Rain again? You have that kissy face again," Leaf laughed.

"I was thinking how our life's gonna finally change for the better!" Viggo said.

Leaf hopped with joy as he ran.

"Wait for me at the safe nest," Viggo said.

"Got it, brother!"

Leaf and Viggo parted ways.

I wonder how Arison and the others are doing. How big is the reward? Viggo pondered.

Viggo hurried around an old building, out of sight from the road, and down the dark alleyway—a path he and Leaf often took when returning to Section 12. He lifted the manhole lid, jumped into the sewer, and navigated its underground mazes. Emerging at the end of the sewer tunnel, he stood and looked up at the cloudy night sky, with the smell of sewage wafting around him as the water ran off the ledge.

Finally! Finally, tonight, everything will change for the better! Viggo thought happily and let out a deep breath.

His breathing slowed down, and his expression gradually grew solemn.

He became serious and thought, *but knowing my luck.*

He glanced downward and could not help but feel excitement surge within him as the Huntsman hideout was hidden below in Section 12. The cold wind whistled through rusty pipes and rattled the loose metal panels, creating a low, rhythmic lullaby for sleepy children and adults alike. Section 12 appeared darker and quieter than usual, even for its eerie nature. There were no signs of giant rats lurking for their nightly treasures in the muddy street, nor was a soul in sight. Malevolent shadows stretched and deepened in every crevice.

Viggo puffed out his chest and clenched his fists, "Everything's on the line! No matter what happens, I will not fail again, not this time! Even if it costs me my life!"

He took a deep breath, then hopped and slid down the pipelines on the side of the mountain, jumping from rock to rock as the frosted blue rays illuminated the way. Viggo leaped off the last pipe and sprinted along the least-used path, which ran parallel to the Street Market. He knew the longer he remained in the open, the more perilous it would become. He froze in his tracks and scanned his surroundings. GLB gangs loitered at every corner, with more emerging as he looked on.

"You finally came home. We have been patiently waiting for you all night," Big B maliciously said.

Viggo stepped back, scanning his surroundings, only to find himself surrounded.

"There are rumors that you're somehow involved with the Totalist Military. I told myself that couldn't be true. Even a street rat of Section 12 wouldn't sink that low."

Voices murmured within the shadow.

Intensely, Viggo scanned for any opening but found all escape routes blocked.

"For some reason, the Totalist Military is suddenly interested in us, and they've captured some of my boys. I was heartbroken for a slight second. But then, there are these other rumors brewing, ones I couldn't ignore." Big B continued as he walked into the blue rays.

Viggo stood his ground and finally stared at Big B, not listening to anything he had said.

"Not so talkative tonight, huh? No worries, I've got a big heart. That is why they call me Big B. I can forget about those boys and what happened. We can always recruit new ones. But this other rumor, you must answer me. What's this mumble jumble I've heard about, some girly bracelets that sell more than gold shins?" Big B chuckled, and his GLB gang's fallacious laughed along.

"Hmmm... still quiet as a mouse. Maybe this will get our conversation started."

They dragged Leaf out from the darkness, his face downturned and blood dripping.

"LEAF!" Viggo shouted angrily and ran towards them!

"Ah ah ah." Big B said as he pulled his knife out.

Viggo stopped in his tracks, "He's got nothing to do with it! Let him go!"

"He talks! Magic, boys! That's why dirty, ruthless tricks are the best!" Big B walked to Leaf and lifted his bloodied chin with the knife, "He remained as silent as a mouse while we each took turns slowly beating him and beating him, and beating him. Not a single squeak escaped his lips. Now I know where he got it from."

They laughed again.

Viggo clenched his fists tightly, gritting his teeth as he observed Leaf's battered face: bloodied, both eyes swollen shut in black and red. His bony left cheek was swollen to the size of a fist, rendering him unconscious. Viggo's eyes blazed with rage, his heart throbbing with anger!

"Boy, for a small, bony guy, he was tough as nails, making our poor bloody fists ache. Then, a big light bulb popped into my big head. Vrat will tell us," Big B stared at Viggo directly, "Wouldn't you?"

A small, hardened blackness grew inside Viggo's chest, filled with potent rage, anger, and pain.

No response.

Big B looked at Leaf, surprised, "Oh no, he must have fallen asleep. Don't worry; we'll happily carry him to you once you hand over the two girly bracelets."

Viggo snapped his focus on Big B and demanded, "Bring him to me first."

Big B glanced around, then met Viggo's gaze.

"It's not like we can run from you," Viggo added.

Big B laughed and nodded. "Of course."

Two GLB gang members carried Leaf and dropped him in front of Viggo.

Viggo gently parted Leaf's bloody hair and stared at his blackened eyes. Viggo fought back the tears at the sight of Leaf's beaten face. He pulled Leaf close to his chest, feeling his fragile bones and cold hands.

Big B walked up to Viggo, "Awe, so touching. Now, about those two bracelets!"

Viggo closed his eyes, cutting off the tears, and took a deep breath. Without looking at him, "I will give you one of the Dream Bracelets now and the other when we reach Borat Edge."

"Why should I listen to what you say? Why don't I take it from you and kill you both right now?" Big B questioned.

Viggo pulled out the Dream Bracelet, holding it to his face. It shimmered in the frosted blue ray, "Because one Dream Bracelet is worth more than all of our pathetic lives combined, and I will gladly break it!"

The Dream Bracelet hypnotized Big B's wide eyes.

"And your boys will have to carry Leaf to Borat Edge."

"Why would we want to do that?" Big B asked.

"It's only fair since you and your boys had beaten him like this," Viggo said, looking at him.

"He's right, boss," Loose Tooth chimed in.

Big B's glare turned on Loose Tooth and snapped, "Did I ask for your useless words to slide out of your toothless brain?"

"Sorry, Boss!" Loose Tooth recoiled, apologetic as he shrank back into the crowd.

Big B signaled two GLB gang members to carry Leaf. Viggo tossed one of the Dream Bracelets to Big B.

Big B's smile stretched uncontrollably as he slipped the bracelet onto his wrist. "Would you look at that? This is worth more than all your useless lives combined! It's pure gold and... and... look at those different-colored crystals!" He raised his arm, admiring the glittering sparks it emitted.

Viggo's gaze was fixated on the Dream Bracelet, a great disappointment sunken into him and anger simmering.

"Let's hurry to Borat Edge for my second bracelet!" Big B commanded in a jolly voice.

They walked back toward Borat Edge.

Big B walked alongside Viggo, "How would a street rat from Section 12 have info about these girly things?"

Viggo ignored Big B and kept walking.

"I know our first encounter wasn't the friendliest, but that's all in the past. Now, we can talk about our future!"

Viggo kept walking.

"How about this: You tell me where you're getting your source from, and I'll make sure no one in Section 12 gives you any trouble for as long as I'm around!"

Viggo's look at Big B.

"And Leaf as well," Big B added with a friendly smile.

Viggo glanced at Big B's ugly smile, then turned around and walked away.

Big B grabbed Viggo's neck from behind and slammed his face into the muddy ground. As Big B lifted his face from the mud, Viggo gasped for air.

"It's SO hard to be nice when being bad is so much easier!" Big B repeatedly smashed Viggo's face into the mud, "Hahahaha!"

The mud covered Viggo's face and neck, making it slippy.

Big B lost his grip.

Viggo turned around, grabbed a handful of mud, and smashed it into Big B's face as they both fell into the mud.

Viggo jumped on top of him, delivering powerful punches against his face. Each strike echoed with loud cracks. "This is for Leaf!"

Crack! Crack!

"If you dare to lay your fingers on him again, I will kill all of you! Even if it cost me my life!"

Crack!

Blood splattered out of Big B's nose as Viggo continued to punch him relentlessly. GLB gang members dragged Viggo off Big B and began to beat him. Viggo fought back fiercely, kicking them away, and pulled out the second Dream Bracelet.

"BACK OFF!" Viggo yelled, a little disoriented, stumbling around. The GLB gang members backed away, and Viggo got up, wiping the bloody mud off his face.

Big B pushed through, "Now that we're both bloody and muddy. I'll say we're even."

Viggo spat blood at Big B's feet.

"Let's keep walking, boys. We don't have all night," Big B ordered as he passed Viggo and shook the mud off his Dream Bracelet.

Viggo walked close to Leaf as the GLB gang members carried him along. They exited an old building and stepped onto the empty road.

"We're here, Borat Edge. Hand over the second bracelet!" Big B's shouted as he stopped.

Viggo scanned the area around Borat Edge's wall, "We haven't reached the destination yet. It's a building two blocks from here."

"This better not be a trap you're cooking. Otherwise, you and your friend will never see another day!"

"No trap. We want to go where more people are around so we can leave safely. Then you can have your bracelet."

"No! We've come far enough! Now give it to me!" Big B commanded.

The GLB gang pushed Leaf into Viggo's arms.

Viggo held him tightly, his desperation evident as he scanned the surroundings for anyone who could help them. But no one was in sight, and his heart sank. His hope faded.

Leaf slowly opened his eyes and looked at Viggo.

He painfully said, "Bro... ther..."

Viggo gave Leaf a stern look and whispered, "Safe nest."

Leaf took a deep breath, clenching his jaw shut as pain gripped his face.

Viggo released Leaf, unzipped his fanny pack, and retrieved the last Dream Bracelet. Big B and the GLB gang smiled at the sight of it.

Leaf grimaced in pain but took off running. The GLB gang chased after him!

"HEY!" Viggo shouted.

Viggo had held the Dream Bracelet high, standing firm. "You want this!"

"Let's that dead bait go! I want that bracelet and Vrat's head!" Big B commanded.

They stopped and faced Viggo.

Viggo's boots pressed firmly into the ground as he faced them fearlessly, "Come and try to pry it from my cold fist!"

They surrounded Viggo, rushing toward him. Two GLB gangs leaped at him from the sides, but Viggo stepped back, causing them to collide into each other. Three others charged at him from the front, but Viggo exploded a bag of hot pepper powder across their faces. They covered their eyes and screamed. Suddenly, Viggo was sent flying forward from a hard kick from behind, crashing into one of them. The cloud of hot pepper stunned his eyes as they fell to the ground. Fists rained down on his head and body! Viggo fought off as many as he could, but numerous punches landed, knocking his head against the hard ground. Brutal kicks to his side ribs stunned him, while the hot powder made him choke. Unable to block anymore, his head repeatedly swung left and right as blood splattered out.

Big B pushed through, and they dragged Viggo up to face him.

"Look at you now. What were you even thinking? I hope it was worth it." Big B laughed.

Big B grabbed the Dream Bracelet, but Viggo held it tightly. Big B pressed his knife against Viggo's left cheek. "Let go," he commanded, slicing it across.

Viggo bit his tongue, staring painfully at him, and still gripped firmly onto the bracelet as blood dripped from his left cheek.

"You willing to die for this?"

Viggo's fierce eyes pierced back at him. Big B saw the undying will in Viggo's eyes.

"Then die, Vrat!"

He swung his knife back.

Leaf pushed through the GLB gang and hurled his body into Big B, sending them both tumbling to the ground.

Heavy Caterpillar knocked aside half of the GLB gang!

"Come back!" His deep voice boomed, directed at Leaf.

He cracked his knuckles and shoulders. Heavy Caterpillar's sheer size intimidated the GLB gang, causing them to release Viggo and back away.

Viggo then lifted Leaf.

The GLB gang and Heavy Caterpillar closed in around them. Viggo looked down at the Dream Bracelet in his hand. Its brilliance sparkled. At that moment, Viggo glimpsed all their dreams coming true in his hand. For that split second, he felt truly happy.

"Bro... ther..."

Viggo glanced at Leaf; they're both were severely hurt. Turning to Big B, Viggo shouted, "You wanted it that bad!" He then threw the Dream Bracelet at Big B, who caught it as he got up.

"Think again." Heavy Caterpillar punched Big B in the face, sending him flying back and knocking him out. The GLB gang members swarmed onto Heavy Caterpillar as Viggo and Leaf made their escaped. Heavy Caterpillar spun wildly like a tornado, shaking off some attackers while others jumped in to take their place.

Viggo lifted a nearby manhole cover, and they entered the sewer, closing the lid behind them. They navigated through dark, maze-like tunnels until they reached a corner. They stopped and cautiously peeked around, finding no one in sight. A half-broken brown brick lay next to the entrance of a dark, circular tunnel.

Viggo leaned Leaf against the entrance, picked up a half-broken brick, and pushed it against another half-broken brick in the wall. The brick slid back, revealing a key nestled inside the dark tunnel. Carefully, Viggo carried Leaf into the tunnel and stopped at its end. He retrieved the key from the exposed brick and unlocked a door disguised as a painted brick wall in front of them. Placing the key back inside the brick, Viggo pushed it back into place, causing the outer brick to fall back outside near the entrance. He then assisted Leaf through the heavy door, which slowly closed and automatically locked behind them.

Inside the room, the four stone walls exuded a chilling aura. A fire flickered and swayed with the air currents emanating from a lantern on the table. Two makeshift mattresses, composed of stacked blankets, softened the harsh concrete floor and faced each other against the wall. Viggo gently laid Leaf on his bed and covered him with a blanket. He then went to the table, poured cold water onto a rag, and cleaned his face. He rinsed off the bloody rag at the side of the table and returned to Leaf's bedside. He carefully wiped away the blood from his blackened eyes and swollen left cheek. He noticed a slight reduction in the swelling.

Leaf barely parted his lips and whispered, "Bro... ther?"

"Rest. I'll get you some water." Viggo returned to the table.

Leaf slowly opened his eyes, and the dimly lit, cold, and somewhat empty room gradually became familiar. He noticed his bed of blankets on the opposite side. A bookshelf near the door held a haphazard assortment of snacks and makeshift traps.

Viggo poured water into a cup alongside his failed trap contraptions. Sitting beside Leaf, Viggo offered him the cup of water. Leaf sipped the cold water, but a sharp pain stabbed at his ribs, causing him to shut his eyes tightly.

"Take it easy, okay?" Viggo spoke softly.

Leaf looked at Viggo, wanting to say something.

"Don't worry about it," Viggo interrupted.

Leaf realized they had lost everything and looked down.

Viggo whispered, "What matters is that you're here and safe. Where does it hurt?"

Leaf leaned to the side and pulled up his shirt. His body showed no fat, only bones, with purple and red bruised ribs. Viggo stared at it. Leaf pulled his shirt down, noticing how it made Viggo feel.

"I'm okay," Leaf murmured, his head shifting slightly. The movement had left his mind exhausted, and his eyelids felt heavy. Leaf lay back down and passed out.

Viggo covered him with blankets, then got up and headed toward the door.

But he stopped.

Leaf's heavy breathing was audible as Viggo stood there with his eyes closed. The airflow struggled through the dried blood and narrow airway. With every other exhale, the breathing halted, followed by a small groan. Viggo stood there, unsure what to do, as the night slowly burned away. The fire in the lantern flickered and fought to stay alive. The room gradually darkened into darkness.

The door opened and closed.

❖

The cold wind howled against Viggo's hoodie as he sat on the rooftop ledge. The cut on his left cheek stung from the bitter cold. He gazed up at Commander Thorik and Commander Raz's statues standing proudly atop Borat Edge, facing the West side with the banners of 'Hope' and 'Perseverance' on their back, fluttering rapidly in the fierce wind. He had clung to those two words for so long. Now, those words felt meaningless and crumbled in his heart. But they are all he has to hold onto—amidst the storm of waves crashing below him.

Viggo stared at the strong facial structure of Commander Thorik's statue, the first to be elected as Commander of the Totalist Nation. He settled the Totalist on the flat mountaintop with vital open viewpoints all around. A great defense against ground attacks from below, especially the mountain's backside, was layered with large, jagged edge rocks against the crashing waves from the Grand Ocean. Forbidding any warships to be near or dock. It had promoted a long-lasting peace.

Two drunken Totalist made a commotion as they stumbled beneath a streetlight, laughing and accusing each other of being drunk. Their daily worries and pains seemed nonexistent, buried in a temporary, safe place. He sat there, watching them support each other to avoid falling as they wobbled along. The comforting notion of drowning his sorrow and laughing away his failures seemed like the answer he needed—an escape from the constant pain of setbacks and struggles.

Then, Leaf crossed his mind.

Viggo turned away from the drunks and surveyed the scene where the fight had taken place. The GLB gangs and Heavy Caterpillar were gone. The Dream Bracelets and tickets had vanished, along with the hope of leaving Section 12 and taking Rain to The Lighting of Dreams Welcome Ceremony. His body ached as he shivered from the cold emptiness that filled his heart. The wind howled harder into his hoodie, prompting him to pull his cloak tighter around himself as he sat in the dark with his arms folded. He closed his eyes and lowered his head. Across the street below, a slow pluck of notes emanated from a hologuitar. A long, gray-haired man leaned against a light pole as he played. The melancholy tune tugged at Viggo's broken emotions and defeated thoughts, and his once strong will now battered and bruised. The wind carried the slow, mournful melody down the empty street.

Viggo lingered late into the cold night.

Chapter 5

Pink Mellow

The morning gray clouds loomed over Section 12, the chaotic Street Market bustling as usual. Viggo's black hoodie partially covered his face as he walked past the storefronts, where the noise of arguments and bargaining for the best deals filled the air. He spotted three young kids up ahead, arguing with an elderly shopkeeper over a rusty fork they were trying to sell. Two boys appeared younger than Leaf, while the youngest girl stood silently. Viggo couldn't help but feel their daily struggles were more daunting than his own. His heart ached at the thought of what lay ahead, but he had no choice; he needed shin to help Leaf get better. It was another grim day for all of them.

Viggo looked down, ashamed to even meet their little faces, and quickened his pace. He bumped into the tallest boy, who watched Viggo retreat. The other younger boy and girl remained unaware of the encounter. Viggo navigated through the crowd, feeling guilty. He darted around a corner and into an alleyway, where he hid behind a trash bin. Voices echoed from nearby: "Do you see him!?" followed by a little girl crying as they rushed past the alleyway.

Opening his palm, Viggo stared at the rusted shin. Anger flooded his heart as he clutched the stolen item and slammed his fist against the trash bin, the heaviness in his chest growing. Closing his eyes, Viggo felt consumed by pain and self-loathing.

The tallest boy attempted to console the two younger children at the end of the street. Viggo approached them and held out his palm with the shin in it.

The tallest boy quickly grabbed it.

The little girl marched up to Viggo, punched his arm, and yelled, "You big meany!"

"I know," Viggo replied without making eye contact.

He handed them a hot pepper bag. "Use this if someone tries to hurt you."

They looked at him, surprised and confused, as he walked away.

Viggo returned to Safe Nest empty-handed. He approached the bed to check on Leaf, but he wasn't there.

Leaf stood before Big B, seated on a large crate in the center of his expansive warehouse. The space was cluttered with various-sized boxes and wooden crates stacked high, and GLB gang members were scattered throughout.

"Are you here to continue the beating?" Big B asked.

"I'm here to take back the three tickets you stole from me," Leaf answered.

Everyone laughed.

"Are you telling me you came here alone, hoping to take something from me while all my boys are around? We barely escaped that maniac of a beast from a good beating, and he stolen my two bracelets! I haven't even had time to think about revenge, and here you are, demanding things from me! You and what army?!"

"Just me."

They laughed, but Big B remained serious, staring at Leaf dead in the eyes. "You ain't getting that. Either you got beaten up so badly that you're brain dead or just stupid like Loose Tooth."

"Thanks, boss!" Loose Tooth blurted out without thinking.

Big B rolled his eyes, "Did spineless Vrat make you come here for it?"

"No. I ..."

"Get lost and go home! I'm tired of beating worthless kids."

"I'm not leaving till I get the tickets back," Leaf stated firmly.

"Now you're starting to piss me off! Go somewhere else if you want to die."

Leaf held up a small metal box. "I'll give you everything I have in here."

Big B laughed. "What does a bony street rat have that I want so badly to give away three tickets to the Lighting of Dreams Welcome Ceremonies? It's a once-in-a-century event!"

Leaf opened the box, and everyone leaned closer to get a better look. "These are my life savings, and I'm willing to give it all to you for the three tickets you stole from me."

"Don't act like you and Vrat didn't steal it from someone else! Acting all righteous," Big B retorted.

Leaf looked down, knowing it was the truth. "My brother told me to keep the tickets safe, and I lost them. The tickets mean so much to him, and I will give you all my life savings for it."

"I don't care! And I pity no one! Put down the box and walk away with whatever value life you have left. If not, my boys will just beat you up again."

"I will not leave, no matter how much you beat me!"

Loose Tooth snatched the metal box from behind and pushed Leaf down.

"Boss, there are only three shins in here!"

"Three shins! You wasted my time over three shins! Give me those three shins and throw him outta here!"

Loose Tooth and two other GLB gang members dragged Leaf into the alleyway. They punched him in the face, and Loose Tooth kicked him onto the sidewalk. Leaf crashed into a black-cloaked man. The man grabbed Leaf by the collar with one hand, tossed him aside, and then turned to face Loose Tooth and the other two gang members.

Loose Tooth, startled and frightened, shouted at Leaf as they ran away, "Don't ever come back!"

A young black girl with large pom-pom afros on each side, covering her small, sharp face, rushed to the hooded man and asked the girl behind him, "O my gosh! Are you OK, Pink Mellow?"

"I'm OK, Leila. Thank you," Pink Mellow replied.

With rainbow-curly pigtails, light brown eyes, and a turned-up nose, the youngest girl pushed the hooded man aside and stood next to Pink Mellow.

"That was closed! Were you hurt?" Ira asked.

"No, thank you, Ira, I'm fine. She would have crashed into me if Lyndon hadn't appeared before me," Pink Mellow replied. "Thank you, Lyndon."

Lyndon scanned around with his deep hazel eyes for any suspicious characters. In this area, nobody seemed to care about what had happened; fights and murders often occurred in broad daylight on the street.

Turning to Pink Mellow to ensure she was not hurt, Lyndon replied, "It's what I do." His tone lacked affection, but his actions suggested otherwise.

They all wore high-quality black cloaks. All three girls were similar in age. Pink Mellow, who was the same age as Leaf, had long dark brown hair, an adorable snub nose, light pink lips, and a petite face. Her smooth, light skin indicated that she was not from the area. Underneath her luxurious cloak, she wore a lavish pink silk blouse. She asked, "Where is that girl?"

"She's over there," Leila pointed at Leaf, lying on the muddy ground. She walked to Leaf and asked, "Are you OK?"

Leaf, covered in mud, grimaced as he rolled over in pain.

"Don't get too close to her. She might be dangerous!" Lelia shouted.

"I'm not a girl," Leaf replied, sweeping his dirty blond hair off his face. Struck by Leaf's captivating and cute appearance, Pink Mellow took several steps back. Their eyes met, causing her cheeks to turn rosy red.

"I'm really sorry! I didn't mean to crash into you guys," Leaf said as he got up and approached Pink Mellow.

Ira stepped in between them and blocked Leaf's path. "Who said you could talk to our Pink Mellow?"

"Pink Mellow? That is a funny name." Leaf chuckled.

Leila stepped in, saying, "It's not funny!" as she pushed Leaf back.

"What's your name?" Ira asked.

"I'm Leaf."

Leila and Ira burst out laughing.

Pink Mellow whispered under her breath, "Leaf," and had a sweet smile on her face.

Lyndon walked away.

"Where are you going, Lyndon? We got to protect our Pink Mellow!" Leila asked.

"If this keeps up, my ears will need protection," Lyndon muttered, heading to the corner and leaning against the tin wall, trying to ignore the chit-chat.

"Are you hurt?" Pink Mellow asked Leaf.

Leaf looked around. "Me?"

Pink Mellow nodded.

Leaf examined his arms and legs.

"Yes, you! Raccoon! He's been fighting, which means he's a bad person," Leila declared.

"Oo, yeah, I kinda got beaten up. But I think I'm okay now." Leaf touched the top of his head with his left hand and his chest with his right, rubbing them simultaneously. Pink Mellow giggled at Leaf's cute gestures.

"Why did they beat you up?" Ira asked.

"They stole three Lighting of Dreams tickets from me and then beat me up. I'm trying to get them back."

Ira turned to Leila. "Leila, aren't Lighting of Dreams tickets for Vellatine City and international invites only?"

"They are. You don't seem to be from either of those places. How did you get those three tickets?" Leila asked.

"My brother Viggo was able to take them from the SKA Rebels and gave them to me to keep safe. But the GLB gangs took them away," Leaf explained.

"SKA Rebels and gangs! We should stay away from him, Pink Mellow. He's big trouble!" Leila grabbed Pink Mellow and Ira's hands and pulled them away, but Pink Mellow swiped her hand away.

"He seems nice to me, and the bad guys hurt him and took his tickets," Pink Mellow said, then turned to Ira and instructed, "Give him three of our tickets."

"We shouldn't. How will we explain what happened to our tickets?!" Leila asked.

"The SKA Rebels," Pink Mellow replied confidently.

"Are you sure?" Ira asked.

Pink Mellow nodded in affirmation.

Ira took out three Lighting of Dreams tickets and handed them to him.

Leaf was shocked and pushed the tickets back, "Thank you, but I can't just take it from strangers."

"We all know each other's names, so technically, we're not strangers anymore," Pink Mellow explained.

"But I don't know you guys, and you're giving me something so...."

"Don't get beaten up anymore over these tickets. Take them. They're yours," Pink Mellow insisted with a smile.

Ira stuffed the tickets into Leaf's hands. Leaf was speechless as he looked at them.

Tears rolled down his cheeks. "No one had ever been so nice to me. I don't know you guys."

"I don't know why our Pink Mellow is so nice to you either. But you better put it away before it gets stolen again!" Leila suggested.

Leaf tucked the Lighting of Dreams tickets into his pocket. "Thank you! I would have given you my life savings, but they took that too."

A thought burst into Leaf mind as a big grin appear and he reached into his pants pocket, took out a rag, and unwrapped his half-torn bun. It still looked good, free of mud. Leaf smiled, then handed it to Pink Mellow.

"Eeww!" Ira screamed. "That rag is dirty!"

"We don't want that!" Leila shouted.

"It's a little dirty, but the bun still smells good. I haven't touched it," Leaf explained.

"Thank you, Leaf, but we're not hungry," Pink Mellow smiled kindly.

"I don't have anything else to offer you. Please take it!" Leaf insisted.

Pink Mellow took the bun. "Thank you. You don't have to give us anything in the future. Maybe we can see you again?"

Leila and Ira looked at Pink Mellow in shocked.

"At Lighting of Dreams Welcome Ceremony? Where will you be?" Pink Mellow asked.

"Uh, I... I don't know. But how will you go if you give me your three tickets?"

"Don't worry about us," Pink Mellow smiled reassuringly. "Why don't you meet us at The Sphere Station Six before tomorrow's celebration?"

"Um, okay. I'll need to ask my brother Viggo first. Do you know where it's located?" Leaf asked.

"It will be at D-One Wall by the Avedon River. Just show them your tickets at Sphere Station Six, and we'll be there," Pink Mellow explained.

"Thank you, Pink Mellow! I really appreciate you!" Leaf said with a big smile.

Pink Mellow blushed, waved goodbye to Leaf, and then walked toward Lyndon. Leila and Ira, still in shock over what had happened, quickly chased after Pink Mellow.

❖

Where are you?

Viggo ran through the Street Market, turning his head left and right, searching. The chaotic scene of faces, merchandise, and tin can buildings rushed past him in a blur. His heart raced faster and faster as Section 12 swirled around him, and everything became too overwhelming. Viggo stopped and leaned against an old tree.

What is happening to me?

Tightness gripped his chest, and a heavy weight bore down on him. His knees gave way, and he collapsed to the ground. The blackness inside him grew gradually, consuming his chest, and he passed out. Others walked past him, unaffected by the typical scene of another dying kid on the street.

A faint whisper called to him, and then a scream echoed in his ears.

"Brother!" Leaf shouted from a distance.

Viggo opened his eyes, feeling his heart rate return to normal. The blurry vision subsided, and he could hear footsteps approaching rapidly. Leaf ran towards Viggo, embracing him tightly. The warmth of Leaf's hug brought a sense of comfort and care—a feeling he had not felt in so long. Viggo took a deep breath, feeling loved. The weight of his worries and the strange sensation in his chest gradually dissipated.

"Brother, why are you on the ground?" Leaf asked.

Viggo snapped back, "Where did you go? Are you OK?!"

Viggo looked at Leaf intensely. Despite his slightly reduced bruised face, he was excited and happy.

"Guess what! Guess what!" Leaf exclaimed as he helped Viggo up.

Still caught up in his worry, Viggo responded, "You had me worried!"

Leaf glanced around, pulled Viggo closer, and whispered, "I got the tickets!"

"What tickets? You mean..."

Leaf nodded and hopped up and down.

"Really! How? Did you go to Big B!"

"Yes, but Pink Mellow gave it to me."

"Pink Mellow? Who? Why? What does he want in return?"

"Nothing! And Pink Mellow is a girl."

"Nothing is free in our world, Leaf. She must be after something!"

"Oh, yeah, she wanted to meet at... um... at some station... I think." Leaf tried to remember.

"Station?" Viggo looked around. "There's no station around here."

"I'm sorry, Brother. I got too excited, and now I've forgotten."

"Don't worry. It might come back to you later. Just make sure you keep those tickets safe, and no more running off by yourself!"

Viggo hugged Leaf tightly. "I'm glad you're Okay. We should also check in on Arison and let him know what happened."

Leaf nodded, and Viggo ruffled his hair.

Arison lived in the middle of the Borat Section, on the third floor of the laundromat store. The damp building had a musty smell. Viggo opened the door to Arison's room. The morning light streamed through a crack in the curtain, illuminating the clean and organized space—just the way Arison preferred things. A small table lamp cast light on an open wound on Arison's upper left arm.

"Glad to see you both alive," Arison said with a pained expression as he threaded the needle through his wound.

"Do you need help?" Viggo asked.

"Nah. I should be done soon," Arison replied, focused on his task.

"That looks like it hurts," Leaf commented.

"It does. A lot of our brothers didn't make it out. I see you both got a bit of a beating as well," Arison said, still stitching his wound.

"We failed," Viggo admitted.

"So did we. Those SKA Rebels are out of our league. We thought our chances would be much higher after they exhausted most of their resources on the heist. But they are still too good and better equipped. White Sting will not be happy with our substantial loss, which will put us back for a good while."

Arison pulled the thread tight and knotted the wound closed. He then rolled down his sleeve and put on his heavy brown metal-button jacket.

"What should we do now?" Viggo asked.

"The International VIPs are scheduled to arrive very soon. Let's check it out from the roof deck. Security is on high alert after last night's heist, and any mistake will be dealt with harshly. We need to lay low and stay out of sight. The final preparations for the Welcome Ceremony are also wrapping up," Arison explained.

"We have three tickets to the Welcome Ceremony," Viggo announced.

"Well, lucky you! You can sell each of them for a pretty silver shin," Arison suggested. "I know a few buyers…"

"Leaf and I will be attending with one of our friends so that we won't sell them," Viggo said.

Arison stood proudly. "Well, I didn't know I was that special?"

"You're not," Viggo replied bluntly.

Arison laughed. "Is that how you treat our friendship?"

"It's for his future girlfriend," Leaf added.

"Ah, well, that makes more sense. I wouldn't want any of you numskulls ruining my shot at a great relationship. Venice isn't cheap, and taking a girl out will cost even more," Arison teased.

"I've got a few shins saved up," Viggo replied.

"There are about eight shins in the top drawer. Take them, and don't forget to invite me to the wedding!" Arison playfully punched Viggo's arm. They smacked their hands together and hugged.

"Now go get yourself a wifey," Arison chuckled.

Viggo retrieved the eight shins and closed the drawer. "Thanks for always looking out for us."

"Shut up, and let's go check out the International VIP before I get too jealous," Arison said, giving Leaf a friendly hug.

"What about you, little man?" Arison asked as they walked to the door.

"Yuck!" Leaf shouted, shaking his head.

"Good. You don't need to be like your brother, wasting all his time and money—unless she's the one," Arison pointed out.

"She's the one," Viggo replied with a smile.

They reached the rooftop deck and gazed up at the sky. Two parallel formations of Hell Raptors hovered above, creating a clear lane for the Totalist Air Fleets and Motherships to pass from the opened Dome Shield to Vellatine City. The entire city erupted in cheers as they welcomed the International VIP. Each Totalist Air Fleet was color-coded to represent the nations they were escorting in the Motherships.

"Brother, look at all the red jets coming in!" Leaf yelled excitedly as they zipped by overhead. The rush of the wind and adrenaline quickly filled their bodies, transporting them back to a childlike state of excitement.

"Wow! It's headed toward Commander Bazyli's statue!" Arison exclaimed as he dashed to the edge of the rooftop deck.

A line of red Totalist Air Fleet zipped by swiftly, their engines roaring as the wind tousled their hair. They streaked across the Sections and raced toward the statue. As they approached Commander Bazyli's statue, the jets split apart, spun to each side, and ascended into the clouds.

Commander Bazyli bore a long scar down the side of his right forehead, trailing into his white beard. His piercing gray eyes seemed to see through the facade of loyalty surrounding him. Standing seven feet tall, he was clad in red military body armor adorned with decorated medals. Proudly positioned at the edge of his statue's finger, his black cape billowed rapidly as the red Totalist Air Fleet zoomed up alongside him on his left.

Patiently waiting on the left palm of the statue stood the Royal Totalist King Roy, sporting a well-trimmed black beard and deep blue eyes. His prominent nose pointed upward with pride, suggesting a life of luxury and indulgence. Despite the passage of years, he still appeared youthful due to his pampered lifestyle and pursuit of countless young ladies over time. King Roy wore his grand Royal Crown, adorned with precious gems, fitting perfectly atop his head.

Beside him stood his most recent and longest-lasting Queen, Queen Glory, epitomizing the true beauty standard of Vellatine Totalist. She possessed light, silky skin, deep, rosy cheeks, stunning emerald almond-shaped eyes, long black eyelashes, a symmetrical button nose, and lush pink lips. Her hourglass figure accentuated her fulsome bosom. King Roy and Queen Glory were draped in long, opulent, deep purple cloaks adorned with lavish sparkling jewels, standing nobly as they observed the red Totalist Air Fleet soaring into the clouds.

Behind King Roy and Queen Glory stood Commander Bazyli's top commanders: Lieutenant General Bradstone, overseeing the Royal Justices; Major General Vic, in charge of the Elite Black; General Crocrovich, leading the Totalist Infantry; Admiral Baylee, commanding the Totalist Ocean Defense and Offense; and Colonel Steel, heading the Totalist Air Fleets. Each officer was impeccably groomed in crisp military attire and stood patiently before a giant hologram of Ourania World.

"That is the power of our Totalist Air Fleet!" Arison yelled.

Viggo and Leaf were in awe as the steady stream of Totalist Air Fleet jets zoomed overhead!

"They're escorting the first International VIP, the Majestic Royal Mothership!" Arison shouted.

"Wow!" Leaf yelled against the rushing wind.

The sheer size of the red mothership cast a shadow over half of the Borat Section, eliciting cheers from the Totalist's people as they welcomed the arrival of the Majestic Royal fighters.

"Are they bringing in that many Majestic Royals?" Viggo asked as the red Mothership flew past.

"No, there's only a small group aboard the Mothership. They serve as protectors and escorts for the two Majestic Royal fighters who will compete in the Lighting of Dreams Battle World!" Arison clarified.

"Battle World?" Viggo asked curiously.

"Every century, two fighters of each participating nation compete to become the next Ourania World Champion!" Arison explained. "So, they are truly the best of the best from their countries!"

The red Mothership deployed a Wing Destroyer down to the statue's palm, where the Totalist leaders awaited.

"Look, Brother! The white..."

The white Totalist Air Fleet zoom! Zoom! Zoom by!

Leaf tumbled backward, and Viggo and Arison laughed as the white Totalist Air Fleet flew by so quickly. A group of eighteen white Gargoyles, led by two white and gold Gargoyles, glided in with great speed toward the statue.

"Are those Gargoyles?" Leaf asked as he got back up.

"I don't know much about them, but it sure looks like it," Arison admitted.

The Gargoyles' faces looked stern and fierce. They stood at least ten feet tall and had massive bodies, with wingspans ranging from twenty-four to thirty feet across. The Totalist below were in shock and awe. They pointed and whispered among each other, and many feared the giant flying beasts above. The cries of babies could be heard amid the commotion.

"They don't resemble the ones from Section 12, all weak and small," Viggo remarked.

"Yeah. These look massive," Arison said.

"Are they also here for the Battle World?" Leaf inquired.

"I believe so. I doubt anyone can take those beasts down," Arison replied, pointing towards the approaching black Totalist Air Fleet. "Look! That's the Ukko!"

"Who?" Leaf asked, puzzled.

Arison leaned closer to Leaf, his excitement evident. "They're the clans of the Ninja from the far Northeast, across the Grand Ocean. They possess strange magical powers that make you search aimlessly for your head for eternity."

"Really?" Leaf asked, visibly scared as he ran behind Viggo.

"Arison is just joking with you," Viggo reassured with a laugh.

"Am I?" Arison chuckled mischievously.

"Is anyone from our Totalist Federation participating in the Lighting of Dreams Battle World?" Viggo inquired.

"Of course, but it's classified. Even White String doesn't have that info."

"Do you know where the Battle World will take place?" Viggo asked.

"Vellatine City, Section 10, at the City of Lights Stadium," Arison said.

"The City of Lights? There's no way we can watch it." Viggo said, disappointed.

"We can't watch it in person, but they're broadcasting it live on top of the whole Avedon River! It'll be a fifty-foot-tall live holoscreen, action-packed!" Arison replied.

"Wow. This is so amazing!" Leaf exclaimed as they watched the last Black Mothership arrive at the Statue of Commander Bazyli.

Chapter 6

Lighting of Dreams Welcome Ceremony

A pink laser cut through the rust on the armor plate of the Hawk Robot. Mr. Hairo blew away the dust and wiped down the shiny armor plate.

"How does it look now, Rain?"

Rain walked over to the table, jumped onto her chair, "Booster looks much better now, Daddy. Can I install the new pulsar power cells in her dual rockets?"

"Yes and be careful."

"I know, Daddy! I'll be careful. I wished you had gotten more of this from the Weaponry and Research Lab in Vellatine City before you left." Rain said as she struggled to open the rocket hatch with a small tool.

Mr. Hairo handed Rain his laser multi-tool, "Used Deca Unlock. It's the perfect setting for it."

Rain scrolled through different holoscreen tools, selected the appropriate one, and flipped the holoscreen to activate the liquid titanium. It contoured to the unique lock on the hatch and solidified instantly into a secure form. She easily removed the hatch on both rockets and installed the pulsar power cells.

"These laser multi-tools saved me many times when I worked on some top-secret projects."

"I rarely hear you talk about your projects, Daddy. Can you tell me about them?"

"O, it's nothing special."

"Well, it's special enough to be top secret, right, Daddy? You don't work for them anymore; it must be old news. Please tell me. Just one!" She made a sad puppy look.

Mr. Hairo took a deep breath.

"Sure, hon, just one." Mr. Hairo smiled, "Back in the day, we were tasked with creating a new type of special ops unit for the Totalist Military to handle challenging operations outside our usual specialties. Our mission was to develop an advanced robot with a human-brain fusion. I was against using our fellow soldiers, but Commander Bazyli was adamant. The process of merging human brains with robotic bodies led to many complications and failures. It was disastrous, resulting in the loss of many good soldiers and significant funding. Then, I secretly developed a fully self-aware robotic design without needing a human brain. Everything worked flawlessly in the projection system, and it could follow basic commands within days. I needed to create a prototype and assemble a team I could trust. I recruited three of the best Totalist I knew. Dr. Jacob was an exceptional conceptual designer, able to detect minor design flaws before construction. Dr. Shield was a prodigy in weaponry and ammunition creation, and Big Paul Jackson was the finest builder in Vellatine City. That's when I also met Helen."

"Mom!"

Mr. Hairo laughed. "Yes, she and I created the main XM Universal Neuro Intelligent Terminal program, which we now refer to as the XM Unit. Once the prototype was complete, we showcased it to Commander Bazyli through the military's most brutal combat scenarios, and it performed flawless. Commander Bazyli was ecstatic, and the project was generously rewarded. However, I knew that such a powerful tool in the military's hands could cause a lot of misery in the Ourania World. During the creation process, I secretly developed a nuke serum as a fail-safe to shut down the XM Unit entirely if it became uncontrollable. Big Paul Jackson installed it into the XM Unit cerebrum."

"Wow, how would you activate the nuke serum, Daddy?"

"Unfortunately, it cannot be activated."

"What do you mean?"

"When Commander Bazyli learned about the nuke serum, he ordered it to be disabled and removed. We complied and deactivated it. Big Paul Jackson removed it. I discreetly relocated the nuke serum of the central trigger system under its left foot using the laser multi-tool."

"You went against Commander Bazyli's order; that could mean death, Daddy!"

"Any rational person would not act recklessly, but yes, I did. From that day on, I began questioning my role as the Head of Weaponry and Research for the Totalist Military. I realized the harmful impact my creations were having on innocent Totalist in the Ourania World. Instead of benefiting them, my inventions were exploited for power and greed."

"Is that why you left, Daddy?"

Mr. Hairo looked at Rain with sad eyes and nodded. Rain hugged him tightly.

Rain held the laser multi-tool and said, "With this, we can begin building a better world. I searched everywhere for a tool like this but couldn't find anything similar."

"That's because this was personally made for me." Mr. Hairo said.

Surprised, Rain looked at the laser multi-tool and discovered a letter H inscribed at the bottom.

"Did mom make this for you?"

Mr. Hairo chuckled, "You've got her quick wit. It's been by my side ever since I can remember."

Rain looked at the laser multi-tool and admired the craftsmanship even more. "Wow, Mom made this," She remarked. Rain then scrolled through the holoscreen tools one at a time.

"I had more hair and less weight before we started dating. Now, I have less hair and more weight."

Rain laughed, "You're still my Daddy. I loved you then, and I love you now even more!"

Mr. Hairo looked at Rain and smiled gently.

"I was going to give you this laser multi-tool when you turn eighteen. But since it's already in your hand, it feels right."

"Really, Daddy!"

"Of course, silly, what's mine is yours."

Mr. Hairo surveyed their old tin can walls, noticing their poor condition. The tiny house was dim and messy, with a single large photo of Mr. Hairo laughing and chasing Rain in the garden when she was four years old hanging on the side wall. Mr. Hairo looked at Rain as she stood by her chair, engrossed in scrolling through the holoscreen tools.

It's been ten years. Mr. Hairo thought.

"Rain," he said, his throat swelling.

Rain turned around. "Yes, Daddy?"

Mr. Hairo looked at her and wondered where the time had gone. He could vividly remember it as if it were just yesterday. She once wobbled her little body, trying to stand on her own two feet, staying still as she sought perfect balance. Now, standing before him was a beautiful young lady.

"I just wanted to say I'm sorry."

Rain looked confused. "For what?"

"For not giving you a better life."

"I don't understand?"

"I didn't realize how long we had been living here." He continued to look around. "I thought if I followed my morals and instincts and took a leap of faith, I could make Ourania a better place. But it's been ten years since I took that chance, and Section 12 has made it difficult to realize my dream. Now, I still have nothing to offer you. If I had stayed in Vellatine City, you would have received a superior education, a better opportunity, and a large home. I could have bought you anything your heart desired." Mr. Hairo choked up, tears rolling down his cheeks. "I still remember that doll you wanted. You cried your little heart out and saying no pained me so much. I promised I would get it for you next time, but that next time never came."

She sat beside him and held his hand, "It's Okay, Daddy. I don't care for any of those things. You've given me what truly matters and taught me invaluable lessons that shin can't buy. Please don't feel sad. I'm doing fine. I'm just happy that we're together."

He tapped her petite nose, "You've always been so understanding and mature for your age. I know you'll make the right decision when that special someone comes along and makes you fall head over heels."

"If I ever feel that, does that mean he's the one?"

"It's a good sign. How you feel is very important—being together and having a good time with that special person. However, what truly matters is whether you can overcome challenges together. You must be willing to fight for this person no matter what, and he must be willing to fight for you as well. Only then can you know if he is the one."

A knock sounded at the door.

They looked surprised.

Rain went to open the metal door, and there stood Viggo.

"What do you want?"

"No, hello? Or missed you?"

"No."

"It's OK. After this, it will all change," Viggo smiled.

Leaf giggled from behind the tree, and Rain rolled her eyes.

"What happened to you? Did you get into another fight?"

"They started it! But the important thing is, we just saw the international VIP arrival, and it was super-duper cool!"

Rain closed her door, but Viggo stopped it with his foot.

"We also have three tickets for tomorrow's Lighting of Dreams Welcome Ceremony! Do you want to go?" Viggo asked, his excitement evident.

"Not interested," Rain said firmly before closing the door.

Viggo stood there, clearly shocked.

There was another knock at the door. Rain hesitated before opening it again.

"Why?"

"Because I'm not interested in any of Vellatine's stuff."

"It was tough to get these tickets! Even Leaf had to put up a fight!"

"Well, I appreciate Leaf for it. But I'm still not..."

"Fine! Mr. Hairo, would you like to go?" Viggo yelled from the door. Laughter erupted from inside.

"That's also a no," Rain laughed.

Mr. Hairo walked to the door, "You are too kind, Viggo, to consider an old man like me. Thank you for cheering me up, but I would just end up dozing through your fun. Rain, why don't you go? Have some fun."

"I don't care for it and would rather be working on mechanical parts with you."

"There will be many days for that, and you can tell me all about this event when you get back."

"That's a great idea, Mr. Hairo! I'll stop by tomorrow to pick up Rain!" Viggo quickly ran away.

Mr. Hairo waved goodbye.

"Hey!" Rain yelled to Viggo.

"Thank you, Mr. Hairo! Can't hear you, Rain!" Viggo yelled as he jumped up and down, shouting, "Wahoo!"

Leaf dashed out from behind the tree, waved goodbye to Mr. Hairo and Rain, and then chased after Viggo.

Mr. Hairo laughed.

"He's not the one, Daddy!" Rain said, her face puffed up with irritation.

"Maybe not. But it doesn't seem like he's giving up anytime soon," Mr. Hairo teased.

Rain closed the door and ignored Mr. Hairo. She then focused on playing with the laser multi-tool, scrolling to the last holoscreen, which displayed a key.

"What is this key for, Daddy?"

Mr. Hairo and Rain walked back to the desks.

"That key is for the box I safely stored on my top shelf. It's a gift made by your mom and me, and we wanted to give it to you when you turn eighteen."

"Can I open it now!?"

"Two more years, honey. That's what your mom and I agreed upon."

"What if I forget in two years?"

"I know you won't."

"Alright, Daddy. I'll carry this tool by my side from now on, just like you did." Rain said cheerfully as she clipped the laser multi-tool onto her belt.

❖

The morning sun cracked the night sky, casting golden rays that shimmered upon the darkness, heralding a new day— a day Viggo Van Hunt had only dreamt of. Everything he had endured—the struggles, the rejections—had led to this day. Today marked the Lighting of Dreams Welcome Ceremony! Viggo sensed it was the beginning of many great things to come, and for once, everything seemed poised to go right.

Viggo, Rain, and Leaf stood on the streets of Borat Section, feeling the excitement grow little by little as each home awakened to this joyous day, marked by the ancient bells ringing for the first time in a century from Vellatine City to Borat Section. Soft, uplifting orchestra music began to play across all the Sections. Flocks of birds soared high in the sky, and the landscape was adorned with festive decorations. Colorful, differently designed glowing spheres of lights decorated each building, while the Dome Shield sprayed mist over the five Diamond Ring Bridges, forming giant rainbow arcs at each ring. Each Section burst into life as food carts fired up their stoves, preparing various foods—from the famous honey-glazed juicy roast beef to sweet cream pudding desserts and exotic fresh fruits. Stores opened their doors, showcasing new Lighting of Dreams toys and regional apparel. Booths with games and prizes, roller coaster rides, street performers, and an animal petting area. Viggo, Rain, and Leaf were in awe of the spectacle before them. Everyone was living in the same rhythm of life, united in pursuit of the same goal and making the same dream a reality—the Lighting of Dreams.

"This looks incredible!" Rain exclaimed.

"Aren't you glad you decided to come on this date?" Viggo asked.

"This is NOT a date. I'm just curious about…"

"You can be curious about me anytime…"

Rain pushed the tip of Viggo's nose upward with her finger, "Don't get any ideas, Vgoo! I am only here because my dad insisted."

Viggo turned his head away from Rain's finger, "Well, I appreciated the sweet scent."

Rain made an angry face, and her finger collapsed into a fist, pushing it toward Viggo's face.

"Look! A flying wishing pig!" Viggo pointed in the sky.

Rain turned and gazed up at the flocks of birds. Viggo grabbed her fist, and they ran through the street together, laughing.

"Wait for me!" Leaf shouted, chasing after them.

They dashed past numerous food carts brimming with fresh, plump fruits, giant rainbow-colored candies hanging all around, and a cart laden with enormous chunks of meat roasting.

Leaf stopped and stared at the sight. "Wow. Brother, have you seen anything like this before?"

A burly Totalist Meat Owner noticed Leaf and said, "Good morning, young customers! Would you like to try Borat Section's juiciest grilled roast beef?"

"O, no sir, I have no shin. I can get full just smelling it; it smells great!" Leaf replied politely.

The Meat Owner stared at Leaf from head to toe as Viggo and Rain approached.

"Those sure smells good! Do you offer any samples, mister?" Viggo asked.

"Samples? Why is there trash from Section 12 here!"

Viggo stepped before Leaf, "Hey, fat mutt butt butt! You're in the presence of greatness! Remember that before you make those rude remarks! I could buy out your whole meat cart and leave you jobless!"

"Broken trash is not welcome here! Pack up your garbage and your little girlfriend and get away from my cart! Sample? Hmph!" snorted the Meat Owner.

Viggo turned to Rain and laughed. "He said you're my..."

Rain punched Viggo, causing him to fall to the ground.

The Meat Owner was taken aback and handed Rain a bowl of meat. "Young lady, I don't want any trouble! Here are some free samples for you and your friends. Please leave here in peace."

"You're too kind, mister!" Rain replied gratefully.

"Thank you, sir!" Leaf said.

Viggo staggered to his feet, rubbing his head. Rain grabbed his hand and pulled him along. Viggo glanced at his hand held by Rain's soft grip; his heart quickened. The pain faded, replaced by a sudden sense of relief. Leaf waved goodbye to the Meat Owner.

Rain handed Leaf and Viggo a large chunk of meat on a stick.

Viggo grabbed it, still smiling at Rain. She gave him the looks, and Viggo took a big bite. The meat was soft and tender, easily pulling apart with sweet, juicy flavors bursting out!

"Holy! The meat just melted in my mouth!" Viggo said as he barely chewed it.

"Is this what meat tastes like? It's so good and juicy!" Leaf spoke with his cheeks stuffed full.

They quickly gobbled down the meat. Rain let out a loud burp. Viggo and Leaf exchanged looks.

"Just be glad it's only the attic," Rain said, lightly bumping her chest with her fist as she walked down the street.

"Wow. What a girl," Viggo said.

They laughed and ran through the streets, passing food carts and stores.

At the 300 feet D-Three Wall entrance, Viggo handed the gate guard three credentials, who scanned each one.

"Viggo LeBest. Age twenty-one. Stocks Management. No match. Allowed," the Female Voice Scanner announced as it scanned Viggo's body.

"You may pass," the Guard said.

"Leaf DeGreat. Age fifteen. Stocks apprentice. No match. Allowed," the Female Voice Scanner announced, scanning Leaf's body.

"You may pass," the Guard repeated.

"Rain Loveheart. Age twenty-one. Special Dancer. No match. Allowed," the Female Voice Scanner stated, scanning Rain's body.

"You may pass slowly," the Guard said, winking at Rain.

They passed the D-Three Wall checked point.

"Special Dancer!" Rain muttered angrily to Viggo as they walked into the Corecrest Section.

"I didn't come up with that title. I just gave them some suggestions. Hey, it works!" Viggo chuckled.

Corecrest Section is a middle-class society within the Totalist Federation characterized by its imaginative, abstract, and futuristic cityscape. It serves as an experimental hub for construction, pioneering advancements in building techniques and telegate transportation. Corecrest is renowned as the birthplace of innovative design, overseeing the entire process from conceptualization to the assembly of buildings and technological components. It is a perpetual manufacturing center fueling the Totalist Federation's ambitious quest for universal conquest and expansion.

Rain looked around at the modern steel buildings and abstract glass towers. Unlike the Borat Section, there is no limit to the creativity in building design here. Some buildings were covered with polka dots, wave patterns, and square and circle merged designs. The buildings were plastered with random colors as if they were done by eight-year-olds. In contrast, others exuded a dark and mysterious aura with hidden doors and intriguing features. Some structures were unconventional, lacking walls, and emitted strange sounds reminiscent of old gastrointestinal rumblings as they shifted left and right in search of a stable foundation. Viggo and Leaf found amusement in the noisy, 'farting' building, bursting into laughter as they held each other in tears while staring at a peculiar brown brick wall. Rain, unamused, walked away to encourage them to move on. Amidst the diverse architecture, propped-up booths filled with games and prizes lined the streets, adorned with giant stuffed animals hanging all around.

"Rain, just let me know which stuffed animal you want, and I'll win it for you!" Viggo said confidently.

"I don't need anything. Save your shins."

"I'm going to get you something; you might as well choose one."

Rain suddenly recognized Viggo's kindness.

"I want a hamster!" Leaf shouted.

Viggo slowly nudged Leaf aside. "No hamster."

Viggo walked toward a shooting game booth adorned with giant killer dragons, crazy buck-toothed sharks, and ten armed giants with glowing three-eyed lights, all roaring menacingly. He placed five shins on the table, prompting a smirk from the young Booth Attendant.

"How many games can I get?" Viggo asked.

The Attendant pointed at the sign with his stick, which read, 'Twenty-five shins per shot.'

Viggo's mouth dropped open in shock.

"Why don't you play a kiddy game like Fishing for Peanuts or Crystal Charm' for foolish kids?"

"What if I throw in some extra items along with my five shins?" Viggo asked.

"Hmm... What you got?" The Attendant raised his eyebrow as Viggo unzipped his fanny pack and emptied its contents onto the table. Among the items were bags of hot pepper powder, spider web strings, marbles, spiky pins, a rat, and Mr. Stinky, a skunk.

"Eewww! Get your junk out of here! Who carries spider webs in their bag along with a rat and a skunk?!" the Attendant shouted angrily, pushing Mr. Stinky away with his stick. In response, Mr. Stinky snarled back.

"Fine, I'll take my shins and valuables to someone who will appreciate them!" Viggo put his stuff back.

"Why do you have a rat and a skunk in your fanny pack?" Rain questioned.

"I don't know how the rat got in there, but you never know when you'll need Mr. Stinky. I found him by the forest near your house before we picked you up."

"No one needs a skunk. Get out of here before you drive off my customers!" the Attendant yelled.

"You're doing a good job of that yourself!" Viggo retorted as Rain pulled him away from the booth.

"I didn't want that stuff anyway. Let's check out the crystal charms he mentioned," Rain said.

"I see it, Rain! It's over there!" Leaf pointed to the tent across the street with crystals hanging outside.

They walked towards it.

"Look! It's only two shins to play; that seems much more reasonable." Rain said as she read the sign on the tent.

"Yeah, but that booth had light-up killer dragons, crazy buck-tooth sharks, and an incredible ten-armed, three-eyed giant! Ten arms!" Viggo shouted.

"I never wanted any of that," Rain replied.

"Are you sure? Don't you want to cuddle with a ten-armed giant that roars while you sleep?"

"I do! I DO!" Leaf's hand flew way up!

Viggo quickly pointed to Leaf to emphasize his point, "See!"

Rain shook her head.

"Okay, fine. I'll get you one of those toy charms," Viggo said disappointedly.

Madam Crystal, wearing a black hoodie with one dead gray eye visible, stood behind them and corrected Viggo in a scratchy old voice, "They are not toys. The crystals choose you before you even think of them."

Viggo, Rain, and Leaf seized up in shock and stepped aside as Madam Crystal walked past them.

Viggo whispered, "She's a creepy old lady! This must be a shady little place. When did she get behind us?"

"You are?" Rain asked.

Madam Crystal pulled off her black hoodies, revealing her short, white, frizzy perm hair and small face that seemed unnoticeable because all their attention was drawn to her dead gray eye or empty black eye socket.

"I am Madam Crystal—unique and unparalleled. My crystals bring upon you good luck, health, and wealth..."

Viggo whispered, "Do you want this fake stuff, Rain? We could spend our shins on more worthwhile things."

"And perhaps even a touch of much-needed, magical love," Madam Crystal continued.

Viggo's ears perked up.

"Not every chance will grant you a crystal. Would you like to test your luck and potentially acquire one of my precious crystals?"

"Here are two shins, old lady. What do I need to do to win the magical love one?"

"It would take more than just two shins from you," Madam Crystal replied, her gaze fixed on Viggo with her eerie gray eye.

Madam Crystal took Viggo's two shins, her rough, cracked hand brushing against his as she passed through the black curtain. Chills ran up Viggo's spine.

He looked at Rain and thought, *what will I do for the chance of love?*

"I like her. This little thrill is worth the two shins already." Rain chuckled.

"I hope you don't turn out like her!" Viggo said.

"If you keep this up, I might just haunt your dreams!"

"You've already been in my dreams," Viggo smiled.

Rain entered the dark tent without a word. Leaf chuckled and trailed after. Within, mysterious shimmers and glitters danced in the shadows. Their eyes adjusted, and sparks flickered in and out of view. Rain glanced up at the ceiling adorned with countless small and large crystals. The clarity and brilliance of these crystals stole Rain's breath.

"Wow," Leaf said.

"How do they shine like that when no lights are here?" Viggo asked in awe.

Madam Crystal sat at the table, accompanied by a giant clear crystal ball.

"Viggo, have a seat," Madam Crystal commanded.

"I don't remember telling her my name," Viggo questioned.

Leaf shrugged his shoulders. Viggo approached the table and sat before the giant, clear crystal ball. Madam Crystal positioned her hands slightly above the ball, slowly moving them around.

"Chan Tal Car Me Ra! RA SHIN TAR! What lies deep within thy scar!" Madam Crystal chanted over and over and over again.

The crystal ball started to glow. Viggo leaned back in his chair while Rain and Leaf stepped back, watching as the crystals around the room and on the ceiling began to emit different colors.

Madam Crystal shook rapidly, one eye closed in alarm, "No! No! No!"

The giant, glowing crystal ball grew brighter. Viggo stared intensely into it, shaking his head from side to side. He could not blink or tear his gaze away from its dazzling brightness.

"Uh, Viggo, maybe we should leave..." Rain said nervously.

"Nooo!!" Viggo screamed.

The giant crystal ball exploded as the crystal shards flew toward them. The force of the explosion knocked them to the ground, and the shockwaves shattered the other crystals around the room.

Rain coughed, dusted herself off, and stood up. Tiny crystal shards covered the floor. She helped Leaf to his feet.

"Is that blood on your chest?"

Leaf touched his chest. "I don't think so."

"Are you hurt anywhere?"

"I don't feel any pain," Leaf replied as he checked himself.

Rain wondered aloud, "Then whose bloods..."

Rain rushed over to Viggo, lifting his head.

"Viggo! Are you hurt? Viggo!" Rain panicked.

He slowly opened his eyes, still in a daze, "An angel whispered in my ear, bringing me back to life. If it had been a kiss instead, I might have thought I was in heaven."

Rain dropped Viggo's head on the floor.

"Ouch!" Viggo shouted as he sat up.

"He's okay."

"For a moment, I think you actually care for me," Viggo remarked.

"You bumped your head too hard." Rain replied.

"I detected a hint of concern when you called my name."

"I thought you were dead!" Rain exclaimed.

"Aha! So, you do care!" Viggo pointed.

"Maybe I need to bump your head harder next time to make sure you stay dead!" Rain made a fist, and Viggo quickly grabbed her hand.

"You'd better handle me gently. Otherwise, you might accidentally break this crystal!" Viggo said as he held up a bluish-purple glowing crystal and placed it in her hand. Rain was mesmerized by the crystal's clear bluish-purple glow and how the sparkles caught her breath in its lights.

"Where did you acquire this?" Rain asked.

"I just pulled it from my chest, and surprisingly, I feel no pain. That old hag wasn't joking about the crystal choosing you."

Rain and Leaf looked at Viggo's chest with a minor wound as the crystal had gone through his brown cloak and shirt.

"But... I saw something... it was... very dark and terrifying," Viggo said.

Leaf stood behind Rain and peeked from behind.

"What did you see?" Rain asked.

"I saw you."

"Me?"

"You were on the ground, not moving. A dark figure stood next to you, its long black hair covering its face to the ground with long black arms..."

Leaf buried his face behind Rain.

"Choking you!" Viggo yelled.

"Aaahh!" Leaf screamed.

"Vgoo, stop! You're scaring Leaf!" Rain demanded as she hugged Leaf, "Don't be scared. Vgoo is just trying to frighten us. He hit his head too hard during the crystal ball explosion."

"But I saw it!" Viggo protested.

"My crystal ball didn't explode." Madam Crystal said softly.

They turned to look at Madam Crystal, seated at the table beside the giant crystal ball.

"Wait! What? We all saw that giant Crystal ball and the myriad crystals on the ceiling..." Rain looked up, observing the crystals suspended above, radiating in various colors. Viggo and Leaf scanned the room; it appeared unchanged from their initial entrance. Viggo checked his clothing and chest; both were undamaged.

"Whoa! What trickery is this?" Viggo exclaimed.

"No trick. What you hold is my precious 'Faith of One,' the strongest of all my crystals."

"Faith of One?" Rain repeated, looking at the bluish-purple crystal in her hand.

"It signifies the unbreakable bond between two lovers. Its unwavering determination to endure even the darkest times makes its power boundless. But..."

A loud explosion of fireworks echoed from outside, followed by an announcement.

"Welcome, everyone, to our centennial event, the Lighting of Dreams Welcome Ceremony! We are thrilled that you could join us to experience this once-in-a-lifetime celebration! We are honored and grateful to host the Lighting of Dreams in our Totalist Federation, welcoming our Ourania brothers and sisters! Please enjoy the wonderful food, games, rides, and the spectacular Lighting of Dreams in the sky at our Sphere Stations at Venice D-One Wall and Vellatine City Skylines! May all your wishes come true!"

Multiple fireworks exploded in the sky.

Leaf's face lit up, and he dashed outside the tent, shouting, "Brother! It's starting!"

"Wait, what about Viggo's injury from the crystal explosion?" Rain remained puzzled as the fireworks continued to burst overhead.

Viggo looked at Rain impatiently, "Rain! Don't worry about all this mumbo jumbo right now! It's just an illusion trick! It's starting! Let's go!"

Viggo grabbed Rain's hand, and together, they ran out into the street to join Leaf. They stood together, gazing at the sky ablaze with fireworks with half of Zephaniah World, the two moons, and the stars behind it.

"It's beautiful," Rain said.

Leaf turned to Viggo, "Brother! I remember now. Pink Mellow

wanted to meet at Sphere Station Six before the celebration started! Do you think we can make it in time?"

"It seems like the celebration has already started, but if we take the Telegate to the D-Two Wall and then the Venice Telegate to the Venice D-One Wall, we should be at the Sphere Stations."

"OK! Let's go!" Leaf shouted excitedly and jumped up with happiness.

Rain stood there, oblivious to Viggo and Leaf's conversation, lost in the fireworks spectacle. For the first time in her life, she felt a deep sense of happiness, all because of Viggo. He had not given up on her, which had allowed her to savor moments like this and experience this newfound warmth. The fireworks painted the ember's sky in vivid hues, casting a morning-like glow on their faces. Rain admired the bluish-purple Faith of One crystal in her hand, cherishing its precious colors and significance.

Could he be the one?

Meanwhile, Viggo and Leaf took off running towards the large arc Telegate up ahead.

"Come on, Rain, let's go!" Viggo shouted.

Rain looked up at Viggo, smiled, and carefully tucked the Faith of One into her pocket before joining them in their sprint.

Suddenly, multiple loud, deep BOOM! BOOM! BOOM! Reverberated through the air as large white spheres launched into the sky from the eight Sphere Stations atop Venice D-One Wall and Vellatine City skylines.

"Look over there and there!" Rain exclaimed, her heart racing with excitement.

Fireworks erupted in every direction, with white spheres floating in the sky.

Rain felt like a little kid again, exclaiming, "Wow!"

If only tonight could last forever. She thought. *And if only Daddy were here to see this—it would have been perfect.*

Madam Crystal emerged outside and gazed up at the magnificent sky. She observed Viggo, Rain, and Leaf running toward the Telegate.

Chapter 7

A Night To Remember

The Telegate stood twenty feet tall, crafted from a gunmetal gray arch. Outer arches were linked to the top of the 'Corecrest West Telegate' sign. Two inner metal arches bent like a bow intersected from top to bottom in opposite directions. The Totalist departed from one side of the Telegate and arrived on the opposite side. Borat, Corecrest, and Venice Section each had Telegates positioned across eight locations: North, Northeast, East, Southeast, South, Southwest, West, and Northwest.

Viggo, Rain, and Leaf reached the Telegate.

"Each Sphere Station was situated near the Telegates. So, when Pink Mellow mentioned waiting at Sphere Station Six on D-One Wall, we needed to head to Corecrest Southwest Telegate, pass through D-Two Wall, and enter the Venice Section," Viggo explained.

"How do you know which Sphere Stations are close to which Telegates?" Rain asked.

"O, there's a pattern," Viggo explained. "Let me tell you, Miss Pretty Little Loveheart. North corresponds to Sphere Station One, Northeast to Sphere Station Two, East to Sphere Station Three, and so on."

"So, we head to the Southwest Telegate?" Leaf double-checked.

"Yes," Rain confirmed.

"And once we're in Venice, we'll take Venice Southwest Telegate to Venice D-One Wall, where Sphere Station Six is located," Viggo explained.

As they approached the Telegate, a Female Hologram Attendant materialized in front of each of them, offering a friendly greeting.

"Welcome to Corecrest West Telegate, Mr. LeBest. Where would you like to go today?" the Female Hologram Attendant asked.

Viggo replied, "Southwest Telegate."

"You're all set, Mr. LeBest. You can proceed right through and have a wonderful evening."

Rain and Leaf also relayed the same information to the attendant.

They passed through Corecrest West Telegate and emerged from Corecrest Southwest Telegate. Then, continuing, they went through the D-Two Wall security entrance and entered the Venice Section.

Venice Section, home of the high-class Totalist, boasted natural beauty with serene garden theme parks, colorful flower beds, lakes, hot springs, and waterfalls. Green rolling hills and snow-capped mountains awaited adventurous explorers. Venice was a nature lover's dream, yet it was renowned as the creator and exporter of the finest fine luxury goods. Their exclusive products were in constant demand, exported only to Vellatine City Section One, Section Seven to Eleven, and other elite regions of Ourania World. At the heart of Venice stood Corporate Skyscraper One, the most famous strip of land encircling the natural environment. Skyscrapers lined each side of the road; each building engaged in an ongoing race to outdo the others in construction and design. Corporate Skyscraper One was strategically positioned amidst this stunning environment, offering a grand vista of the Avedon River, the Vellatine City Skyline across the way, and the monumental Statue of Commander Bazyli in the center. Over the Avedon River, the five Diamond Ring Bridges sparkled brilliantly, connecting Venice D-One Wall to Vellatine's five outer Sections.

Vellatine City, the crown jewel of the Totalist Federation, encompassed eleven sections. Section One served as the heart of Vellatine, hosting the monumental Statue of Commander Bazyli. Sections Two to Six remained shrouded in secrecy, undisclosed to unauthorized personnel, forming the innermost circle. Sections Seven to Eleven constituted the outer circle. The Totalist in Sections One to Eleven do not recognize the Venice Section, Corecrest Section, and Borat Section, even though they fall under the umbrella of Vellatine City. Especially the shameful Section 12, which was a failed establishment for The Totalist Federation due to the constant struggle for control against the SKA Rebels. The Totalist Federation has abandoned and removed it from their list of Vellatine City. Since then, Section 12 has become a haven for refugees from around Ourania. Due to the mix of criminals, rebels, and foreign beings, it has been a place of misery and a hell pit for many. The Totalist Military still exerts little control in some areas, but its influence has dwindled over the years.

Vellatine City Section Seven served as the Weaponry and Research Center, focusing on advancements in weapon development, bio healthcare, and space research. Section Eight housed the Gamma Ray Power Plant, responsible for energy creation, renewal, transportation, and storage throughout Vellatine City. Section Nine functioned as the Military Academy, providing training for special forces, combat tactics, intelligence planning, and reconnaissance. Section Ten was dedicated to entertainment and hosted the City of Lights Stadium, where major celebrations, events, tournaments, and the Lighting of Dreams Battle World would occur. Section Eleven specializes in advanced manufacturing, producing weapons, air and ground vehicles, and cutting-edge technology.

Many high-class Totalist in Venice enjoyed the celebration in their luxurious surroundings. Some picnicked in parks or colorful flower beds under the fireworks, while others watched from Snowcap Mountain around the campfires with friends and associates. Some relaxed in hot springs with chilled bottles of wine, and families boated on the lakes. Children with waterproof rocket packs soared above and into the water. Meanwhile, older couples savored a quieter evening in the comfort of their skyscraper condos. The luckiest few experienced it from the very top of Vellatine's sky, surrounded by fireworks, and had the opportunity to make their dream wish come true inside the white spheres.

Sphere Station Six was an open round platform extending over the top of the D-One Wall, featuring four massive neon cannons aimed at the sky over the Avedon River. These neon cannons were specially crafted for the occasion, and giant white spheres with glass tops were slowly loaded into them from beneath the platform. Totalist with Lighting of Dreams tickets lined up at the neon cannon boarding zones. On either side of the Sphere Station platform, pathways led to a lower viewing deck beneath the neon cannons. Several Totalist gathered there, awestruck by the breathtaking view of Vellatine City's Skyline, rainbows over the Diamond Ring Bridges, and the fireworks illuminating the sky. Some Totalist, filled with pride, even saluted as the neon cannon fired the white spheres into the atmosphere—one after another. BOOM! BOOM! BOOM! BOOM!

Viggo, Rain, and Leaf arrived at Sphere Station Six, where they joined a crowd of high-class Totalist exiting the area. Leaf looked around curiously, unable to see over the crowd due to his short height.

"Do you think she's still here waiting?" Leaf asked anxiously, "What if she left or thinks I intentionally ignored her?"

Rain replied in a soothing tone, "I believe she's still around."

"How do you know?" Leaf pressed.

"Well, the fact that she gave you three tickets suggests she likes you. I'm sure she wouldn't just leave without trying to see you."

"Really?" Viggo and Leaf were both surprised by Rain's statement.

"O no! I don't know what to do if she likes me. I know nothing about girls!" Leaf panicked, looking around nervously.

"Well, well, you lover boy! I didn't know you had a girlfriend... before me!"

"I don't have a girlfriend and didn't ask for one, brother!"

Viggo laughed, ruffled Leaf's hair, and teased him, "Don't worry, little buddy. You've got the chick expert right here. I'll show you all my cool and slick moves. She'll be eating out of your hand in no time!"

Viggo gave himself a thumbs-up with a smirk.

Rain smacked Viggo on the head and asked, "Am I supposed to be eating out of your hand?"

"It's just a figure of speech!" Viggo shouted, rubbing his head. "Stop advocating violence!"

"Stop advocating childish schemes!" Rain retorted.

Viggo ignored Rain and turned back to Leaf. "Now that I think about it, she seems pretty well-off if she can give you three Lighting of Dreams tickets. I wonder if her parents are from here. If she's rich, then we're set!" Viggo ducked and glanced at Rain as her hand passed by his head.

She glared at him with anger. "Don't listen to Vgoo, Leaf. What matters is the person, not what they have."

"You sound like Mr. Hairo, but I understand what you mean," Leaf replied.

Rain chuckled. "I'll take that as a compliment. We can thank her properly once we see her. Do you know what she looks like?"

"Ummm... I think she's shorter than me, and um." Leaf paused, squinting as he rested an index finger on his chin.

"Shorter? I don't know if we'll spot her among all these tall Totalist," Viggo remarked, scanning the Sphere Station and boarding zones.

"Oh, yeah! She also has three friends: two girls and one older man."

"Do you remember what they look like?" Viggo inquired.

"I don't remember, but I should be able to pick them out if I see them. They seemed nice when I almost crashed into her."

"It's okay. We'll walk around, and if you spot them, give us a heads-up," Rain said, smiling reassuringly at Leaf.

Leaf felt relieved and nodded in agreement.

"That's a great plan, and we can also check out that cool neon cannon!" Viggo exclaimed, pointing ahead.

They walked toward the boarding zone and noticed how out of place they were. Everyone around them was well-dressed. The men wore fitted suits and vests, some even sporting top hats. The ladies were all dolled up and filled with excitement. Some wore long, satin, backless dresses, while others donned sparkling ball gowns adorned with jewels that matched their high heels. Everyone looked stunning—a perfect match for a memorable evening. A Totalist soldier walked up and stopped them.

"This event is by special invitation only. Leave the premises immediately," the soldier ordered.

"Special invitation?" Viggo raised an eyebrow, holding up three Lighting of Dreams tickets. "You mean these special invite tickets that WE received to attend?!"

The soldier scanned it and looked at them.

"I apologized. Please follow me, and I'll show you to the best seat in the house."

Their faces lit up. Viggo winked in response and proudly followed the soldier. They walked past the line, onto the platform's edge, and down the hallway.

"We seem to be going farther away from the boarding zone," Viggo asked, looking around.

"We've arrived," the soldier replied confidently, opening the doors to the viewing deck. "See? Just as I told you—best seats in the house!"

They walked to the platform edge and looked up at the neon cannon from below. BOOM! BOOM! The white spheres launched into the sky.

Rain and Leaf had never been so close to a cannon, and the loud BOOM! Shook their little hearts.

"Wow!" Leaf shouted as the white sphere blasted into the sky.

Viggo approached the soldier and whispered, "This is great! Thank you for showing us this. After we're done here, should we head to the boarding zone?"

The soldier smirked, "For you, this is as good as it gets."

"But our tickets allow us access to the white sphere!" Viggo argued.

"I don't know where or who you stole that from, but consider yourself lucky. I let you in here," the soldier retorted.

Viggo realized his intention. He unzipped his fanny pack and took out a silver shin, which the soldier promptly snatched from his hand.

"It's most of my savings. I would really appreciate it if you could get us into the white sphere! I brought my date and my little brother. It's our first time experiencing this. Please bring us up there. It should be enough for your trouble."

The soldier held the silver shin, tucked it into his side pocket, and grabbed Viggo's cloak tightly. "Listen, trash digger. I'll be straightforward with you this time. Beggars can't be choosers. The way you all look and smell, you're lucky I noticed you first. Be grateful you're even here. If you keep pushing, you and your little girlfriend will face worse consequences than I'm offering. Now, go and make some cute memories!" The soldier then pushed Viggo away, adding, "Oh, this should add some love points. Don't think your silver didn't get you anything."

The soldier threw some glow sticks at Viggo and walked away. Viggo watched as the soldier closed the gate and picked up the glow sticks with one hand. Viggo opened his other fist and revealed a spider web string with a silver shin dangling at the end. He stashed the silver shin and a glow stick into his fanny pack before returning to Rain and Leaf. Viggo hopped onto the ledge and sat beside them, handing Leaf a glow stick.

He waved it around, "Thanks, brother! This view is so cool! We're so lucky to be here. When that cannon goes, boom! It feels like we're right in the middle, zooming through the sky, and then KA-BOOM! Big fireworks everywhere!" Leaf laughed as he jumped off the ledge and ran around the courtyard like a sphere with his glow stick. Viggo watched him and felt a pang in his heart.

"Yeah, this is pretty cool." Rain said softly.

Viggo looked down over the ledge at the Avedon River. The waves calmly move along.

"You don't have to pretend to be nice and try to make me feel better."

"What are you talking about? I genuinely think it's been pretty cool, except for what you said earlier."

"Well, it was a joke. If I were like that, I would have tried to find a rich girl to marry instead of falling head over heels for you."

"Was that supposed to make me feel special?"

"Sorry."

Rain was surprised to hear the apology and noticed that he looked unhappy, "I'm sorry for hitting you on the head earlier. I appreciate your effort and for letting me experience this... with you."

Viggo looked at Rain and saw her big blue eyes looking back at him. Her long, greasy blond hair swayed in the wind, and he sensed her sincerity.

"Am I dreaming again?" he tapped his cheek.

"You're such a goof. I'm not always mean, and I can be nice sometimes. I'm glad you didn't just give up on me."

A glow stick crept up in front of Rain's face and emitted a green glow.

Viggo handed her the glow stick and sprang onto the ledge. "You're right, Rain! Sometimes, we must create opportunities, even if there aren't any! Let's go!"

"Go? Aren't we supposed to be watching the fireworks?"

Viggo extended his hand. "Trust me!"

She gave him a strange look at his words, then smiled and took his hand. With great strength and speed, he pulled her up and held her tightly against him. The tight squeeze between their body made Rain blush, her face flushing red. She suddenly felt warm, and it felt right. He held her tighter, spun off the ledge in midair, landed on the ground, and finished with a stylish dip. She held onto him, gazing deeply into his light brown eyes. She had never realized how beautiful and mesmerizing light brown eyes could be. Behind him, big fireworks exploded with crimson colors. Their surroundings felt frozen in time; the fireworks fell slowly, and their hearts beat in unison. This moment was captured in their hearts. Rain closed her eyes, her moist lips slightly parted. Viggo closed his eyes and leaned down to kiss her.

"That was so cool!" Leaf shouted from a distance.

It startled Viggo, and Rain fell to the ground.

"Can you spin me too, Brother?" Leaf asked, and he ran toward them while Rain laughed from the ground.

Viggo realized what had happened.

I was so close! He thought.

Turning to Leaf, Viggo picked him up and spun him around wildly. Leaf spread his arms and shouted, "Wooaahhh!"

The two collapsed onto the ground in laughter. Suddenly, BOOM! BOOM! White spheres launch into the sky, catching Viggo's attention.

"Let's ride those spheres!" Viggo said with determination.

"Can we?" Leaf asked.

"Why not?" Viggo replied with a smile.

"Yay!" Leaf shouted and jumped up and down in excitement. Viggo and Rain glanced at each other, and she smiled. But this time, her smile appeared different.

Viggo, Rain, and Leaf stood in line behind a group of young ladies in elegant ball gowns. The girls giggled and pointed at Rain, dressed unladylike in pink punk combat boots, but Rain ignored their stares. Viggo unzipped his fanny pack and released a rat. The rat scurried under one of the young lady's ball gowns, and she screamed. The rat popped its head out between her cleavage, causing all the young ladies in the group to scream and scramble to escape. They stumbled over each other hastily, leaving behind high heels and even a fallen wig. Meanwhile, the rat returned to Viggo's fanny pack. With the commotion settled, Viggo, Rain, and Leaf found themselves first in line to board the white sphere.

They approached the boarding zone, and a young sphere attendant greeted them and collected their three Lighting of Dreams tickets. "Good evening, young Madam and young Sir. Welcome to Sphere Station Six. The doors will open when the white sphere arrives, and you can safely steps inside."

"How do we get back down once we're up there?" Rain asked.

"When the white sphere reaches its designated height, it will orbit around Vellatine City. Eventually, it will descend back to Sphere Station Six, and you can exit at the platform below."

The white sphere arrived, and its doors opened.

They entered the spacious sphere cabin, and the doors closed behind them. The walls were lined with white leather sofas, and glass windows stretched overhead, offering panoramic views. In the center of the cabin were three high round tables adorned with food and a bottle of wine. Viggo, Rain, and Leaf hurried to their respective tables. Viggo wasted no time; he grabbed a slice of roast beef and stuffed it into his mouth. Then, he unzipped his fanny pack and tossed some fruits inside. Mr. Stinky and the rat popped their heads out, eagerly devouring the fruits.

Viggo looked over and saw Rain and Leaf enjoying their meal. "What a life!" he laughed with food in his mouth. "I wish they had this event every day!"

"Ye...ah!" Leaf attempted to speak, but his cheeks were stuffed and round with food.

Rain noticed a pink bottle illuminated in the middle of the table. She grabbed it and poured herself a glass.

"This tasted funny but good!" Rain said and laughed after several more sips.

Leaf eyed the red bottle at the center of the table, just out of reach. He jumped up and down to grab it, but it remained elusive. Viggo chuckled at Leaf's antics while Rain took a few more sips and laughed louder and louder.

"Is it that good?" Viggo asked.

Before Rain could answer, a young female hologram dressed in a light-yellow gown appeared at the sphere's center. She was surrounded by five different colored orbs rotating around her.

"Welcome to our Lighting of Dreams Welcome Ceremony at Sphere Station Six. I'm delighted you could join us for this wonderful evening. Please make yourself comfortable and enjoy the complimentary meals, drinks, and magnificent views. Once airborne, feel free to select one of the wishing orbs floating around me and make your wish in them. When our glass windows open, release your wishing orbs into the sky, and hopefully, it will come true one day. Enjoy your time here!"

The young female hologram vanished.

The white sphere accelerated as it entered a dark tunnel, then BOOM! It shot into the night sky. Gradually, it slowed to a gentle rotation and began to orbit around Vellatine City. The glass windows retracted and opened the top half of the sphere. Viggo and Rain could see Zephaniah World, the two moons and the stars. They had never felt so close to them before.

It was like a dream!

Leaf dashed around the sphere, taking in the various views below. Meanwhile, the wind tousled Rain's hair as she closed her eyes, smiling in the frosty air.

"This is incredibly refreshing." Rain said softly.

"It does feel nice," Viggo replied softly.

"I feel so free up here. Today has been unbelievable, and I can't imagine anything topping this breathtaking moment." Rain said, opening her blue eyes.

Fireworks exploded in front of their white sphere, and she held her breath in amazement.

"Well, there might be one more thing."

Rain turned to Viggo, "Do you have the Faith of One?"

She took it out of her pocket and handed it to him. He retrieved an old, tarnished, dull necklace from his fanny pack and connected the Faith of One to it. Mr. Stinky and the rat looked at the Faith of One, mesmerized. Holding it up, he admired its bluish-purple shimmer before stepping forward and placing the necklace around her neck.

"I hope you are happy," Viggo said softly in her ear.

He stepped back, and tears rolled down her face.

"Did I say something wrong?"

"It's beautiful," she said, placing her hands under the crystal.

"Then what's wrong?"

"No one had ever been this kind to me before."

"Well, maybe if you give it a chance."

Rain looked up at Viggo, and their eyes met. Her heart beats irregularly as her mind transcended into an unfamiliar warmth. She leaned forward and kissed him on the cheek, causing Viggo to stumble backward and hit his head on the couch.

"Brother, is that the skyline of Vellatine City?" Leaf questioned, pointing at Vellatine City below. But when he didn't receive a reply, he turned around to see Viggo on the floor. Leaf ran over to them.

"Brother! Have you eaten too much?" Leaf asked as he helped Viggo up.

With a big smile, Viggo turned to Leaf and said, "I think my wish came true."

"What! You made your wish already?!" Leaf whined.

"No, I was just expressing my appreciation, and then he fell," Rain explained.

Viggo, squatting slightly, widened his stance and stomped his feet on the floor for a better grip.

"You totally caught me off guard! I wasn't prepared at all! It happened in a flash! I think I blinked out for a second. Could you do it again? But this time... really... really... slow. I want to experience the full impact of your plushy lips!" Viggo leaned toward Rain, cleared his throat, and licked all around his lips.

"Why do you have to ruin the moment with that sleazy look!"

"The moment is not ruined! We can still recreate this magic again!" Viggo said quickly, trying to salvage the moment.

Rain took Leaf's hand and walked to the other side. "Yes, that's Vellatine City. If you look around, you'll notice statues of our past Commanders at Borat Edge, safeguarding the city."

"You're so smart, Rain!" Leaf said.

"If you keep asking all these questions, you'll be smart, too!" Rain replied.

Different colored orbs flowed into the sky from other nearby spheres.

"O! Look! They're making their wishes!" Leaf exclaimed.

They rushed to the center where the rotated orbs were.

"Leaf, which color orb would you like to make your wish in?" Rain asked.

"They're as large as my head!" Leaf said, while pointing randomly at the rotating orbs.

"This one!" Leaf shouted as he grabbed the yellow orb.

Rain selected a pink orb, while Viggo opted for a red one. They exchanged glances.

"Leaf, what will you wish for?" Viggo asked.

"I can't tell you, brother."

"Of course, you can. We don't keep secrets from each other," Viggo chuckled.

"I want it to come true," Leaf replied.

"Then, I hope it does," Viggo said sincerely, giving Leaf an encouraging smile.

Leaf nodded. Viggo looked at Rain.

"I don't mind telling you since I know it won't come true," Rain said.

"Is it me you're wishing for?" Viggo teased, "If you try hard enough, maybe it will come true." He winked playfully.

"You wish!" Rain laughed, "I wish my Daddy and Mommy were here. I wanted them to experience this magical moment with me."

"That's a great wish!" Leaf said.

"A meaningful wish. Your parents would be super happy if they heard this." Viggo said.

"What about you?" Rain asked.

"My wish already came true!" Viggo laughed and winked at her again.

"Don't push your luck. Otherwise, you might forget this whole thing ever happened."

Rain closed her eyes and brought the orb close to her mouth. It glowed bright pink.

"Whoa," Viggo and Leaf whispered in awe.

They both closed their eyes and held the orbs close to their lips. When Rain opened her eyes, she saw the red and yellow orbs glowing beautifully.

"Do we just let it go?" Leaf asked.

Rain nodded. They released their grip, and the glowing orbs floated higher and higher, gradually dissolving into the atmosphere, leaving shimmering dust trails behind. They watched in awe.

"How do we know if it will come true?" Leaf asked.

"You'll know when you have it," Viggo replied.

As the white sphere rotated above Vellatine City, fireworks exploded around them. They continued eating and drinking, admiring the stunning night lights of the city's sections below. Down on the streets, the Totalist were out in force, dancing, singing, laughing, and celebrating the Lighting of Dreams.

Leaf laughed, saying, "I see, tiny! Little tiny Totalist!"

Viggo and Rain laughed as they continued drinking. Rain pointed unsteadily at Section Seven and slurred, "That's... that's where Daddy used to work!"

Viggo turned to look at where Rain was pointing and laughed. "Your... Daddy used to be... tiny..."

Leaf laughed and rolled off the white leather sofa. Viggo and Rain looked at Leaf and burst into uncontrollable laughter. They tried to help him up but kept stumbling onto each other and ended up falling to the ground, while laughing. Meanwhile, the glass window rose and sealed shut as it descended back to Sphere Station Six. The doors opened, revealing an empty bottle rolling in next to the door while the table's food had been mostly eaten, leaving just a few bones behind. The Young Sphere Attendant walked in and saw Viggo, Rain, and Leaf on the floor, rolling around in laughter.

"Uh, young Madam, and young... SIR!"

Viggo stumbled; he accidentally threw up on the Young Sphere Attendant's shoe. He screamed and awkwardly hopped away. Other Totalist emerged from the white spheres, curious about the commotion. Meanwhile, Viggo, Rain, and Leaf stumbled out, still laughing uncontrollably.

"I am so sorry!" Viggo shouted, hiccuping as he hopped after the Young Sphere Attendant with one of his dirty brown boots in his hand. "You can have my boot! Wait!"

Rain and Leaf chased after Viggo.

A Totalist man grabbed Leaf's shoulder from behind, stopping him abruptly. Rain heard Leaf shout, "Hey!"

"Viggo! Leaf is in trouble!" Rain shouted, and Viggo stopped!

They ran back to help Leaf, pushing through the crowd.

"YOU!" Leaf hugged the Totalist man, feeling happy but a bit woozy!

"Are you OK, Leaf?" Viggo shouted as he jumped in, attempting to push the Totalist man back, but he couldn't. The man grabbed Viggo's hand and twisted it.

"Ouch!" Viggo shouted and collapsed to his knees.

"Lyndon." Pink Mellow said.

"These are the friends I've been looking for!" Leaf shouted, and Lyndon let go of Viggo.

"Ooo... Nice to meet you all! I apologize for Viggo's behavior. We thought you were trying to harm Leaf." Rain said.

"You are?" Leila asked.

"This is Rain and my brother, Viggo. We were trying to find you guys earlier," Leaf said, turning to Pink Mellow. "I want to thank you very... very much for the tickets!"

Pink Mellow looked at Leaf and softly said, "You're welcome."

"Yes! Thank you very much! We had an amazing time!" Rain added.

"I hate to interrupt this overly sentimental greeting, but who are you guys, and why did you give Leaf your three tickets? What do you want in return? Who are your parents? And why do you have an old man with you..."

"Viggo!" Rain interrupted.

"Why don't we find a more private place to talk instead of drawing attention here?" Leila suggested.

"I know a perfect place!" Ira shouted, "Hold our hands and repeat after me. BON!"

"Hold your hands? Bon?" Rain sounded confused.

"Yes," Leila exclaimed as she grabbed Rain's hand. Lyndon took hold of Leaf's hand while Ira grabbed Viggo's hand.

"BON!"

They all disappeared, leaving the crowd scattered in confusion from what had just happened.

Chapter 8
The Emerald Gala

Viggo, Rain, and Leaf glanced around, enveloped by the gentle illumination cast by Zephaniah World, the dual moons, and the sparkling stars above. No bursts of fireworks or booming cannons filled the air, but the soft murmur of running water nearby soothed their senses, though the meandering stream leading into the pond eluded their sight. The tranquil ambiance brought a sense of peace. Rain and Leaf caught sight of a family of deer by the pond while several others reclined amidst the lush greenery. Unperturbed by the group's sudden presence, the deer exuded no hint of fear or alarm.

Lyndon took the lead toward the pond, the rest of the group trailing behind him.

"How did you do that? Is it magic?" Rain inquired.

Ira chuckled loudly, "I wish! That would be incredibly duper awesome!"

"Then how did you manage to bring us here?" Rain asked.

"It's Vellatine Point." Leila raised her hand, displaying a delicate bracelet adorning her wrist. "It's similar to a telegate but portable. With the coordinates captured just once, this device allows us to visit it again from anywhere in Ourania. Anyone who thinks of the destination and holds onto their hands will travel along."

"And we have to say bon?" Rain questioned, a hint of confusion in her voice.

"No. It's BONNNN!" Ira exclaimed excitedly, bouncing around.

"I don't see anyone with this Vellatine Point bracelet. Is it a new release or coming out soon?" Viggo inquired.

"It's been out for about three years." Leila answered.

They arrived at the pond, where the reflection of Zephaniah's World shimmered magnificently, casting a sizable and vivid image. Lyndon stretched out on the lush grass, settling himself in, and closed his eyes, surrendering to the tranquility.

"Now we can talk peacefully without others nosing in on our conversation," Leila remarked.

Viggo wasted no time getting to the heart of the matter once more. "Who are you guys? Pink Mellow can't be your real name?"

Ira asked, "What makes Rain and Leaf a real name?"

"Ah, fair point," Viggo laughed. "Why did you give Leaf your three tickets? Do you expect something in return? We have nothing to offer you."

"We don't want anything! Our Pink Mellow is just too kind-hearted, and she wanted to help him," Ira explained.

"Thank you, Pink Mellow," Leaf said softly.

Pink Mellow smiled and nodded.

"Handing over three highly sought-after tickets to a stranger is a little too nice. And considering you still have three tickets for yourself, it suggests your parents are either super rich or very important. Which is it?" Viggo questioned.

"Or both," Rain added.

Leila, growing irritated, interjected, "Hey! Pink Mellow was being kind! Why all these questions..."

Pink Mellow interrupted, "I find the name Pink Mellow quite charming. It has a certain sweetness and is a moniker I frequently go by when I'm out and about. My real..."

"Pink Mellow." While gazing at the sky, Lyndon interrupted the conversation.

"It's all right, Lyndon," Pink Mellow intervened, kindly stepping forward. "My name is Princess Kayla, and my family belongs to the Royal Totalist."

Viggo, Rain, and Leaf gasped and were shocked.

Princess Kayla continued, "When I saw Leaf, it was evident that someone had roughed him up, yet he apologized for bumping into us. He was also resolute about retrieving his tickets. That's when I offered him ours so he wouldn't have to fret about his stolen ones. I assure you, no deceit was intended towards him or you."

"I am terribly sorry, Princess," Viggo said, "Will we face execution for our rudeness?"

"Yes!" Leila shouted.

"CHOP! CHOP!! CHOP!!!" Ira chimed in as she bounced around, her hands chopping up and down.

In fear, Viggo instinctively grabbed Rain, who promptly pushed him away.

"No," Princess Kayla corrected gently.

"Only if you disclose information about our Princess or cause her harm!" Leila asserted firmly.

"How can we be certain you're truly a Princess and not just a wealthy girl? Can you provide proof? Anyone can claim royal lineage," Rain questioned.

"We don't need to prove anything. If you doubt our words…" Leila began.

"The chances of encountering a member of the Royal Family are as slim as visiting Zephaniah," Rain interjected.

"Or obtaining not just one, but three Lighting of Dreams tickets?" Leila replied.

Rain was momentarily speechless, and then Leaf stepped forward, his voice unwavering. "I believe. I believe you, Princess Kayla."

"Me too. If it weren't for Princess Kayla, I wouldn't have had the chance to give Rain and Leaf such a memorable night. Thank you," Viggo added.

"I apologize for my earlier skepticism, but if you truly are a princess, what motivates you to reveal your identity to a group of strangers?" Rain asked.

"Yeah, Princess?" Ira asked.

Leila looked at Princess Kayla for her response.

"Because it felt like the right thing to do. I sensed I could trust Leaf, Viggo, and you," Princess Kayla replied sincerely.

"But revealing your identity could put you in danger if the wrong person finds out," Viggo pointed out.

"That's why she has us!" Ira declared proudly.

"You're just a kid and so much smaller than me!" Viggo said.

"Exactly! I am smarter than you!" Ira countered with a laugh, darting around them playfully.

"That's not what I said."

"Ira's size doesn't define her when she's the clever one in our group. Leila serves as our medical specialist, and Lyndon is our loyal and kind protector," Princess Kayla affirmed.

Lyndon let out a loud snore.

Princess Kayla then presented a half Royal Emblem, a solid gold piece bearing half the royal double crown. "This is the Royal Emblem of our family. I possess one half; the other belongs to my older brother, Prince Jaden Knight."

"Wow, a real princess!" Rain said. "Thank you for placing your trust in us, Princess Kayla."

Rain bowed down to the ground. Viggo and Leaf quickly followed.

"Please, there's no need for formalities, especially when we're out together. We're friends. Treat me like any of your friends," Princess Kayla insisted.

Rain, Viggo, and Leaf straightened up, acknowledging her words.

"Great! Because I'm not used to all this bowing and stuff. So don't worry about Leaf and me. We'll treat you just like one of us! Though I must warn you, Rain might not treat you the same way she does to me," Viggo laughed and blew her a kiss. Viggo took off as she chased him. They all laughed.

"So does that mean we're all just friends now?" Leaf asked eagerly.

Princess Kayla smiled warmly and nodded in affirmation.

"Yay!" Leaf exclaimed joyfully, pulling Princess Kayla into a hug. Leila and Ira looked on, surprised and momentarily frozen by the unexpected display of affection. Princess Kayla blushed.

"I was so nervous the whole time, and now everything feels normal again!" Leaf said.

Ira whispered to Leila, "This is the first time anyone has touched Princess Kayla! A hug?! Do you think he'll get the death penalty?"

"I hope so!" Leila whispered back, a mischievous glint in her eyes.

Princess Kayla, her voice soft, turned to Leaf and asked, "Would you like to go to The Emerald Gala tomorrow?"

Leaf scratched his head, "Um. I think Brother and Rain would like that."

"I can only invite one person," Princess Kayla said gently.

"Um…" Leaf hesitated, glancing around for guidance, his eyes searching for Viggo.

"Of course, he'll go!" Viggo's voice rang out from a distance as he darted away from Rain, a playful escape from her grasp.

"But…" Leaf began, still unsure.

"What time and where should he meet you?" Viggo interjected Leaf.

Rain stopped and caught her breath. Viggo crashed onto the soft grass, breathing heavily.

Princess Kayla turned to Leaf, "Do you want to go?"

"I'm sorry…" Leaf began, but Viggo cut in before he could finish.

"No need to be a baby turtle, Leaf! This is a rare opportunity, and I understand, you'd want us to experience it, too. But it's okay! As Mr. Hairo said, 'Tell me about it later.' So go ahead and enjoy yourself," Viggo reassured him.

Leaf pondered for a moment, then turned to Princess Kayla. "Thank you, but I don't want to go without my brother, and I would rather not go if I had to leave him."

Princess Kayla nodded understandingly. "I understand. But if you change your mind, show this to the guard at the Diamond Ring Bridge tomorrow night. They'll escort you to The Emerald at Section Ten, City of Lights." She gently placed the Dream Bracelet in Leaf's hand, closing his fingers around it.

Rain glanced around, taking in the serene atmosphere of the trees and the gently flowing water. Nearby, a family of rabbits hopped along the water's edge while an owl settled on a branch, observing the scene with keen interest.

"So, what exactly is this place?" Rain inquired.

"This is the Pond of Reflection," Leila explained.

Rain, Viggo, and Leaf walked to the Pond of Reflection and looked at the dark water.

"Sure is a Pond of Reflection," Viggo said jokingly as he glanced at their reflections in the pond.

The water rippled slightly; Viggo leaned in for a closer look.

"I think something…" Viggo whispered and leaned in closer. A pale face of a little boy staring back at him from the dark water. Viggo stumbled and backed away from the water.

Nervously, Viggo turned to Leaf and Rain. "Did you see that?"

"See what?" Rain asked.

"I didn't see anything, brother. Was there something in the water?" Leaf inquired, scanning the area as he approached where Viggo stood. Viggo grabbed Leaf's arm and pulled him back.

"Don't go there. Leaf!" Viggo's attention shifted to Leila.

"What exactly is this Pond of Reflection?!" Viggo's tone demanded an answer.

"It reveals what's been buried deep within," Leila replied.

"How do we get out of here?" Viggo asked.

"Is there something you're concealing or attempting to evade?" Leila's inquiry cut through the tension.

Viggo regarded Leila with a solemn expression. "We're leaving. Let's go."

"Where would you like to go? Leila can take you back." Princess Kayla said.

"Section 12, Princess Kayla," Viggo said.

"What did you see, brother?" Leaf asked again.

Rain regarded Viggo with intrigue.

"It's probably nothing. Let's go." Viggo said.

"Alright, hold on to each other hands and say BON!" Leila instructed.

They clasped hands tightly and exclaimed, "BON!" They vanished into thin air.

Princess Kayla made her way to the pond, with Ira hopping alongside her. Gazing at the tranquil sky's reflection in the water, Princess Kayla remained contemplative. Lyndon rose from his spot and joined Princess Kayla and Ira.

"Lady Spectra," Princess Kayla said softly.

A gentle breeze swept across the water's surface, causing ripples to dance and swirl. The water began to rise, coalescing into a large bubble at the pond's center. Within the bubble, a luminous blue soul emerged from the water.

"Welcome back, Princess Kayla," Lady Spectra greeted.

She stood petite in stature, adorned in a blue sparkling translucent gown. Her long, curly blue hair cascaded, partially veiling her sharp features.

"Thank you, Lady Spectra. Is there anything of concern we should be aware of?" Princess Kayla inquired.

"Viggo harbors a shadowy past."

"Can you shed some light on it?"

"A young boy."

"A young boy? What's the significance of a young boy?"

Lady Spectra stood in silence, surrounded by glowing sparkles.

Princess Kayla turned to Ira, her expression troubled. "Do you believe that young boy could be Leaf?"

"I hope not, considering it's a dark past," Ira replied.

Princess Kayla then directed her attention back to Lady Spectra. "What are your thoughts on Leaf, Lady Spectra?"

"Alight in the ashes to a fiery might. Soft, tenderhearted brings a glow of hope."

Princess Kayla repeated what Lady Spectra said, "Alight... in the ashes... to a fiery might. Soft tenderhearted... brings a glow of hope."

Ira thinks out loud, "Alight... might... hope?"

Princess Kayla asked, "What does it mean?"

Ira pondered deeply in the recesses of her mind, "I'm not a word weaver, but it seemed to suggest that Leaf has the potential for great strength, and if he maintains his belief, it will be true."

Princess Kayla nodded.

Lady Spectra, adorned in her ethereal bubble, began to dance gracefully. A long yellow light ribbon extended from the bubble, gliding gently through the flowers, grass, and among the animals. It wrapped around Princess Kayla, twirling her in its luminous embrace, eliciting a joyful smile from her. Everywhere it touched, it brought upliftment and a sense of serenity. Simultaneously, a long red-light ribbon emerged from another direction, carrying water from the pond. It flowed gracefully around the trees and flowers. As it passed, it poured a small amount onto a leaf for the rabbit's family. A light blue ribbon danced around with a refreshing breeze, gathering up torn, old, fallen leaves and broken branches scattered about the area. It carried them back to the pond, restoring harmony to the surroundings. Fishes jumped out of the water and dived back in like a dance around the pond.

Princess Kayla asked, "What about Rain?"

"Love a touch unreachable. Love of pain unspeakable."

Ira mulled over Lady Spectra's words, then slowly repeated, "Love... unreachable... pain... unspeakable... that doesn't sound good."

"Who would desire to break her heart?" Princess Kayla asked.

"I don't know. She's like a piece of heaven that's fallen from above! If I keep listening to Lady Spectra, I might become a word weaver of love!" Ira chuckled.

Princess Kayla turned her attention back to Lady Spectra, "Could you provide further insights into Viggo?"

"The dying sun births into darkness, igniting a new dawn of power, but gone is its light."

"We ought to tread cautiously around Viggo, Princess Kayla," Ira said.

Princess Kayla nodded gracefully and expressed, "Lady Spectra, your precious time is invaluable. Rest well."

The dance slowly ended, and the rainbow light ribbons flourished in their environment. Everything returned into the bubble, which popped, and Lady Spectra vanished. The Pond of Reflection regained its calm and peaceful demeanor once more.

Viggo, Rain, and Leaf arrived at her home. Rain opened the door. "You've been awfully quiet since we left. Everything alright, Viggo?"

"Yeah," Viggo said unconvincingly.

Rain paused by the door momentarily and spoke, "Well, I thoroughly enjoyed myself. Thank you," before closing the door.

Viggo and Leaf strolled down the street. Leaf glanced at Viggo several times, noticing his preoccupied expression.

"Princess Kayla gave me the Dream Bracelet. Do you want to give that to Arison?" Leaf inquired.

Viggo remained silent and kept walking.

"Brother?" Leaf called out.

Viggo halted, responding, "Yeah?"

"I have a Dream Bracelet with a double crown marking. You can get a gem for it, right?"

Viggo looked at Leaf momentarily, "Why don't you attend the Lighting of Dreams Gala Party?"

"I don't want to go without you."

Viggo crouched down to Leaf's height and met his gaze. "Opportunity doesn't come often around here, especially to someone like us. If you let it go, this moment will never come back again. I know you always want to be with me. But sometimes, we might have to be apart for a bit, and that's alright."

"You could sell this Dream Bracelet and finally achieve what you've always dreamed of brother!" Leaf exclaimed excitedly and placed the Dream Bracelet into his hands.

Viggo gazed at the beautiful gold design adorned with multicolored crystals and delicate lace, their brilliance captivating his eyes. It differed from the other Dream Bracelet he had seen; it bore a distinctive double crown marking, registering as a royal guest and adding exceptional value.

Leaf's selflessness tugged at Viggo's heart, filling him with sadness. "I see something so rare that it would be wrong of me to take it away from you. I might not understand what you and Mr. Hairo said about shin and love. However, the time we spent together tonight—I wouldn't exchange it for any sum."

Viggo gently returned the bracelet to Leaf's hand. "Why don't you put it away? There will be another opportunity for us, but I'm not sure how many chances there will be to see a princess."

Viggo pointed to Leaf's heart. "I'll always be here, and you'll always hold a place in my heart."

Leaf glanced down at his chest, feeling his heartbeats against Viggo's finger.

"Be happy, baby turtle. Now you have someone who cares about you beside me, and you should treat her kindly. She sees you for who you are and wants nothing more."

"She doesn't have to be nice to me; just don't be mean to me."

"Nobody must be nice to anyone. But very few will do it because they want to... and care."

Leaf give a slight smile and asked, "She is nice, isn't she?"

"You're lucky. Now let's go home," Viggo replied.

They walked through the foggy Street Market, and Viggo's mind drifted once more as he gazed up at the two moons in the sky.

"Brother!" Leaf shouted by the side entrance of the Diamond Ring Bridge gate. Viggo ran, huffing and puffing as he reached the gate. Exquisite ladies and well-dressed gentlemen enter through the Diamond Ring Bridge gate.

"Try this on," Viggo said, holding out a sleek black dress coat. "I just bought it."

"Brother, you didn't have to spend your shin! My cloak is fine."

"No way! This will make you blend in with those Totalist over there."

Viggo removed Leaf's cloak, put a black dress coat on him, dusted it off, and buttoned it up.

"They told me it's made from the finest wool and was once worn by a nobleman of Vellatine!" Viggo said excitedly.

Viggo stepped back and looked at Leaf. The oversized coat hung off his shoulders, his fingers barely visible. It didn't look as well-tailored as the gentlemen nearby. Several interior areas were ripped, with a big hole under the left armpit, and the inside pockets had fallen apart with strings hanging out. The black fabric was noticeably faded. Leaf's long, dirty blond hair was unkempt, and his face had brown smudges. Viggo licked his thumb and rubbed off the smudges. He ran his fingers through Leaf's hair, pulled it back, yanked out a string from the inside pocket, and tied his hair back. Viggo rolled up his sleeves and noticed the Dream Bracelet on his wrist.

Viggo smiled and stepped back to admire his handiwork. Although Leaf's black coat didn't match his brown pants and boots, Viggo couldn't help but feel proud. "Wow, you look great!" he exclaimed.

Leaf tried to smile.

"I could barely tell you apart from those guys over there, and I think you've even grown taller!"

Leaf tried to hold his tears back as he looked down. Viggo noticed it.

"You silly baby turtle! Go on now! Don't make a princess wait for ya. I'll be waiting right here by the rocks. No need to worry, alright?"

Leaf nodded and instantly hugged Viggo tightly, squeezing him affectionately. Viggo felt a knot in his chest and fought back the emotions.

They walked alongside the guest line until Viggo stopped at the gate, waving goodbye. Leaf continued his path, returning Viggo's wave before disappearing into the crowd.

A Totalist soldier glanced at Leaf, scrutinizing him from head to toe. Leaf responded with a smile, lifting his hand to reveal the Dream Bracelet. The soldier scanned both the bracelet and Leaf himself.

"Leaf DeGreat, fifteen years old, stocks apprentice. No match. A Royal guest of Princess Kayla," the Female Voice Scanner declared.

The crowd murmured in surprise, "Royal guest?!"

The soldier waved his hand by his nose, recoiling from the unusual stench, then double-checked to ensure the scanner was correct and scanned Leaf again.

"Proceed to the first War Vehicle. It will transport you to The Emerald at the City of Lights."

"Yes, sir." Leaf started to walk away but paused, turning back. "Thank you, sir."

The soldier ignored Leaf.

A line of black military war vehicles awaited to escort all the guests. Leaf approached the first vehicle, where a soldier stood tall with his automatic rifle by his side, opening the side door for Leaf's entry. Leaf stepped in and found other guests already seated inside. The door closed, Leaf heard the window rolling down, and the other guests scooched farther away from him. The war vehicle accelerated, zooming across the bridge over the Avedon River. Leaf rolled down the window, peering out to behold the platinum Diamond Rings ahead, the Rainbows adorning the sky, and the vibrant Vellatine Skyline. The fresh, cold wind brushed against his face. He felt thrilled and nervously excited.

The war vehicle came to a halt at The Emerald, a circular three-story glass building boasting an open skylight ceiling and an outside balcony encircling the third floor.

Leaf was shoveled out of the vehicle onto the red carpet. Lights flashed all around, blinding him momentarily. The guests hurried past, brushing him aside as they made their way onto the carpet and into the building. Murmurs and giggles permeated the crowd.

"So, I can show up looking like a beggar and still get into the Gala?" a crowd member chuckled.

"What is that revolting smell?" a voice from the crowd exclaimed.

Leaf could feel the weight of countless eyes fixed on him, and the waves of laughter rippled through the crowd as he dashed past other guests toward the building entrance. A hand seized his shoulder from behind and tore his sleeve. Leaf halted and spun around, the laughter and flashing lights swirling around him. Before him stood a man in a black suit, holding his torn sleeve. Though tears welled up, Leaf fought to suppress them, reaching out to retrieve his torn sleeve. Three more men in black suits swiftly descended upon him, wrenching him away from the red carpet and toward the side of the building, away from the reveling crowd. Despite his struggles, Leaf found himself overpowered by the men's strength. A man in a black suit ripped the Dream Bracelet from his wrist.

"Hey! That's mine!" Leaf shouted, struggling to break free. The man in the black suit scanned the Dream Bracelet.

"He's identified as one of Princess Kayla's Royal guests, sir!" the Security guard exclaimed.

"That's no Royal guest! Throw him back in the war vehicle and send him back out. Fire the security guard who let this in!" the Head of Security shouted.

"What about Princess Kayla?" the Security guard inquired.

"The Princess? If my understanding is correct, this was stolen in a recent heist! Let's pray Commander Bazyli is too occupied to see this live broadcast, or your heads may not remain intact by the end of this!"

They dragged Leaf and hurled him into a war vehicle, his shoulders slamming against the unforgiving metal interior door.

"Please, can I have my sleeve back? My brother just bought this for me!" Leaf pleaded, tears streaming down his face.

"Throw that rag in there, too," the Head of Security ordered as the other man threw the rippled sleeve in. Leaf quickly grabbed it. The vehicle zoomed away toward the D-One Wall.

❖

VIP guests passed through the towering twenty-five-foot-tall, ten-inch-thick double glass doors, intricately engraved with details of past Commanders' holoscreens. Holding their flags aloft, they exchanged greetings with each guest. Upon reaching the front entrance, guests paused to pose for the live digital holoscreen broadcasted throughout Vellatine City. Stepping inside, they found themselves on a path of 10,000 red rose petals, stretching from the entrance to the dance floor at the center of the ballroom. The Gala Ballroom, circular in shape, was enveloped in deep royal red walls embossed with intricate floral patterns. Life-size wax candles depicting romantic couples in silhouette illuminated the space with a soft glow. Surrounding the circular dance floor were hundreds of decagon marble tables, each adorned with a white satin pleated skirt. Plates, glassware, and silverware, all crafted from glass, were meticulously arranged atop each table. The golden royal double crowns were etched within the glassware, adding regal elegance to the setting. The centerpiece of each table was a grand ice sculpture depicting an open clamshell filled with large pearls and exotic fruits, with a towering rainbow chocolate fondue fountain at its center. Some guests had taken their seats and indulged in the sweet treats. Above, the expansive open skylight ceiling bathed the Gala Ballroom in a cascade of blue, sparkly rays, fully illuminating the space and lending it a truly magical atmosphere.

On the second floor of The Emerald building, chefs and entertainers stood ready to serve and perform. Servers dressed in white tuxedo lined up, each carrying trays of hors d'oeuvres, descending the bifurcated white marble curved staircases adorned with intricate gold railing designs and deep green jade handles. Hundreds of servers presented guests with delectable appetizers representing various regions alongside selections from Ourania's top ten rare wines and champagnes. Guests' glasses were magically filled from their chosen selections and automatically refilled or changed as needed.

On the third floor, a grand circular balcony was reserved for Commander Bazyli and the Royal Family, flanked by two Royal Justices standing guard. These Royal Justices held the highest rank within the Totalist military divisions and were tasked with the strict protection of all high-ranking officials and the Royal Family. Proficient in various weapons and expert in close and ground combat, they were prepared to sacrifice their lives to safeguard their charges. As a result, they remained unmarried and childless. Adorned in long, deep royal red cloaks, easily pushed aside to reveal their concealed weapons, they were fully armored in white and gold, epitomizing their elite status.

Flanking each side of the grand circle balcony, cascading waterfalls illuminated in white flowed down the walls, encircling the ballroom as they descended to the first floor. Adjacent to the waterfalls, seven private balconies were designated for each fighter and their guests. Eight long banners, alternating in red and white, extended from the base of each balcony to the middle of the first floor.

The last guest walked in and took their seat at the table. The double glass doors closed, and the round skylight partially shut, dimming the Gala Ballroom. The only light now focused on the dance floor, where a suited holographic male announcer appeared.

"Welcome, distinguished guests of Ourania, to our Totalist Lighting of Dreams Gala. We are honored to host this momentous event! We hope you enjoy the delectable treats and the delightful company around you. Tonight is a significant celebration for us all, marking a new beginning for Ourania's young, aspiring future leaders and protectors! Every century, we reflect on who we are and what we can achieve to better our land and world. The Lighting of Dreams unites the four great nations to celebrate our peaceful existence, engage in the thrilling and fair competition of Battle World, and crown the next grand champion of Ourania! Without further ado, let me introduce our first fighter!"

Clapped and cheers exploded around the tables.

"White Death from the Koi Ka Chi region of Ukko! Rule by the iron fist of Emperor Razen!"

The holographic male announcer introduced each fighter, and he stepped away from the circular dance floor. A three-dimensional representation of the fighter materialized on the dance floor, towering up to the third floor and rotating slowly in a dramatic pose. Each banner will be engulfed in flames, and the fighter's name will be displayed once introduced.

White Death, clad in all-white masked attire, one of the two ninja fighters of Ukko, stood proudly with his arms crossed inside his balcony as the elite crowd below applauded.

"Moving toward the left balcony, joining us is the formidable Azriel, hailing from the proud land of Sleeping Tear in Gailstone!"

Azriel, a monstrous Gargoyle, barely fit inside the balcony, but he happily waved into the crowd below, his large fangs exposed in a smile. Gasps of fear rippled through the crowd as his wings expanded, whispers of awe accompanying the sight of the three-dimensional Azriel.

"Next up, we have the sole female competitor in Battle World, the beautiful Lixia Ziva, representing Justice of Majestic Royal!"

The ladies in the crowd murmured to each other in critique and admiration as they beheld the beautiful three-dimensional figure of Lixia Ziva. Her light skin, complemented by long, thick brown hair shimmering under the lights, framed her large almond green eyes, slightly curved button nose, and bright red lips, forming a perfect smile on her heart-shaped face. With a graceful wave to the crowd below, she wore a chrome diamond breastplate snugly fitted with red shoulder plate armors and a flowing red cape. At her side hung her long-trusted Swift Sabre, while a Majestic Royal steel curved dagger with a glass center rested comfortably behind her back. Renowned for its unbreakable craftsmanship, Majestic Royal Steel ensured she wielded the finest weapons.

The crowd erupted in supports at the sight of her, their cheers resounding loudly below.

"Next up, hailing from our Venice Section, we have the fearless and indomitable Bronx, representing the Elite Black of The Totalist Federation!"

With a formidable presence, Bronx boasted a large, muscular frame and a rugged appearance, accentuated by his stubble beard and a demeanor that exuded a bad-boy attitude. Hailing from the esteemed Elite Black military team, he wore thin, well-fitted black body armor, its surface marred by scratches and faded from years of battles and neglect.

His double boom joy shotgun was fitted comfortably to the back of his armor, capable of firing sixteen rounds before requiring reloading alongside a grenade launcher. Renowned for his expertise in close-quarters combat, Bronx carried nine-inch combat knives with a black cloth tied at the end, strapped to each side of his leg. Completing his ensemble was a large metal utility belt, meticulously organized to hold all his ammo and necessities. Bronx's eyes were a deep, dark brown, capable of vanishing in low-lighting conditions. Positioned on his balcony with two women draped around him, he remained oblivious to his introduction. Bronx affectionately rubbed his stubble beard against their overly exposed cleavage, eliciting giggles from the ladies as laughter filled the air.

"Once more, I am pleased to introduce the daredevil Bronx of The Totalist Federation!" The holographic male announcer's voice resonates loudly.

Bronx laughed heartily as he seized his ladies, leaping onto the balcony ledge with them in tow. With a playful flourish, he swung them around in a joyous display. A three-dimensional hologram of Bronx materialized with a smirked face as it rotated around, wielding his double boom joy shotgun and a grenade launcher.

"Wooah! LET'S DO IT!" Bronx let out a wild scream as he leaped off the balcony, his two frightened ladies clinging to him tightly. With a thunderous crash, they collided with the ice centerpiece on the table below, shattering it upon impact.

"WOOAH!" Bronx let out an exhilarated scream as his lady friends clung to him tightly, sharing in the thrill of the moment!

"Let's give another round of applause for the daring Bronx, ladies and gentlemen!"

Slow clapping could be heard.

"Next up, we have Black Death from Gai G by Ukko!"

Black Death stood silently inside his balcony, clad in all-black, masked clothing. Despite his imposing presence, the crowd did not greet him with applause.

"Now, presenting the mighty Thanatos from Sleeping Tear of Gailstone!"

Thanatos, the largest of all Gailstone Gargoyles, bore battle scars on his wings and a prominent scar that traversed his face from the middle of his right eyebrow to his left cheek. Despite his imposing appearance, he stood fearlessly on his balcony, eliciting only a smattering of applause from the crowd.

"Now, introducing Adonis Belacaro from Ironstead of Majestic Royal!"

Adonis Belacaro commanded attention with his tall, muscular frame, deep hazel eyes, and chiseled facial features, earning him admiration from many. His neatly trimmed full beard complemented his long blond hair, adding to his rugged allure. Draped in a dark brown mane-collared cape, his large, muscular, hairy chest and abs were proudly displayed, every sinew visible beneath his attire. He wore dark brown pants with a fur belt and fur boots adorned with leather knots at the back. Proudly brandishing a giant battle-axe crafted from Majestic Royal steel strapped to his back, Adonis Belacaro waved to the crowd below, earning thunderous applause.

"Now, with great pride, allow me to introduce our esteemed leader of The Totalist Federation and the Royal Family at the grand circle balcony! None other than our illustrious Commander of The Totalist Federation and the reigning champion of the last Lighting of Dreams Battle World—Commander Bazyli!"

Excitement pulsating through the room, all the guests rose to their feet, clapping vigorously. Each fighter bowed gracefully, paying their respects. The grand circle balcony illuminated, and Commander Bazyli made his entrance, taking his seat in the top row. Adorned in his signature two-piece red body armor and a flowing black cape, he exuded authority and presence.

"Presenting our esteemed Royal Family: the great King Roy and the epitome of grace and beauty, Queen Glory of Vellatine!"

King Roy and Queen Glory entered; the room hushed in reverence. Taking their seats in the second row, they radiated regal elegance. King Roy, adorned with a majestic crown, and Queen Glory, resplendent in her royal crown, both wore opulent cloaks befitting their status. Queen Glory's attire was particularly striking, with a pure dark blue silk velvet dress adorning her beneath the royal red cloak, accentuating her regal presence.

"Please warmly welcome our beloved Princess Kayla, our beacon of grace and youth!"

Tonight, Princess Kayla exuded a newfound maturity, her dark emerald silk gown adorned with light green lacing hugging her figure flawlessly. The top of her gown sparkled with fine gemstones while exotic white feathers gracefully spread upward from both sides of her temple, adding a touch of ethereal to her ensemble. Her hair was elegantly styled, twirled on each side, and her gold tiara shimmered harmoniously with the jewels adorning her hair. Princess Kayla sat serenely, casting her gaze below. All the young suitors stood proudly, their chests puffed out, and each one flashed a charming smile, revealing sleek, glossy white teeth. They turned gracefully from side to side, causing their tailored suit to twinkle in the light, vying for her attention.

Princess Kayla looked around and did not see Leaf.

"And now, it's my pleasure to introduce our final contender for Battle World, the valiant young royal, Prince Jaden Knight!"

The banner burst into flames, and Prince Jaden Knight's name illuminated beneath the grand circle balcony, mesmerizing the guests. Multiple flames spiraled upwards from the dance floor, leaving everyone in awe. Young Vellatine ladies gasped and pointed upward as Prince Jaden Knight descended gracefully from the skylight. Clad in a sleek black leather suit that gleamed under the lights, he sported a striking red velvet vest. A seamless white flame ran up the side of Prince Jaden Knight's arms, flaring up at the back of his shoulder, adding an element of mystique to his entrance. His blond hair was meticulously parted in the middle, cascading perfectly below his piercing blue eyes, which held a commanding presence that captivated all the young ladies in the room. His handsome, clean-shaven face, with its sharp features, seemed to halt every heartbeat in the room. The sight of him prompted screams from the young ladies, with a few fainting and others shedding tears, realizing their chances with him were nonexistent. Some had to be escorted away in their overwhelmed state. Prince Jaden Knight, holding a white rose in one hand, descended gracefully onto the shoulder of his three-dimensional model, further adding to the spectacle of his entrance.

The crowd erupted into applause.

Prince Jaden Knight leaped onto the edge of the grand circle balcony and bowed graciously to the crowd below. With a tender gesture, he kissed the white rose, transforming it into a vibrant shade of red. Turning away from the crowd, he tossed the rose over the balcony and stepped off. Below, screams mingled with shattering glassware as young ladies clamored to claim the coveted red rose. The frenzy intensified, resulting in several guests and tables being hastily removed from the chaotic scene.

"Hello, Father and Mother," Prince Jaden Knight said with reverence.

"My young Prince Jaden, this is a significant event. It was unnecessary to make the young ladies unladylike," Queen Glory said.

King Roy chuckled, "That's because he inherited my royal looks!"

Prince Jaden Knight bowed respectfully to Commander Bazyli, "Good Evening, Great Commander Bazyli."

Commander Bazyli nodded in acknowledgment.

The flames disappeared as Prince Jaden Knight took his seat beside Princess Kayla. "You look especially lovely tonight. Is there a special gent?"

Princess Kayla remained quiet; her gaze averted.

"Without further ado, let the festivities commence!" The holographic male announcer in formal attire vanished, and regal music filled the room.

Two lines formed at the top of the second floor with Golden Totalist Warships, each carried by six white-clothed chefs descending the bifurcated white marble curved staircases, and atop the vessel rested a colossal roasted beast adorned with majestic horns of wisdom, a generous gift from Emperor Razen of the Ukko. The sight left all the guests in awe, marveling at the grandeur of the feast presentation.

At the tables, guests pointed to their desired portion of the roast beast, which promptly materialized on their plates. The tender and juicy meat, its flavor unknown but undeniably exquisite, delighted their palates. The skylight opened once more, and ladies adorned in elegant gowns spun down one by one in a graceful double helix pattern from above onto the dance floor. Below, their gentlemen partners awaited, ready to whisk them away into the enchanting rhythm of the dance. Once the romantic couples dispersed throughout the ballroom, they gracefully ascended into the air, spinning in perfect synchronization to form multiple circles of ten.

Amidst the collective awe over the fantastic food and mesmerizing performance, excitement buzzed in anticipation of the upcoming fights.

However, Princess Kayla appeared visibly disheartened amidst the revelry, her mood markedly subdued.

Prince Jaden Knight spoke gently. "If you seek a specific boy, he's currently absent."

Princess Kayla stayed quiet.

"Ah, had he been present, your demeanor would likely differ," Prince Jaden Knight remarked with a smirk.

Princess Kayla looked away.

"Little sister, allow me to share something I know too well: the art of breaking hearts. Allow him to come to you. Let him recognize your true worth."

Princess Kayla's gaze finally shifted to her older brother; her surprise evident in her expression. Never had she received any advice from him; he had always appeared too preoccupied and disinterested in her affairs. Yet, at this moment, his sincerity was unmistakable. A sudden warmth enveloped her, offering a sense of unexpected comfort.

Prince Jaden Knight chuckled before rising to his feet. "Father, it seems a young man has caught Kayla's eye."

"Off with his head!" King Roy exclaimed, stunned by the revelation.

Taken aback and seething with embarrassment, Princess Kayla shot a glare at him. "No, there isn't!"

"Where are you off to, my young Prince Jaden?" Queen Glory inquired.

"I have fulfilled my duty. Commander Bazyli," Prince Jaden Knight replied, placing his hand over his heart and bowing his head.

Commander Bazyli nodded in acknowledgment.

Prince Jaden Knight walked out of the grand balcony, flanked by his two female bodyguards, Elixir and Lux. They stood at the ready, their formidable and unwavering presence.

Viggo sat by the banks of the Avedon River, the rhythmic crash of waves against the rocks filling the air with a haunting melody. The river's dark waters, barely visible in the dim light, seemed to hold secrets within their depth. Above, the bright lights of the Diamond Ring Bridge danced and shimmered, their reflection casting undulating patterns upon the water's surface. The night deepened, and the wind grew colder, chilling Viggo to the bone. He wrapped his cloak tightly around himself, seeking refuge from the biting cold. He watched as the last war vehicle disappeared into the distance, heading toward Section Ten, the City of Lights.

Fifteen years ago, the Venice Section remained unconnected to Vellatine City, with no bridge spanning the divide. Borat Edge, too, was yet to be established. Vellatine City stood isolated, its connection to the surrounding sections severed. Without proper support or protection, the three major sections grappled with rampant crimes, leading to widespread unrest among the local Totalist against The Totalist Federation. Persistent threats and rumors of overthrowing Vellatine City loomed large, fueled by the demand for formal inclusion and protection under its jurisdiction.

To uphold the peace and bolster the confidence of The Totalist Federation, King Roy implored Commander Bazyli to initiate the construction of the five Diamond Ring Bridges and Borat Edge. This grand gesture served as an engagement with the Venice Section, Corecrest Section, and Borat Section, ensuring their formal inclusion under the Vellatine City's protection. In the years since, they have thrived, enjoying prosperity and security. The morale and support of the Totalist have never been more crucial or steadfast.

I hope Leaf is having a great time. Viggo thought as he took a bite of stale jerky, finding the taste bearable despite its minimal meat flavor, mainly derived from leftover plants. Despite the less-than-ideal meal, Viggo smiled as he reminisced about the delicious food from the previous day, persevering through the chewing of the stale jerky. He gazed at the dark water; memories of the young boy's face resurfaced in his mind, causing him to grip the jerky tightly. His once-happy expression quickly faded, replaced by a somber demeanor as he averted his gaze from the water. Struggling to swallow, he heard a faint voice calling, "Brother!"

Startled, he shook his head in an attempt to dispel the sound. "Brother!"

As the sound grew louder, Viggo felt a hand on his shoulder, which caused him to startle and jump away.

"Brother?" Leaf's voice quivered as tears welled up in his eyes.

"Leaf! Why are you here? What's the matter? What happened to your sleeve!"

Viggo walked to Leaf as he stood there fragile.

"What happened? Did someone hurt you?"

Leaf retrieved the ripped sleeve and handed it to Viggo.

"Who did this to you?!" Viggo demanded, his grip tightening on the torn sleeve.

"They said I don't belong there."

"Who?! Did you show them..."

"They took the Dream Bracelet," Leaf sobbed, tears cascading onto the rocky ground.

Viggo's anger flared as he glared at the soldier stationed at the bridge. "We'll report this to Princess..."

"No! I may have already caused her enough trouble, and now I've lost the Dream Bracelet!"

Viggo was taken aback, seeing Leaf in such a vulnerable state. "Leaf..."

Princess Kayla stood on the balcony outside the Emerald building, her gaze fixed across the Avedon River. Above, clouds obscured portions of Zephaniah World, masking the visibility of the two moons and dimming the stars to mere glimmers. The cold wind swept against her soft, beautiful, yet somber visage, adding to the melancholic atmosphere around her.

Chapter 9
Battle World!

The City of Lights, Section Ten, has long been revered as the epicenter of entertainment in Ourania, boasting a rich history spanning many centuries. Tonight, however, marks a historic occasion as it hosts its grandest event. The City of Lights Stadium is the battleground where the four nations of Ourania will unite to compete in Battle World for the coveted title of Ourania World Champion!

The City of Lights Stadium stood as a perfect dome arena, renowned for its unparalleled ability to evolve into various battlegrounds. Its transparent shield provided impenetrable protection for the spectators, ensuring their safety throughout the competition. No attacks or abilities could breach or damage this formidable barrier, allowing the audience to witness the intense battles unfold without fear.

The stadium has eight sections.

Next to each section of the stadium, stone column of statues of young maidens delicately pouring water from jugs down into the stream that encircled the edge of the circular battleground. This serene feature lent a calm and tranquil atmosphere to the surroundings before the battles began. With twenty-five levels of seating, the stadium offered ample accommodation for spectators. Above the twenty-five rows is the pinnacle of the Royal Levels, comprising the next top three levels. Each suites within these Royal Levels stood twenty feet high, enclosed by impenetrable glass, affording spectators an unobstructed view of the battleground below, ensuring an unparalleled viewing experience for the esteemed guests.

Eight stone pillars were embedded around the stadium wall, reaching high above the Royal Levels. Stone-carved statues of each fighter were positioned atop of the pillar. Below their respective statues, the fighters sat in their stone chairs, except Bronx was nowhere to be seen.

The stadium allows spectators and individuals from around Ourania World to actively participate in selecting the battleground landscapes. Through a voting system, attendees and viewers can vote for the preferred landscape. The landscape with the highest number of votes will then be selected as the battleground for the fighters to compete in, ensuring that the audience has a stake in shaping the course of the battles.

In the early days of Battle World, the first Champion of Ourania World hailed from the esteemed Majestic Royal Justice, marking a historic milestone. However, they have not claimed victory since their initial triumph. Subsequently, the following eight victories were alternated between the Gailstone and the Ukko, with the Gailstone securing three wins and the Ukko emerging victorious on five occasions. The most recent Champion of Ourania World was Commander Bazyli of the Totalist Federation, who made history as the youngest champion at age twenty-five. However, amidst mounting anticipation, this time, the Ukko has been overwhelmingly favored in the voting process, poised to potentially claim the championship once again.

As Battle World unfolds, the exhilarating action will be broadcast live to spectators across Ourania World, captivating audiences far and wide. A special screening awaits those in attendance along the banks of the Avedon River, with live holoscreen projections showcasing the intense battles as they unfold over the water. Each holoscreen fighter will loom an impressive fifty feet tall, bringing the excitement of the competition to life in stunning detail. With both sides of the river teeming with spectators and fans eagerly awaiting the spectacle, excitement fills the air. Among them, Arison secures prime seating atop a spacious flat rock positioned at the heart of the action. Soon joined by Viggo, Rain, and Leaf, the group settles in, ready to witness the thrilling clashes.

"Great seats, Arison!" Viggo remarked.

"Yeah, that's cause I've been here all night to snag this sweet spot!"

"You slept here all night?" Rain inquired, surprised.

Arison gazed at Rain, momentarily struck speechless by her beauty.

He nudged Viggo with his elbow and whispered, "Where did you find this goddess?"

Viggo pushed Arison back, "She's taken! So don't get any ideas," he declared, settling beside him.

"O, I didn't notice a ring. Maybe I should get her one," Arison teased.

Viggo attempted to punch Arison, but he swiftly dodged it, laughing. "Alright, alright! Does she happen to have a sister or a friend just as stunning?" Arison joked.

Rain chose to ignore the immature comment and switched seats with Leaf.

Now seated between Rain and Viggo, Leaf asked cheerfully, "Who do you think will be fighting first?"

"I don't know, but I know who will crush this competition! My hero! Bronx of The Elite Black!" Arison shouted.

"I hope he does!" Leaf said.

"I heard our Prince Jaden Knight will be competing. Rumor has it he's incredibly handsome!" Rain added with a smile.

"This competition isn't just about looks. It's about brutal skills, where limbs are torn apart, and blood splattered everywhere!" Viggo interjected, throwing his hands up and punching the air.

"You sure know how to charm a lady," Arison teased, winking at Rain, "What's your take on Lixia Ziva, Viggo?"

"She's so hot!"

"I thought looks didn't matter?" Rain questioned with a playful smirk.

"They don't, but she's still hot!" Viggo laughed.

"I second that. Do you think she stands a chance at winning?" Arison inquired.

"I hope so. She's the only female fighter qualified, and I'm rooting for her to take the whole competition!" Rain added with determination.

"I hope so, too!" Leaf quickly added with a smile.

"Didn't you just say you wanted Bronx to win?" Arison asked.

"Yep," Leaf laughed in response.

Viggo shook his head, "I don't know. Her chances seem pretty slim when you consider the other fighters. They look too dangerous even to breathe around. I can't imagine having to fight any of them!"

❖

A faint, slow, deep beat of the drums resonated through the City of Lights Stadium, gradually intensifying in volume and tempo. Echoing around the arena, the rhythmic drumming stirred the crowd into a frenzy of excitement. Spectators and fans alike cheered and clapped in unison, their enthusiasm reverberating throughout the stadium. Waves of hands swept across the stands, creating a visual spectacle to complement the pulsating rhythm of the drums. The beats quickened, the stadium seemed to come alive, the drumbeats becoming the very heartbeat of the arena, pounding faster and faster with each passing moment! Then, with a triumphant flourish, the sound of trumpets erupted proudly in harmony with the drums, heralding the start of Battle World with a majestic and heroic theme that resonated throughout the stadium, igniting the spirit of competition and anticipation among all in attendance.

A fifty-foot Hologram Announcer appeared on the battleground, saying, "Ladies and gentlemen, esteemed beings of Ourania World, welcome to Lighting of Dreams Battle World! Each contender has proven their mettle before you, but only one shall emerge victorious at the top, earning the coveted title of Champion of the Ourania World! In Battle World, there is but one rule: win. As a new century dawns, our fighters stand poised and prepared. Are you ready? Now, let us rise and extend a warm welcome to the rulers of Ourania!"

As the anticipation peaked, all the spectators rose to their feet, erupting into thunderous cheers and applause! Drums and trumpets reverberated throughout the stadium, their melodies filling the air with grandeur and excitement. The glass window of Royal Level Two opened, and four royal seats descended gracefully down to the battleground and rotated around slowly.

"Ruler Belvedere of The Majestic Royal!"

Ruler Belvedere stood resplendent in gleaming chrome armor, adorned with a flowing white cape. At his side, a sword of purest white, intricately embellished with jewels and gems, caught the light with every moment. As he rose, he radiated an aura of magnificence, waving graciously to the spectators.

"King Prime of Gailstone!"

King Prime ascended from his royal seat, with his great wings spread wide as he gazed across the assembled spectators below.

"Emperor Razen of Ukko Nations!"

Emperor Razen donned a menacing full black helmet and armor adorned with spikes from his fists to his shoulders. Multiple incarnations of Emperor Razens materialized across the battleground, hovering in midair with their arms crossed, casting an ominous presence.

"Lastly, presenting Commander Bazyli of The Totalist Federation!"

Commander Bazyli rose to his feet. Fireworks lit up the sky, and three rows of arrow-shaped red Totalist Air Fleet flew across the City of Lights Stadium.

The drums beat more dramatically!

"Now, it's time to select the battleground landscapes for our inaugural battle! None of our fighters have seen or set foot on any of the landscapes in our selection. Are you prepared for struggles and the loss of hope?" The Hologram Announcer's inquiry echoed through the arena.

A hologram of Bronx vs. Black Death posed against each other.

"Are you ready to feel and witness the agony of a bone-crushing combat with your own eyes?"

A hologram of Adonis Belacaro vs. Azriel faced off against each other.

"Are you ready for victory or death!"

Another hologram depicted Thanatos and White Death in a confrontational stance.

"Are you ready for Battle World!"

A holographic projection materialized, depicting the duel between Lixia Ziva and Prince Jaden Knight appeared.

The crowd erupted in a unified roar, causing the glass dome ceiling to shatter and cascade onto the transparent shield. Undeterred, the spectators cheered even louder, their excitement palpable.

"Ladies and gentlemen, please give a warm welcome to our first fighter, Bronx, representing The Elite Black of The Totalist Federation!"

Bronx, an Elite Black member, was among the best in the Totalist Military. Known for his unorthodox methods, he always got the job done. However, he was not in his seat beneath his statue. The spectators, puzzled by his absence, mumbled to each other in confusion.

The Hologram Announcer looked around and finally shouted,

"Bronx of the Elite Black!"

Bronx entered the battleground with two young ladies in red miniskirts on each arm. The spectators cheered and whistled, giving him a standing ovation and feeling relieved by his arrival.

Bronx surveyed the stadium, a sense of pride swelling within him as he represented the Totalist Federation and the Totalist. He swung his arms up and down, amplifying the crowd's cheers to an even greater volume.

"Now, please welcome Black Death, the assassin team from Gai G in the Land of Ukko!"

Black Death rose from his stone chair atop the pillar and instantly appeared in the center of the battleground.

"Ooo!" The spectators exclaimed, followed by a smattering of applause.

Bronx swung his double boom joy shotgun and fired a shot. Multiple bullets struck the ground near Black Death's feet, but he remained unfazed.

"This is a one and only warning. Any further hostile action before the fight begins will result in disqualification." The Hologram Announcer said as he disappeared.

Bronx noticed his opponent's calm and serious demeanor. He smirked and laughed, "Remove that stick out of your soft bum, Mr. Announcer! I was merely extending a friendly greeting, and he didn't even notice."

Bronx spitted, turned to Black Death, "Hey there, little man! Do you want a warm-up with one of my lady friends before we start?"

The young lady in a red miniskirt slapped him on the chest.

Bronx laughed and teased her, "Be careful what you touch on my body; something might go boom!"

Bronx playfully slapped her bum and lifted her with his palm over his head. Then, he threw the second young lady over his shoulder, slapping her bum to the rhythm of the drums as he hopped around in a barbaric dance. Walking along the edge, he showcased his young lady friends as they waved to the whistles and hooting from the spectators.

Bronx leaned back and roared.

The stadium erupted in loud foot-stomp rumbles and rhythmic clapping. Bronx put the young ladies down, dipping them both simultaneously and kissing each one slowly. As the last of the fireworks exploded above the City of Lights Stadium.

"That's my cue to win, ladies!"

The young ladies blew good luck kisses and gracefully catwalk off.

Bronx made his way to the center of the battleground, where Black Death awaited.

"Our audience had chosen the battleground landscape: the Towers of Stone! Let the battle commence!" The Hologram Announcer exclaimed through the speakers.

The sand shook violently, and the ground cracked apart as massive stone pillars burst through the sand and ascended into the sky. Bronx walked to the edge of the stone tower and looked down, observing the tiny spectators and fans below.

"Looks like quite a drop. Things just got serious, real fast!" He laughed.

Bronx returned to the middle of the stone tower, his gaze fixed upon Black Death, whose eyes were closed. He exuded a calm readiness, his aura tinged with a palpable sense of danger.

Bronx took a deep breath, his chest swelling as he allowed the air to flow through his body. He felt invigorated!

"Let's break something." Bronx slammed his fists together and stretched his arms upward, four solar jet packs emerge beside his double boom joy shotgun and grenade launcher. Bronx jetted toward Black Death!

I can't give him any opportunity for any counterattack! He thought.

Bronx appeared before Black Death, who opened his eyes just in time to evade Bronx's punches. Black Death disappeared and appeared quickly at random locations. Despite Black Death's rapid movements, Bronx stayed by his side, each strike causing explosions, and the pillar collapsed. Utilizing his solar jet pack, Bronx locked on his target, tracking and calculating Black Death's every move. With precision, he smashed his fist into the stone, but Black Death vanished at the last second, causing an explosion as the tower of stone collapsed.

Bronx landed on another stone tower and adjusted himself. "Getting tired of chasing this little chicken around," he muttered.

Black Death instantly appeared before him. Bronx caught only a fleeting glimpse of the dragger's edge out of the corner of his eye before it sliced across his chest and triggered the booby traps. The resulting explosion sent them both hurtling off the stone tower. Black Death managed to twist mid-air as they fell, hurling his dagger into a nearby stone tower with a rope attached. Using the momentum, he swung around, deftly ran up to the top of the tower, and effortlessly whipped his rope dagger back to him. Meanwhile, Bronx soared into the air, protected by a gel layer shielding him from the blast. Drawing his grenade launcher from his back, he activated it and synchronized the target tracking system.

"Let's see how fast those little legs of yours can dance," he chuckled and fired nine rounds into the air, each seeking its target automatically. Bronx then swapped his grenade launcher for his double boom joy shotgun and drew his large black combat knife from the side of his leg.

Eight Towers of Stone blew up across the stadium, leaving only three standing. Black Death breathed heavily, blood dripping from his side and leg.

Bronx landed beside him and laughed, "I might have overdone it and clipped one of your little chicken wings."

Black Death materialized above him from behind, wielding a dragger aimed downward. Bronx's solar jet pack propelled him around to confront Black Death, and he swiftly blocked the attack with his giant black combat knife.

Bronx jammed his double-boom joy shotgun into his stomach, smirking as he quipped, "How you doin'?" before blasting Black Death across the stone.

Smoke steamed from the barrel as he holstered it away, a big grin spreading across his face. Pulling his second large black combat knife, he floated slowly toward Black Death. He pressed his combat boot firmly against his bloody chest.

"You don't look so good. Is this the best you've got?"

Coughing up blood, Black Death laughed, "My dagger will slice your head off!"

Unamused, Bronx slammed his two knives into Black Death's shoulders, driving them deep into the ground.

"Sweet dream," Bronx whispered.

He flew away as the last grenade fell from above, exploding in a fiery blast on Black Death. Behind him, a massive fireball engulfed the background as the stone tower collapsed. The crowd erupted into a wild cheer, the roar echoing across the stadium. With all his might, Bronx bent backward and screamed into the sky, celebrating his proud victory!

The loud cheers became muffled, and everything slowly faded into the quiet stillness of the aftermath.

❖

Bronx lay in bed, a grin spreading across his face as he mumbled softly. The doctors hovered over him, diligently checking his vital signs and scanning for any signs of brain damage.

"He's waking up, doctor!" the Nurse said.

Bronx opened his eyes, feeling disoriented as he looked around the room. Puzzled, he attempted to sit up, but the nurse and doctors held him down.

"What are you doing?! Why am I here?! Let me out!"

Bronx yanked the medical device sensors and tore the cables from his body.

"The battle ended an hour ago. You were unconscious and defeated," the Doctor stated.

"NO! I won! What are you talking about!"

The doctor pointed to the holoscreen, displaying a replay of an earlier battle. The stadium responded with a loud foot rumble and rhythm claps as Bronx roared at the crowd, and the fireworks exploded in the sky. The scene showed Bronx standing, facing Black Death as the battle commenced. Black Death approached him and swiftly sliced his head off before kicking his body off the stone tower. Bronx's head and body tumbled to the bottom as the battle concluded. Black Death was declared the winner, qualifying for the semi-final fight. Bronx's statue crumbled, and his pillar collapsed in the aftermath.

He watched in disbelief.

"Fortunately, our clandestine medical team was prepared for scenarios where you or Prince Jaden Knight might face critical injuries!"

"That is not what happened! I killed Black Death! I WON!" Bronx shouted as he rose from the bed, seizing the doctor's neck and lifting him into the air with one hand.

The doctor gasped, "That's the truth! Release me this instant, or you'll answer to a court-martial!"

As Bronx dropped the doctor, leaving him choking on the ground, an older doctor standing by the monitor system spoke: "Your head has been successfully reattached, all the fractures have healed, and your vital signs are stable. Major General Vic requests your presence at the Royal Chamber Level. Please proceed there immediately."

Bronx pulled the remainder of the sensors off him.

"Let's hope Prince Jaden Knight puts up some resistance, at the very least."

Bronx overheard one of the nurses say as he stormed out of the medic bay.

❖

Bronx approached the Royal Justices who guarded the high-ceiling double doors made of black marble with intricate gold trim.

"I'm here on orders from Major General Vic."

The Royal Justices pushed the imposing high-ceiling double doors, which swung open to reveal a spacious Royal Chamber. The room was dimly lit, with a striking carpet featuring alternating dark and light silver rectangles covering most of the floor. In the center, a pathway of long white marble tiles led to Commander Bazyli's half-circle black marble table. As Bronx entered, his gaze was drawn to the large window panels before him, offering a view of the stadium below. Glancing to his left, he noticed chandeliers hanging high from the ceiling, casting a warm glow down the room's length.

Four oversized leather chairs surrounded the half-circle black marble table, while on the opposite side sat Commander Bazyli's chair, positioned to face the holoscreen wall.

The double doors closed behind him.

The Royal Chamber remained dimmed as Bronx strode down the long white marble path toward the table, paying no heed to the window panels lining his right. With each step, the chamber echoed his movement. Spaced along the left side of the wall were four large fireplaces, each burning and crackling, their flame casting flickering shadows. Passing under each chandelier above him, Bronx noted the intricate design, crafted with eight tiers of light blue crystals that illuminated his path, accentuating his sense of shame. The Ourania World News echoed through the vastness of the large Royal Chamber as he drew closer and closer.

"In the eagerly anticipated first round of Battle World, hopes were high for our formidable Elite Black to secure victory. However, their performance left much to be desired, casting a shadow of doubt over the reputation of our Totalist Federation. The untimely demise of Bronx only added to the disappointment felt by Totalist across Ourania, dealing a crushing blow to our aspirations of triumph. As we grapple with this setback, all eyes turn to our young Prince Jaden Knight. Can he lead us out of this deficit and summon the miracle we so desperately need to prevail?"

Bronx nervously glanced at the massive chair on the table's other side. Placing his right hand over his heart, he lowered his head respectfully and spoke, "Commander Bazyli, sir."

Silence.

There was no response or movement from Commander Bazyli's chair.

With his hand still over his heart, Bronx turned towards King Roy, who sat in the middle of the table, and respectfully lowered his head, "Your Highness, King Roy."

King Roy remained silent; his attention fixed on the holoscreen.

Bronx shifted his gaze to the right side, where Lieutenant General Bradstone sat. "Lieutenant General Bradstone, Sir."

Bronx bowed to him.

Lieutenant General Bradstone, adorned in a red cloak with full-body chrome armor accented by gold trim, exuded an aura of authority. As Commander Bazyli's right hand, he controlled the Royal Justices. With commanding brown eyes, a rigid square face structure, and a quiff hairstyle peppered with salt and pepper, he cut an imposing figure. His pointed ducktail beard added to his stern demeanor. Upon noticing Bronx's left sleeve, which was not buttoned, Lieutenant General Bradstone offered no response. Instead, he turned his attention back to the holoscreen, his focus unwavering.

In frustration, Bronx gritted his back teeth before turning to Major General Vic, who sat on the left side. Still, with his hand over his heart, Bronx bowed respectfully and greeted him, "Major General Vic."

He rotated his oversized leather chair away from the holoscreen and nodded.

Though short in stature, Major General Vic possessed a round face adorned with a thinning, balding white head. His tiny grey eyes were set above a prominent nose and a small mouth. Draped in an honored black military suit, he carried an air of authority. Major General Vic spearheaded the creation of the Elite Black task force, propelling them to the zenith of the military hierarchy. Serving as Commander Bazyli's left hand, he had a softer, more compassionate demeanor than Lieutenant General Bradstone. However, he understood that capital punishment was always an option for those deemed deserving. His gentle face had seen many regime changes and futile wars.

Bronx bowed respectfully to Admiral Baylee, addressing him, "Admiral Baylee, sir."

Admiral Baylee, the Totalist Ocean Defense and Offense commander, was the youngest to attain such a prestigious status. His shoulder-length blond hair partially obscured his pristine white military uniform, adorned with medals on each side of his shoulders and gold chains connecting to his elbows. With a sharp, clean-shaven face, he wore a smirk that twitched his crooked nose while his keen green eyes remained fixed on the holoscreen. "Pathetic."

Major General Vic broke the awkward moment, rising to his feet before finally addressing Bronx. "What happened, Bronx?"

"I engaged in combat with Black Death, and he proved no match for me. I emerged victorious! But then, the next moment, I found myself in the medic bay. I do not understand, sir."

Bronx's eyes followed Major General Vic as he walked to the window, gazing at the stadium below. "We dedicated countless hours to training, eagerly anticipating this moment for a very long time. As one of our most skilled members of the Elite Black, your loss in less than a minute is disheartening. It undermines the efforts of our Totalist Federation, making us appear inept. Smearing our great Federation into your clown show!"

Bronx's gaze fell upon the undamaged Towers of Stone visible outside the windows, causing him to lower his head.

"Such humiliating loss warrants death!" Without glancing at Bronx, King Roy burst out with a commanding tone.

"We do not deny that option, my King," Major General Vic bowed respectfully, his hand over his heart. "However, with over 532 successful missions, numerous honors, and fifteen years of unwavering loyalty, coupled with the expertise of the finest individuals, wouldn't it be prudent to allow for an opportunity for evaluation? Won't you agree, my King?"

Bronx gripped his chest.

"We lost all respect from the elites of Ourania!" King Roy's voice boiled with frustration.

"We still have our formidable Prince Jaden Knight, your son, my King, if we can uncover what happened to Bronx, we may better prepare him for future battles."

"I thought we had comprehensive intel on everyone's abilities and power? Do we not?"

"The Ukko possess thousands of years of enigmatic abilities, and our intel teams have barely scratched the surface, Bronx, if you can offer any hints about what occurred, inform us immediately. As of now, you may go." Major General Vic said.

"A punishment will be decreed tomorrow. Await further instructions in your quarters," King Roy declared sternly, his gaze fixed on Bronx.

Bronx replied, bowing his head respectfully. "Thank you, King Roy, Lieutenant General Bradstone, Major General Vic, Admiral Baylee, and Commander Bazyli." Bronx turned and walked out of the Royal Chamber.

"Intel Unit," Major General Vic ordered.

An Intel Unit holoscreen appeared in the center of the table.

"Yes, Major General Vic," Intel Unit replied.

"Please ensure I receive a thorough analysis, scan, and cross-intel reports of the fight by tomorrow. Replay every angle and seconds of the stadium footage before Black Death enters the battleground and provide comprehensive details of each action taken during the battle."

"Yes, Major General Vic," the Intel Unit replied, and the holoscreen disappeared.

Lieutenant General Bradstone ordered, "Colonel Steel, report to the Royal Chamber at the City of Light Stadium."

Colonel Steel appeared, placed his hand over his heart, and bowed, "Commander Bazyli, King Roy, Major General Vic, Admiral Baylee," he greeted each in turn. Then, looking at Lieutenant General Bradstone, he continued, "Lieutenant General Bradstone, you requested?"

Colonel Steel wore a light grey cap and suit embellished with gold medals and chains. His long eyelashes cast shadows over his weary light brown eyes, and a stubble beard covered his exhausted, drawn face.

"Prepare a live report of the Timeless Island mission and the X Chamber failure once Lighting of Dream Battle World concludes," Lieutenant General Bradstone ordered.

"Yes, Lieutenant General Bradstone."

"I believe my Advisory Kin was with you during your X Chamber failure?" King Roy asked.

"He was, my King." Colonel Steel replied.

"Great, I will have him attend as well. You may dismiss."

"Thank you, Commander Bazyli and King Roy." Colonel Steel turned to Lieutenant General Bradstone, Major General Vic, and Admiral Baylee, "Good day, gentlemen," he greeted. They nodded in acknowledgment as Colonel Steel promptly disappeared.

Lieutenant General Bradstone ordered, "General Crocrovich, report to the Royal Chamber at the City of Light Stadium."

General Crocrovich appeared with his hand over his heart and bowed, "Commander Bazyli and King Roy, I am honored and proud to announce that we have discovered a Stone Rune in the name of The Totalist Federation!"

Commander Bazyli swiveled his massive chair around, his gaze intent. "Where is it currently?"

"At the Weaponry and Research Lab undergoing thorough examination, my Commander Bazyli," General Crocrovich said with a happy bow.

Commander Bazyli nodded.

"How did you find the Stone Rune?" inquired Major General Vic.

"It was no easy feat, Major General Vic. I had to confront formidable adversaries in Section 12 and endured significant damage during the struggle. Fortunately, my resilience prevailed, and the notion of disappointing my Commander Bazyli was inconceivable!" General Crocrovich explained as he lower his head towards Commander Bazyli.

Admiral Baylee said. "No one from Section 12 or any other section can match our military might. It's hard to believe you sustained such heavy damage, good old General."

General Crocrovich's expression hardened. "A tone of resentment, do I hear?"

"A tone of lies doesn't go uncontested," Admiral Baylee retorted, a smirk on his lips.

"The fact remains that we now possess the Stone Rune. We appreciate your loyal and dedicated efforts, General Crocrovich. However, I must inquire: How did the adversaries manage to acquire it? " Major General Vic queried.

General Crocrovich paused briefly before responding, "The interrogation process is still ongoing. Rest assured, as soon as I have the answer, I will report directly to Commander Bazyli."

"General Crocrovich, what is your current report on the search for X?" inquired Lieutenant General Bradstone.

General Crocrovich swiped up five layers of topography for Vellatine City, along with the hologram of Vellatine Forest beside it, on the table. Commander Bazyli focused his attention on the Vellatine Forest hologram. He then scrolled through various topography holograms from different regions. Among them, he observed blue Totalist soldiers and large robotic droids scattered across multiple areas.

"All my men and resources are being utilized to the fullest across all sectors and regions. The Lighting of Dreams Battle World event has significantly slowed our progress due to the large number of attendees and the need to protect our VIP and Elite members," General Crocrovich explained.

Commander Bazyli pulled up the topography holograms for Section

12 and Borat Section. Blue soldiers were interrogating white Totalist civilians while large robotic droids searched the area.

"King Roy will double your army and resources." Commander Bazyli removed the Black Onyx Emblem of Vellatine from his wrist and tossed it to General Crocrovich. "I want results!"

"Yes, Commander Bazyli! Thank you, King Roy. Good day, gentlemen." General Crocrovich gleamed brightly, placed his hand over his heart, displayed the Black Onyx Emblem of Vellatine, and bowed as he disappeared.

"You're using the Black Onyx Emblem of Vellatine?" King Roy asked.

"Failure is not an option," Commander Bazyli said.

"And you want to put more of our resources into Project Firelights?" King Roy questioned.

"We have been pouring our resources for five years!" he continued angrily. "Even our allies could barely match a quarter of our contribution!"

"A monetary loss now will be rewarded ten thousandfold in the presence of a greater vision," Commander Bazyli responded.

"I hope you're right. Otherwise, the great Vellatine City will become the next slum of Section 12," King Roy said.

Commander Bazyli slanted a grin. "In time, my king, in time," he replied, turning back to watch the holoscreen wall.

Chapter 10

Decapitation!

The crowd by Avedon Rivers was in an uproar, throwing rocks at Bronx's holoscreen in the river!

"Unbelievable!" Arison's voice echoed with fury as he flung a rock at the hologram. "He just stood there and got his head chopped off!"

"You think he threw the fight?" Viggo asked.

"There's no way Bronx will betray us for any amount of shins or gems!" Arison said.

"I don't know. I would," Viggo said.

"Of course, you will. That's why you're not up there making the big shin! You're too busy picking up every little scrap off the floor. You've missed the big opportunities flying right over your head," Arison remarked, smacking Viggo on the back.

"Hey, you're sitting right next to me, so spare me the lecture on missed opportunities!" Viggo retorted.

"Arison, do you think he was searching for his head?" Leaf pondered.

Arison paused, his expression brightening as if a light bulb had just gone off above his head.

"That must be it! He must have been caught under some magical power! You're a genius, Leaf!" Arison shouted.

Leaf grinned widely and scratched his head.

"But does that even matter anymore? The fight's over, and Bronx is already dead," Rain questioned.

"I don't know about all these rules, but maybe they can overturn them," Arison mused.

"The only rule is to win!" Viggo said.

Arison, wearing a defeated expression, nodded silently.

"The Ukko are cheaters! That wasn't even a fight!" Viggo exclaimed.

The drums beat again as the second battle was about to start.

❖

The stadium spectators' excitement waned after the Totalist's disappointing loss. Their disappointment lingered until a ten-foot white Azriel descended from the sky onto one of the Towers of Stone. Murmurs spread among the spectators as they pointed at Azriel.

"Ladies, gentlemen, and inhabitants of Ourania World, welcome to the thrilling second battle of our main event! Without further ado, let's begin the spectacle! Tonight's chosen battleground is none other than the fearsome Octo Maelstrom, The Aquatic Monster!" The Hologram Announcer's voice boomed excitedly, setting the stage for an electrifying showdown.

The spectators were in awe.

Fear quickly overcame them as the landscape tore apart, and Octo Maelstrom, the Aquatic Monster, formed before their eyes. The Towers of Stone trembled as the sands below swirled faster and faster, cascading into the growing black hole. Water surged in, crashing against the Towers of Stone. Fragments of the stones shattered and collapsed into a monstrous spiral whirlpool. Large stone pieces were carried along a spiral path, colliding with each other. Only three Towers of Stone remained standing.

"Let's give a round of applause for Azriel the Gailstone, hailing from Sleeping Tear Island!" The Hologram Announcer's voice echoed from the speakers.

Azriel hovered in midair, flapping his massive wings, and glanced up at Adonis, standing at the edge of his pillar. Azriel then looked down at the terrifying Octo Maelstrom below as it grew, swallowing the deafened water into darkness. Some spectators clapped, but most were gripped by fear. Azriel landed on a large stone swirling along the top of the whirlpool, one knee and fist on the ground. With his head bowed, his wings slowly closed.

Adonis glanced over to where Lixia Ziva was seated. Their eyes met, and Adonis smirked before leaping off the pillar towards the Octo Maelstrom below. A white horse, fully decorated in white and purple velvet caparison, soared from the battleground's edge, catching Adonis midair before landing gracefully on a stone at the top of the whirlpool. The horse trotted confidently around the stone's edge, displaying no fear of the Octo Maelstrom before rearing up excitedly.

"Now, Adonis Belacaro strides into the battleground, representing the Ironstead of The Majestic Royal!" The Hologram Announcer's voice boomed, eliciting cheers from the spectators!

Adonis dismounted his loyal horse and whistled. Its nodded and snorted before trotting off and leaping back onto the safety of the battleground edge.

"Are we playing hoppy?" Adonis remarked as he surveyed the scene, noting the many large stones slowly swirled towards the bottom of the whirlpool.

He glanced at Azriel as he pushed his left fist off the ground and slowly rose to his feet. His muscular physique and chiseled abs revealed as he unfurled his thirty-foot wingspan.

"What a masterful sculpture—truly a formidable beast. I will hang your head along side my many worthy trophies!" Adonis exclaimed with delight, effortlessly pulling his labry battle axe from his back with one hand. The double-bitted axe head was as large as his broad chest. He slammed it into the ground with a powerful swing, causing the stone to crack from the heavy impact.

"Don't count it. You disadvantaged!" Azriel said.

"It will only make your head more worthy," Adonis smirked confidently.

"Let the Battle World commence!" The Hologram Announcer's voice thundered.

The crowd roared in excitement.

"Let's give this crowd a show, shall we? Now, which shall I slice off first? Your wings or your head?" Adonis laughed.

He charged forward, his battle axe slicing through the concrete stone effortlessly as it split into two. With his battle axe trailing behind, he leaped toward Azriel, swinging it over his head at the last second as he came down. However, Azriel remained calm and proud, not moving an inch as he looked up at Adonis. Azriel's palms pressed against the hot Majestic Royal steel, halting it in front of his face. Adonis, expecting nothing less, swung his whole body down with significant momentum and delivered a powerful kick to Azriel's chest, causing him to stagger back a few steps from the impact. Azriel held the brown leather-wrapped steel hang of the battle-axe with one hand, smiling as he brushed the dust off his chest. He admired the beautifully carved steel bit, a masterpiece crafted with 2,000 hours of intense hammering by a skilled axe master.

"Gorgeous!" Azriel exclaimed as he swung the axe side to side, slicing the air into a perfect triangle.

"Fit good." Azriel tossed it back to Adonis.

"I get from Ironstead," Azriel laughed.

Adonis looked up at Azriel, who towered four feet taller than him, smirked, and nodded. "You don't have to wait. If you defeat me, Mightis will be yours!"

"Mightis! A fitting name. I not know Majestic Royals give up easily."

"No one has ever taken Mightis from me."

"What you want if I lose?"

"I've already told you. Your head."

Azriel's expression hardened, and his muscles swelled larger with determination. "Mightis mine!"

The spectators cheered and rumbled the stadium.

Without hesitation, Azriel flew straight toward him. His arm pulled back. Adonis tossed Mightis backward, quickly hopped back, dodging side to side to evade Azriel's powerful punches, then ducked and countered with a mighty punch to Azriel's ribs!

Adonis jumped above him, delivering a powerful straight-down punch to his stone cheek, causing it to crack. Azriel crashed and landed near the edge of the stone, water splashing onto him, a stark reminder of their proximity to the bottom of the whirlpool.

"There's more to me than just a piece of steel," Adonis rotated his fist side to side and blew at it while walking toward Azriel.

The force of the punch from someone smaller than him took Azriel aback. The crack on his cheek sealed and turned back into stone once more.

Adonis effortlessly caught Mightis with one hand, "Now, let's see what you're made of."

He swung Mightis towards Azriel's chest, but Azriel rolled to the side just in time. Mightis sliced off the corner of the stone. Adonis swung it sideways without hesitation, cutting into the concrete stone toward Azriel as he spun himself off the ground. Azriel's claw was instantly reinforced with stone, halting the momentum of Mightis bit. Adonis roared in frustration, gripping Mightis with both hands. He sliced through the claws and slashed across Azriel's chest with a mighty effort!

Azriel's wings popped open and flew backward, blowing dust into Adonis's eyes. Azriel touched his chest, and blue blood leaked out. Taking a deep breath, he exhaled, and the stone sealed the slash, resolidifying his stone chest and claws.

"I suppose I'll have to cut you in half now," Adonis advanced toward Azriel, swinging Mightis left and right. Azriel roared in response, baring his fangs as his claw grew six inches longer, transforming into razor-sharp stone.

"Did I break your nail? Now, onto those wings!"

Azriel folded his wings and charged at him on all fours, ripping chunks of stone from underneath his claws as he advanced. Adonis stood his ground, bending his knees and firmly pushing his feet against the ground. Azriel lunged at him, snapping his massive jaw toward his head. He countered by pushing Mightis's hang into Azriel's jaw, preventing the bite. Azriel's relentless charge forced him to slide backward. Adonis glanced back and noticed the edge of the stone approaching rapidly. Simultaneously, other stones began to disappear into the darkness of the whirlpool!

With the momentum, Adonis dropped backward, leveraging his weight to kick Azriel's body over him, flip him over the edge, and into the whirlpool. Adonis quickly scrambled to his feet, running and hopping from stone to stone, desperately trying to escape being swallowed by the darkness below.

Adonis hopped halfway to the top of the whirlpool, finding a smaller stone to stand on. He glanced back but saw no sign of Azriel.

The stone Adonis stood on was suddenly pulled under, causing him to plummet into the water below.

Underwater, Adonis witnessed a giant tentacle wrap around the stone dragging it deeper before crushing it. At the heart of the whirlpool lay a massive black mouth lined with razor-sharp teeth, shredding and devouring everything that went in. The water rushed into the mouth's wall as it swallowed relentlessly. Multiple giant tentacles pursued Adonis, but he fought back fiercely, wielding Mightis to slice at the tentacles, attempting to ensnare him. With each strike, the chopped tentacles fell into the gaping maw, where the teeth shredded them to pieces. However, to Adonis's dismay, the giant tentacles regenerate their appendages.

That's going to be annoying. Adonis thought.

A shadow loomed above him, and Adonis saw a massive stone. He swam toward it, then leaped out of the water, driving Mightis into the side of the rock wall, and began his ascent. Three tentacles whipped out of the water, coiling around his legs and body, yanking him back down. His right hand slipped off the rock but clinging tightly to Mightis's hang. Adonis gritted his teeth from the sharp pain. The tentacles squeezed tighter, their sharp needles digging into his flesh.

A painful scream echoed through the stadium.

The side of the stone tilted toward the water from the powerful pull, three tentacles were sliced off, causing the stone to swing to the other side. Launching Adonis into the air with Mightis in hand and landed at the top of the stone, the severed tentacles attached to his body twitching. He ripped them off his body as he ran and jumped from stone to stone as other giant tentacle arms followed closely behind, slamming down onto the stone like hammers and shattering it into pieces.

Adonis leaped toward the large stone before him, but multiple tentacles destroyed it, and more awaited for him in the water below. As he descended, other tentacles lunged into the air after him. Adonis gripped Mightis tightly, preparing for a confrontation. He caught sight of a dark figure above him from the corner of his eye. Without hesitation, he raised his arms. Azriel swooped down, grabbing hold of Mightis hang, and together they ascended, soaring up to one of the three remaining Towers of Stone.

They landed safely, and Adonis walked to the edge, peering down as the Towers of Stone shook from the tentacles' relentless assault.

"I didn't need your help, and perhaps you could have won," Adonis stated.

Azriel walked over and stood beside him, gazing down at the chaotic scene below.

"Not victory."

Adonis chuckled. "Victory belongs to the last one standing. Don't tell me you, Gailstone, believe in honor?"

The Towers of Stone shook once more, cracks began to formed, and a piece of the stone broke off, plummeting downward. Azriel gazed towards the sky and declared, "Honor is our way."

"Honor is for suicidal fools!"

The Towers of Stone shook again, and more stones fell into the whirlpool.

"I don't think this tower can withstand much more of this," Adonis shouted as he sprinted and leaped towards the next Towers of Stone, with Azriel following closely behind as the tower crumbled beneath them.

"What plan? We fight?" Azriel asked.

Adonis landed on the second tower and said, "We can. Or we can take on that," pointing towards Octo Maelstrom with Mightis.

Azriel looked below, "How?"

"The only way we know how," Adonis exclaimed as he punched his fist into Mightis, the Majestic Royal steel ringing out with a loud, high-pitched sound.

The second Towers of Stone shook.

"You see that dark void in the center? That's its mouth," Adonis said. "If we take it out, there will be no more interference."

Azriel gazed at the gaping black mouth below as the Towers of Stone trembled under the relentless assault of the tentacles. Feeling the warm sunlight on his face, Azriel closed his eyes and tilted his chin upwards towards the sky. With a deep breath, he opened his massive wings, stretching them wide. Reaching his right arm into the warm sunlight, his sharp claw slowly twirled around as if grasping the light. As Azriel exhaled, he grew larger and more formidable. He focused intently on the gaping black mouth below, his gaze unwavering. With determination, he lowered his arm and clutched his claws. His entire body and wings were enveloped in hard, concentrated stone layers. He walked off the edge and plunged straight into the maw of Octo Maelstrom. Folding his stone wings to create maximum speed, he thrust his arms forward, slicing through the air like an arrow. The tentacles hurling large stones from all directions, he zipped past them. Two massive rocks flew into the spectator areas, shattering against the transparent shield. The spectators erupted into a cacophony of screams and roars, filled with fear and excitement!

"A suicidal fool! I love it!" Adonis laughed.

Azriel exploded into the center of the giant black mouth, his sharp claws piercing deep into its soft muscle.

"Roooaaarrrrrhhhh!" Octo Maelstrom uttered a monstrous scream as its tentacles thrashed wildly, lashing out at everything in sight. Two of the tentacles shattered the Towers of Stone Adonis was standing on. He leaped from stone to stone as they collapsed beneath him.

Azriel's razor-sharp claws tore deep into the rough flesh, ripping off chunks of meat and opening large wounds. Teeth quickly grew into the wounds, attempting to chew into his stone body, but Azriel swiftly dug them out. Tentacles whipped around and attacked Azriel from above, but Adonis kicked the fallen stones into those tentacles, providing cover for Azriel.

Large stones crashed into the tentacles and the black mouth surrounding Azriel, raining down like a meteor storm from the sky. Holding a large stone over his head, Adonis hurled it into the mouth, where it slammed down next to Azriel. Landing on the stone beside Azriel, Adonis stood firm. Octo Maelstrom roared in pain, and shook violently in response.

The spectators cheered at the edge of their seats!

They both fought ferociously against the teeth and tentacles surrounding them. A tooth bit down into Adonis's back, but it grinded across Mightis's steel instead, emitting a sharp, high-pitched sound that reverberated into the rough flesh, stunning the surrounding teeth. Adonis retaliated by punching the teeth around him, breaking them in half. However, for every tooth he destroyed, three more slowly grew in their place. Undeterred, Adonis repeatedly punched into the rough flesh. Octo Maelstrom roared in agony, and the flesh ruptured under Adonis's assault. Three tentacles wrapped around Adonis's arms from above, yanking him upward, while the teeth below bit into his legs, holding him down. He yelled out in excruciating pain as his body was being pulled in opposite directions.

Azriel witnessed Adonis getting ensnared by the tentacles and acted swiftly. His wings, flung outward and he flew toward the giant tentacles, determination blazing in his eyes. With a powerful swipe of his claw, he ripped one of the enormous tentacles off of Adonis's arm. Two more tentacles remained tightly wrapped around him, still threatening to tear him apart.

As Azriel's claws grew longer and sharper, twelve tentacles dived at him from behind. Four tentacles wrapped around each of his wings, and two held onto each arm, leaving Azriel suspended in midair, his body pulled in different directions. Despite the strain, Azriel summoned all his strength, pulling his arms together and leaning toward Adonis with all his might. His protective stone cracked around his left wing and arms as he struggled against the overwhelming force. With fierce determination, Azriel yanked his claws across each other, slashing the tentacles to pieces and freeing his arms. But a sickening, tearing sound ripped off his left-wing.

Azriel let out a thunderous roar of agony as he grabbed the tentacles around his right wing and tore them apart. The tentacles continued to crushed his left wing before dropping it into the gaping black mouth below, where it would be consumed.

With a mighty leap, Azriel surged towards the tentacles ensnaring Adonis's arms. He viciously shredded them apart and freeing Adonis's hands. Adonis shattered the teeth that bit into him. Azriel fell along with the shredded tentacles into the mouth below. Inside, more razor-sharp teeth closed in around him, crushing into his stone body and right wing. Azriel roared angrily and fought back fiercely. Swinging his claws and twisting his body, he shattered the teeth that threatened to consume him. Eventually, he managed to get back on his feet, but razor-sharp teeth pierced into his stone legs, adding to his agony.

Adonis stood on the stone with Mightis in hand, "Azriel!" and threw Mightis to him.

He caught and swung it around him, cutting through all the teeth.

Adonis pulled Azriel onto the stone. He bled profusely and lost consciousness as Mightis fell onto the stone.

"Today is not your suicidal day."

Summoning every ounce of this strength, Adonis held Azriel tightly, his grip unyielding. With a mighty roar, he spun Azriel around and hurled him out of the black mouth, launching him to the top of the last standing Towers of Stone.

Adonis retrieved Mightis, but as he did, the teeth grew around the stone, gnashing and chewing into it, causing it to crumble beneath his feet.

Adonis held Mightis aloft with both hands, his voice boomed in a godly command, "Final Judgement!" even as the teeth and giant tentacles descended upon him.

A blade of light descended from the sky, illuminating Mightis with a radiant glow.

"DECAPITATION!"

Adonis swung Mightis in a slow, complete circle, slicing Octo Maelstrom and the landscape in half!

Octo Maelstrom roared in agony as half its form slid into the plummeting landscape. Adonis's hair whipped up from the sudden rush of wind and water that surged into the air from the newly formed chasm below. Half of the stadium's spectators leaned to one side of their seats as the blade of light descended, yet they remained shielded by the transparent barrier. Adonis sheathed Mightis, eliciting a standing ovation from the audience as half of the landscape vanished into the abyss below.

Azriel slowly opened his eyes to the loud cheers and claps below. Pain radiated from everywhere; his legs, torso, and wing were punctured and bleeding, with teeth still embedded in his body. Azriel pushed himself up, limped to the edge of the Towers of Stone, and looked down. Half of Octo Maelstrom was gone, its lifeless form causing no more whirlpools, with some tentacles slumped over the cliff. Azriel was astonished and glared at the spectators, all on their feet, applauding. Then, he saw Adonis below, looking back at him.

"I honor to fight Adonis Belacaro!" Azriel declared to the spectators below, who responded with cheers.

Azriel jumped off the edge, dug his razor-sharp claws into the side of the Towers of Stone, and slid down to the bottom. The last Towers of Stone split in half and crumbled. Azriel limped toward Adonis.

"You look terrible," Adonis said.

Azriel chuckled. "Feel terrible," he paused to take a deep breath, his face contorting with pain. "I fight now."

Adonis briefly glanced up and down at Azriel. "You're missing a wing, and some teeth are still pierced in your body. You could barely stand. Your head is not worth anymore."

Azriel stood tall, displaying tremendous grit as he yanked out the teeth embedded in his body and flung them onto the ground. Adonis turned away from Azriel, "You saved me, and I will not fight you."

"Give crowd... good show," In great pain, Azriel continued to extract the last teeth from his body.

Adonis raised his head, "This is not a good show nor a fight worth fighting."

Azriel took a deep breath, exhaling loudly. His stone chest expanded with each, while his wounds rapidly healed and his right-wing regained strength. As he continued to breathe deeply, a growing shadow covered Adonis. Turning back, he beheld Azriel, now twice his size, towering over him. The swift recovery took aback Adonis.

Cracking the stones on his neck, Azriel declared, "Feel better!" His body instantly transformed into stone. "Need real Champion!"

Azriel slammed his fists into the ground, sending a quake hurtling toward Adonis, splitting the ground in half. With a swift leap to the side, Adonis narrowly avoided the tremor, causing half of the cliff to crumble away.

Adonis smirked, nodding in agreement before whispering, "Let's tango."

Azriel leaped onto him, and punches rain down at him. Adonis attempted to evade and dodge, but each powerful punch from Azriel created small craters that shook the ground. Adonis misstepped on the crumbled earth; he stumbled and fell. Azriel seized the opportunity and punched through the gap between Adonis's arms, smashing into his face. Adonis was dazed, allowing Azriel to quickly strike his ribs and midsection repeatedly. Adonis managed to evade several punches aimed at his head but couldn't escape the final powerful blow, and his head slammed into the ground. Azriel grabbed Adonis's legs, leaped to the cliff's edge, and swung his body over his head. With a sickening crunch, Adonis's back cracked against the sharp edge, leaving him breathless and motionless over the cliff's edge.

Such speed and strength! Adonis thought.

"Draw Mightis!" Azriel yelled.

Adonis rolled over, blood spilling from his mouth. "Why stop?"

Slowly, he rose to his feet, wiping the blood from his face. "I've always said there's more to me than my Majestic Royal Steel. I can defeat you without relying on Mightis!"

"Cannot defeat me," Azriel strode forward confidently, his chest thrusting outward as he shed loose stones from his back. With each deep breath and exhale, he grew larger and larger. Meanwhile, Adonis dashed alongside Azriel's leg, delivering punches to his stone knee to halt his expansion. Shards of stones flew in all directions but quickly regenerated, growing thicker with each blow.

Azriel laughed.

Adonis now stood only as tall as Azriel's knee. Azriel lifted his foot without hesitation and brought it crashing down onto Adonis and the rocks beneath him. Everything was crushed, and a cloud of dust billowed outward. Azriel lifted his foot and surveyed the scene, there was no sign of him. Unbeknownst to him, Adonis had climbed around and onto Azriel's broken wing, his arm raised in preparation. He slammed his elbow into the weakened stone, shattering it further. Azriel roared in agony, staggering towards the cliff's edge. His attempt to reach for Adonis was futile. Desperately, Azriel spun from side to side, trying to shake his adversary loose. Adonis clenched his fist tightly, drawing it back with all his strength before driving it into the wound, shattering the scapula bone and severing nerves. Azriel lurched forward and tumbled over the cliff's edge. Adonis jumped off, landing on the cliff edge, and stood on the giant tentacle while Azriel clung desperately with his right claw; his left arm hung limp. With Azriel's weight bearing down and his razor-sharp claw, the giant tentacle slowly began to tear apart.

"Now, do you want to keep fighting, or are you ready to admit defeat?" Adonis asked with Mightis in hand. As the sunlight caught the blade, it gleamed brightly, reflecting into Azriel's eyes. He turned away, his gaze shifting downward into the abyss below.

"That's where all the so-called honor warriors end up. It's harder to do what's right every day and live purposefully. It is easier to give your life away. Live Azriel. Live another day to make a difference for yourself, others, your people, and the world. That's a true honor and the mark of a real warrior."

Azriel glanced at Adonis and then, with a resigned gesture, returned to his average size. "I concede."

Adonis hoisted the dead tentacle upward, bringing Azriel along with it. Once at the top, he help Azriel up.

"Ladies and gentlemen, put your hands together for the victor of this incredible match, Adonis Belacaro!" the Hologram Announcer shouted.

Adonis lifted Azriel's right arm triumphantly, eliciting thunderous cheers from the spectators. Adonis's white horse elegantly trotted into the battleground towards him, and he gracefully mounted it.

Azriel's statue and pillar crumbled into dust.

Adonis looked up at Lixia Ziva, who clutched her fist tightly.

"A stunning victory for Adonis! He's now advanced to the semi-finals and will go head-to-head against the formidable Black Death!" the Hologram Announcer shouted.

Black Death seated, unfazed, as Adonis's white horse reared up. Adonis drew Mightis from his back and hurled it at Black Death. Mightis spun straight upward, slicing the head off Black Death's statue, which crashed to the ground below. Black Death remained unperturbed, still seated comfortably.

"They're poised and ready to go!" the Hologram Announcer shouted.

The spectators roared in excitement!

"And tomorrow, prepare for an electrifying showdown as the beautiful Lixia Ziva takes on the valiant Prince Jaden Knight! Thanatos verse White Death! Who will emerge victorious and secure their spot in the semi-final Battle World?"

Viggo, Rain, Arison, and Leaf, along with everyone along the Avedon River, rose to their feet, applauding Adonis Belacaro's victory.

"That was an amazing fight!" Viggo said.

"That light sliced through Octo Maelstrom like a hot knife through butter!" Arison exclaimed.

Struggling to carry a large rock by his side, Leaf tossed it forward. It landed among other stones, and he spoke. "Wow. I could barely throw the rock into the river, and… he cut the land in half!"

"I had no idea people were capable of that," Rain commented.

"Azriel had his wing torn out, yet he still managed to save Adonis Belacaro!" Viggo said.

"He might have stood a chance at winning if it weren't for that wound," Arison said.

"So, he sacrificed his chance to win to save a competitor?" Rain asked.

"Looks like it," Viggo said.

Everyone discussed the incredible fight and its greatness as they departed from the Avedon River.

"Shall we meet here again tomorrow? Same time, same spot?" Viggo asked.

"Hopefully," Arison said.

"Nice to meet you, Arison," Rain said politely as she made her way up.

Arison grinned and called out, "Bring a cute friend next time!"

"She already has," Viggo replied, and they all laughed.

Chapter 11

Heart of The Dream

A curtain remained tightly shut in a small quarter, yet a soft glow emanated from the early morning light filtering through. Against one wall sat a small bed, its perfectly pressed white sheet illuminated in the corner. The edges were neatly tucked underneath, and the pillow remained fluffed and unused. A fist-sized crack marred the middle of the glass mirror, its fracture lines spreading outward. Below the mirror were empty alcohol bottles on top of the drawer. At the center of the room, perpendicular to the bed, Bronx lay on the bench press amidst the scattered bottles strewn across the floor.

Beads of sweat trickled down his forehead as he pushed the 600-pound weights up and down. The door swung open, and three Totalist soldiers entered. Two burly soldiers clad in full military gear flanked a smaller soldier with a high-pitched voice. He inquired, "Bronx of The Elite Black?"

Bronx paused, then resumed his workout without replying. The two soldiers approached either end of the barbell, exerting maximum force to push it down. It slowly descended, pressing against his throat. More sweat beaded on Bronx's forehead, his face flushing with rage. He tightened his hold on the barbell with a fierce grip and exerted all his strength. The barbell began to rise. as they struggled to keep it down. Enraged, Bronx let out a roar and angrily hurled the barbell and weights into the wall. Half of it crashed into the neighboring quarter while the rest crushed his bed.

Bronx sat up amidst the clatter of the alcohol bottles on the floor, he coughed roughly. He reached for a bottle from the side drawer, popped it open, and chugged it down.

"Are you Bronx of the Elite Black?" The squeaky little soldier asked again, this time with a smile.

Bronx rose to his feet and approached the small soldier. Towering over him, Bronx gazed down at him. Sensing tension, the muscular soldiers interposed themselves between the two.

"Ya," Bronx replied, punctuating his response with a long, loud burp.

The little soldier swallowed nervously, unrolled a piece of paper, and began to read it. "By the decree of King Roy, a judgment has been rendered, Bronx of the Elite Black, you are hereby stripped of your rank and relieved of all duties, effective immediately. Surrender your gear and your authorized clearance badge at once." He nervously looked up from his paper, glancing at Bronx, who stood looming over him, breathing heavily.

"Please turn over your gear and auth..."

Bronx took alcohol bottle from his side pockets, pressed the bottle caps against each other, and popped them open. He offered the bottles to the muscular soldiers before him, but they ignored his gesture and stared at him emotionlessly. Shrugging, Bronx chugged one of the bottles, downing it all in one go.

"We can do this the hard way..." the diminutive soldier said.

The two muscular soldiers approached Bronx, and the one on his left side pulled out his steel baton. Bronx raised his second bottle of alcohol and began chugging it. It was shattered by the steel baton, instantly triggering Bronx's reflexes. Bronx smashed his other empty bottle into the head of the soldier on his right and kicked him into the hallway.

Bronx twisted the wrist of the soldier holding the steel baton, flipped him over, and stomped hard on his face with the heel of his boot, driving it into the ground. He then sauntered to the smaller soldier, effortlessly flipping his double-boom joy shotgun and pressing it against his pants. The little soldier trembled nervously, wetting himself in fear. Bronx holstered his shotgun, removed his clearance badge, tossed it onto the wet floor, and departed the room.

"We... we need your gear... sir?"

Bronx continued walking and left.

❖

Avedon River was even more crowded than yesterday, and their usual spot had already been claimed. Viggo scanned the area but couldn't spot any available space or Arison.

"It's so full," Rain said.

"What should we do?" Leaf asked.

"It doesn't seem like there's much we can do," Viggo remarked as he scanned the area one last time. Some Totalist cast cold glances as they passed and climbed over the fence barrier.

"But we're not going to miss the fights!" Viggo said, "If Pink Mellow were here, she could probably hook us with one of those swanky spots, with cool air and amazing food, to catch all the action."

"Brother, I don't want to ask her for things anymore," Leaf said.

"Why? You still hurt from that?"

"No. I'll just feel guilty."

"Guilty? You don't need to feel bad. It doesn't cost her anything to help us. If you're too scared, I'll ask her."

"No, brother. It's wrong."

"Since when do you hate freebies?"

"It's not about that. She's already too kind to us. I don't want to take advantage of her generosity."

Viggo looked at Leaf and felt his kindness, "OK, let's see what else we can do then."

"Thank you, brother."

"Don't worry about it, baby turtle. I won't ask her for anything anymore. Unless you want me to."

"Glad Leaf is always by your side to keep you on the right track," Rain remarked.

Viggo leaned closer to Rain's face and looked deep into her blue eyes, "You're absolutely right."

She was surprised by his response.

Viggo ruffled Leaf's head and continued, "If it weren't for Leaf's kind heart, I might be an ugly, grumpy man."

"Except for the man part," Rain laughed.

The slow, deep beat of the drums interrupted Viggo before he could respond. Growing louder with each thud, it signaled the start of the second day of Battle World! Spectators lining the bank of the Avedon River erupted into applause and cheers!

"O no! It's starting!" Leaf panicked.

Viggo glanced around anxiously, whispering, "Arison, where are you?"

The Totalist soldiers patrolled along the fence barrier, waving for them to move on.

"Viggo!" Arison shouted, running from a distance.

They met him halfway.

"You're late!" Viggo shouted.

"White String needed to talk to me."

"About what?"

"We'll discuss it after the battles."

The drums beat louder, signaling the impending battles.

"The fight's about to start!" Arison exclaimed.

"The riverside is packed," Leaf added.

Arison surveyed the riverside before walking to a soldier. After a brief conversation, Arison handed him something and then gestured for them to come over. They following the soldier and made their way down to the river. Upon reaching the bottom of the large rock, the soldier directed some spectators to clear a space. They thanked him before settling down.

"Voila! Front seats," Arison said with a smile.

Leaf hugged Arison.

"Thanks, Arison," Rain expressed her gratitude.

"Man, I wish I had your knack for making things happen!" Viggo remarked wistfully.

"Simply take care of them, and they'll take care of you," Arison advised.

"But I don't have anything to give in return."

"Start small," Arison encouraged.

The fifty-foot holoscreen appeared over the Avedon River, prompting cheers from everyone!

❖

"Ladies, gentlemen, and beings of Ourania World, welcome back to day two of our Battle World!" the Hologram Announcer's voice boomed through the arena. "I hope you enjoyed yesterday's thrilling battles! Today heralds a fresh start with new challenges and new victors! As the qualifiers progress, anticipation mounts for tomorrow's semi-final, where contenders will vie for coveted spots in the final showdown!"

The spectators stomped with excitement!

"Everyone, it's time to cast your votes for the battleground you desire. Mean while, allow me to introduce our first inaugural contender. Please join me in extending a warm and gracious welcome to the illustrious Lixia Ziva, representing the Majestic Royal Justice!"

The spectators applauded and stomped their feet!

Lixia Ziva rose from her stone chair clad in her chrome diamond breastplate, red shoulder plate armor, and flowing red cape. Her battle-worn metal scabbard hung at her right side, while a small dagger was tucked horizontally against her lower back for easy access by her left hand. As the spectators waved from below, she strode to the edge of the pillar and threw her red cape into the sky as it flutter away. The spectators roared with excitements! She had finally made it here and the looks on her face is determine. She leaned over and dove head-first toward the battleground. Her scabbard bent against the ground as she pushed off it and landed safely. She shifted her hip to one side. The crowd erupted into a standing ovation, clapping and whistling in admiration. Lixia Ziva glanced up at Prince Jaden Knight, who applauded from the edge of his pillar.

"Next is our young Prince Jaden Knight of the Totalist Federation!"

The spectators went wild!

A cloud of dust burst from the ground, gradually settling as Prince Jaden Knight stood tall on the battleground, resplendent in a well-fitted black ensemble. His attire included a rugged leather topcoat, a deep blue button-down vest, gloves, a golden crown buckle adorning a black magnetic belt, and sturdy black leather boots. His Stetson sat slightly askew, partially covering his eyebrows and blond hair. With fierce blue eyes, he locked gazes with Lixia Ziva and tipped his Stetson to her as flames flared on the side of his arms. The sudden appearance of Prince

Jaden Knight left the spectators stunned by his striking appearance.

"The votes are in, and the battleground landscape has been chosen! Behold the magnificent Ukko Sanctuary!"

The battleground trembled, and snow-covered mountain peaks burst through from underneath, piercing toward the sky. Two parallel lines cracked across the land splitting between Lixia Ziva and Prince Jaden Knight, elevating the ground they stood on high into the atmosphere. Peering down from the edge, they beheld a frozen river whose water came from the waterfall at the peak of the snow-covered mountain. On Lixia Ziva's side, an old traditional Ukko architectural-style village emerged from the snowy landscape. The small village comprised wooden structures with roof tiles covered in snow, while the front paper sliding doors were painted with black and pink flora. Pots of plants hung at the front entrances. Each home stood closely built, fostering a sense of community. In front of Lixia Ziva, a wooden bridge spanned the gap, connecting her to Prince Jaden Knight at the other side of the cliff. Two additional wooden bridges materialized on each side.

The Ukko Sanctuary lay blanketed in pure white powdered snow. Lixia Ziva gazed around the snow-covered village, her warm breath chilling in the cool air, crystalizing in its stillness. A smile graced her lips as she admired the serene and peaceful white beauty surrounding her.

"Fighting against a beautiful lady and shattering her dreams in this picturesque setting is cruel and unfortunate," Prince Jaden Knight remarked as he gently touched the soft white powdered snow coating the wooden handrail of the bridge.

"My dream will not be the one shattered."

"I commend for your bravery and the journey that brought you here. I will offer you a chance. Surrender."

"Just cause you're a Prince doesn't mean you're immune to a proper spanking," Lixia Ziva replied confidently, standing firm and tilting her Swift Sabre slightly forward.

"I don't want to scar your beautiful face, for which you would need to find a husband who will care for you after."

The Hologram Announce roared excitedly, "Things are heating up, ladies and gentlemen! Now, let the battle begin!"

The spectators cheered!

Prince Jaden Knight stretched his arms upward and leaned his head back while Lixia Ziva stared at him cautiously.

It appears he's not carrying any visible weapon. Perhaps he's skilled in hand-to-hand combat? I'll keep my distance for now, especially considering how he had just appeared from the top of the pillar. Let's see what you can do, young prince.

Snow flew up from the ground, covering Prince Jaden Knight as he stomped down. A fist descended inches above Lixia Ziva's head. Black metal pieces materialized around his fist and arm, connecting to form protective armor. She instinctively swung her head and body back at the last second, narrowly avoiding his arm as it went straight down with flames flaring up. His furious punch exploded the ground upon impact, sending her flying backward into the snow. The snow cloud settled around him, his fist resting on the ground as he slowly rose. Lixia Ziva observed his fist, noticing the absence of the black metal armor.

He can teleport?! Lixia Ziva thought as she got up.

She ducked her head to the right and left as the black metal fist passed by her face, Prince Jaden Knight appearing before her in an instant.

But I could feel and see his attacks within my area. Lixia Ziva thought as she hopped back from side to side. Her long Swift Sabre sliced through the air, creating space between them and forcing him to back off. Its needle-like blade could cut even the toughest rock into the thinnest sheet of paper. She instantly closed the distance with quick dashes and thrust the blade forward at his midsection. He blocked its tip with his black metal hand and seized it. She swiped it to the side swiftly, causing sparks to fly off his hand and across his chest. Then, she aimed and thrust straight at his black metal armor chest plate where his heart should be. But her blade couldn't pierce through. His black metal forearms attempted to snap the blade in half by forcing it to bend in opposite directions.

"It's a Majestic Royal blade," Lixia Ziva said as she slithered her blade back out between his forearms. The blade scraped against the black metal armor, sending sparks flying. She launched her Swift Sabre toward his face, but he dodged from side to side. Undeterred, she leaped into the air and spun her body around in circles, slashing downward multiple times against his left forearm with each rotation. She stood tall and swiped the blade to her side. It appeared sharper, and its shined intensified as it grated against other metals. He lowered his arms, revealing deep cuts in the black metal armor. The cut vanished as the black metal armor rebuilt itself.

"Your speed and reaction were quite impressive, but there are levels to this," he remarked.

"You..."

Before she could speak, Prince Jaden Knight's black metal fist smashed into her chrome diamond breastplate, sending her flying back ten feet before she rolled in the snow. Grimacing, she quickly pushed herself up to the side, coughing up blood.

He stood there.

She rose to her feet, wiping the blood away, and ran toward the house's front doorstep. Prince Jaden Knight appeared at the top of the steps just as Swift Sabre instinctively slashed across the wooden paper door where he stood. A long slit formed across the door, causing it to fall apart and reveal the snow-covered square garden inside. She walked inside as he stood in the middle of the garden.

His movements are much faster now! A minute ago, I could sense his attacks and was able to kept up with his speed. But now, I couldn't even sense it.

"Don't lose focus!" As Prince Jaden Knight stood before her, his black metal fist whizzed past her head, and a shocked wave exploded by the side of her head from the force of his punch. She was propelled to the side of the garden, sliding across its surface. The black metal armor on his arm dissipated. Rotating his fist, he opened and closed his fingers, stretching his arm as the flame flared, and spoke, "Last chance."

❖

Young Lixia Ziva shook her head, disoriented. Her left ear rang loudly as an older, familiar voice echoed, "Last chance." She lifted her head from the hard wooden floor and recognized the blurry figure of the old Majestic Royal knight. He stood before her, holding a large, mighty sword that had seen decades of battles. A disappointed expression creased his battled-aged face as he peered down at her. With a roar of pain, young Lixia Ziva pushed herself up and weakly swung her long sword at the blurry image. Her long sword clashed with his mighty sword, and they looped in a circular motion, the blades sparking against each other and ringing loudly. With a powerful swing, his mighty sword redirected her long sword into the air and slashed deep into her shoulder armor. She cried in pain, and her weak knees gave way as she collapsed.

"Let my blade carve the truth into your foolish dream of carrying my legacy! No daughter of mine could ever replace my only deceased son," her disappointed father said as he swiped her blood off his mighty sword and walked away.

The cold snowflake stung Lixia Ziva's rosy cheek, jolting her back to reality. She swung her Swift toward Prince Jaded Knight in multiple directions and yelled defiantly, "Never!"

Her eyes flared with anger as she spotted him, charging at him, with Swift gripped tightly in her hand. She slashed from multiple angles, aiming from the top to the side, but he dodged each strike, countering with his punches. Swift swung upward to block his attack, then from the left and right sides. Her blade slid against the inside of his right metal arm, sparks flying as she roared in fury. He halted the blade's trajectory with his left black metal hand just before it could cut into his right shoulder. Swift then slashed down and across with immense force as sparks erupted as her blade penetrated the black metal armor deeply. Spanning from his right shoulder to his left hip. She followed up with a kick to his stomach, but he vanished before she could connect. Whirling around, she spotted him atop the roof tiles at the far end of the square garden.

"Will you keep vanishing, or will you stand your ground?"

Prince Jaden Knight observed the delicate snowflake descending before him, his fingers tracing the deep slashes etched into his metal armor chest. He glanced upward as more soft white snowflakes drifted down from the sky.

She put Swift into the scabbard.

"You stand no chance of winning. I'm barely tapping into ten percent of ..."

Multiple snowflakes in front of him split in half as a pink energy blade was only inches away from his face, before he deflected it with his right black metal arm, sending it into the house beside him. The structure exploded, crumbling to the ground. The impact shattered his black metal armor and sent him hurtling through the roof tiles.

He sat up amidst the rubble, wiping a trickle of blood from his left cheek and examining it closely.

What was that? Was it from her long sword, but it was still in her scabbard, and she didn't move.

White and Black Death eyed her intensely and looked at each other.

Lixia Ziva stood there, surprised, and thought, *He deflected my blade energy! His reaction was incredibly fast!*

"Don't lose focus," Lixia Ziva called from outside.

Prince Jaden Knight chuckled, brushing off the dirt as he regained his footing. "That was a close one."

He scrutinized his right arm, observing the severe damage to his black metal armor. Electric sparks sputtered as disconnected pieces attempted to reconnect, and the armor malfunctioned. With revolve, he pressed his thumb against the black metal armor on his right shoulder blade. A green glow emanated around his thumb, accompanied by a spinning red light around his right shoulder. The damaged black metal armor detached and clattered to the ground. He flexed and clenched his fist, and new nano-black metal pieces seamlessly materialized around his right arm and fingers.

"Not bad. Your power took me by surprise. But whatever that was, it's inconsequential now."

He materialized before her with his left metal fist, driving deep into her stomach. She was launched off the ground, her body folding halfway forward from the impact. He clutched his right metal fist and unleashed a powerful straight uppercut to her chin, sending her hurtling backward. In a seamless motion, he appeared mid-air beside her, gripping her face tightly, slammed her into the snow, and ran her head into the ground.

He tore her scabbard away, casting it aside with disdain. As she rolled over, half her face smeared with blood, and she lifted her gaze defiantly.

"I wouldn't move if I were you. You're hurt badly," Prince Jaden Knight declared as he towered over her, the flames on his arms flickering out.

The snow continued to fall on them.

"I don't recall Majestic Royal having such ability."

Despite the injury to her head, her gaze remained determined, and a fearless expression adorned her face as she met his eyes in silence.

The frigid air from the snow-covered mountain cascaded downward in a swirling spiral toward them.

Prince Jaden Knight stepped back, "I despise fighting against a lady, especially one as lovely as yourself."

Spectators pointed skyward; their expressions filled with awe. Lixia Ziva, too, observed the phenomenon, noticing how the snowflakes crystallized around the chilled air, freezing together like a long finger extending down from the sky above them.

"Do you wish to know, or shall I demonstrate it once more?" she asked.

Prince Jaden Knight laughed.

"It's Ko."

White and Black Death looked at each other.

"I don't recall any Ko from the Majestic Royal employing such fighting strategy."

"That's because it originates from a renowned swordsman, not the Majestic Royal."

The ice encased the top of his Stetson and spread out around it. A sudden chill enveloped his ears, causing him to jump back in surprise as his Stetson froze.

"What is that?" Prince Jaden Knight queried; his gaze fixed on the elongated ice formation in the sky.

She rolled to the side and quickly got up.

The ice extended downward, reaching the ground and spreading outward. It froze his boots solid, prompting him to deliver a powerful punch. The ice exploded, shattering halfway into the sky along with his frozen Stetson.

Lixia Ziva swiftly drew her dagger from behind and unleashed a flurry of swipes at him. He deflected the pink energy, causing it to detonate, damaging the surrounding houses and pushing him backward, the impact taking a toll on his already damaged black metal armor. Seizing the opportunity, she dashed towards her scabbard, executing several backflips and somersaults before flipping into the air and slashing at him with her dagger. As she landed, she snatched up her scabbard.

The pink energy detonated where Prince Jaden Knight had stood, but he reappeared behind her instantly. His fists surged forward, aiming for her back, but she swiftly intercepted with her dagger, blocking the attack. With a fluid motion, she spun around, using her scabbard to fend off his subsequent punches, then forcefully pushed him backward. Standing face to face beneath a vast cloud of glittering crystallized snowflakes, the compound started to bond.

The spectators applauded and cheered!

"Ladies and gentlemen, you have just witnessed a rare phenomenon within Ukko Sanctuary, known as Ice Death! Anything it touches will freeze instantly and perish slowly over a few minutes!" the Hologram Announcer said.

Some spectators gasped at the thought that it might kill their Prince Jaden Knight.

Without hesitation, Lixia Ziva flipped her dagger against her left forearm, positioned the curved blade outward, and drew her left arm close to her side. She flung her scabbard toward his face. He reacted quickly, swatting it away, but Swift emerged from the blindside of her scabbard, slicing across his right cheek. He instinctively tilted his head away from the blade. Before she could follow up, her small dagger flew across his chest, but he vanished into thin air. The front wall of a nearby house exploded from the force of the pink energy. Undeterred, she exited the garden and headed towards the front of the house, where he stood waiting at the end of the middle bridge.

"That's two strikes to your face, my Prince. The next one will pierce your heart," Lixia Ziva spoke as she walked toward the middle bridge.

"No lady has ever gotten close to my heart."

"My blade is no ordinary lady."

Prince Jaden Knight smirked and pointed upward. "If the announcer is right, I'm not the only thing that will bring you down."

Lixia Ziva glanced up at the sky. The clouds of snowflakes had transformed into a massive frozen fist descending toward them.

"Surrender..." Prince Jaden Knight's voice faded into the cold air as he spoke. A small snowflake brushed against her face. She closed her eyes as memories flooded her mind in a fleeting rush.

❖

Young Lixia Ziva pressed against her damaged armor, her wounds seeping blood as she struggled through the dense forest of Dahhar. Each step was a battle against the heavy snowfall that blanketed the landscape.

Dahhar, situated between the lands of Justice and Melchior of Majestic Royal, was an island characterized by its rugged terrain and extreme weather conditions. Encircled by towering mountain ranges, it remained primarily uninhabited by Majestic Royal citizens due to the relentless onslaught of rainstorms and blizzards that besieged it throughout the year.

She hacked through the dense undergrowth, cleaving thick bushes in half with her broken sword, stomped it down, and pressed through. Her battered and swollen face bore testament to the hardships she endured. Deep cuts marred her arms where a piece of her missing armor once provided protection, blood seeping from multiple slashes on her chest plate. The snow on her body turned red. Though her body was shocked and weakened, her eyes blazed with fierce determination, and her heart surged with the indomitable will forged in her first battle.

Young Lixia Ziva yelled defiantly, "I will never surrender!"

Standing weakly in the Majestic Royal battle arena, Lixia Ziva tightly gripped her long, battered sword in her bloody hand. Despite her depleted strength, she faced the Majestic Knight with unwavering resolve.

"The esteemed Ziva name shall fall from grace," the Majestic Knight replied.

She valiantly blocked his relentless onslaught, but the Majestic Knight's massive sword proved too much for her battered defenses. With a powerful blow, it cleaved through Lixia Ziva's sword and tore deep into her body armor, leaving her vulnerable to his merciless slashes. Despite her efforts, she was overwhelmed, collapsing to the ground amidst a pool of blood. Defeated, she was unceremoniously dragged off the battle arena and discarded in a back alley, left to die.

Blood trails seeped into the snow as she ascended deeper into the mountain. The scent of blood attracted numerous large predators, which shadowed her every move, lurking around the corners, beneath the ground, in the water, high in the trees, and the sky. However, they maintained their distance, their instincts cautioning them of the imminent danger ahead.

She entered an expansive, snow-cleared area with a river stretching out before her. To her far left stood a quaint wooden cabin flanked by stacks of chopped wood and a steaming pot of water suspended over a crackling campfire. Though the allure of warmth, rest, and food briefly tempted her, she resolutely turned away, pressing on through the river's frigid waters. The icy embrace of the water jolted and numbed her wounds, offering a fleeting yet welcome reprieve.

Perched upon a tree branch several feet above the icy river's midpoint sat a man with long gray hair. A black mask concealed half of his face while adorned in a thick black fur outfit. Despite her approach, his eyes remained closed, deeply engrossed in meditation. He had sensed her presence before her arrival, attuned to the myriad large and perilous predators concealed in the surroundings. He noted how they maintained a cautious distance from her.

A strong warrior. Ryoku thought.

Unfazed by his presence, Lixia Ziva pressed forward, forging her path across the icy river and into the forest's depths.

She halted before a secluded enclave encircled by rugged rock walls tinted in hues of red and brown, offering a panoramic view of the open sky. She surveyed her surroundings and basked in the warmth radiating from the crimson walls. Here, devoid of snow, towering oak trees stretched skyward, providing sanctuary to myriad small birds and animals. Mounds of earth dotted the landscape while a tranquil pond nestled in one corner. She knew she had found her place to heal, hone her skills anew, rebuild her broken sword, and reinvent her sword skills. She is determined to reclaim her family's name, restore her father's pride, and maybe his acknowledgement.

A campfire crackled beneath the overhang of a massive flat rock jutting out from the side of red mountain. Lixia Ziva tended her wounds, wrapping them in makeshift bandages crafted from leaves. Venturing to the nearby pond, she beheld a wealth of freshwater fish darting through the crystal-clear waters, crabs scuttling along the sandy bottom, and clams and oysters. She kneed down and dived her head into the icy water, washing away the dry blood and dirt.

She felt relieved and clean.

The clams and oysters diligently filtered the pristine water, imparting a subtle sweetness to its taste. Drawing her broken sword, Lixia Ziva deftly snared a fish from the pond's depths, preparing it for the evening's meal over the crackling campfire. Sated from dinner, she climbed to the apex of the flat rock, perched along the mountainside. Stretching out upon its surface, she gazed upward, immersing herself in the celestial spectacle above the twinkling stars, the dual moons, and the distant presence of Zephaniah. The warmth emanating from the rock wall enveloped her, soothing her weary body amidst the lingering ache of her wounds. As she closed her eyes, her mind surrendered to the tranquil embrace of the cool evening breeze, merging seamlessly with her surroundings. In that moment of serene surrender, she found liberation, plunging into the boundless expanse of the night with a sense of newfound freedom.

As the cold, snowy weeks drifted beyond the confines of her secluded sanctuary, Lixia Ziva's wounds gradually healed. Her unwavering resolve to recuperate and fortify herself manifested in tireless days and nights of rigorous training. Utilizing her battered steel armor and her fractured sword, she engaged in a relentless pursuit of improvement. Through a crevice in the rock wall, where molten lava simmered, she channeled her efforts, melding her damaged armor and forging her shattered blade anew. With each strike of the molten metal against the hot anvil, her sword underwent a metamorphosis, gradually sharpening layer by layer as the rock pounded against the hot steel.

Perched atop the rugged mounts, Lixia Ziva engaged in relentless training with her newfound long-needle sword. She traversed the uneven terrain with fluid grace, seamlessly transitioning from sprinting to climbing, executing spins and flips with effortless precision. Her blade sliced through imposing boulders as if they were mere parchment, cleaving them cleanly in half. She flipped backward while cutting the small leaves in half and flung them toward a shadow in the wood.

Ryoku emerged from the shadows, holding the split leaves as he stepped into the light. "Not bad."

With her sword leveled at him, Lixia Ziva demanded, "You are not of Majestic Royal. Who are you?"

"A foe?" Ryoku replied as he drew his sword.

She stood firm, her grip on the sword unwavering as Ryoku darted toward her with swift agility. With precision timing, her blade descended toward him as he closed the distance. Yet, he effortlessly sidestepped her attack, smoothly sliding to her flank. In a lightning-quick motion, he tapped her hand with his sword and delivered a swift kick, sending her hurtling across the clearing until she crashed into the imposing red wall. She looked up, and her sword spun in a circle on the tip of his sword.

"Looks like there's still much to learn."

Lixia Ziva's eyes snapped open, fixing her gaze on Prince Jaden Knight. With a subtle shift in her stance, she leaned forward slightly, her movements fluid and poised. In a deft motion, she flipped her small dagger in her left hand behind her, "How could someone who's never been given a chance to face failure or sacrificed anything that is everything to them truly grasp the concept of surrender?"

Her right hand clenched tightly around the hilt of Swift.

"By studying the downfall of a thousand empires and their hubris, one can recognize when they're overpowered."

"What worth do you hold when your soul echoes the emptiness of your words?"

Swift split the wooden bridge handrail, thrusting it through the wooden structure, and flung the shards at him from the broken handrail. Prince Jaden Knight appeared behind her, as she had predicted, and spun around with Swift twirling at him. She directed her attacks toward his arms and chest. His metal arms blocked them, sending sparks flying with each impact. She twisted Swift and drove it into his right metal shoulder. He grabbed the blade with both hands, halting its advance.

As she released Swift, a small dagger appeared beneath it. Gripping the dagger tightly with both hands, she drove it forcefully into the black armor with all her strength. It sliced deep across his chest plate under his left arm, tearing it wide open as electrical parts and sparks erupted. Though he attempted to grasp the dagger, her right hand intercepted his, pushing it aside. With the blade now poised by his heart, she slammed her right palm into the dagger's hilt, thrusting it straight into his heart. Prince Jaden Knight screamed in agony!

"Ziva Rise!"

A streak of pink energy from her small dagger went through him as she reappeared several feet behind him. A massive explosion erupted. He toppled backward into the soft snow as his body seared and burned. Gasps and screams erupted from the spectators, terror gripping many of them.

Lixia Ziva, breathing heavily, rose to her feet with deliberate effort. She spun her small dagger skillfully before tucking it behind her back. Turning, she approached him steadily. With a firm grip, she extracted Swift's hilt from his burning hand. She grimaced as she observed the flesh melting away, the bones on his fingers crumbling into the flames.

She lowered her head, "Rest in peace, young Prince."

Ice Death's fist descended from above, striking the tall trees and roof with a thunderous impact. Ice fragments exploded into fine crystal particles, enveloping everything around them and crystalizing the surroundings.

"A perfect execution," Prince Jaden Knight said from behind.

She was startled by his voice and quickly turned around.

"How?!" Lixia Ziva yelled angrily as the burning body smoldered beside her.

"As I mentioned earlier, there are levels to this."

Ice Death fell onto them and right above her.

"I won't falter, even if I have to die!" Lixia Ziva shouted, her voice trembling with anger.

In one smooth motion, she swiped her small dagger the pink energy sliced through Ice Death's fist shattering into millions of particles. The foggy glitter covered the Ukko Sanctuary as ice particles began to form around Prince Jaden Knight and Lixia Ziva, slowly freezing them in place.

"A picture-perfect place to immortalize two beautiful individuals," Prince Jaden Knight remarked with a smile.

With all her might, she hurled Swift at him. The twirling air trail froze behind her sword as it sliced through the cloudy crystallization. Its tip halted inches before his throat, freezing midair. Prince Jaden Knight and Lixia Ziva remained frozen in place.

The spectators gasped and mumbled in confusion.

"What happens now?" a male spectator queried.

"Is it a draw?" an elderly spectator inquired.

"My Prince Jaden Knight! Is he alright?" a young female spectator called out in concern.

They watched as both fighters remained frozen in place. Sparks flickered around Prince Jaden Knight's shoulders, and flame flared up on each side of his arms, burning through the ice. He moved his arms as the ice melted around him.

Tears streak down her cheeks and froze in place. Unable to move as she watched him approach.

"By now, seventy-eight percent of your blood should be frozen, and your heart will cease in ten seconds, sweet dream." Prince Jaden Knight said as he stopped before her.

She loss conscious.

He shattered the ice surrounding her, and her body slumped against him. He then enveloped her in his arms, drawing her close to his warm chest. The flames on his arms continued to flare, providing warmth for them both.

Lixia Ziva's statue crumbled, and her pillar collapsed.

"Ladies and gentlemen, the victor is Prince Jaden Knight!" the Hologram Announcer shouted, and the stadium erupted in joyous cheers!

"How did Prince Jaden Knight survive?" an old spectator inquired.

"Who cares! My Prince is alive and well! He's so caring! That's all that matters!" the young female spectator exclaimed.

Prince Jaden Knight and Lixia Ziva vanished from the battleground, reappearing in the Medic Bay. He carried her to the waiting doctors and nurses, "Please take good care of her."

The female nurse smiled uncontrollably as they nodded.

"Son, come to The Royal Chamber Level," King Roy ordered through secure communication in Prince Jaden Knight's ears.

Chapter 12
A Thousand Deaths!

Prince Jaden Knight appeared, his hand over his heart, as he bowed his head before Commander Bazyli, King Roy, Lieutenant General Bradstone, Major General Vic, and Admiral Baylee.

King Roy opened his arms and tightly embraced his son, shouting, "Well done, my son! You've made the Federation and me incredibly proud!"

"Thank you, my King, but I did it for myself, not for the Federation," Prince Jaden Knight replied.

"The Federation had provided you everything, from your head to your precious little toes," Lieutenant General Bradstone remarked.

"Indeed, but the Federation had taken more than what my family had dedicated their lives to," Prince Jaden Knight responded.

"You're merely a boy barely taking his first step into adulthood. One misstep your foot could easily get chop off," Lieutenant General Bradstone warned.

"A boy he is! Now, apologize to Lieutenant General Bradstone," King Roy scolded.

"I said what I said," Prince Jaden Knight replied firmly.

Lieutenant General Bradstone huffed, "A boy who approaches their battles with frivolity, displays a feeble heart, commits numerous errors, and carelessly loses their double cannot be deemed fit to lead the future of the Totalist."

"Don't be too harsh on the lad. He emerged victorious," Major General Vic said.

"He lost his trump card," Lieutenant General Bradstone reminded.

"A trick that serves me no purpose," Prince Jaden Knight said.

"Then let it be," Lieutenant General Bradstone replied coldly.

"And risk the safety of my son?" King Roy slammed his fist on the table as he interrupted. "I demand ten additional doubles for Prince Jaden Knight!"

"Each double typically requires up to eight weeks to perfect, my King. We only have one more available for our young Prince," Major General Vic explained.

"I will not hide behind such useless toys," Prince Jaden Knight declared.

"Such useless toy is burning in the ground instead of you, my young Prince," Major General Vic reminded him.

"I wasn't anticipating a second blade," Prince Jaden Knight responded.

"You'll never know until it's too late, my young Prince," Major General Vic said.

"That's precisely why it's crucial for you to utilize the second double!" King Roy insisted.

"Take flight, Prince Jaden Knight. Prove your worthiness to your fellow Totalist and win their hearts. Forge the path you wish to tread," Commander Bazyli spoke.

"But Commander!" King Roy said, his expression filled with concern.

Prince Jaden Knight smiled and bowed to Commander Bazyli, "Thank you, Commander Bazyli."

"He's, my son! I demand…"

"Commander Bazyli is right. Let our young lion roar and win their hearts just like he does with the young ladies," Admiral Baylee smiled warmly as he patted Prince Jaden Knight on the shoulder.

Prince Jaden Knight moved his shoulder out of the way, unimpressed by the gesture. "If there are no other pressing matters, I'll excuse myself."

Commander Bazyli nodded.

Prince Jaden Knight bowed and then disappeared.

❖

The crowd at Avedon River jumped up and down, cheering loudly for their Prince's victory!

"Our hope lives on!" A Totalist shouted!

"I love you!" Young Totalist ladies screamed excitedly at the hologram of Prince Jaden Knight on the river.

Everyone danced and embraced each other in celebration.

Viggo, Rain, Leaf, and Arison joined the celebration with the crowd.

"I am fully committed to our Prince!" Arison screamed.

Viggo gazed at Prince Jaden Knight's hologram. "Some people seem to have it all: the looks, the wealth, the love, and now, the entire country."

"Are you jealous?" Arison asked.

"I'm just stating the fact."

"The fact is, we don't know what it took for him to reach where he is," Rain remarked.

"If he hadn't been born with a golden spoon in his mouth, he might have been just like one of us," Viggo speculated.

"Even with a golden spoon in your mouth doesn't mean you can get my respect," Arison stated firmly.

"It seemed like he earned it." Rain chimed in as the chanting of Prince Jaden Knight's name grew louder and louder.

"I think it's jealousy." Arison chuckled.

"It's just not fair," Viggo said, sounding disappointed.

"Then do something about it! Get your dirty hands dirtier. Sacrifice anything that stands in your way if you want it that bad!" Arison pressed on, "You've mentioned wishing you could do what I do, make things happen. It doesn't happen overnight. I've had to work hard for it, sacrificing many things along the way. That's why I don't have what you have: a girlfriend, I mean a female friend."

Arison turned to Rain, "But that doesn't mean I'm not interested in having female companionship."

Viggo gazed at the water splashing against the rocks, "Is it wrong of me to feel jealous and desire what others have?"

"You don't want it badly enough. That's why you don't have it," Arison remarked.

"You have us," Leaf said, casting a reassuring glance at Viggo.

"That's right, Leaf." Rain said and smiled at him.

"Yeah! We're worth more than any fancy clothes or jewels. Our friendship has no limit!" Arison said.

Viggo looked at them gratefully, "Thank you, guys. I think I understand what you're saying. There's still so much for me to learn."

The sound of drums started.

"Welcome to the second bout of the evening, ladies, gentlemen, and beings of Ourania World! Who will emerge as the final challenger to advance to tomorrow's semi-finals? Will we witness two formidable Ukko contenders battling for the coveted title of Ourania World Champion, or shall Thanatos rise as the beacon of hope, the proud Gailstone so needed? Are you ready?" the Hologram Announcer asked.

The spectators roared and clapped.

"Now it's time to select the next battleground landscapes! Please join me in welcoming White Death of Koi Ka Chi!"

White Death, clad in a completely white outfit and mask, vanished from his stone chair and emerged from the snow on the battleground. Blending seamlessly with the white backdrop of Ukko Sanctuary, he stood tall and gazed at the glittering, sparkling sky as they vanished.

Two white swords crossed on his back.

"Next up, let's give a warm welcome to the biggest Gargoyle, Thanatos from Sleeping Tear of Gailstone!"

A giant stone-carved statue of Thanatos loomed over the pillar. Its fierce visage roared down into the stadium below, its stone claws firmly gripping the sides of the pillar while its wings stretched out menacingly.

Thanatos rose from his seat, strode to the edge, and peered at White Death below. Without unfurling his wings, he stepped off the pillar, causing the snow to billow up as he landed five feet deep into the ground. Thanatos emerged from the hole, snow falling around him.

The spectators rose to their feet, eager to catch a glimpse of Thanatos, who stood twice as tall as White Death. The two figures locked eyes, and a hush fell over the crowd as they watched in awe.

"The battleground landscape is now locked in! Let the Trampling of Wrath begin!"

The deep rumble echoed in the distance, causing the snow on the battleground to tremble. Three black Ukko Beasts charged through the houses, heading toward White Death. Each beast was larger than a house, with long pointy horns spiraling outward. White Death slowly grabbed the hilts of his white swords, his eyes never leaving Thanatos. Leaning forward, he gradually drew his swords, spun them, and stepped aside.

A Ukko Beast ran past him.

White blades of light sliced through the beast's front and back left legs, severing them cleanly. The beast toppled onto its side, crashing into the snow and sliding toward Thanatos before coming to a halt several feet away from him.

The second and third beasts charged side by side, emitting huffs and puffs of smoke as they blew out from their nostrils. Their large heads bobbed up and down, and their sharp spiral horns lowered menacingly for the attack.

White Death watched them charged at him.

He hurled his sword from under his hip into the left eye of the charging beast on his left. The creature's head plowed into the snow, its spiral horns piercing into the ground and flipping its body over. White Death ran and leaped onto the second beast, stabbing his other white sword into the back of its neck. He dragged the blade down to its tail, splitting it wide open. He flipped off as it crashed into the snow.

White Death's foot pressed against the other beast's head, wrenching his white sword from its left eye as it roared in agony. He drove the blade into its neck, slashing it open, crimson blood pouring into the snow. He spun his swords, casting off the blood before slowly sliding them into the scabbards on his back.

The rumbling persisted as a massive herd of stampeding black Ukko Beasts thundered through the Ukko Sanctuary Village, shattering the once peaceful and beautiful scenery into pieces. White Death and Thanatos stood facing each other, unflinching, their gazes locked as the beasts parted in the middle of their path, avoiding the fallen creatures. The ground shook beneath their feet as the beasts raced past them from both sides, kicking up clouds of snow dust as they surged toward the cliffs and bridges. The weight of the Ukko Beasts proved too much for the bridges, causing them to collapse into the frozen river below while others plunged off the cliff. The stampede was deafening, the wind howling against White Death and Thanatos as the beasts rushed by. Amidst the swirling snow dust, White Death vanished from view, yet Thanatos remained calm and unfazed.

Emerging from the snow before him, White Death launched himself at Thanatos, his swords slashing across Thanatos's neck. The blades shattered upon contact with Thanatos's solid stone form, leaving barely a scratch. Thanatos retaliated, his claws tearing into White Death's white outfit and skin. White Death spun his body, kicking Thanatos's arm away which tore his white collar. In a blur, White Death vanished back into the snow. Thanatos examined the torn, bloody piece of clothing in his claws, taking a deep breath. Grinning, he tossed it aside, spreading his razor stone claws wide and slashing into the running beasts from the side. His claws sliced through their thick skin, causing sudden pain that sent them careening off course, colliding with other beasts nearby. The chaos ensured as they tripped and fell upon each other, some meeting a grisly end under the stampede's merciless hooves. As blood dripped from his claws, Thanatos advanced, his imposing figure casting a dark shadow over the snow. Coming to a halt, he raised his left muscular stone arm into the sky, its bloody claws spread wide, before plunging it into the snow. With a powerful tug, Thanatos pulled White Death out from the depths of the snow by his head, lifting him high into the air.

White Death plunged two daggers into Thanatos's left arm with lightning reflexes, but the blades barely penetrate the stone. Undeterred, White Death seized Thanatos's bloody claws with both hands, wrenching his body upward, and kicked the daggers deeper into the shattering stone. Thanatos roared in agony and let go of White Death as his arm flew upward. Seizing the opportunity, White Death somersaulted away from Thanatos's grasp and swiftly retrieved three small sticky bombs from his sleeves and hurled them at the wound. The bombs detonated exposing the flesh littered with broken dagger shards. Thanatos grimaced in pain as he yanked the shards from his flesh, casting them aside in a display of defiance.

White Death smirked.

The stone instantly enveloped the exposed flesh, shielding it from further harm. Thanatos spread his arms wide, a grim invitation to the looming threat in front of him. His stone chest expanded, towering over him like an impenetrable fortress.

The Ukko Beasts diverted from their path along the cliff and charged toward them. As the stampeding beasts surged toward Thanatos, White Death vanished into the snow, evading their path.

Thanatos seized the horns of the oncoming beast, halting its charge with his powerful grips, and forcing it back. The beast rotated its head from side to side trying to get loose. Despite its struggles to break free, another beast rammed into it from behind, sending it airborne. Undeterred, Thanatos maintained his hold on the creature's horns, using its momentum to spin it around before hurling it back toward the approaching herd. Several beasts were sent tumbling backward, but the relentless charge continued unabated. Thanatos spread his wings wide and soared backward, retreating over the safety of the cliff as the stampede thundered even closer.

Five metal chains shot out from the snow near the cliff's edge, ensnaring Thanatos's wings, wrists, neck, and ankles, immobilizing him. Thanatos struggled against the chains, but his efforts only seemed to strengthen them, each pull causing the metal to grow larger and more resilient. White Death emerged from the snow, brandishing a sleek white diamond-edged sword. He sprinted along the length of the metal chains to the top. The beasts ran over the metal chains as their legs tangled and fell into the snow.

White Death stood resolute at the apex of the metal chain, and his gaze fixed squarely on Thanatos.

"This time, this sword will cleave your head from your shoulders," White Death said as he raised it above Thanatos's head.

The Ukko beasts dashed to the side, but some became entangled and collided with the fallen ones caught in the chains. The beasts were rammed off the cliff's edge. The metal chains dragged Thanatos down as the blade swung at his neck, narrowly missing. However, it severed the metal chain on Thanatos's right wrist as he deflected the attack. He then gripped his claws into White Death's left leg, pulling him down with him. They crashed into the frozen river, followed by other beasts from above. The weight of the dead beasts ensnared in the metal chains pulled them deeper into the freezing, dark water below. The river depth appeared bottomless as Thanatos laughed triumphantly. Air bubbles flowed into White Death's face, blocked his view of Thanatos, and the freezing water stunned his body and wound. White Death screamed as air bubbles and blood escaped his mouth. Thanatos clawed deeper into his leg and crushed his bones. With a painful, determined look in White Death's eyes, he sliced his leg off along with two of Thanatos' claws, enabling him to escape.

Thanatos pulled on the chains, flew out of the frozen river, and alighted on the opposite side of the Ukko Sanctuary cliff. Folding his wings, he examined his two missing claws. They slowly began to regenerate. He clutched his fist, observing a trail of blood in the snow. Following it, Thanatos dragged the metal chains up the cliffside, each link trapping dead beasts, and hauled them across the snowy terrain.

Thanatos could walk no farther. He glanced at the metal chains stretched taut across to the opposite side of the cliff as hundreds of beasts continued to plunge off the edge.

"This is as far as you'll get." White Death said, standing shirtless with a bloody white shirt tied around his missing leg.

The metal chains slowly pulled Thanatos back as he struggled against them. His resistance was futile as the chains grew bigger and stronger.

"You'll lose more than I ever did!" White Death spoke calmly as he flew out of the snow before Thanatos, delivering powerful Trifecta Palm Strikes on Thanatos's arms and body. The impact unleashed a powerful force that blew out from behind and cracked the solid stone. Thanatos swiped his right claw at White Death's left side, but he agilely flipped his body to the side, deflecting the attack with his right kick. Landing back on one foot, he continued his assault on Thanatos's body and legs. Each trifecta palm strike blasted the stone, cracking it further. He vanished into the snow and reappeared behind Thanatos. Thanatos's wings snapped open, swung back, and propelled him away as White Death's palm struck against them. He flipped back and vanished once more into the snow. Thanatos flew upward, getting a bird's eye view, and scanned the snowy landscape. Thanatos dived as his right claw plunged deep into the snow upon landing, seizing hold of White Death and pulling him out.

"How do you know where I was!"

"Blood scent," Thanatos replied as large stone pieces fell off his back.

He felt a sudden surge of pain coursing through his body as his exposed back flesh turned purple and red. The loose metal chains quickly reeled and yanked him back, causing Thanatos to lose his grip on him. He plummeted face-first into the snow and dragged backward toward the cliff.

"Are you finally feeling the effects?"

Thanatos grunted, straining to halt the relentless pull of the metal chains.

"The daggers that pierced your arms earlier were laced with a potent, colorless, and odorless poison of my creation. A mere trace could decimate an entire population. Yet, despite its effects, you've managed to endure and continue our duel this far. The Trifecta Palm Strikes further facilitated its dispersion throughout your body, triggering your death timer," White Death laughed mercilessly.

The metal chains dragged Thanatos across the snow at an accelerating rate. He dug his claws into the ground but still got dragged back. The dead beasts tumbled over the cliff and yanked him off. Swinging across, his exposed back smashed into the cliff wall, slowly scraping upward as his blood smeared against the surface. Herds of beasts continued to plummet passed Thanatos into the frozen river below.

White Death knelt at the cliff's edge, withdrawing his white diamond-edge sword from the snow before pushing himself upright. Raising the gleaming blade, he fixed his gaze on Thanatos being reeled up. With a deep breath, White Death's chest expanded, his biceps bulged, and gathered the energy within him.

"Ko," White Death said.

He swung his diamond-edge sword slowly, the blade slicing through the air particles in half. This set off an electrical chain reaction of white light that slashed into the cliff walls. The motion grew rapidly, sending waves of white energy slicing through the air, striking the beasts, the cliff wall, and Thanatos.

The Ukko beasts falling before Thanatos were sliced into pieces. They absorbed most of the energy, but it still cut deep into Thanatos's stone body, shattering his stone armor and metal chains.

White Death spun his diamond-edge sword and slammed it into the snow. An enormous outward explosion erupted from every part of the cliff, casting a dark silhouette of White Death against the fiery backdrop. The land where Ukko Sanctuary stood, crumbled and collapsed into the frozen river below.

White Death looked below as the dust of Ukko Village and rocks settled over the frozen river. He raised his hands and glanced around the stadium, where only a few spectators clapped. He turned his gaze to Thanatos's stone pillar, which stood tall, signaling that no winner had been declared. Lowering his hands, White Death looked down at the rock-covered river.

Impossible!

Thanatos's lifeless body sank, the last traces of purple poison blood flowing from the deep cut and neutralizing in the cold water. With his arms, right leg, and half of his chest missing, the freezing water slowed and eventually stopped the bleeding. Organs began to regrow, bone structures formed, large muscular flesh enveloped them, and rough, hardened skin covered the wounds. The significant, deep cuts sealed and healed themselves. Thanatos's body and wings blackened, but then he opened his eyes.

White Death picked up his diamond-edge sword. Frozen razor claws dug into his neck, lifting him off the ground. He glanced down at the hole in the rocks below that exploded outward. Thanatos, his black wings spread wide, hovered midair by the cliff, gripping White Death's neck as he struggled to breathe. White Death's left hand tried to pry Thanatos's claw from his neck. He swung his diamond-edge sword. Thanatos caught his right arm and ripped it off, then used it to sever White Death's other leg. Thanatos tossed White Death's right arm to the rocks below and hurled White Death's body onto the snow, leaving him with only his left arm.

White Death coughed up blood, "How!"

Thanatos landed before him, his massive wings blowing the snow aside, and folded, "You saved me."

White Death laughed and laughed louder!

"The likes of you will not kill me!"

His left hand gestured multiple signs across his chest before slamming his bloody palm into the snow. Four white ninjas wielding swords appeared at each corner of White Death. Black Death stood beside him, gripping his dagger tightly.

"Emperor Razen, accept a thousand deaths as my apology!" White Death's voice echoed, his eyes shut, and head bowed in contrition.

Four white ninjas flashed diagonally across each other, leaving trails of red blood before disappearing. Black Death's dagger cut clean of blood and disappeared as White Death's head fell off.

"What an honorable way to go! Ladies, gentlemen, and beings of Ourania, I present to you the champion of tonight's contest: Thanatos of Gailstone!" the Hologram Announcer's voice resounded with fervor.

The stadium erupted with screams and applause as the statue and pillar of White Death crumbled to dust. Only four statues remained standing!

Chapter 13
Advisory Kin

The wooden door creaked open, revealing a dark and ominous room illuminated only by old lamps scattered along the stone walls. Mischievous eyes peered out from beneath dark hoodies, tracking the movements of Arison, Viggo, Rain, and Leaf as they entered. They passed a unconscious man, who's slumped over the round wooden table. At the rear of the room, a burly, bearded bald man stood behind the bar counter, his gaze fixed on them as they approached.

"Brotus! Please put four red spirits on my tab. Is the side room available?" Arison handed him the empty bottles on the bar counter as he asked.

Brotus retrieved the key from under the bar counter and passed it to him. His white tank top barely concealed his array of body tattoos, and his gaze lingered on Rain.

"I wouldn't stare if I were you. She's off-limits," Arison added as he grabbed the key and headed to the other end of the bar, where the room was located.

"In my bar, nothing is off-limits," Brotus replied in a deep, heavy tone.

Viggo walked up and locked eyes with Brotus, "Don't even think about it."

"What's a weak weasel gonna do?" Brotus asked, towering over Viggo by a head.

Rain stood beside Viggo, wearing a sweet smile, "I'm a big girl now."

Brotus glanced at Rain, revealing a grin marred by blackened teeth. He licked the bottom of his lip with his wet, thick tongue and said, "You catch that, weasel? She's a big girl, and it takes a real man to handle a bundle like her."

"Once I see one, he can stare all he wants," Rain said as she walked away.

Brotus laughed heartily, then slapped Viggo on the shoulder with a resounding thud, "Ah weasel, you don't stand a chance!"

Viggo pushed Brotus's hand off his shoulder, "I respect her, unlike you, and I will marry her someday."

Brotus met Viggo's gaze squarely, sensing the seriousness in his expression.

Leaf interjected into the conversation, vaulting himself onto the bar counter, "Hi! I'm Leaf. It's nice to meet you!" Leaf gave him a big smile.

Brotus stared at Leaf and burst into laughter, "What are you dragging around, Arison?"

"Friends I can trust," Arison replied as he opened the door to the room. He then proceeded to turn on the lamps adorning the stone wall. Casting a glance around, he pulled out the chairs individually as he circled the round table. "Take a seat. Brotus will bring us our drinks once they're ready."

"Are the drinks even safe?" Viggo asked.

"That's the good thing about Brotus. He may appear like he just broke out of prison, but beneath that rugged exterior lies a heart as tender as a newborn's. We've been through thick and thin together, lost comrades, and faced hardships, but his loyalty has never wavered. You'd expect him to squander every shin he earns, but surprisingly, he's a penny-pincher, saving every hard-earned one. He always talked about having a place where people could afford decent drinks and unwind. A place where they can feel safe. After numerous small successful heists, he saved enough to open Old Rust Bar."

The door swung open forcefully, and Brotus entered, placing four large glasses of red spirit on the table. "Don't ruin my good image," Brotus smirked as he removed a plate of salted peanuts from atop one of the glasses and placed it at the center of the table.

Arison chuckled. "Can't do any more damage than it already has."

Brotus chuckled at the thought, "Damn right," as he walked out, pulling the door shut behind him.

Leaf reached for the peanuts and tossed them into his mouth.

Rain sipped the red spirit, and her eyes lit up, "It's sweet and bubbly!"

They all took a sip and felt refreshed.

Viggo asked Arison, "Earlier, what did White String want with you?"

Arison finished his sip, "He has been getting small strings of whispers about some Stone Runes. He wants us to dig into it and fetch it for him."

"Stone Runes?" Viggo repeated, the phrase sounding oddly familiar.

"What's a Stone Rune?" Leaf inquired.

"It's a stone with some kind of carving on it," Arison replied.

"I don't know if it's related, but General Crocrovich once asked me how I obtained a Stone Rune," Viggo recalled.

"You got a Stone Rune?!" Arison exclaimed, rising from his seat with excitement.

"No. I'd never seen one. I don't know what he was talking about," Viggo said.

"General Crocrovich? What exactly did you tell him?" Arison questioned.

"I told him maybe the GLB might know something about it, but it doesn't seem like they do," Viggo replied.

"What is so special about a stone anyway?" Rain asked.

"I don't know, but White String believes there's something of immense value to them. The Totalist Military devoted half its resources to finding it. Now that General Crocrovich is also interested, those whispers carry more weight. White String wants us to secure it before they do. He promised a very handsome reward to whoever brings it to him," Arison explained.

"What kind of reward are we talking about?" Viggo asked eagerly.

"A safe passage anywhere in Ourania World to the person who delivers the Stone Rune. A new life," Arison said, taking another sip.

Viggo's eyes widened as he absorbed the news. "A new life..." and realized what it meant.

Viggo reconfirmed, "But just for one person."

Arison nodded.

Viggo's excitement surged as he glanced at Leaf. "This is the chance we have been waiting for, Leaf! This is your way out of this pit-hole! I'll do whatever it takes to secure that Stone Rune!"

Rain looked puzzled, "But it's only for one person, Viggo."

Leaf turned to Viggo; his expression of concern etched on his face.

"Brother, I don't want to go anywhere without you!"

"Don't be a silly turtle. This is the chance we've been waiting for! It's finally here! We cannot let this slip away!"

"And you're okay with leaving Leaf alone, wherever this place is?" Rain questioned.

"Anywhere is safer and better than Section 12, wouldn't you agree?" Viggo countered.

"Safer, perhaps. Better without you? No," Rain replied firmly.

"Beggars can't be choosers, especially when it comes to a once-in-a-lifetime opportunity," Viggo asserted resolutely.

"We all have choices, and another opportunity will come along." Rain said.

"It's been thirteen years, Rain!" Viggo's voice cracked with frustration. "Not one opportunity has come our way, not a glimmer of hope to escape this misery. Thirteen long years! You don't know what it's like being out here, day in and day out, and worrying about what will happen next? Will there be a meal for us today? Or a beating tomorrow? You don't know how hard it is to worry constantly!"

"Brother..." Leaf's voice quivered with sadness.

"I would not let this opportunity go. This I know for sure!"

"I know abandoning Leaf is wrong!" Rain said.

"I'm not abandoning him! I'm trying to give him a chance to live! To breathe! You won't understand! You have your father to give you everything!" Viggo's voice rose with frustration, his words punctuated by anger.

"Brother..." Leaf's voice was soft, but the heated argument drowned it out.

"And I will never leave my father, no matter how great the opportunity is!" Rain yelled back, her anger matching Viggo's intensity.

"You are both right, and I think we should calm down and see what Leaf thinks about this," Arison intervened, his voice steady and calming.

Viggo and Rain ceased their argument and turned to look at Leaf, waiting for his response.

"I don't want to leave you, brother," Leaf said, his voice trembling slightly, tears welling up.

"Great! Now let's have another drink," Arison declared, lifting his crimson glass and took a sip. He understood the significance of this opportunity for Viggo, who seemed tense and isolated. Setting his drink down, Arison affirmed, "Viggo's correct, Leaf. I'll do whatever it takes to help both of you escape from here."

"How?" Leaf inquired; curiosity evident in his voice.

"Whenever an opportunity arises, I'll do everything in my power to ensure a smooth and safe passage," Arison assured them.

"But what if there isn't another opportunity for brother?" Leaf's concern was palpable.

"You should understand, living in Section 12, opportunities are as rare as they are valuable. The likelihood of another one presenting itself is almost nonexistent. Viggo grasps this reality and is prepared to sacrifice everything, even his chance, to secure a new life for you. Sometimes he struggles to convey his emotions properly," Arison explained.

"Why aren't you seizing this remarkable opportunity for yourself, Arison? Why are you telling us about it instead?" Rain queried.

"I could've, but the chances of finding it were less than one percent. However, when sharing it with those closest to me, those odds were slightly improved. Besides, I have no intentions of leaving here."

"What's your plan then?" Rain inquired.

Arison took another sip of his drink.

"He's aiming to join the Totalist Military Academy and become the first Commander from Borat Section," Viggo said.

"A Totalist commander? That's even harder," Rain said.

Arison set his glass down. "That's precisely why I'm committed to do everything in my power to help Viggo achieve his!"

Leaf gazed at Viggo with teary eyes, but Viggo avoided his gaze.

"But we need to take the first step and that is finding this Stone Rune. We can discuss the reward later," Arison said.

"Do you trust White String to fulfill his promise?" Rain inquired.

"As odd as it may sound, we thieves uphold a code of honor among ourselves. If that code was ever broken, you'll lose more than any heist, even your life. So yes, I trust him. He's been looking out for me since I was three. Everything he had said and done been genuine," Arison explained.

Viggo rose from his seat, and they slapped their hands together in agreement, "And I trust you. Let's find this Stone Rune!"

Prince Jaden Knight, Elixir, and Lux appeared in the hidden half-circle Royal Room of the three-story V.I.P. nightclub in the Borat Section. Before them, a towering glass wall extended to the top, dominating half the space of the nightclub. The Royal Room boasted two levels, each adorned with long black onyx bar counters positioned opposite of each other, accompanied by black onyx tables and luxurious white fur furnitures crafted from the hide of the great beasts. Massive white marble dance floors graced each level, while the smoothest, purest black walls provided a striking backdrop, accented by neon lighting fixtures blended perfectly behind the abstract paintings. Live, beautiful, and seductive hologram dancers swayed to the pulsating beats of the club music. Their bodies moved across the wall. A natural hot spring pool nestled against the one-way glass window on the lower level, offering a panoramic view of the bustling nightclub below.

Over the years, the V.I.P. hidden rooms had been privately reserved, and their accommodations were tailored uniquely to each guest's demands and desires.

Prince Jaden Knight strolled along the pathway encircling the hot spring, nearing the one-way glass. From this vantage point, he observed the young and affluent partygoers below, reveling in the exclusive experience atop the six rotating white circular platforms. Each circular platform, bathed in colored laser lights, provided a unique setting for the privileged guests. Accessible only through a special teleportation from the first level, these platforms offered an elevated experience. Directly beneath them, a massive water sphere float in the center, descending to the first level. The V.I.P. nightclub boasted three levels, each dance floor enveloping the water sphere in its unique ambiance.

Young partygoers frolicked within the confines of the water sphere. Anyone could dive into the sphere, even leaping from the circular platforms above. As the water splashed outward, the sphere's design ingeniously drew it back in, maintaining the aquatic spectacle within.

Inside the V.I.P. nightclub, the glass walls reflected the partygoers' beauty, excitement, and youthful energy. White furniture and bars adorned the space, illuminated by neon blue and green lights, adding an extra cool layer. On the first level, the main dance floor occupied the center, surrounded by bars and white furniture along the glass wall. The dance floor had the unique capability to transition from a flat surface to undulating waves, syncing perfectly with the pulsating beats of the music.

"Congratulations, my young Prince!" Lux exclaimed, dancing beside him with infectious joy.

Lux's short, light brown hair frames her face, complementing her piercing green eyes, small lips, and delicate button nose. She exudes a formidable presence in sleek black metal armor tailored to her hourglass figure. Two thick black gloves encase each hand while a small mechanical circular gear adorns her right shoulder. Her attire starkly contrasts with that of Prince Jaden Knight's black armor, showcasing a unique style and individuality.

"Yes, congratulations, Prince Jaden Knight. However, may I offer a suggestion?" Elixir asked politely.

Elixir possesses long, blond hair, piercing blue eyes, and a captivatingly pretty face, with a figure that mesmerizes most. She dons bright red armor adorned with multiple side pockets, accompanied by a hardcover backpack and a blade strapped to her right leg. A white cross embellishes the shoulders of her attire. Renowned as one of the finest young medics in Vellatine City, Elixir is also adept in close combat. Lux is a rising star within the Vellatine Special Op. Both have served as Prince Jaden Knight's bodyguards for five years, since he was twelve. Their lethal proficiency is matched only by their striking appearances.

"Must you?" Prince Jaden Knight asked.

"As your health specialist and closed combat mentor, yes. Your strike requires total concentration and flawless execution. Moreover, I don't believe coming here is wise, especially on the eve of your semi-final," Elixir advised, her gaze sweeping the Royal Room.

"This is precisely why I'm here," Prince Jaden Knight responded.

Lux peered through the glass, excitement radiating from her as she danced to the pulsating music. "This is what relaxes our young Prince."

Lux gracefully danced towards the black onyx table, where pink and yellow neon bottles rose in the center as she approached. She reached for the pink bottle, poured its contents into three glasses, and spun to the music as she returned to her companions.

She handed each of them a drink. "Let that music bounce through your sexy body, Elixir!"

"But what if…"

"That's precisely why I have you both," Prince Jaden Knight interjected, raising his glass in a toast.

Lux emptied her glass, raising it high before exuberantly screaming, "Wooah!"

As she spun and danced to the music, Prince Jaden Knight couldn't help but smile, feeling a sense of relaxation wash over him. The alcohol coursing through his veins warmed his body, complementing the enjoyable vibe of the music.

"Lux, despite being only a year apart, we're so different," Elixir remarked as she surveyed the bustling dance floors. Young women shrieked and playfully struggled against the young studs who carried them towards the water sphere, where they would be tossed in. Some chased each other around before leaping into the water sphere themselves. Holding her pink glass close to her chest, Elixir pondered. *Perhaps this could be good for him—a bit of relaxation after his big win.*

As the empty bottles were lowered away, two new ones replaced them. Prince Jaden Knight laughed and spun around, trails of lights swirling around him. Elixir and Lux became blurred figures, and then he blacked out.

The soft morning light filtered through the expansive window wall. Prince Jaden Knight's eyes fluttered open, greeted by the sight of the intricately gold-decorated crown molding lining the skylight ceiling, with birds soaring overhead. He luxuriated in the comfort of his soft feather comforter, enveloping him in warmth and coziness. The high-end wooden frame of his bed boasted intricate details meticulously carved by Corecrest's finest craftsmen. The white veil surrounding his bed was drawn closed, with King Roy and Queen Glory standing beside him. Prince Jaden Knight attempted to sit up but was met with a numbing sensation coursing through his body. Queen Glory gently placed her hand on his shoulder, urging him to recline. Lieutenant General Bradstone and Major General Vic stood sentinel by the heavy double doors.

"Why are you in my room, my Queen?" Prince Jaden Knight asked.

"You don't remember, my young Prince Jaden?" Queen Glory asked, her tone weary.

He rubbed the side of his head. "Not much. I was relaxing with Elixir and Lux last night."

"Elixir and Lux are currently in Vellatine Medic Emergency Center. Both are in critical condition and have not regained consciousness," Lieutenant General Bradstone voiced.

"What happened?!" Prince Jaden Knight exclaimed, attempting to rise but hindered by the numbed sensation coursing through his body and hand.

"We were hoping you could tell us that. They both did a fine job bringing you back with minimal harm. According to the ongoing investigation, an assassination was attempted on your life last night, my young Prince," Major General Vic said.

Prince Jaden Knight was shocked as he lay in bed.

"Who dares! I want their heads!" King Roy's voice thundered angrily as his frustration mounted, "Do you have any inkling as to who would wish harm upon you, my son?"

Prince Jaden Knight shook his head, confused.

"Can you recall anything that might help?" Major General Vic inquired.

"The V.I.P. nightclub..." Prince Jaden Knight recollected.

"It's been blown up. Whoever is behind this has taken extreme measures to eliminate you at any cost. They likely don't want you to compete in today's semi-final," Lieutenant General Bradstone interjected.

"It must be those filthy Gailstone!" King Roy exclaimed in anger.

"It's too conspicuous to point fingers at them, especially since he's set to face Thanatos today," Lieutenant General Bradstone remarked.

"But that doesn't rule them out as suspects," King Roy countered, his tone resolute.

"I need to see Elixir and Lux!" Prince Jaden Knight demanded, pulling the soft comforter aside.

"Will you be fit to battle today?" Lieutenant General Bradstone asked indifferently.

"But the poison hasn't been fully eradicated," Queen Glory interjected.

"Poison?" Prince Jaden Knight echoed; his voice tinged with surprise.

"The Royal Doctors are investigating the type and origin of the poison. They mentioned that everyone would have perished if it hadn't been for Elixir's quick action in administering the anti-poison serum earlier. They assured us that the numbing sensation should subside before the start of the first semi-final," Major General Vic explained.

"Then I'll fight that Gailstone!" Prince Jaden Knight replied, retorted angrily.

"Shouldn't you rest, my dear Prince Jaden?" Queen Glory inquired with concern.

"I'll be fine, my Queen," Prince Jaden Knight assured her.

"Then I insist you utilize the double!" King Roy demanded.

"A slight numbness will not change my will," Prince Jaden Knight asserted.

"Major General Vic, choose two of your best Elite Black and assign them to Prince..." King Roy began.

"No one can replace Elixir or Lux! I'll visit them immediately," Prince Jaden Knight interrupted firmly.

"Is there anything else you could share with us, my young Prince?" Major General Vic inquired.

Prince Jaden Knight shook his head before vanishing from the room.

King Roy roared with frustration: "That boy's stubbornness will be the death of him!"

"A reflection of you, my King," Queen Glory remarked calmly.

"Have you forgotten what happened to White Death?" King Roy's voice thundered.

Queen Glory closed her eyes and turned her head aside.

"Perhaps someday, this stubbornness will aid him in conquering his trials. It can be a formidable trait, my King Roy," Major General Vic said.

"Don't attempt to placate my fury on his behalf. I demand a comprehensive investigation immediately! If the Gailstones are responsible, I want them brought to their knees and executed!" King Roy declared, his gaze fixed on the window.

"What about the Borat kids?" Major General Vic inquired.

"Where are they currently?"

"At Royal Level One, my King," Major General Vic responded.

"Send Advisory Kin to attend to them. Ensure they are not permitted to depart until the investigation exonerates them. If they are deemed guilty, their fate will be the most severe," King Roy commanded.

"Understood, my King Roy. Also, a report regarding Bronx versus Black Death has been received from intelligence," Major General Vic informed.

King Roy nodded and then turned to Queen Glory, saying, "Excuse us, my Queen."

Lieutenant General Bradstone, Major General Vic, and King Roy bowed their heads with their hands over their hearts before vanishing from the room.

A worried expression creased Queen Glory's face as she clasped her hands tightly.

At the Royal Chamber Level, Commander Bazyli observed Major General Vic activate the report hologram. A holographic projection of Section 10, City of Lights, materialized and rotated around Black Death as he swiftly traversed through the events leading up to the tournament's commencement.

A female voice reported, "According to our surveillance and thorough background checks on all attendees in the stadium, there's no indication of any conspiracy involving a third party or any traps set prior to the battle. We've meticulously reviewed the backup databases four times, analyzing recorded abilities, powers, and the history of the Ukko.

However, we couldn't find any record of the ability used during the Bronx versus Black Death battle."

A holographic representation of Black Death approached Bronx and swiftly decapitated him.

"We've determined this is a new ability not previously recorded in our databases. It appears this ability was activated when Black Death closed his eyes. However, we're still uncertain about when or how Bronx became ensnared by it. At present, we don't have a solution to counteract this ability."

The female voice concluded the report.

"These Ukko are enigmatic and perilous!" King Roy remarked.

"If Bronx's claims are accurate, how do we confront someone possessing such capabilities?" Major General Vic questioned.

"White Death relies more on physical combat, while Black Death seems to be a mental fighter using visual techniques. We must devise a new defensive mechanism..." Lieutenant General Bradstone suggested.

"Let's wait and observe Prince Jaden Knight's performance in the semi-final first," Commander Bazyli interjected.

"But we can start developing a countermeasure device for such abilities..." Lieutenant General Bradstone halted abruptly.

Commander Bazyli turned around, stating firmly, "Petty mind games do not trouble me. A true fighter must possess both a robust physique and an unyielding mind."

Prince Jaden Knight appeared in the Vellatine Medic Emergency Center alongside the medical staff. They were performing surgery on the naked bodies of Elixir and Lux's within a sealed, sanitized glass chamber. Substantial quantities of bloody-stained bullets were extracted from their bodies and deposited into glass containers beside the chamber. A laser scanner meticulously traced the deep lacerations and bullet wounds across their bodies, gradually reconstructing the missing tissue and sealing the wounds.

"How are Elixir and Lux, Doctor?" Prince Jaden Knight inquired; his gaze fixed on them as they lay motionless in the glass chambers.

"They're in critical condition, and we're uncertain of their prognosis. However, we've managed to control the massive bleeding, which ceased five hours ago. Fortunately, they were brought here promptly. Had it been twenty minutes later, we might not have been able to intervene," the doctor explained, focusing on operating the lasers without glancing at Prince Jaden Knight.

Prince Jaden Knight's fists clutched, and he vanished.

The City of Lights Stadium comprised three royal levels: Royal Level One, Royal Level Two, and the Royal Chamber Level, which was situated at the pinnacle.

Viggo, Rain, Leaf, and Arison stood at the entrance of the imposing black marble double doors adorned with gold handles, rendered speechless by the grandeur of the Royal Level One room. It served as an exclusive waiting area for special guests. High vaulted ceilings showcased past commanders depicted in dream-like pastel hues, while the gold-trimmed reflective white marble flooring guided visitors to the room's center. The floor encircled the expansive black marble fountain, extending seamlessly to the room's left and right sides. Proudly positioned on the fountain were nine statues of the commanders, crafted from dark red chrome, each exuding a sense of stoic determination. At the heart of the water feature, a fierce, unyielding flame dancing wildly.

To the right of the fountain, white marble stairs descended gracefully to the seating area below, while to the left, matching stairs ascended to the seating area above. Both staircases were adorned with red carpet runners boasting intricate gold-crown patterns. Large round tables were meticulously arranged along the glass window wall on each seating level, offering optimal views of the stadium below. Each seat was crafted for supreme comfort and automatically elevated to an unobstructed height, ensuring a perfect viewing experience for all guests.

Dirty footprints marred the pristine, reflective white marble floor as they walked slowly to the center of the room in awe. They clashed unpleasantly with the environment. Rain gazed up at the vaulted ceiling, where white chandeliers hung along the pathway, flanked by white marble columns.

Leaf glanced around, "Are we in the wrong place?"

"I hope not!" Viggo replied.

"They escorted us here. I guess this is the waiting room," Arison said.

The heavy double doors of black marble swung open, and Advisory Kin strode in, flanked by two Totalist soldiers wielding automatic assault rifles.

Advisory Kin, clean-shaven and impeccably dressed in a black suit adorned with prominent shoulder pads and a gold tie, commanded attention as he stopped before them. His straight, shoulder-length gray silk hair gleamed in the light. With a flourish, he tapped his translucent fluid cane against the white marble floor, exuding style and authority. Small red and blue orbs flowed around each other within his translucent cane, adding to his enigmatic presence.

"Ah, the Undying Spirits of Totalist. A great contribution to our great leaders," Advisory Kin admired the dancing flames of the fountain, his gaze fixed upon their mesmerizing movement.

He turned his attention to them, "My apologies," Advisory Kin began, his voice carrying a tone of deference. "I am Advisory Kin, a loyal right-hand servant to King Roy. Welcome, young ones, to Royal Level One. I am here to assist you with any needs you might request, and I've arranged room accommodations for each of you to rest as long as you require."

Advisory Kin bowed gracefully to Rain. With a subtle twist of his wrist, a vibrant red rose materialized, and he extended it to her with a flourish. "To our esteemed VIP lady."

Rain was surprised as she took the bright red rose, "Thank you."

Viggo's thoughts drifted sadly to the torn blue rose petal, Rose Du Pare. The red rose's sweet scent whisked him back from his memory. Despite the bittersweet nostalgia, he couldn't help but smile as he looked at Rain, standing beside him in happiness. They were within Royal Level One of the City of Light Stadium, a place he never thought he'd set foot in, let alone share with Rain. It felt like a dream come true, a blessing he never expected. Returning Advisory Kin's smile, Viggo felt a sense of gratitude wash over him. "Thank you very much for your kind greeting. We would be delighted to stay a while longer."

"I can't stay," Rain said softly, her voice tinged with worry. "Daddy would be so worried. He'd think something terrible had happened to me."

"No need to concern yourself, my lady." Advisory Kin said reassuringly. "A message can be swiftly delivered to your father, informing him of your whereabouts. Here in Vellatine City, under the great care of King Roy, you can safely and comfortably enjoy the nights."

"The King... Vellatine City..." Viggo said in awe.

"Thank you, Advisory Kin. Please convey my sincere gratitude to King Roy for his generous offer, but I must decline," Rain insisted firmly.

"You don't want to stay with us?" Leaf asked, sounding disappointed.

Rain gently placed her hands on Leaf's cheeks, her touch tender. "I love every moment of seeing your cute face," she said as she squeezed and rubbed his bony cheeks up and down.

"If you keep doing this, I won't be cute anymore," Leaf quipped, playfully pushing her hands away. Laughter rippled through the group.

"Everything is grand, unbelievable, but I must go home," Rain said.

Advisory Kin bowed respectfully. "Whatever my lady desires, I am here to make it happen. However, would you prefer to stay until the semi-final is over?"

"Please stay till then!" Leaf pleaded earnestly.

Rain smiled and nodded in agreement.

"Then please help yourself to the food and drinks," Advisory Kin gestured towards the back wall by the entrance, drawing their attention to a long line of tables adorned with an extravagant display of fresh, steamed, and grilled foods featuring an array of meats, fruits, and vegetables. A tantalizing tower of desserts stood proudly at the end of the table, promising indulgence. Each food station boasted a personal chef, diligently serving and replenishing the offerings to ensure a continuous supply of fresh delicacies, even in the absence of guests. Gleaming gold plates, silverware, and neatly folded gold cloth napkins awaited guests at the beginning of the table, adding a touch of opulence to the culinary experience. On the opposite side of the entrance, long tables showcased an impressive selection of wines, juices, and specialty drinks, accompanied by an assortment of large and small glasses, catering to every preference.

"We've reserved these tables specifically for you, offering a perfect view of Battle World. Once the battle concludes, I'll personally return to escort each of you."

A deep, slow drumbeat resounded loudly from below, it's clear, raw sound amplified in the live setting. The anticipation was palpable as Battle World was on the brink of beginning.

"It's about to start! Let's get the food and drinks!" Viggo exclaimed eagerly, his excitement palpable.

They dashed towards the food tables, hastily grabbing plates and piling them high with an assortment of delicacies, paying no heed to the stunned chefs who watched in disbelief. Viggo swiftly unzipped his fanny pack, tossing fruits and meat for Mr. Stinky and the rat. Another plate of food was added to Viggo and Leaf's already-laden dishes.

Chapter 14
Assassination

The Hologram Announcer's voice boomed through the stadium. "Ladies, gentlemen, and beings of Ourania World! Please stand and show respect for your semi-finalists!"

The crowd, stretching from the stadium to far reaches of the remote regions, surged to their feet, their applause resonating with pride and excitement.

"Great fighters of Ourania World, please stand and receive our heartfelt appreciation for your success. We wish you the best in the battles ahead!"

Adonis Belacaro, Black Death, Thanatos, and Prince Jaden Knight rose from their stone seats, commanding attention as they ascended. Below, spectators erupted in cheers, applause, and waves of enthusiasm. Adonis raised Mightis skyward, its glint catching the sunlight. Black Death, arms crossed, offered a subtle nod of acknowledgment. Thanatos unfurled his great wings, his right fist clenched in determination. Prince Jaden Knight, his charm unyielding, tossed a red rose to the crowd, inciting wild screams of adoration.

"Please lock in the battleground landscape for our first semi-final battle! Let me welcome the formidable Adonis Belacaro from Ironstead of The Majestic Royal!"

Adonis leaped from his pillar, landing in the battleground with his fist pressed into the ground. Rising slowly, sand trickled through his fingers.

"Next, let's give a thunderous applause for the fearsome Black Death of Gai G, Land of Ukko!"

Black Death appeared on the battlefield, arms wide open, locking eyes with Adonis.

"Your gazed doesn't intimidate me, nor does your cheap hypnosis,"

Adonis challenged, unflinching.

"And how can you be sure you're not under its spell right now?" Black Death retorted.

Darkness engulfed Adonis. He was in total blackness, unable to see even his own hands.

Is this what happened to Bronx? He thought.

Concentrating intently, he discerned a shadowy figure lurking in the distance, watching with lethal intent. Mirroring its movements, he shifted cautiously.

"A strong mind," Black Death's voice echoed. The darkness gradually faded, revealing the stadium again.

"Brain and brawn, I possess both," Adonis chuckled.

"But I doubt this will be a lengthy affair," Black Death stated coldly.

"Is that so? I certainly hope you're right," Adonis shot back.

"The battleground landscape, 'Silver Lake Lava,' is now locked in!" The announcer's voice boomed through the arena. "Let the semi-final battle begin!"

The crowd erupted in cheers of excitement!

Adonis and Black Death scanned the sandy battleground, finding no trace of lava or melting sand. A meteor hurtled from the sky and crashed into the center. The sheer force of the explosion instantly blew everything into the sky, and they were hard-pressed against the searing surface of the burning rocks. Black Death strained to push himself upward as the rock grew hotter. Adonis lifted his face from the scorching surface and leaped from rock to rock as they vaporized from the extreme heat. Black Death disappeared, reappearing on successive rocks ascending higher into the atmosphere, closely following Adonis Belcaro from behind.

Under the intense heat of the shattered meteor, the sandy ground liquified into lava. The freezing, chilled air swept across the top of Silver Lake Lava, freezing and hardening the top surface into an ice sheet.

The large rocks ascended to the top of the Ourania atmosphere, and their pace slowed. The air grew thin, making it difficult to breathe. Adonis landed on a colossal rock. Black Death appeared behind him, crouched at a low angle, and lunged forward with his dagger, slashing into the back side of his adversary. Adonis leaped away from the blade, but a rope whipped around his neck from behind, forcefully yanking him down and slamming the back of his head against the rock. A dagger plunged from above toward his face. Adonis tilted his head to the left, barely avoiding the blade as it stabbed into the rock. Black Death pressed his knee against Adonis's right temple, immobilizing him, and then sliced his dagger sideways. Sparks flew against the rock and cut across his right cheek.

Adonis seized Black Death's right wrist, executing a deft roll on the ground as he twisted his opponent's arm and forced him to flip over and tumble alongside. He hammered his fist into Black Death's right hand until the dagger was relinquished. Adonis rolled backward and flipped on top of him as he was still face down. He locked his arms around Black Death's waist and suplexed him into the rock. Black Death's head slammed into the hard rock. Stunned.

Without hesitation, Adonis flipped over his adversary once more, securing his arms around Black Death's waist for another suplex. As they hurtled off the rock, plummeting from the sky at breakneck speed, Black Death's upper back and head crashed into the hardened ice sheet, resulting in a dislocated left shoulder. The impact caused shards of ice to spike up along the lines of the cracked ice sheets.

Adonis rose to his feet.

Black Death disappeared and reappeared at a distance, his hands and knees pressing against the icy surface. Blood seeped through his face mask, forming dark stains as it dripped onto the frozen expanse.

Adonis rolled his shoulders, cracked his back, removed the rope encircling his neck with the dagger at the end of it, and tossed it to Black Death.

"You still have the energy to move after I slammed you with that double suplex? Especially from that height?"

Black Death drew a deep breath, his eyes betraying the intensity of his pain as he reached for his left shoulder, gritting his teeth against the agony. He pressed his dislocated arm against the unforgiving ice, then slowly rotated his body until a loud pop echoed, signaling the joint's realignment. Black Death took a few quick, short breaths as the pain disappeared, then retrieved his dagger from the ground.

"You'll need a bigger pocketknife to cut me," Adonis spoke as he drew Mightis from his back. Large rocks crashed beside them, shattering through the ice sheet and spilling lava into the sky. Black Death turned to face him. He lifted his dagger, its tip glinting menacingly.

He zigzagged toward Adonis, deftly evading the splashes of hot lava as they seared onto the icy surface. With a fluid motion, He whipped his dagger ahead, the steel tip slicing through the ice spikes and propelling them into the air. He appeared at each ice spike, kicking, punching, and spin-kicking them toward Adonis at great speed. Some smashed into Mightis as Adonis Belcaro blocked and cut down the ice spikes. One managed to pierce through his upper left shoulder and flew out the other side. The instant chill went through his wound, followed by the sharp, gripping pain that contorted Adonis's face.

The dagger appeared, its clash with Mightis igniting sparks upon impact. Each strike was meticulously aimed at Adonis's vital points. Stepping on his rope, Black Death spun it around his foot, launching his dagger directly at Adonis. The blades clashed fiercely, causing the rope end to whip around and strike Adonis's cheek with a sharp crack.

Adonis turned away, feeling a sharp sting on his cheek as it instantly reddened. The dagger spun dangerously close to his neck, but Mightis deflected it. The rope snapped loudly against Adonis's inner thigh. As Black Death turned, the rope's end slapped Adonis's other cheek, and the dagger swung upward, slicing across his chest.

Blood seeped through the open cut.

His speed was too great for Adonis to react and was unable to block both attacks.

Adonis raised his left arm. Seeing an opening, Black Death sliced at his left side. However, Adonis quickly dropped his arm, securing Black Death's right arm in place while swinging Mightis down onto Black Death. Sparks flew across his right arm and chest.

Armor! Adonis thought.

He swung Mightis at his head, but Black Death whipped Adonis's right wrist with the rope end and kicked Mightis away. Black Death's long shirt dematerializes, reforming instantly into a night sword in his left hand. The sword clashed with Mightis several times. On each impact, the blade wrapped around Mightis and cut Adonis's right hand and arm. During the clash, the sword coiled around Mightis again. Adonis released Mightis and seized Black Death's left wrist, pulling him in, then smashed his forehead into his face.

Stunned and in pain, Black Death watched as Adonis leaned back again and threw his forehead toward him, but a fierce kick flew between them, smashing Adonis's chin and sending him flipping backward, landing on the ice. Adonis shook his head and looked at him as he got back up. Black Death swiftly placed his dagger at his side and looped the rope behind his back. Turning around, he retrieved his sword and Mightis, glancing at them.

Adonis observed black tattoos covering Black Death's entire body.

At the center of his chest was a fine detail of a Dark King who wore his crown in full armor with a fur cape looming over his shoulders. He rested his hands on a large double battle axe, which stood up to his chest. A Black Viper wrapped around Black Death's left arm, its head resting on the back of his hand. At his upper right arm was an Ice Beast; its horns and black body were outlined in blue ice. On his back was the Wings of Misery. A wrinkly, aged woman with bloodshot, wide eyes stared intensely back. Her long, thin, wavy white hair framed her old face, revealing rotten teeth. She wore a long dress with ripped holes covering down to her bare feet. Transparent fire wings with thick veins running through them behind her.

Black Death hurled Mightis back to him, the blade embedding into the ice sheet before him. Adonis retrieved Mightis. Blood dripped from his hand and splattered onto the ice. Below the ice, Adonis could see the lava flowing.

A black tongue flickered the air from the back of Black Death's left hand.

"You want this prey?" Black Death asked as he lifted his arm and pointed his night sword at him. The Black Viper tattoo slowly coiled, its head emerging from his arm. It slithered off the tip of the night sword and onto the ice sheet, growing larger and larger as it encircled itself. Its glossy black scales reflect the light, and a spiky spine rose on the back of its head.

Adonis gazed up at the towering Black Viper, its red eyes slitting open to peer down at him. Black Death stood amidst the serpent's encircled body, staring down at Adonis.

"What illusion is this?" Adonis asked as he watched in disbelief.

Black Death vanished.

The viper flicked its tongue and lowered its head toward him, who stood motionless. Its tongue, as large as Adonis himself, flickered in front of his bloody chest.

It scented his blood.

Its jaw opened, revealing eight rolls of sharp, inward pointing, hooked teeth. Adonis could smell the foul, bitter venom emanating from its mouth, which could melt tissues and bones. Black Viper leaned its head back and instantly snapped at him, but he ducked under its chin. Then punched it upwards, slamming its mouth shut. The serpent's head flew upward, swaying side to side before it looked back down at him. Undeterred, Adonis stood fearlessly with Mightis in his right hand. He raised his left thumb and two fingers taunting the creature, waving it to come at him again.

It hissed, and two large fangs flicked out like switchblades. The viper dove low to the ice surface, slithered across with great speed, and snapped multiple times at him. Adonis dodged left and right as the viper's triangular head aimed its fangs at him, but it quickly darted away as Mightis swung into the ice.

Adonis ran past the holes, dragging Mightis through the ice as the viper slithered closely. Adonis slid and skated around, kicking up ice particles, facing the incoming viper with its jaw wide open. Adonis grinned and charged at the viper. The ice split open as lava erupted from behind Mightis. Black Viper lowered its mouth to swallow him, but he spun to the side and swung Mightis sideways with all his might to slice its mouth wide open. Black Death appeared with his sword inside the viper's mouth, clashing with Mightis! Lava flew off Mightis, splattering across the right side of Black Death's face and into the viper's mouth!

The impact blew them apart!

Black Death covered his face, screaming in agony, before disappearing as the viper closed its mouth, twisting and coiling in pain. Adonis was thrown several yards away.

Black Viper thrashed against the cracking ice around it. The gash Adonis had cut earlier with Mightis broke apart when the viper chased him. The ice beneath Black Viper collapsed, and lava splashed onto its body. Adonis watched from a safe distance, clutching Mightis. Black Viper roared in great pain, leaping from the lava and lunging towards him, its mouth and fangs wide open. The lava had burned off chunks of flesh from Black Viper's head, but its scaly body remained undamaged. Adonis spun Mightis from his right hand to his left, took a deep breath, and his chest expanded as he jumped high. The viper leaped after him and consumed him.

Mightis spun in a circle and split Black Viper's jaw wide open. He leaped from its jaw high into the air, drew his right fist back with all his might, and punched the top of the viper's head. The impact exploded, sending its head straight down through the ice into the lava below. Its body was flung upward and followed into the lava. Adonis landed far away.

Waves of lava crashed against each other, splashing onto the ice sheet before slowly calming down.

Black Death stood at a distance; half his face burned off. His right cheekbone and half his jawbones were exposed.

"You don't seem to be giving up anytime soon," Adonis said.

Black Death stared at him intensely.

Black Viper's spiky skull burst through the ice sheet before him!

It's still alive! Adonis thought.

The viper swiftly swooped to the side, wrapping around him and coiling its body tightly. Despite Adonis slashing Mightis against its scaly armor, the viper continued constricting around him. Hundreds of tiny black needles on its scales pierced deep into his back, causing intense pain. With every squeeze, Black Viper compressed him further, crushing his arms against his rib cage and making it difficult to breathe. Adonis and Mightis were immobilized and unable to move. As blood stopped flowing to Adonis's brain, it began to seep from his open wounds. Black viper's spiky, hollowed skull loomed ominously above him, patiently waiting.

Adonis lay still.

The viper opened its split jaws and snapped at him. Its fang pierced through his back and emerged from the front of his chest before retracting. The hooked teeth then gripped his chest and back, pulled his body into its jaw, securing him tightly as it slithered towards the lava.

Black Death appeared on the opposite side of the lava just as the viper slithered closer to it. The lava bubbled, and Black Viper's large, triangular, spiky skull leaped into the air, diving down into the lava.

"DECAPITATION!"

A blade of light beamed into Black Viper's skull, split it apart! The blade of light spun around, slicing its body in half and vaporizing it. Adonis stood on a piece of ice, holding Mightis aloft. The landscape of the ice sheet shattered into pieces and scattered apart. Mightis cut into the ice in front of Adonis as he fell to his hands and knees, head bowed. His body had turned purple, and his flesh shriveled like a prune and rotted. Green pus and black blood spewed from his wounds.

Black Death appeared before him, his white eyeball with blood vessels peering down from its bone socket, "Death is upon you."

Slowly, Black Death picked up Mightis and raised it into the sky. Beside them, lava exploded upward.

Black Death looked at it admiringly. "Decapitation!"

There was no blade of light beaming down into Mightis. Black Death chuckled as Mightis sliced down through the air toward Adonis's neck.

Sharp metals clashed against each other, and Mightis flew out of Black Death's hand, embedding itself into the ice along with Swift.

The spectators gasped.

Lixia Ziva stood at the edge of the battleground, dagger in hand, and shouted, "He's mine!"

Black Death glared at Lixia Ziva.

Adonis collapsed onto the ice.

His white horse trotted nervously around the edge, shaking its head and rearing up, then neighing loudly. Adonis's statue crumbled and collapsed.

"You've won. He's worthless to you!" Lixia Ziva shouted.

Black Death glared down at him with his white eyeball, his night sword materializing in his right hand. He raised it high, a wide grin spreading across his face.

The night sword swung down, quickly turned sideways, and deflected the pink energy toward the spectators.

A massive explosion erupted behind Lixia Ziva as she stood with her dagger held high.

"He's mine!" she declared loudly.

"Lady, gentlemen, and esteemed beings of Ourania world, I present to you the victor of the first semi-final—Black Death!" the Hologram Announcer shouted.

The spectators weren't sure to cheer or clap!

Black Death smirked and then disappeared.

❖

"Black Death was terrifying before, but now, he's downright horrifying!" Rain said.

They shook in agreement.

"I like Adonis Belacaro. I'm glad she saved him," Leaf said, watching as the dust settled around the statue of Adonis Belacaro.

Arison breathed deeply, "He's lucky."

"Think Ukko will win the tournament again?" Viggo asked, leaning forward.

"I hope not," Rain said.

"Black Death is badly hurt. Hopefully, this will give our next fighter a chance," Arison added.

"I hope Prince Jaden Knight will win," Leaf said.

"I don't know, especially after what happened to..." Viggo said.

"Shhh... You don't want to end up like Adonis," Arison interrupted Viggo, glancing around to ensure they were alone.

Viggo relaxed, sinking back. "I need a drink and more food before the next fight."

"Great idea, brother!" Leaf shouted, jumping out of his seat.

Viggo stood up. "Do you want anything, Rain?"

Rain stared at the statue of Prince Jaden Knight, unaware that Viggo had asked her a question.

"Rain?" Viggo asked again, following her gaze.

"I'd be full just looking at that piece of art," Arison joked.

"Do you think our Prince stands a chance against that beast?" Viggo asked.

Arison's face betrayed his lack of confidence.

"Me, too," Viggo said.

❖

Major General Vic stood at the window, "The Ukko's strength is extremely strong. The probability of them winning is now up to eighty-seven percent. Even if Prince Jaden Knight makes it to the final, his odds are slim. The Ukko is truly a terrifying being to fear."

"How do we stand a chance against someone like that?" King Roy asked, his eyes fixed on the replay from his oversized black leather chair.

"Fight until you win," Major General Vic declared, returning to the table and eyeing the four hologram black tattoos on Black Death.

"His fighting skills are top-notch, and those strange black tattoos of his, they could come alive!" King Roy remarked, glancing at the old woman and the dark King, "I can't even imagine what they're capable of."

"Are we getting ahead of ourselves, gentlemen?" Commander Bazyli asked.

The room became silent.

"Every battle is captured, analyzed, and stored, including counter-attack simulations where available. We'll provide our best strategy if Prince Jaden Knight reaches the final. But for right now, Thanatos is our priority. I'm particularly concerned about his regeneration speed. Even when severely cut into pieces, he recovers remarkably fast," Lieutenant General Bradstone explained, pulling up Thanatos's hologram.

"Not to mention his strength, size, and ability to fly," Admiral Baylee added.

"Is there a solution?" King Roy asked, his expression filled with concern.

"Intel ran millions of scenarios, and the best outcome showed a seventy-three percent chance of winning," Lieutenant General Bradstone stated.

"What is it?" King Roy asked.

"SolBoom," Lieutenant General Bradstone replied.

King Roy's eyes widened. "Is that permitted?"

"If Prince Jaden Knight activates it, then it is," Lieutenant General Bradstone clarified.

"That's overkill! Wouldn't our Prince Jaden Knight also get hurt?"

Major General Vic questioned.

"Not if he appears at a specific longitude in the atmosphere before it strikes," Lieutenant General Bradstone explained.

"Send him the details immediately," King Roy ordered.

Lieutenant General Bradstone, Major General Vic, and Admiral Baylee looked at Commander Bazyli's chair as it rotated.

"How is our Prince?" Commander Bazyli inquired.

"He is well but stubborn," King Roy replied.

"He is in the Battle Room preparing for his upcoming battle," Major General Vic said.

Commander Bazyli observed Thanatos's hologram and remarked, "A great, wise warrior is carved from the harsh paths they've walked."

Lieutenant General Bradstone and Major General Vic nodded in agreement.

"This is my son we're talking about! This is your Prince of Totalist Federation and future King! His safety must be our top priority!" King Roy exclaimed.

"Yes, our Prince's safety is paramount, but not to win a battle by simply pushing a button," Commander Bazyli asserted.

"I will personally reinspect all of his gear and armor before the battle, my King," Major General Vic promised, placing his hand over his heart and bowing respectfully.

King Roy silenced and nodded.

Commander Bazyli dismissed Thanatos's hologram with a swipe and brought up the exterior of the V.I.P. nightclub. "What's the report?"

"Our investigation into who is behind this is still ongoing, but our records have revealed what happened," Lieutenant General Bradstone explained as they watched the hologram replay.

The exterior V.I.P. nightclub hologram zoomed through the building into the Royal Room, where green square holograms tracked Elixir, Lux, and Prince Jaden Knight. Screens appeared beside them, detailing their health statuses.

A female hologram reported, "Prince Jaden Knight, Elixir, and Lux have exceeded the average alcohol limit, and there was also evidence of poison in their systems."

Prince Jaden Knight collapsed into Elixir's arms. She struggled to support him, feeling dizzy herself and stumbling. Elixir's eyepiece transformed over her right eye as she checked Prince Jaden Knight's and Lux's health statuses.

"Poison?" Elixir exclaimed.

Everything around Elixir spun. She swiftly retrieved her injection gun from her side pocket and shot it at Prince Jaden Knight, Lux, and herself, halting the poison's full effect.

"We need to get out of here now!" Lux exclaimed.

"We can't use our Vellatine Point," Elixir said as she hoisted Prince Jaden Knight onto her shoulder. Red square holograms appeared around a large group of unidentified fighters armed with submachine guns, who appeared in front of them. Their black armor gleamed with robotic enhancements.

Major General Vic paused the replay and zoomed in on the red square hologram fighters, rotating them. The details on the screen beside them are displayed as unknown. "There's no affiliation symbol, weapon trace, or identification from their eyes. Our system detects multiple blockers, disabling the Vellatine Point. They've managed to infiltrate the Royal Room with their technology. Whoever they are, they know our system inside out."

"Could they be SKA Rebels?" King Roy inquired.

"There is no trace of their signatures. It seems this assassination is an outside job," Admiral Baylee said.

"Admiral Baylee, we do not make assumptions. This situation runs deeper than what's apparent on the surface," Lieutenant General Bradstone asserted as he resumed the replay.

Elixir grabbed Prince Jaden Knight and carried him to safety behind the bar. Lux quickly followed, while running backward, extending her left arm to activate the Glove of Justice. A holographic blue bow materialized on her glove; its targets locked. The assailants fired their submachine guns, shredding furniture and walls and hitting Lux's body armor. Blood spewed from her mouth. Lux pulled back her right arm and rapidly fired five yellow arrows, each hitting its mark with a perfect bullseye at the head of each assailant. The arrowheads detonated, causing the explosion to blow out the windows of the Royal room into the nightclub. Two circular platforms collided with each other amidst flames wrapping around the top of the water sphere. Young partygoers screamed and fled for their lives!

The unidentified fighters rushed into position, firing relentlessly. Lux leaped behind the bar as bullets peppered the stone wall.

"You're badly hurt!" Elixir said.

"It'll get worse if we don't leave right now!" Lux replied.

Half the bar was blown apart, revealing Elixir and Prince Jaden Knight. Lux threw herself in front of Elixir and Prince Jaden Knight, bullets piercing her front armor.

Four grenades landed beside them!

Lux gripped the feathers of her red arrow tightly, shaking uncontrollably. She released it just as a sphere shield closed behind the feathers.

The V.I.P. nightclub building exploded. A green square hologram chased a fireball across Borat Section and crashed through the side wall of Old Rust Bar. It zoomed into the room of Old Rust Bar. The fire sphere shield opened, shrinking into a small white ball that rolled beside Elixir's hand as she stowed it away in her pocket. Quickly, she glanced through her eyepiece at Prince Jaden Knight and Lux. Prince Jaden Knight's health status was okay, but Lux lay unresponsive and in critical condition.

"Leaf! Rain! Are you guys, okay?" Viggo shouted between coughs, the dust swirling around them.

"I think so, brother. It's a good thing Arison was there to stop me from hitting the wall," Leaf said with relief.

"I'm not okay," Arison admitted, collapsing from the wall.

Rain assisted Elixir to her feet. "Are you hurt?"

"Please help me get them out of here! Bring them to Borat Edge; the Totalist soldiers will know what to do!" Elixir urged urgently.

As the dust settled, Viggo squinted and recognized Prince Jaden Knight, "Isn't that the prince?!"

"Please! Now!" Elixir yelled.

Unidentified fighters marched through the broken wall, brandishing their submachine guns. Elixir retrieved her knife from her boot, skillfully stabbing through their robotic armor at the armpits and back of the neck, flawlessly severing critical nerve points to incapacitate them instantly. She engaged them in combat, forcing them out of the room, but more unidentified fighters emerged outside the breached wall.

Viggo, Rain, Leaf, and Arison dragged Prince Jaden Knight and Lux out of the room into the main bar area. The sound of loud submachine guns firing could be heard from the other side of the room.

"We got to save her brother!" Leaf said.

"Do you not hear those gun fires!" Viggo yelled over the noise.

"She's the one who saved us from them!" Rain said.

"What can we do?" Viggo inquired.

"I know!" Leaf shouted, darting back into the room.

"LEAF!" Viggo yelled, and they chased after him.

Leaf rushed into the room. Viggo immediately dove on top of him, shielding him from the flying bullets. Leaf handed Viggo the submachine gun.

"Never do that again! Go back to the other room while we help her!" Viggo yelled, snatching the submachine gun away from Leaf.

Leaf smiled, "Thank you, brother!"

Rain and Arison grabbed the submachine gun.

"Do you guys know how to use it?" Arison inquired; his voice tinged with concern.

"Point and shoot," Rain replied calmly, raising the gun to eye level, firing, and striding out.

"How does she know..." Viggo began, trailing off with uncertainty.

"Go! Go! Go!" Arison interrupted as he fired.

Twelve unidentified fighters lay dead on the ground as they walked out, shooting at the remaining assailants. Elixir managed to stab one of the unidentified fighters, but her body was riddled with bullet holes as another assailant knocked her to the ground and aimed a submachine gun at her. The barrel flared as bullets tore into Elixir's chest armor. Viggo quickly fired at the last assailant, killing him. Rain rushed to Elixir while Arison provided cover from the side.

The replay stopped.

King Roy pulled up the Royal Level One hologram and observed Viggo, Rain, Leaf, and Arison. "Well damn."

Commander Bazyli leaned forward and looked at Rain closely.

Chapter 15
My Way

Major General Vic appeared in the Observation Room, silently watching Prince Jaden Knight. Four Holo Airbots targeted Prince Jaden Knight, their bullets piercing his black metal armor. He gritted his teeth against the pain as they circled back around. Prince Jaden Knight appeared and disappeared across the Battle Room in a flash. He reappeared atop one of the Holo Airbots, smashing his bloody, black-armored fist through its metal casing, ripping it apart before disappearing again just as it crashed into the wall.

Prince Jaden Knight appeared on the side of the wall, sprinted alongside a Holo Airbot, and broke its wing with his hand. He appeared before it, using his legs to spring back and kick it into the Holo Airbot behind it. He landed on the wall, ran briefly, jumped off, rolled on the ground, and walked away.

A massive explosion erupted above him.

Angrily, Prince Jaden Knight looked up at the last incoming Holo Airbot firing at him.

He gripped his black metal fists, pulled his arms back, and gritted his teeth for impact! Multiple bullets ricocheted off his armor, but two struck his right leg, and three pierced his chest. In great pain, Prince Jaden Knight's eyes followed the Holo Airbot as it flew by. He tried to stand firm, but his right leg buckled. Blood poured from his wounds. The Holo Airbot circled back. Prince Jaden Knight gritted his teeth, painfully stood up, and pressed his feet firmly against the ground.

The Holo Airbot flew low to the ground, took aim, and locked onto him, firing rapidly. Dirt exploded into the air as bullets shredded the ground toward him at great speed. The Holo Airbot exploded in front of him. Through the smoke, Prince Jaden Knight stared in astonishment at the back of Major General Vic, who stood before him with his hand crushing the remnants of the Holo Airbot. He had stopped it with his bare hand!

"There is no need to bear such pain. What happened to Elixir and Lux is not your fault," Major General Vic said, tossing the Holo Airbot aside.

"I do not need your help," Prince Jaden Knight replied, his voice strained with pain.

Major General Vic turned, placed his hand over his heart, and bowed. "My sincere apologies, my Prince Jaden Knight. Your safety is our top priority."

Prince Jaden Knight disappeared.

Major General Vic followed and appeared in the Recovery Room.

"Would you like me to summon the medic team here?" Major General Vic asked.

"No."

Major General Vic watched as Prince Jaden Knight activated the nano patch on his wounds. The patch adhered to the injury, emitting hundreds of red lasers that scanned through the damaged tissues and sealed the wounds with precision.

"Your heart is in the right place. If you want positive results, focus your energy in the right direction. Each of us has limited luck until that one unlucky day," Major General Vic said.

Prince Jaden Knight rotated his arm, and the wounds were now healed. "Regardless of luck, I won't let it happen again."

Major General Vic smiled as he watched his black armor repair itself. "That's an amazing armor. How high can the defense be set?"

The black armor disappeared, revealing the bullet holes in the back of Prince Jaden Knight's red vest. "Why are you here?"

"King Roy still strongly believes the Gailstone was behind the assassination attempt, but our investigation is ongoing."

Prince Jaden Knight clutched his fists.

"Ah, I almost forgot. Here's a small token of my support." Major General Vic took a small purple glass ball from his side pocket and handed it to him. "If you ever need a small assist, best of luck, my young Prince."

Major General Vic placed his hand over his heart, bowed, and disappeared.

Prince Jaden Knight lifted the purple glass ball to the light, revealing swirling dark purple gases. He opened the buckle of his golden crown and placed the ball inside. With a smooth motion, he grabbed his rough leather topcoat from the wall hanger, spun it into the air, and effortlessly slid his arms through as he turned and walked out.

❖

"Ladies and Gentlemen, and beings of Ourania World! Welcome to our last Semi-Final! Please select the battleground landscapes you would like," the Hologram Announcer declared.

Three stone pillar statues stood tall: Prince Jaden Knight, Thanatos, and the headless Black Death. Prince Jaden Knight and Thanatos stepped forward to the edge of their pillars while Black Death, covered in a black hood, sat in his stone chair, observing.

"And now, give a big, warm welcome to our Prince Jaden Knight of the Totalist Federation!"

The spectators stomped on the stadium floor and roared with excitement. The ladies screamed, waved frantically, blew kisses, and released thousands of heart-shaped balloons into the sky. Each balloon displayed holograms of themselves winking and kissing.

Prince Jaden Knight looked around the stadium as the heart-shaped balloons ascended passed him. He glanced at Thanatos, who seemed more prominent and stronger than before. Confidence radiated from Thanatos's face and body, standing proudly as the lights glowed behind him.

Prince Jaden Knight turned and looked at the Royal Chamber, put his hand over his heart, and bowed.

This battle meant everything to both of them.

Prince Jaden Knight appeared at the battleground, making a bold and confident entrance. He stabbed the Totalist Federation flagpole into the ground, dust swirling around him. He stood stylishly, his topcoat billowing in the wind. The red flag, with a white circular background and a golden royal crown in the middle, waved proudly above him. His demeanor and the flag's imagery created a powerful scene of determination and pride.

"Aww!" the young ladies exclaimed, placing their little hands over their hearts.

Other spectators rose to their feet, applauding proudly as the deep drum reverberated loudly throughout the stadium.

Thanatos landed on the battleground and rose slowly, preempting the Hologram Announcer's introduction. His imposing presence silences the stadium as he unfurled his enormous wings. An aura of anticipation and intimidation stirs around the stadium. Whispers and murmurs spread among the spectators, who pointed out the stark difference in size.

"Is my Prince going to be okay against such a monster?" A young lady asked nervously.

"I don't think so," an older man replied.

"He's crazy to fight such a beast! If I were him, I would stay in my golden bed and enjoy eating golden grapes all day with all my beautiful Vellatine servants!" another old man added.

His old lady laughed, "Thank goodness you're not him. He's doing it for us! For the Totalist Federation!"

Other onlookers also express similar disbelief and concern, suggesting they prefer a life of luxury and ease rather than engaging in such a perilous battle. The contrast between the danger Prince Jaden Knight faces and the comfort they imagine highlights the stakes and the bravery required for him to confront such a formidable opponent.

The Hologram Announcer appeared above them, "Give a big round of applause to the powerful Thanatos from Sleeping Tear of Gailstone!"

Few spectators clapped while roses, flowers, and panties were tossed into the battleground around Prince Jaden Knight.

"The battleground landscape is now locked in. Now rise, the Grandeur of Hope Tree!"

A powerful tremor shook the arena as a frenzy of fissures raced around the battleground's outer edge. The ground quaked violently, freeing the massive circular platform to float upward into the sky and slowly hover above the clouds. Lush green grass sprouted in waves across the sandy landscape. At the heart of the battleground, a single red sprout emerged and grew into a towering dark red tree. It grew taller and taller until it soared at a magnificent height. Its canopy unfurled, shading the battleground beneath with dark crimson branches adorned in delicate pink cherry blossoms. They swayed gently in the wind while some drifted down and scattered onto the newly grown grass around them. Prince Jaden Knight plucked a pink cherry blossom from the air and held it delicately between his fingers, studying it.

A smile crossed Thanatos's face as he soared swiftly above the canopy, taking in the breathtaking sight. The dark-red branches were heavily laden with pink cherry blossoms while white clouds rolled gracefully beneath the floating arena. Warm sunlight kisses his face, and the cool wind brings solace to his soul.

Closing his eyes, Thanatos found peace within himself.

The surreal and serene presence of the mighty Grandeur of Hope Tree took them aside. It added a mystical and symbolic element to the setting, creating a visually striking backdrop. The tranquil yet charged atmosphere juxtaposed the impending battle between them.

Prince Jaden Knight appeared at the top of the canopy, scanning the surroundings until he spotted Thanatos hovering in the air.

Now they stood face to face.

"Without further ado, let's get it on!" the Hologram Announcer bellowed.

No words were exchanged; only their intense gazes spoke volumes. Prince Jaden Knight furrowed his brow, locking eyes fiercely with Thanatos.

He swept the sides of his rough leather topcoat up to his hips, the garment snapped into place. His coarse leather topcoat billowed wildly in the wind, and a golden crown buckle gleamed on his thick black magnetic belt. His arms swung past his hips, snapping forward as black metal armor materialized around them, each arm locking into position with a revolver in each hand.

Aimed.

Fired.

Bullets exploded against Thanatos's chest and left wing.

Thanatos pushed back from the impact, eyes fixed on the damage to his wing and torso. His stone armor slowly regenerated over the wounded areas as he thought, *Slow.*

Thanatos folded his wings and dove downward. Prince Jaden Knight vanished and reappeared on different branches, pursuing Thanatos relentlessly and firing his revolvers. Each bullet shattered the stone armor on Thanatos's back. Despite spinning and maneuvering through tight branches, Thanatos couldn't shake Prince Jaden Knight, who continued to hit him with precision shots.

Thanatos grabbed a large branch before him, snapped it off mid-flight, spun around, and hurled it at Prince Jaden Knight, but before he could, it exploded into fragments, knocking Thanatos down faster. Prince Jaden Knight flew through the explosion, reappeared on Thanatos's chest, and unloaded all his rounds into his chest.

Thanatos's chest muscles were exposed as his back broke through the branches, creating a funnel of pink cherry blossoms swirling around them. He spun his revolvers sideways in his hands, gripped the handles, popped the cylinders open, and ejected the spent cartridges as new bullets appeared. He slammed the metal cylinders against each other, creating a quick clicking as they spun back and locked into place. He took aim and fired at Thanatos.

Thanatos crashed into the ground, creating a small crater. Bullets rained down, exploding on his wings and forcing him down. There were bullet wounds all over him, and his stone armor was gone. Prince Jaden Knight appeared behind him. Blood spewed out of Thanatos's mouth as he struggled to rise, black palm prints visible on his arms and chest. It reddened and bled out. Despite his efforts, he fell to his knee, and his right fist pushed against the dirt. Blood was running down his arms—a revolver barrel pressed against his temple.

Prince Jaden Knight cocked the hammer and coldly said, "Die."

Thanatos's head exploded, and his body collapsed to the ground.

The smoke wisped from Prince Jaden Knight's revolver barrel as he spun them slowly back into his side holsters, and the holsters disappeared on his golden crown black metal belt.

Spectators, amazed by the speed of Prince Jaden Knight's victory, rose to their feet and cheered wildly!

Thanatos's skull regenerated, flesh covered his head, and the stone slowly reformed over his body. Blackened palm prints marred his wings and torso where the stone hadn't yet recovered. The spectators fell silent as Thanatos stood, towering over Prince Jaden Knight, cracking his neck and gazing down.

"Never lost," Thanatos said in a deep voice.

"Is that so?" Prince Jaden Knight replied.

Their fists collided with tremendous force. The stone around Thanatos's fist shattered halfway up his arm and didn't regenerate. Thanatos lifted his right hand and stared at it, puzzled.

It had turned black.

Black Death stood, looked at Thanatos's hologram in the battleground, and thought, *to last this long.*

Prince Jaden Knight's anger intensified at the memory of Elixir and Lux. "You done?"

Thanatos looked at him, took a deep breath, gripped his right fist, and pounded his chest, "Come."

The stone on his chest crumbled.

Prince Jaden Knight snapped his left finger, catching his attention. Instantly, he appeared in midair, his right fist aimed at Thanatos's face, shattering his left stone cheek. Thanatos's right knee buckled, and he collapsed to the ground. Prince Jaden Knight delivered another punch to his bloody face, then reared back his right fist and struck with all his might. The shockwave from the punch blew away the stone fragments, sending him crashing to the ground.

Thanatos writhed in agony, his face blackened and cracked, fissures spreading down his body. His eyes stared at the sky as he lay motionless on the ground. Pink cherry blossoms fell from the branches and fluttered past him as the pain slowly ebbed away.

His heartbeat stopped.

Thanatos's chest jolted upward, light bursting through his lifeless form, which disintegrated before the spectators' awe-struck eyes.

A strong wind swirled around Prince Jaden Knight, tousling his blond hair and flapping his topcoat wildly. His eyes closed, he tilted his head toward the sky, savoring the cool breeze. The last pink cherry blossom fell from the Grandeur of Hope Tree, and as the wind subsided, it gently settled on the ground. The battleground was now blanketed in pink cherry blossoms, casting a pink glow.

Prince Jaden Knight felt a warm energy enveloping him. He looked around the ground as each cherry blossom lit up gracefully and withered into the air, dissipating the pink glow until the warm energy faded.

Quiet and still.

Prince Jaden Knight's head smashed into the tree!

His vision blurred with pain.

A giant claw seized his neck tightly, propelling him upward against the rough bark. He crashed through branches at breakneck speed, the tree bark tearing his topcoat and scraping against his black armor. Sparks ignited, flames racing up his now-burning topcoat as he ascended toward the tree's apex. His topcoat burnt off as the wind blew against his bloody face. He blinked against the sunlight, and Thanatos's face loomed into focus, blocking the light.

"How..." Prince Jaden Knight choked, blood spewing from his mouth. His left claw tightened around his throat as they hovered high above the Grandeur of Hope Tree.

Thanatos inhaled deeply, his stone armor chest expanding. "Don't know. I'm new. 300 younger."

Prince Jaden Knight chuckled weakly, "How many times must I kill you?"

Thanatos laughed as Prince Jaden Knight's blood dripped onto his claw. "Surrender?"

"That's... my... line..." Prince Jaden Knight struggled to say.

Thanatos seized Prince Jaden Knight's left black metal arm and pulled forcefully. The nano metal armor stretched and fractured with a high-pitched sound. Sparks flew as electrical connections strained to hold. Prince Jaden Knight screamed in agony. The black metal armor instantly doubled in size, its power surging tenfold. Prince Jaden Knight slammed his right fist into Thanatos's left arm, freeing his neck from his sharp claw, pushed it away, and swung down to his hip, and his right holster instantly appeared with his revolver. It ejected into his right hand. Two shots rang out point-blank, striking Thanatos in the face and right arm, causing explosions that released Prince Jaden Knight.

He plummeted from the sky, crashing through the burning branches until his back slammed into the green grass below.

He blacked out.

Thanatos's feet landed heavily over Prince Jaden Knight's black metal arms, claws digging into the ground. His wings folded back, and the stone on his face and right arm solidified instantly. Prince Jaden Knight lay motionless, blood seeping from five puncture wounds on his neck.

Thanatos snatched the revolver from Prince Jaden Knight's hand, crushed it into a small metal ball, and cast it away. He clenched his claws and hammered them into Prince Jaden Knight's black armor chest. Each blow dented the armor inward, and he dug his claws into it. Thanatos's muscular arms bulged with strength.

Prince Jaden Knight suddenly awakened, screaming in agonizing pain! Electricity sparked wildly as the black metal armor was forcefully ripped from his chest and tossed aside. Deep claw marks marred Prince Jaden Knight's chest and abs.

The spectators gasped in shock. Many screamed, "No!" and "Boo!"

The young ladies looked away from the brutal scene, tears streaming down their faces.

Thanatos stared at Prince Jaden Knight. "No one saves you. Surrender and live."

Prince Jaden Knight gasped for air, blood bubbles in his throat.

"I will... Avenge them!" he choked out, spitting blood into Thanatos's eyes.

Thanatos stumbled back, blood trickling into his eyes as he tried to wipe it away with his right claw. Prince Jaden Knight reached toward his left hip, his holster appearing as his revolver jumped into his hand. He fired at Thanatos's right claw and left forearm. The explosion from the shots caused Thanatos's right claw to smack against his face while his left arm recoiled.

The spectators erupted in screams of excitement!

Prince Jaden Knight slammed his black metal fist into the ground and rose. Blood streamed from the claw marks on his muscular chest and abs.

"Oo my..." the young ladies fanned themselves, blushing with hidden smiles.

"Avenge?" Thanatos asked, flinging the blood off his claw. His right arm returned to normal, the stone instantly recovering.

"You, Gailstone, have no honor to face me and hired shady weakling to assassinate me! But you hurt my protectors, Elixir and Lux, instead!" Prince Jaden Knight accused.

"We, Gailstone, honor. No us," Thanatos retorted.

"Lying will not free you from your fate!" Prince Jaden Knight warned.

"Surrender... little boy," Thanatos said coolly.

Prince Jaden Knight clenched his right black metal fist, appeared before Thanatos, and locked eyes with him. Thanatos could feel the fury and anger radiating from Prince Jaden Knight's gaze.

"You will die," Thanatos declared as his wings spread outward, shielding the sun.

Prince Jaden Knight stood in his shadow, "Third time's the charm."

A fist came from the side, crushing his right shoulder's black armor, sending him flying across the grass.

How did I not... Prince Jaden Knight thought, more blood leaking from his neck.

"No!" the young ladies screamed.

Prince Jaden Knight's body was hurled into the air and crashed back to the ground, his left black metal armor torn from his arm, leaving deep, bloody gashes.

Everything blurred.

His body thrashed around and smashed into the flaming Grandeur of Hope Tree. Thanatos picked up the revolver and crushed it.

Prince Jaden Knight struggled to focus, dark, winged images crossing his vision. Thanatos raised his right black metal forearm, slammed it against the burning tree, and lifted Prince Jaden Knight off the ground. His golden crown buckle popped open, and a purple glass ball dropped into his bloody left hand.

Prince Jaden Knight screamed as the fire seared his flesh. Thanatos, unmoved by his agony, picked up a wooden stake and rammed it into his black metal palm, shattering the stake into pieces.

"Surrender," Thanatos demanded, breaking a burning branch off and pressing its sharp end against his throat.

Major General Vic watched the holoscreen, murmuring, "Use it."

Prince Jaden Knight felt the purple glass ball in his fingers, "Never!" he shouted, defiance blazing in his eyes.

He stabbed the wooden stake into Prince Jaden Knight's throat.

The spectators gasped, some clutching their necks in horror.

Blood gushed out of his mouth and wounds, his blond hair falling over his eyes as his head dropped forward.

Thanatos coldly pulled the burning branch from Prince Jaden Knight's neck, blood spurting out.

The purple glass ball rolled off his lifeless fingers, cracked as it bounced off the root of the Grandeur of Hope Tree, and rolled under the grasses.

Thanatos stared at the lifeless Prince Jaden Knight, his body still burning. "Honor death," he muttered, tossing the body aside.

His wings popped wide open. He pulled his fist back and roared victoriously!

Thanatos turned around and flew toward the edge of the battleground.

"Booo!"

The sound echoed all around, growing louder.

Dark purple gas crept underneath Prince Jaden Knight's lifeless body. Electricity sparked within the dark purple gas, racing along his body. The electricity surged through his organs, nerves, and wounds, healing the injuries and restarting his heart. The dark purple gases solidified into nano metal pieces, and the electricity connected and attached to his right black metal arm and body.

The spectators erupted in cheers, screaming, "Prince Jaden Knight!"

Thanatos stopped midair, turning to face him.

Prince Jaden Knight stood in a new, dark purple armor from head to toe, glaring back.

A spark flashed, and in an instant, Prince Jaden Knight was above Thanatos in midair, wielding a purple magnum revolver in each hand, both aimed at Thanatos's head. Thanatos knew his sharpshooting skills were unparalleled. He flew at Prince Jaden Knight, grabbing the muzzles and clawing at the revolvers. The guns fired, blasting through Thanatos's palms, causing the battleground below to explode. Giant rocks crashed into the spectators, shattering against the transparent shield, and slid off.

The crowd roared with excitement!

The holes in Thanatos palms sealed quickly, and the stone reformed. His claws crushed the purple magnum revolvers, ripping them apart. However, the revolvers turned into dark purple gas and reformed into brand new purple magnum revolvers in Prince Jaden Knight's hands as his arms swung wide open and aimed at Thanatos's wings.

The eighty-caliber bullets blew off both wings, blasting two large chunks of land into the spectators. Thanatos spun backward from the force, plummeting head-first.

Prince Jaden Knight appeared on Thanatos's back, examining the open wounds where his wings had been. The wounds moved and slowly healed. Electricity crackled around the magnum revolvers, transforming them into a long lightning bolt in his hands.

"This is for Elixir and Lux!" Prince Jaden Knight shouted, stabbing the lightning bolts into each wound, which pieced through his stone chest, he crushed six feet into the ground and creating a small crater.

Prince Jaden Knight walked to the crater's edge, looking down at his fallen foe.

Thanatos roared in agony!

Due to the relentless electric shock and burn, his wounds were unable to heal! Thanatos grabbed the lightning bolts, but they seared and electrocuted his claws. The stone covering his body cracked, crumbling and falling away as his flesh burned from the inside out.

"Surrender or die," Prince Jaden Knight demanded.

Thanatos, on his knees, arms outstretched, bent back, roared defiantly at Prince Jaden Knight.

"Then let this be your burial ground." Prince Jaden Knight replied solemnly.

Black Death stood up, watching intensely as Prince Jaden Knight ascended above the burning Grandeur of Hope Tree. He lifted his left palm overhead, his dark purple armor morphing into purple gas. It swirled around his left arm and coalesced into a massive ball above his palm.

Prince Jaden Knight held a super large purple gas ball aloft, observing Thanatos as flames engulfed his body. Prince Jaden Knight snapped his fingers. A spark lit up his abs and muscular chest. The immense dark purple gas ball ignited into a ball of lightning!

Floating high above the fiery chaos of the Grandeur of Hope Tree, Prince Jaden Knight held the ball of lightning above his left hand.

All the spectators stood up and watched in awe.

He threw the ball of lightning downward toward Thanatos. It struck with devastating force, vaporizing the Grandeur of Hope Tree and triggering a cataclysmic explosion across the battleground. The brilliance of the blast forced everyone to shield their eyes inside the City of Light Stadium.

After several minutes, the blinding light subsided into darkness. The floating land disintegrated into millions of tiny fire sparks, falling gently from the sky and fading before reaching the depths below.

"There!" a spectator shouted, pointing to the center of the deep hole.

The spectators erupted in thunderous applause and wild cheers as Prince Jaden Knight withdrew the lightning bolts from Thanatos, who lay dying on the ground. Prince Jaden Knight glanced upward, where the falling fire sparks illuminated their faces and bodies in a haunting glow.

Thanatos looked up at the fire sparks, his voice heavy with defeat. "You win. Why save?"

"Death is too easy. If the Gailstone is behind the assassination attempt, I will personally take everyone down, with or without the justice system." Prince Jaden Knight replied, his voice firm.

With a swift motion, Prince Jaden Knight drove the lightning bolts into Thanatos's statue and stone pillar, shattering them into fragments.

"Ladies and gentlemen, and beings of Ourania World, I proudly present to you the winner of this semi-final, our Prince Jaden Knight of the Totalist Federation!" the Hologram Announcer bellowed.

The spectators erupted in cheers. The young ladies frantically waved their handkerchiefs in the air with great relief and joys. Black Death was standing by the edge staring down at Prince Jaden Knight. They exchanged glance and Prince Jaden Knight disappeared.

"Tomorrow is the final fight for Ourania World Championship Battle World! Black Death vs. Prince Jaden Knight! Who will be crowned Ourania World Champion?"

The Hologram Announcer's voice echoed through the stadium as the crowd roared with excitement!

❖

Prince Jaden Knight stood shirtless by the glass chambers, gazing at Elixir and Lux. They lay together, lifeless, covered by a white sheet over their body. His hand touched the glass, cold and unyielding, his heart heavy with grief. Clenching his teeth, his broken black metal hand tightened around two bouquets of blue roses. The doctors and nurses stood outside; heads bowed in silence.

The glass of the chambers retracted.

Elixir and Lux's faces were pale but serene, their expressions peaceful in death.

Prince Jaden Knight placed a bouquet of blue roses beside their hands and leaned forward to kiss Elixir's forehead.

Elixir suddenly popped up with her head down, exclaiming, "I'm so sorry, my Prince!"

Startled, Prince Jaden Knight jumped back.

"Elixir! Why did you ruin it? He was about to kiss us!" Lux yelled as she jumped out of the chamber.

Prince Jaden Knight looked at the doctors and nurses, who kept their heads low.

"I told them to play along or else!" Lux declared, flexing her nonexistent biceps and growling at them.

Relief washed over Prince Jaden Knight upon realizing they were alive.

"My Prince, is the ceiling leaking? There's water on your cheek?" Lux asked, leaning toward his face.

He didn't realize his tears had rolled down his cheek and wiped it away, "I was so worried about you two."

"Really?!" Elixir and Lux both exclaimed joyfully.

"See! I told you it was worth it," Lux declared proudly.

Elixir smiled and exited the chamber, "Sorry to made you worry, Prince Jaden Knight."

"Maybe there should be a punishment for playing a joke on your superior. You will not get these beautiful roses," Prince Jaden Knight teased as he grabbed the two bouquets of blue roses and handed them to the nurses.

"Awww! Can we get one at least?" Lux begged with her big green eyes.

Prince Jaden Knight paused and smiled, "Just one."

Elixir and Lux's faces lit up with big smiles as he handed each of them a blue rose.

"We also have to thanks the young kids who saved us," Elixir said.

"What kids?" Lux asked, puzzled.

"They followed my instructions. That's how we're still here," Elixir explained.

"Do you know where they are?" Prince Jaden Knight inquired.

King Roy appeared. "They're at Royal Level One."

"King Roy!"

Everyone in the room held their hands over their hearts and respectfully bowed.

King Roy nodded and approached Elixir and Lux. "You both performed exceptionally well! Beyond the call of duty. I want to thank you personally. Your loyalty to your Prince has been proven. I now appoint you both as his permanent bodyguards."

"Thank you, King Roy!" Elixir and Lux exclaimed with excitement.

"I'd like to meet these kids," Prince Jaden Knight said.

"Certainly, but first, I need to address a few matters. Royal Doctors, I want a comprehensive body analysis of our Prince for any irregularities."

"I am fine, my King," Prince Jaden Knight assured.

"You gave us quite a scare when you were injured. Are you absolutely sure?" King Roy pressed.

"Yes."

"You were fortunate that Major General Vic lent you, his Deus Armor. You should express your gratitude," King Roy suggested.

Prince Jaden Knight nodded solemnly.

"The Deus Armor were a legendary armor, but no one had ever witnessed it in person until now! You looked magnificent in it, my young Prince!" Lux praised enthusiastically.

Prince Jaden Knight ignored her compliment but felt a weird slight tingling left inside him.

"Do you still have the armor, my young Prince?" Lux asked.

"No. I believe it was destroyed during the fight."

"That brings me to my last point. Major General Vic ordered Section

Seven, Weaponry and Research Lab, to create new custom Holo Gears for you. They will be expecting you."

"Maybe it would be wise to do that first before we visit those kids," Elixir suggested, blushing as she glanced at Prince Jaden Knight's muscular chest and abs.

Lux noticed her shyness and poked his chest and abs, "These are dangerous! Maybe he shouldn't stay shirtless..."

Lux couldn't contain her amusement and burst out laughing, "Better cover-up, my young Prince! Otherwise, our doctors and nurses will be overwhelmed in the ER."

Prince Jaden Knight, Elixir, and Lux appeared at Section Seven, Weaponry and Research Lab test center—a large, white, open room. No furniture or plants, just a heavy double door.

It opened.

"Congratulations on winning the semi-final, Prince Jaden Knight! I hope our new gear would greatly assists you in the final." A voice approached.

An older lady said, wearing a white lab coat, approaching with two male assistants. "How rude of me. I am Dr. H., a senior weaponry developer. It's an honor to assist you with your new Holo Gear. They are my assistants. Shall we?"

Dr. H. nodded to her assistant, who did not seem much older than her. He grabbed Prince Jaden Knight's right hand. The assistant's finger popped open to the side, and long wires instinctively connected to his black metal hand. It lit up in sequence, and the black metal armor separated into nano pieces and spun into a black metal ball. Dr. H. grabbed it and handed it to her other assistant, who placed it in a clear container. Prince Jaden Knight lifted his right hand and looked at it. It was bruised, with burn marks.

Elixir walked beside him, placing a red orb near his hand. "This should fix it."

The orb scanned and spun around his hand, healing it.

"Great, please follow us," Dr. H. said.

They walked through three heavy metal doors. Between each small room, they were scanned and sprayed for any contamination. They entered the last room, where four giant, heavily armed Holo Bots stood by the metal doors and scanned them.

"Access granted. Please proceed," one Holo Bot ordered.

They entered the final, empty white room. The walls were pure white, and the high ceiling had a clear protective shield. There were steps leading to an elevated platform.

"Please stand on the circular ground before you, Prince Jaden Knight," Dr. H. ordered.

"You will see three Holo Gears we specifically created for you. The first is our latest nano metal armor," Dr. H. said.

The semi-transparent armor rotated around, scaled to size, and overlaid perfectly on Prince Jaden Knight's body.

"Unlike your previous armor, this one can change into any color, pattern, and shape you like just through your thoughts."

Prince Jaden Knight disappeared.

"And yes, it can even make you invisible," Dr. H. smiled.

Prince Jaden Knight reappeared in a pink suit, and his right arm transformed into a knife, then into a heavy machine gun. It instantly retracted and became his arm again. He scrolled to the next Holo Gear, two matted metal gray revolvers, and they appeared in his hands. He spun them and held them up to his line of sight.

"It was noted that our Prince has a passion for revolvers. We created a lightweight poly metal capable of firing 100-caliber rounds. It's also indestructible, given what had happened to your previous ones," Dr. H. smiled.

Three Holo Airbots appeared above. Prince Jaden Knight appeared on the platform, away from the group. The Airbots flew down, firing at him. The bullets ricocheted off his armor. He spun his right revolver and fired one shot at the incoming Airbots. The first Airbot exploded, and the metal pieces splintered into the other two, causing them to malfunction and crash into Prince Jaden Knight. A big explosion forced the group to take covers. Prince Jaden Knight walked out of the flame in his pink suit, unharmed, and approached the platform's edge.

"There's one more Holo Gear," Dr. H. smiled and nodded to her assistant.

A red Holo Supercar burst through the white wall, equipped with tripled turbo boosters and rocket engine thrusters in the back roaring with blue flames. The supercar swerved left and right at great speed and agility, riding along the wall and passed them multiple times. It leaped off, spinning donuts around the platform and creating fire trails of figure eight behind its flaming wheels. It skidded across toward Prince Jaden Knight and halted in front of him.

Its engines revved quickly and loudly.

Elixir and Lux's hearts dropped, but their faces lit up with big smiles.

The red armor retracted to reveal the bulletproof windows, and the top popped up and slid back, exposing a large, comfortable one-seater inside.

Elixir and Lux sadly said, "Aww!"

"A self-aware Holo Supercar with the toughest armor ever created," Dr. H. Began. "Armed with a 120-caliber machine gun on each side, mini energized nuke pellets underneath, and..."

The red Holo Supercar's tripled-energized turbo booster and rocket engine thrusters merged into one, and red metal wings opened from underneath.

"A private jet. It is waterproof, rustproof, and self-cleaning. It can turn into any color you like. Already programmed to your neural network and ready to go," Dr. H. said.

"No need," Prince Jaden Knight replied.

Confused. Dr. H. looked around and asked, "Is there anything you want us to change or add? Or are you happy with just these two Holo Gears?"

"I only need you to fix my black metal armor and old revolvers," Prince Jaden Knight said.

"If you do not like these, we have hundreds more selections for you to choose from," Dr. H. Said, pressing a button. A large selection of Holo Gears appeared on the white walls.

Elixir and Lux looked in awe at the weapons, armor, and vehicles. Prince Jaden Knight disappeared.

Lux slammed her hand on her forehead and shook her head.

She approached Dr. H. and laughed, "Our young Prince is a bit old-fashioned. He doesn't toss his old things away, even when they're broken. He'd want them fixed. When will they be ready?"

"It will be delivered to Prince Jaden Knight's chamber later today," Dr. H. said, disappointed.

"Great!" Lux smiled.

"Love those Holo Gears, though," Elixir said.

"His next fight will be more dangerous, and his enemy's skills remain unknown. If he doesn't switch to the new..." Dr. H. started.

"He has strong principles that he follows closely," Elixir interrupted.

Elixir and Lux smiled and disappeared.

Prince Jaden Knight appeared in the middle of Royal Level One. Elixir and Lux appeared beside him. Prince Jaden Knight wore a long, white, loose silk shirt with flared cuffs and black leather pants. Leaf bumped into him with food stacked high above his head.

Leaf peeked from the side, "Sorry. I didn't see you."

"What is your name," Prince Jaden Knight asked.

"It's you!" Leaf shouted.

Prince Jaden Knight smiled.

"You're that girl who saved us!" Leaf exclaimed.

Elixir laughed, "Yes, and you're that kid who saved us as well! We want to..."

"Come on! Everyone will be glad to see that you're OK!"

Leaf hurried down the stairs, trying to keep the pile of food on his plate from dropping.

Rain noticed Prince Jaden Knight at the stairs as he walked down. She lowered her silverware, "It... it..."

"The Prince!" Arison shouted.

They stood up in shocked.

Leaf ran to the table and placed his plate down, "Brother, it's that girl!"

"Yeah, and the prince!" Viggo said excitedly.

"What are your names?" Prince Jaden Knight asked as he stood before them.

"I... I... am..." Rain stuttered.

"That's Rain, my future ..." Viggo began, but Rain's hand missed his head as he dodged and jumped to Leaf, "This is Leaf, my little brother, Arison, our great friend, and I am Viggo Van Hunt!"

Prince Jaden Knight looked at Rain with his blue sapphire eyes, "Will you be here to watch tomorrow's fight?"

Rain blushed, unable to meet his intense gaze. "I... I should go... home."

"I understand," Prince Jaden Knight replied.

He knelt on one knee and bowed, "Thank you, Viggo, Rain, Arison, and Leaf, for saving our lives. I am truly thankful for your brave, heroic act."

Everyone gasped.

Viggo helped Prince Jaden Knight up. "It was Leaf who deserved it. He risked his life to return to that room, and lucky for us, it all worked out."

Lux picked up Leaf and kissed him, "Thank you, my little brave warrior!"

"What about us? We were brave, too!" Arison asked, and Viggo nodded in agreement.

Rain shook her head.

Everyone else laughed.

Elixir turned to Prince Jaden Knight and whispered into his ear.

"Unfortunately, my time is always limited. I will pay my debt when the time comes. Thank you," Prince Jaden Knight said.

They disappeared.

"What debt?" Viggo asked.

"You think he means saving him?" Arison wondered.

They looked at each other, unsure, as they returned to their table. Mr. Stinky and the rat were eating happily on the table.

Viggo sat down and looked at his plate of food. "I am very blessed and thankful to have this great meal, to be in this Royal room, and to meet the prince. Maybe being good will get us better rewards than stealing?"

"Having you guys, I feel blessed!" Leaf said with a big smile.

They looked at each other and nodded.

❖

Prince Jaden Knight appeared at the Royal Chamber with his hand over his heart and bowed his head, "My King, you requested?"

"We received confirmation you will not be using any of the new Holo Gears. Why is that my son?"

"My current Holo Gears is all I need."

Lieutenant General Bradstone tapped the black marble table with a steel pen. "Your current Holo Gears are destroyed and would not be efficient enough to battle against Black Death."

"The selected Holo Gears are ten times superior to your current ones and would greatly increase your chances of winning," Admiral Baylee added.

"What I've decided will not change. I am content with my current Holo Gears, which are being remade as we speak," Prince Jaden Knight replied firmly.

"This isn't just a choice you can make lightly. It's not about my pride or your. This is the final of the Lighting of Dreams Battle World. All of Ourania will be watching. If we fail or succeed, every powerful nation will judge us accordingly," Lieutenant General Bradstone's steel pen snapped in his grip.

Major General Vic added solemnly, "This is bigger than just you, King Roy, or Commander Bazyli, my young Prince. It means everything to our Totalist and all the young ones who look up to you. We strongly recommend it."

Prince Jaden Knight looked down at his hands. "Every decision I've made has brought me to this point, and the path I choose is the path I will walk."

"You're walking blindly into the face of death. You only got to where you are because of luck!" Lieutenant General Bradstone said sternly.

"I do not rely on luck. My skills and decisions have brought me…" Prince Jaden Knight began but was coldly interrupted.

"You've been lucky most of your life, born into the role of a Royal Prince. Twice, you rejected the tools we offered, which saved your life, and twice, you nearly lost the battles. Now, you want to risk it all the third time?" Lieutenant General Bradstone scolded while projecting a hologram of Black Death.

"Do you think victory will come easily, or will luck decide your fate? He's a deadly elite assassin, trained to kill even his own. He's studied your fighting style and your Holo Gears. You're handing him an easy victory!" Major General Vic said.

Prince Jaden Knight pondered his words and met their gaze.

"Each of us faces limited luck until that one fateful day. Time mends old wounds and breeds new courage. I place no faith in luck, only in myself! If I am destined to fall, I'll embrace it. If I soar, I'll inspire those who couldn't. But above all, I will do it my way. Thank you, gentlemen, Commander Bazyli and my King."

He turned to Major General Vic, adding sincerely, "Thank you, Major General Vic."

Major General Vic smiled warmly. Prince Jaden Knight bowed, hand over his heart, then vanished.

Lieutenant General Bradstone fumed, "Stubborn! Ungrateful—"

"A boy can only be a true man if he took the path he carved, not a path made by others," Commander Bazyli interjected.

"A foolish boy risking everything! Commander Bazyli, will you condone this?" Lieutenant General Bradstone demanded.

"I endorse the growth of our Totalist," Commander Bazyli replied, glancing at King Roy, who looked down, unsure.

Major General Vic intervened diplomatically, "I believe in the future of our young Totalist. With our guidance, the Federation's future looks promising."

"Yes, but those who stray from our guidance may lead us into dark days, especially those with the power to alter our course," Lieutenant General Bradstone warned.

Chapter 16
The Final

The blue rays streamed into Prince Jaden Knight's expansive bedroom through the skylight, casting a dim, chilly glow over his bed. His Holo Gear arranged on the table neatly nearby. Prince Jaden Knight stood on the balcony, gazing at Zephaniah World and its distant moons; tonight, they seemed farther away. The weight on his shoulders felt heavier than before, doubts creeping in like unwelcome shadows in the loneliness of his room.

He closed his eyes against the cold wind that tousled his silky blond hair, inhaling deeply. When he reopened his deep blue sapphire eyes, they gleamed with renewed determination and focus.

"Ladies, gentlemen, and beings of Ourania World, welcome to the seventh and final day of the Lighting of Dreams Battle World! We, the Totalist, are privileged to represent this era in the ultimate spectacle of combats. It has been a long journey of triumphs and tribulations for each warriors! Let us give a thunderous applause and a warm welcome to our finalists! The glorious victories and heartbreaking defeats! Now, brace yourselves for the final showdown! Black Death of Gai G. verse Prince Jaden Knight of the Totalist Federation!" the Hologram Announcer screamed.

The spectators in the stadium and across Ourania World rose to their feet, cheering and applauding enthusiastically.

Fireworks erupted around the stadium, drums thundered with intensity, and three red Totalist Air Fleet streaked across the sky above.

The stadium resonated with the electric buzz of anticipation and excitement!

"The being who strikes fear and pain into his opponents—the one and only Black Death of Gai G!" the Hologram Announcer's voice boomed across the stadium.

Black Death rose from his stone chair and approached the edge of the pillar. Cheers and waves of excitement rippled through the crowd below. His hooded cloak concealed his face as he looked up toward Royal Level Two. Emperor Razen nodded in acknowledgment.

Black Death threw his right fist downward, vanished, and then reappeared at the base of the battleground, smashing his fist into the ground. He scooped up a handful of sand and rose to his feet, igniting a wave of exhilaration among the spectators.

"Now, let's welcome the youngest finalist, who has inspired millions of aspiring fighters! I give you the charming and deadly Prince Jaden Knight of the Totalist Federation!" the Hologram Announcer's voice rang out enthusiastically.

Prince Jaden Knight stood from his stone chair and appeared at the battleground, facing Black Death. His topcoat billowed in the wind, and his Stetson cast a shadow over his determined eyes. Male spectators cheered while concern etched across the faces of the young ladies in the audience.

Black Death looked on with a disdainful thumbs-down gesture as the sand sifted through his fingers.

Prince Jaden Knight remained steadfast.

"The final battleground landscape has been chosen and locked in! Morbel Dreams!" the Hologram Announcer declared.

In the distance, a towering black mountain emerged from the sand, stretching into the starry night sky, and the sand sunk beneath the black ground. Rolls of colorful rocky coral reefs grew around them and swayed against the air. Prince Jaden Knight extended his hand and touched the anemones, causing them to retract. Black Death looked up and saw trails of rainbow lights marking the passage of a vibrant school of fish. A pair of giant stingrays, each the size of a stadium section, glided above the spectators. A serene pink whale swam by them. Its massive eye observed the unfolding spectacle as it swam peacefully around the black mountain.

High above, a colossal white shark glided slowly.

"The Lighting of Dreams Battle World final will officially begin!"

The spectators screamed and rumbled the City of Light Stadium. They were in awe and excited at the sight.

A dagger flew and stabbed in between Prince Jaden Knight's eyes.

Gasps echoed through the crowd.

Black Death appeared before him, slamming his palm against the dagger handle and driving it through his skull. He fell, and Black Death stood triumphant over him.

Prince Jaden Knight clenched his left fist, sharp pain shooting through his left hand.

He opened his eyes, surrounded by darkness.

The blackness around him shattered, and he plummeted through it.

He woke up and saw Black Death standing at a distance.

Shaken, Prince Jaden Knight staggered back, only to be ensnared by anemones gripped of his left hand. He pulled his left fist, triggering the nano-black metal armor to materialize, slicing through the venomous tentacles and connecting to his arm. He tore free, and his metal armor disappeared, leaving round red spots across his arm.

Black Death appeared before him, his dagger slicing off a piece of blond hair as his head tilted to the right to avoid the sharp dagger. A rope wrapped around Prince Jaden Knight's right hand and yanked it forward, preventing him from reaching for his hip.

Black Death thrust a powerful low-kicked to Prince Jaden Knight's left leg, sending him sprawling. A roundhouse kick followed, slamming into his right temple and his head crashing to the ground.

For a fleeting moment, he blacked out as the dagger narrowly missed his face. His metal armor reappeared, protecting him as he rolled across the rigid black rocks. The dagger spun around by the rope and cut across the armor. Sparks flared as the blade tore the metal apart. He caught a glimpse of the stingrays in the sky and disappeared.

Black Death spun his dagger, scanning the area.

Prince Jaden Knight rolled atop a giant stingray. Sensing fear, the other stingray parted ways. He ran his fingers across his metal armor chest, feeling blood seeping through.

The metal armor repaired the deep slashes, resealing itself.

He hasn't even used his tattoo. How are we so far apart in levels? Prince Jaden Knight pondered, his mind racing.

Black Death lowered his hood, his eyes darting around as he observed the flying fishes above.

Prince Jaden Knight stood up. The last sparks sealed his metal armor together. He placed his right hand near his hip. His revolver appeared and ejected into his grip. Spinning the gun skillfully with his trigger finger, he aimed at Black Death. The bullet whizzed through the air with incredible speed, and Black Death effortlessly dodged it, causing it to shatter against the ground.

The stingray turned and flew towards him.

Prince Jaden Knight walked to the top of the stingray's head, drawing his second revolver and firing. Black Death spun his dagger by the rope, sparks flying as he deftly blocked every bullet.

The giant stingray passed over him.

Prince Jaden Knight popped both revolver chambers open, spun them against each other as it reloaded, and popped them back in. A dagger pierced through the stingray's head, yanked down by a rope. Prince Jaden Knight ran and leaped from the falling stingray tail, hurtling toward Black Death with his right metal fist fully pulled back.

The giant stingray skidded across the rugged black rocks, tearing open its soft underbelly with a tremendous crash that shook the ground and caused a minor quake.

Spectators gripped each other nervously, watching the intense battle unfold.

The ground quaked and fractured as Black Death struggled to regain balance. Prince Jaden Knight descended upon him, their fist colliding with a thunderous shockwave that sent Prince Jaden Knight staggering back and Black Death crashing several feet into the ground. He burst out of the ground, brandished his long black sword, swiped it to his side, and fixed his gaze on Prince Jaden Knight.

"Never bring a knife to a gunfight," Prince Jaden Knight taunted.

"My blade has already done more damage to you and doesn't need to reload," Black Death retorted coolly.

Prince Jaden Knight spun his revolvers in his trigger fingers and unleashed two shots. Black Death deflected the first bullet with his sword and sliced the other in half. A revolver pressed against Black Death's back, but a small dagger blocked its barrel. Another revolver gently touched his right temple with the hammer cocked.

"Now, do you think your knife does more damage than my bullet?" Prince Jaden Knight challenged.

Black Death smirked.

A spark ignited in the revolver barrel, and a bullet surged forth, striking the side of Black Death's temple. Blue ice and blood burst from his right temple, the explosion scorching the side of his head. Black Death disappeared and reappeared behind Prince Jaden Knight's right side, slashing across his back upward.

Prince Jaden Knight disappeared.

The sword pointed at the night sky, blood dripping from its blade. On the back of Black Death's ear was an Ice Beast tattoo. Slowly, its horns and black body receded to his right shoulder.

It was bleeding profusely.

Its paw and head creeped out of Black Death's lower neck, and it walked on top of his right shoulder. A trail of blood was left behind as it stood at the edge of his shoulder and leaped onto the ground, growing larger and larger.

A large chunk of Ice Beast's ribs area was missing and severely damaged, its body half-burnt with a pool of blood forming below. Blue ice rapidly grew over the burnt and wounded areas, Solidifying and halting the bleeding. Ice Beast matched Black Death in height, its glowing blue eyes and drooling green saliva framing its rock-like jaw, razor-sharp blue ice fangs protruding menacingly.

Black Death swiped his sword, and blood flew before Ice Beast. It lowered its head, sniffing the blood and lifted its head to smell the air. It growled and charged toward a section of rocky coral reef with powerful, muscular paws that crushed into the rigid ground, each step shaking and cracking the earth as Black Death vanished.

A long gash ran from Prince Jaden Knight's thigh to his midsection, the split black metal armor sparking as it attempted to repair itself in vain. The bleeding continued unabated. Sensing imminent danger, he leaped backward just as the rocky reef exploded into debris.

Ice Beast emerged through the dust; jaws wide open with razor-blue ice fangs. Prince Jaden Knight flashes side to side as he leaped backward, narrowly avoiding its snapping jaws. Ice Beast turned around and lunged at him as he reappeared. Its outer blue ice fangs shattered against the black metal on his right forearm, but the inner black fangs pierced through, tearing the armor apart as it swung its head forcefully, throwing him through the rocky coral reef. As Ice Beast lunged again, Prince Jaden Knight turned his right shoulder to its mouth, and flames flared into its mouth, engulfing its head in fire. Ice Beast recoiled, shaking violently from the burn.

Blood ran off the tip of his fingers, and sparks and electricity flew around the front and backside of his right arm. It tried to repair itself, but the gash was too large. Ice Beast swung its horns at him. Prince Jaden Knight seized them, pushing with all his strength. Its head turned from side to side, tossing him around, but he held on tenaciously.

Prince Jaden Knight's blood covered his right metal hand and glinted faintly against the Ice Beast's blue ice horn. Despite his efforts to resist, Ice Beast pushed him back relentlessly. Digging his feet into the ground proved futile as he slid backward, his back colliding painfully against the hydrothermal vent reef wall, cauterizing his wounds with searing heat. Agonizing screams escaped him as the hot black smoker vent erupted above.

Struggling against the pain, Prince Jaden Knight's bloody metal hand slipped, and the ice horn punctured his right abdomen, lifting him against the reef. Gritting his teeth, but the pain from the burn and puncture wound was too excruciating. He screamed painfully!

His right hand reached for his hip, his revolver leaping into his hand. Unloading bullets into Ice Beast's head, the blue ice exploded on its head, multiple shots penetrating its skull. Roaring in agony, Ice Beast retaliated, thrusting Prince Jaden Knight through the hydrothermal vent reef wall.

The black smoker erupted with tremendous force, blasting them airborne. Prince Jaden Knight slid off Ice Beast's horn, crashing into the corner of the rocky reef wall before rolling aside. His Stetson fell from the sky.

Prince Jaden Knight lost consciousness.

Ice Beast soared high, but the extreme heat melted its blue ice exterior, causing unbearable burns. Squealing in agony, it was suddenly intercepted by a monstrous white shark. The shark's jaws crushed Ice Beast's midsection and violently shook it from side to side. The shark swiftly tore Ice Beast in half, flew around, and chomped down the two remaining body parts.

Blackness enveloped Prince Jaden Knight.

A sharp pain tore through his right arm.

Distance cries echoed softly.

Another surge of pain seared through his left arm.

Cries growing louder.

With a sudden jolt, Prince Jaden Knight's eyes shot wide open as he screamed in agony. Black Death held his sword upside down, stabbing it into his stomach and pulling it out mercilessly.

"No!" the Spectators cried in despair.

Prince Jaden Knight turned his gaze to his severed arms, blood pouring from his wounds and mouth. Unable to speak, he could only stare up at Black Death standing over him, blood dripping from the sword in his hand while Prince Jaden Knight's revolver rested in his other.

"Death by my sword or your trusty revolver?" Black Death's voice cut through the chaotic scene as he aimed the revolver at Prince Jaden Knight's head.

Prince Jaden Knight stared into the barrel, his body shaking uncontrollably from the overwhelming pain.

Suddenly, the ground beneath them shook violently. The rocky coral reefs exploded all around, sending shockwaves through the stadium. Spectators screamed and clung to each other as the quake rattled them side to side. Continuous loud rumbles echoed from below, followed by a sudden thunderous BOOM!

At that moment, the top of the black mountain erupted upward. Plumes of black and gray shot into the sky, raining large rocks down upon the spectators, shattering on top of the protective shield, and rolling off to the sides.

Screams and cheers filled the stadium.

Black Death blasted the larger rocks with the revolver and deflected the smaller ones with his sword. School fishes darted wildly through the falling debris, some crushed under the massive stones, while others split apart by Black Death's precise strikes.

Large black and gray clouds formed above them, obscuring the starry night sky. Lightning crackled and rolled under the darkened clouds, striking around the black mountain. Molten lava surged through the dark clouds, cascading down like rivers of fire!

Turning his attention to the spectacle, Black Death watched the orange and red glow atop the black mountain.

"A beautiful sight of birth and death." He remarked with a chilling calm.

Black Death smirked as the volcanic rocks crashed beside them. He turned to Prince Jaden Knight. "Crushed by volcanic rocks or slow, painful death by molten lava?" Black Death let out a menacing laughter.

Beneath Prince Jaden Knight laid his pool of blood sparkling. Black Death stared at it.

The ground cracked open around them, and two massive statues shot through the dark clouds with them upon it.

Black Death surveyed around.

Molten lava glowed in the distance above the clouds, with red sprite lightning cracking upward into the outer atmosphere. Black Death walked to the edge and peered down at Lord Burrus's statue. Across from him stood Morbel's statue, facing each other with their right hands pressed against the rotating hologram of Ourania World.

"Morbel," Black Death smirked, raising his arms. A menacing laugh grew louder and louder against the wind. "Witness your new Ourania World Champion!"

Static noise and electric pops crackled behind him as he lowered his arms. It grew louder and louder. Red sprite lightning cracked nearby and shot up into the outer atmosphere. He turned around; Prince Jaden Knight stood before him, arms intact, clad in a new mixture of black and purple armor.

"How?" Black Death screamed angrily.

Black metal fingers gripped Black Death's cheeks and lifted him, cracking his cheekbone into multiple compound fractures.

Gritting his teeth from the pain, Black Death fired rounds into Prince Jaden Knight's chest. The fragments exploded and ricocheted, piercing into Black Death's chest, neck, face, and burning his body. There was no damage to Prince Jaden Knight's black and purple metal armor.

Black Death lunged his sword at Prince Jaden Knight, but his whole body was swung to the side at great speed like a rag doll and hurled into the nose of Morbel's statue, causing it to crumble and collapse. Bullets rained into Morbel's head as it exploded. Black Death's body fell through the debris and into the dark clouds below. The purple revolvers morphed into a swirling purple mist that integrated with Prince Jaden Knight's black metal armor.

A dagger pierced the left eye of Lord Burrum's statue, followed by a swinging rope that catapulted Black Death up behind Prince Jaden Knight. He aimed his revolver at Prince Jaden Knight's head and pulled the trigger.

Clicked. Clicked. Clicked.

Black Death tossed the useless revolver into the air and split it in half.

They both vanished, and random sparks of metal flickered in their wake.

Faster and faster.

Prince Jaden Knight deflected sword strikes with his metal arms and retaliated with a barrage of shots. Lord Burrum's statue's head exploded under the intense battle. Black Death leaped, vanished, reappeared on falling rocks, and zipped at Prince Jaden Knight with his sword. He vanished again before a bullet could hit him, causing a nearby rock to explode. Utilizing his rope, Black Death leaped from one exploding rock to another.

Prince Jaden Knight landed on Morbel's statue's right hand, and Black Death landed on Lord Burrum's right hand. The Hologram Ourania World rotated between them as they squared off.

"Summon your other two." Prince Jaden Knight demanded.

"For a mere boy?" Black Death scoffed.

"Then die." Prince Jaden Knight said coldly.

Black Death spun his dagger, drawing it across his chest. "I will show you the difference between our levels."

The bloody dagger flew through the rotating Ourania World's hologram as red sprite lightning struck upward behind Prince Jaden Knight. The area lit up in a bright red flash before plunging into darkness, leaving a long crisscross sparks slash from Prince Jaden Knight's shoulders to his hips as Black Death stood before him with his long sword.

Black Death seized his incoming dagger, twisted his wrist, and sliced into his black and purple metal abs. He stabbed Prince Jaden Knight's right chest, but the dagger pierced through the metal palm and into his chest. As Prince Jaden Knight blocked, Black Death launched a midair spin kick into his head. Prince Jaden Knight spun off Morbel's arm.

The rope sawed against the stone, whipping around as it was pulled down. Red sprite lightning surged through Prince Jaden Knight's body, arcing into the upper atmosphere.

Black Death leaped after him, grabbing his rope.

Prince Jaden Knight's back slammed against the top of the pink whale. Black Death landed on its side, struggling to hold on, and stabbed his sword into its flesh to steady himself. He gazed below; the ground was consumed by an ocean of lava, with only a few large rocks remaining.

The pink whale let out an deep agony muffled, echoing loudly, tilting to its right side from the pain, forcing Prince Jaden Knight to slide toward Black Death. He pulled the dagger out from his palm, plunged it into the pink whale's side, his body spun around, and stood on the dagger. Black Death rushed toward Prince Jaden Knight, his sword ripping the flesh like butter.

It cried echoed in agony.

Leaning against the pink whale, Prince Jaden Knight extended his arms, summoning his purple revolvers from their holsters. Bullets ripped through the air and split into two as the blade sliced them in half.

The revolvers transformed into two bolts of red lightning, clashing fiercely with Black Death's sword. Electrical sparks exploded around the long sword as they rapidly struck against each other. The pink whale slumped to the side, blood pouring out. Its head crashed into the side of the black volcano, spewing lava onto its body.

Prince Jaden Knight and Black Death appeared on the black rock below.

Black Death spun his rope around his right forearm, and his dagger flew around and snapped into his hand. The lava-covered pink whale soared overhead, diving into the ocean of molten lava.

Tsunami waves of lava crashed over the stadium seating, splashing high up to the Royal Levels. Spectators screamed with excitement as the lava wave rolled off the protective shields.

Prince Jaden Knight appeared before Black Death, a faint trace of lightning trailing behind him. He raised his right hand with the lightning bolt and struck against Black Death's sword. Thunder roared from above, and a flash of lightning from the dark clouds instantly struck down into his lightning bolt with blinding intensity. A white light exploded! Hurling Black Death to the edge of the black rock, his whole body seared with fourth-degree burns as he lay there. The light subsided, revealing the purple flame flaring up on Prince Jaden Knight's shoulders as he levitated above.

"Behold! Your Death God!" Prince Jaden Knight declared as he hovered above him.

Black Death met Prince Jaden Knight's fiery gaze defiantly. "You're no god! You're... just a mere boy with toys!"

Electricity crackled around Prince Jaden Knight's right hand, and a lightning bolt formed in his hand, "Let's see how this 'toy' feels."

A rolling thunder echoed above.

Prince Jaden Knight descended upon Black Death, the lightning bolt sizzling through his burnt right chest and into the ground. Black Death screamed in agony, his hands burning as he gripped the electrified bolt.

Electricity sparked once more around Prince Jaden Knight's right hand, another lightning bolt materializing. He lowered it menacingly towards Black Death's heart. "Surrender or face death."

"Looking at you," Black Death sneered defiantly.

Prince Jaden Knight raised the lightning bolt and launched it into his chest. A lightning flashed down from the sky, striking the lightning bolt itself!

The explosion blew Prince Jaden Knight several feet back. Black particles fell to the ground like snow and a black body outline was incinerated into the ground.

Nothing remained.

Prince Jaden Knight suddenly clutch his hand against his chest. He began coughing and gasping for air.

"By now, you are fully incapacitated. The black particles in your blood stream is consuming every precious oxygen you have. Depriving your organs of it, leading them to fail and to your death. My Dark King, your sacrifice is not in vein. Now victory is within my grasp." Black Death laughed menacing as he stared at the body outline on the ground and Prince Jaden Knight could only starred in frustration.

A dagger stabbed through Prince Jaden Knight's left knee. Black smoke swirled around him as Black Death materialized within it and appeared behind him. He twisted Prince Jaden Knight's right purple flaming arm and made three quick succession stabbed up his shoulder. Leaving the dagger lodged between the shoulder joint with his arm up. Black Death vanished into a cloud of black smoke and he reappeared in front of him. His sword appeared out of the black smoke and sliced through Prince Jaden Knight's left arm; following in one continuous fluid motion, he stabbed into his abdomen. The sword shattered halfway against the resilient black and purple armor. Black Death screamed with anger and slammed his palm against the hilt of his sword, thrusting it through and slicing across his stomach.

Prince Jaden Knight staggered, Black Death fully emerged from the black smoke and faced him, pulling his dagger out of Prince Jaden Knight's shoulder and plunging it into the side of his neck. The flames surrounding Prince Jaden Knight flickered and died as he collapsed onto the ground.

The spectator held their breath in shock.

The black smoke formed into an old woman with wings.

"Be proud boy. You forced me to summoned my Dark King and Wings of Misery." Black Death said.

Prince Jaden Knight's statue and pillar crumbled.

"Ladies, Gentlemen, and Beings of Ourania World, I present our Lighting of Dream Battle World Champion, Black Death!" the Hologram Announcer proclaimed.

Fireworks burst into the sky, accompanied by a tumultuous mix of cheers and boos echoing throughout the stadium. Black Death glanced around as the boos gradually drowned out the cheers. His eyes bore into Prince Jaden Knight, who looked back at him in pain.

"I am Death God!" Black Death shouted with intense anger!

"I will show you what is worse than death!" Black Death spun his broken half sword, driving it into Prince Jaden Knight's spine and splitting it down his back.

The spectators screamed in horror, and the young ladies turned away, tears streaming down their faces.

Six Royal Justices appeared around Prince Jaden Knight. Three swiftly intercepted and blocked Black Death's sword from moving any farther with their blades and axes. Two Royal Justices shattered the broken blade, while the last Royal Justice removed it from Prince Jaden Knight's spine.

Black Death struggled to breathe, thrashing as he slammed his fists against Admiral Baylee's white glove hand, which gripped tightly around his windpipe.

Admiral Baylee effortlessly hoisted him high off the ground with his right hand. "Wrong move," he stated calmly.

His white-gloved hand glowed with power, and he discharged a blast that sent Black Death hurtling across the lava and crashing into a large black rock.

Struggling to stand, Black Death emerged, his skin and hair burned away, revealing only his bloody red skull. He glared at Admiral Baylee with intense rage.

"Maybe we can play again," Admiral Baylee smirked, snapping his fingers. In an instant, they all vanished, along with Prince Jaden Knight.

Chapter 17
A Deep Wound

An uncomfortable silence swept over the crowd. Black Death clenched his fists with intense anger. In the distance, the volcano spewed molten lava high into the clouds. Drums began to beat, and trumpets soon joined in, heralding the triumphant celebration of the Ourania World Champion.

The statues of Morbel and Lord Burrum crumbled into the ocean of lava, creating mesmerizing swirls and curves that splashed upward. The molten rock surged into the air, instantly solidifying into a massive platform. As the stones broke apart, they revealed a large, circular diamond surface above the lava, forming a majestic new foundation.

The lava surged, cooled, and solidified before Black Death, creating steps leading to the circular diamond platform. A beam of sunlight pierced through the dark gray clouds, shimmering them apart like the grand theater curtains.

Black Death ascended to the top.

Sunlight bathed the smooth, sparkling diamond, casting a rainbow of colors beneath the red swirls and curved foundation. Black Death stopped at the center, gazing at the eleven towering jade bronze statues of the Ourania World Champions. At the center stood a statue of Black Death, arms stretched high into the sky, with the golden bronze Ourania World rotating slowly above it. Black Death took a deep breath, feeling a surge of pride.

Four golden Totalist air fleets appeared above, descending vertically and landed before him. Each air fleets lowered its platform to the ground, revealing the four great leaders. Behind each of them were two highest-ranking officers, six Royal Protectors, and four Royal Guards carrying a golden chest, their presence exuding grandeur and authority.

Ruler Belvedere of The Majestic Royal emerged, accompanied by Sir

Knight Monti Targo and Lady Crimson, his most trusted guards. Sir Knight Monti Targo, clad in three-inch-thick battle armor, wielded a long sword as tall as him and carried a towering wall shield. He's the most powerful knight in Justice. Lady Crimson, wearing a helm adorned with red wings, had a beauty as sharp as the blood-red Raven sword at her side. Her crimson-red peacock armor dress trailed elegantly behind her.

King Prime of Gailstone was flanked by Battle Lord Baraskor and the Great Galar, both ancient beings whose profound wisdom and vast power enabled their young king with unwavering loyalty. Battle Lord Baraskor, a towering giant marked by countless battle scares, had proved his worthiness through endless wars. The Great Galar, the most decorated fighter among all Gargoyles, boasted 5,000 victories and only one defeat. He had vowed to follow the true king who could best him in battle and possessed a kind heart. King Prime earned his allegiance by defeating him in a one-on-one combat.

Emperor Razen of Ukko Nations stepped off the platform, followed by General Dakkor and General Kimor. These generals controlled the vast underground networks that kept Ourania World running smoothly, handling everything from assassinations and takeovers to smuggling high-end items and personnel. General Dakkor, clad in an all-white ninja outfit, ruled the Koi Ka Chi region and led the White Ninja. In stark contrast, General Kimor, dressed in black, was as wise as old wine and as lethal. He commanded the Zino region and led the Assassination Ninja.

Lastly, Commander Bazyli of The Totalist Federation stepped forward, accompanied by Lieutenant General Bradstone and Major General Vic.

The four great leaders stood before Black Death, their presence commanding respect and attention.

Black Death dropped to one knee and bowed his red skull.

"Ladies, gentlemen, and beings of Ourania World, please stand and give a big round of applause to our great leaders for making Lighting of Dreams a reality and ensuring the success of Battle World!" the Hologram Announcer proclaimed.

The spectators erupted into wild applause and cheers at the rare sight of all the leaders gathered together.

"Black Death, rise, for you have earned your place among the greats.

Your incredible skills, abilities, and hard-earned victories have led you to this outcome. Continue to hone your talents and provide exceptional services to your nation!" Ruler Belvedere proclaimed.

He unbuckled his white scabbard from his side. Its surface was adorned with gems, and the Majestic Royal symbol of an axe and sword clashed near the red jasper handle. Ruler Belvedere grasped the handle, drew forth the blackest blade of the Majestic Royal Steel, and raised it high. The sword absorbed the sunlight into its abyss, consuming its energy, a masterful creation of a weapon and unparalleled beauty.

"I present this sword, fit only for the mightiest of all! Red Justice!"

Black Death's eyes widened at the sight of such insidious beauty.

Ruler Belvedere carefully sheathed Red Justice in its white, gem-encrusted scabbard. A Royal Protector stepped forward and reverently handed it to Black Death.

He accepted the offer, bowing his head in appreciation. As he gripped the top of the white scabbard and slid his hand down its length, it gradually transformed into a deep, inky black, and the rich-colored gems gleamed in their perfect fitted sockets.

"I expected nothing less of you," Emperor Razen stated, holding an old paper ball in his palm and crushing it. Dust clouds billowed from his hand, revealing an old ancient scroll. Black Death knelt before the Emperor, accepting the ancient scroll with its red wax seal.

"Ancient. Learn it with great caution," Emperor Razen said.

Black Death bowed his head in acknowledgment.

King Prime clapped his claws. The Royal Guards from each leader brought forth large chests and placed them before Black Death. They opened the chests, each filled to the top with gold bricks.

"Each treasure is from the partaking nations. I congratulate you," King Prime said. He spread his white wings and raised his right hand to the sky, which shimmered. "I reward you, Black Pearl of Wings."

A shimmer appeared on Black Death's shoulder blade as black wings grew and expanded outward. Black Death flapped his Black Pearl of Wings, rose into the air, and let out a loud, menacing laugh.

"Each reward is of the highest value, and I shall give no less. I'll give you Nightmare!" Commander Bazyli said.

A black jet materialized beside Black Death.

"It's the only jet ever produced. It is fully loaded with our latest weapons and has a neuro connection that instantly obeys your every command. Give it a try," Major General Vic added.

Black Death flew high into the sky, around the black volcano, and passed the exploding lava. Nightmare followed closely behind at every turn, dive, and ascent into the outer atmosphere. Black Death stopped, flapped his wings, and turned to look at Nightmare as it hovered in perfect stillness before him. Black Death's wings disappeared, and he fell rapidly from the atmosphere. Nightmare dived down, opened its cockpit, swooped him in, and closed it.

Nightmare spun through the sky like a bullet, leaving multiple sonic booms behind! It flew into the exploding lava, followed it into the sky, and shot out at the top. Nightmare looped around, locked onto the black volcano, launched a missile, and flew past it. The volcano exploded into millions of pieces and flattened into a plain.

Nightmare opened its cockpit, Black Death leaped out and dived toward the platform. He disappeared and reappeared at its center.

Black Death looked up at large volcanic rocks showering toward them.

He placed his hand over the red jasper handle and smirked.

He disappeared, zipped across the sky, and reappeared before the leaders as his Black Pearl of Wings popped wide open and slowly folded. Red Justice clicked securely back into its scabbard. Fine black powder fell over them, and Nightmare flew by and blew it all away.

"Ladies, gentlemen, and beings of Ourania World, give a big welcome to your new century Ourania World Champion, Black Death!" the Hologram Announcer exclaimed.

The spectators cheered in amazement!

"As Lighting of Dreams comes to a close, it is a reminder to open your mind and chase after your dreams. It's a long, horrendous path with many failures, but keep hammering your iron will and resharpen your focus along each step. Maybe someday you might reach the front step of victory like the few who stood before you. Even if you don't get there like many, when you look back on the day you started your journey, you will be a different and better being. You will have grown, wisened from failures, and become much stronger! Maybe we will see you in the next century!

Light your dreams!" the Hologram Announcer exclaimed.

The Lighting of Dreams had come to an end. The City of Lights Stadium stood empty, and Vellatine City finally quieted down after its big night of celebration. Hell Raptors circled above, maintaining peace and order. A few flew by Princess Kayla's tower.

Blue rays illuminated Princess Kayla's bedroom, casting a glow on her untouched bed. On the balcony, she gazed at the night sky with its moons and stars. The dreamy view usually brought her peace, but tonight, her heart was heavy with sadness, and her mind unsettled. She knelt, lowered her head, and clasped her hands tightly, praying to the glorious world of Zephaniah and its two moons. Tears rolled down her cheeks, and she softly whispered, "Great god of Zephaniah and your two sons of war and peace. I have never prayed to any beings or gods, but here I am, begging you to save my brother's life. If you can help him through this critical time, I will leave my world of royalty and serve truth and love as long as I live."

Blue rays glittered on Princess Kayla as she gazed at the majestic Zephaniah World, which dominated half of the night sky. A shooting star beamed across the faint blue glow on the horizon, heralding the early morning rise.

"Poor Princess Kayla, I don't know how she could keep her eyes open." Ira yawned.

Leila and Ira stood below Princess Kayla's balcony in the Royal Garden.

Ira glanced at Lyndon, who lay under the tree with his eyes closed. "I could snooze on this grass right now. Is there any update on Prince Jaden Knight?"

"With the damage he sustained, I'd be surprised if he survived," Lyndon said, eyes still closed.

"We have the best of the best attending to Prince Jaden Knight," Leila said.

Ira sat down on the grass, resting her chin on her knees, and sighed sadly. "I hope he's OK."

The Vellatine Medic Emergency Center was heavily guarded. Elixir and Lux stood watch at the front entrance of the operating room. Above, King Roy and Queen Glory held each other closely, watching anxiously. Admiral Baylee, Major General Vic, and Dr. Waski, the head doctor, stood nearby.

"How is he doing, Dr. Waski?" Queen Glory asked.

"At this stage, I honestly don't know, my Queen, but we do detect his faint fighting spirit," Dr. Waski replied.

"Our son will recover in no time, my Queen," King Roy reassured her.

"The extensive injuries sustained throughout his entire body mean this operation will take about two months to complete," Dr. Waski explained.

King Roy turned to Dr. Waski, "You're telling me my boy won't be fine by tomorrow?"

Dr. Waski looked to Major General Vic and Admiral Baylee for assistance, but they remained silent. "My King, we will do our best to help Prince Jaden Knight. However, time is needed."

"I want him back on his feet and well!" King Roy demanded.

Dr. Waski took a deep breath and lowered his head, "Given the way the spinal cord is split in the middle and down to his lower back, Prince Jaden Knight would be paralyzed from the neck down."

Queen Glory was in shock. Tears quickly streamed down her face. She looks at King Roy for any kind of hope.

Her tears ignited King Roy's anger, and he shouted, "If you value your life, that word will cease to mentioned again! I want to see my boy, your future King, walk again in one week!"

"My King Roy, unfortunately, we do not perform miracles, but we will do everything in our power to help Prince Jaden Knight undergo the best rehabilitation. It will all depend on his body and the circumstances then."

"If you and your doctors cannot heal my boy, I will have all your heads!" King Roy shouted angrily.

Major General Vic intervened, "My King Roy, we have the best doctors in Ourania, and Dr. Waski is our head of Vellatine Medic Center. I believe he will do his best to give you a good outcome. There should be no fear, my Queen. Let the good doctor do what he does best."

"In one week, Dr. Waski," King Roy insisted, turning to Queen Glory and wiping her tears away. "Our boy is strong, and we shall be, too. His stubbornness will not allow him to just lie there. Everything will return to normal; I, King Roy, promise you, my Queen."

Queen Glory tried to smile and nodded.

King Roy's face grew serious as he turned to Major General Vic, "See to it that Black Death pays with his life for this!"

"My King, the tournament has no rules. Even death is permitted," Major General Vic said.

"True, the tournament had no rules during battle. But it was over, and the winner was announced. Yet, Black Death chose to harm our Prince when he was down and defeated for his evil pleasure. That act itself warrants death, my King Roy," Admiral Baylee said.

"Agreed!" King Roy shouted.

"But it could wage an unnecessary war between two great ally nations. Please reconsider, my King," Major General Vic bowed his head.

"Do you not agree with Admiral Baylee's observation?" King Roy asked.

"What was done was uncalled for, but please take my word for it, King Roy. If there is an opportunity, I will personally give him the same treatment," Major General Vic said.

King Roy looked at him and said, "Very well, Major General Vic. I will be waiting patiently till that day."

❖

Viggo frantically pushed his arms through the dense water, desperately trying to escape the dark abyss below. He forcefully reached as high as he could and pushed his arms down with all his might. Yet he could not reach the surface. Air bubbles escaping his panicked face as he slowly drowned.

Viggo screamed! His eyes opened facing a park. His family was having a picnic along the Avedon River. He saw his parents laughing and romantically teasing each other. His mom looked as beautiful as he remembered, and his dad, young and handsome, had just been promoted to Captain of the Totalist Navy. It was a happy time, celebrated on this beautiful day. The picnic blanket was covered with fruits, bread, home-cooked meals, sweet wines, and strawberry chocolate drinks.

It was his and his older brother Ben's favorite drink.

"Viggo!" Ben shouted as he ran into baby Viggo, who stood there motionless.

Ben, five years old and a year older than baby Viggo, was slightly taller. He had chubby cheeks, large brown eyes, and light blond hair like their mother's. He had his father's white captain hat on his little head.

The two boys wrestled on the ground. Viggo watched his younger self grab the captain hat, put it on, and run.

"That's my hat! Daddy gave it to me!" Ben shouted, getting up and chasing after baby Viggo along the riverbank.

Baby Viggo panicked and giggled as he ran, half his face was covered by the captain hat, anchored down by his little hands.

Viggo ran after them as fast as he could but couldn't catch up. No matter how hard he tried, they were always out of reach. He stumbled over a root and fell on his face. Familiar laughter and an angry voice echoed from the distance. Viggo opened his eyes, tears streaming down uncontrollably, and saw them by the water. Baby Viggo had fallen, and the hat floated on the river's edge.

Viggo screamed, "NO!"

The sound did not escape his mouth.

Viggo got up and ran toward the two little silhouettes by the river. He could hear his younger self crying.

"Daddy is going to be mad!" Baby Viggo cried.

Ben's angry face softened as he saw his little brother's tears and calmly said, "Don't worry. I will get it for you, and Daddy will not be mad."

Baby Viggo stopped crying and looked at Ben, who helped him up.

Ben gave him a big smile.

That smile has been etched in his mind ever since.

Viggo's heart ached painfully as he looked around and screamed, "HELP! PLEASE SAVE THEM! PLEASE!!!"

Again, only silence echoed out of his mouth.

Ben ran along the river following the hat, with baby Viggo close behind.

"There!" Ben pointed at the bridge ahead and ran as fast as he could.

Baby Viggo got on the bridge beside Ben, trying to catch his breath. Ben's little body squeezed through the metal railing and lowered himself over the edge, his left hand holding the rail. His little right hand reached down as far as he could, but there was a big gap between his hand and the rushing water.

The hat was coming!

Fear overtook baby Viggo as he watched helplessly.

Ben let go of his left hand and fell toward the rushing water, his two feet pressed against the railing to stop him from falling further. The tip of his fingers blocked the hat from floating by it, bounced back and forth against his fingers. Baby Viggo looked surprised, and relief came over his face as his head poked through the railing.

Ben's fingers couldn't grip the smooth top part of the hat. He only pushed it back. Ben tried his hardest and accidentally pushed it too far back, causing the hat to float to his right and past his fingers.

Ben's brave little heart leaped for the hat and grabbed it with both hands.

A big splash echoed, and baby Viggo looked to his side.

Ben was gone.

Baby Viggo turned, ran to the other side of the bridge, and looked through the railing.

Ben's little arms reached out of the water, splashing, splashing.

His face was barely above the surface.

Then he disappeared.

His little hand was visible for a second and gone.

The chaos ended—only the rushing river's sound remained.

Baby Viggo stood there.

No reaction.

Emotionless.

A month later, heavy night rain poured onto baby Viggo as he stood there, soaked, watching his parents argue on the bridge. The metal railing was the only thing that separated them. His mother stood at the edge, crying, facing the terrifying darkness and loud rushing water below.

"Why! Why are you like this? We can get through this together!" his father exclaimed.

"I can't live like this anymore. I missed my Ben so much!" his mother cried.

"But this is not the answer! Please come back to the other side! I need you!"

Baby Viggo could barely see his mother's face as she turned to look at his father, not even a glance toward him. He couldn't tell if it was tears or rain on her cheeks. "I've been on the other side since that day."

She let go of the railing and fell backward.

"NO!" his father screamed.

"Mommy!"

No splashed. Just the loud violent water rushing by.

Baby Viggo screamed and cried as every big raindrop hit his little head and body. He felt the pain, raised his hands to block it, and yelled at the top of his lungs. His body flung side to side. With a sudden calmness, he lay bleeding in a pool of blood, heavily bruised. He barely lifted his swollen eyes and saw a blurred figure walking away into the darkness. It was the last time he saw him. The heavy rain continued to beat on his little body, but there was no more pain.

Everything became cold.

Very cold.

❖

Viggo sat up in bed, drenched in sweats, and looked around. The flickering flame in the lantern barely illuminated the semi-dark, cold room. Everything seem normal, but his body was cold. It had been a nightmare that had occurred more often since the night at the pond. He felt a tear roll down his right cheek, landed. He wiped the tear away and glanced at Leaf, sleeping soundly under the blanket.

Viggo buried himself back under the blanket. His heart ached, his lips pressed tightly together, and he thought, *Why... Why am I the one alive? I don't know how to make this life better.*

He closed his eyes, listening to his pounding heart. A hard blackness grew in his chest. The orange and yellow flame flickered its last breath and died. The cold room became dark.

Viggo leaped off the rope and landed in front of Mr. Sill's Metalware shop, with Leaf landing beside him. Mr. Sill wiped a dirty rag over a reflective metal plate.

"Good morning, pop!" Viggo greeted.

"Not good. We lost the championship, and who knows if we still have a Prince?" Mr. Sill said sadly.

"Don't worry about the big things your little head can't handle. You're given yourself a headache," Viggo replied, pulling out three gold plates, two gold napkins, and two silverware from Leaf's back and placing them on the table. "Let's talk what actually matters."

Mr. Sill held a gold plate against the light, its surface shimmering and reflecting his image. He bit the edge of the gold plate, leaving a slight indent. Mr. Sill gathered the items and walked to the back of the room. Viggo and Leaf looked at each other and exchanged a smile.

"Come on!" Viggo said excitedly.

They followed him into a small back room filled with boxes and a large dirty rug near the back wall. To the right was a lamp on the wall and a long table cluttered with broken metalware and other pieces. Mr. Sill placed the items on the table, turned around, and looked at Viggo and Leaf seriously, "Who did you kill? If the Totalist scrums catch you boys, there is no hope."

Viggo laughed, "We didn't kill anyone, old man! We've been walking on the road of luck and luxury!"

"There is no luck here, especially luxury. I won't tell anyone if you boys..."

"Look, old man! We might be thieves, but we ain't ruthless killers!" Viggo stared intensely into Mr. Sill's eyes.

Mr. Sill leaned back slightly with relief, "OK."

"So, how much?"

"I don't know," Mr. Sill replied, wiping his forehead with his dirty rag.

"What do you mean?"

"This is a gold plate! No one buys gold plate in Section 12! I might even get hanged for having it."

Viggo stared at the plate.

"Does that mean we can't sell it?" Leaf asked.

"I wouldn't," Mr. Sill replied.

"What about the silverware? You could at least do that, right?" Viggo asked.

Mr. Sill examined the silverware, "If we rough it up a bit, maybe."

"How much?" Viggo asked quickly.

"Five."

Viggo smiled, "Ten shins! Deal!"

"Five for both," Mr. Sill corrected.

"Both?! I got three for that silver platter, and you want to give me five for both new high-quality silverware?"

"I did not give you three. It was that old lady. This is a business, and I need to make a little."

Viggo looked at the silverware and turned to Leaf. He nodded.

Viggo took a deep breath, "Five for each, and I will throw in the golden napkins as well."

Mr. Sill laughed and said, "Why don't you work for me, boy, and you can make more than five shins a month. It's a decent job, and maybe someday you can own a store like mine?"

Viggo laughed, "I am not staying in this dump! There are more opportunities for us to do what we're doing than living in this hellhole every day."

"More opportunities to get locked up, boy! That is no life for a young, slick, annoying tongue like yours."

"Is that a compliment? Cause I don't need it. It doesn't give me shin or a ticket out of here. So if you want to help us get outta here, old man, pay us ten!"

"I can't even get myself out of here, boy."

"OK, fine! Five for both and no gold napkins."

Mr. Sill hands Viggo five shins, and Viggo tucked the rest away.

"What will we do with the other stuff, brother?" Leaf asked.

Viggo smiles and ruffs Leaf's hair, "We'll dine like kings on these gold plates and wipe our precious lips and buns with gold napkins after we buy something yummy!"

Leaf likes the idea.

They ran out of the Metalware shop and crossed the street.

Viggo and Leaf walked along the semi-dark alleyway and saw a hooded old woman walking toward them.

Viggo bumped into her. Her dry, rough hand grabbed his, which scared him as her eyeless face looked straight at him. He dropped the bag on his foot and kicked it to Leaf, who caught it and walked away.

"Sorry, ma'am."

"This is not by coincidence," her eyeless face leaned closer to his, "But fate. Care of the words you'll hear. It will be worth more than what you have in your hand."

There was a small black mirror in his hand.

He looked into it, tossed it onto the ground, and it shattered, "Crazy old woman!"

She pulled him up to her face, smelled him, and whispered, "Atop you flow... down to the abyss you go."

Her hands trembled as she let go of him and walked backward, laughing hysterically.

Viggo watched her as she disappeared into the dark alley, "Curse you, old hag, with your twisted phrases!"

Viggo met up with Leaf. He opened the bag, and roaches ran out.

"People here are sure poor," Viggo said, tying the bag and putting it in his fanny pack.

"What did you see in the mirror?" Leaf asked.

"It was a trick mirror with a black shadow. Let's go find Rain!" Viggo said, pretending to be unbothered by it.

❖

A knock echoed against the metal door.

Mr. Hairo opened it. "Good day boys, are you here to see Rain?"

"Yes, sir," Viggo answered, peering around to see if he could see her.

"It's Mr. Hairo." He smiled and added, "She left for the Street Market to handle deliveries and errands not long ago. Would you boys like to come in for some bread?"

"Yes, Mr. Hairo," Viggo and Leaf replied simultaneously.

They settled at the dinner table and helped themselves to the bread.

Viggo paused, looking up. "Mr. Hairo, how did you and Rain end up here?"

Mr. Hairo seemed taken aback by the question, laughing lightly. "That's quite a question for early morning."

He observed their attentive expressions as they continued to chew on the bread. They were genuinely interested in his story and were waiting for it to be told.

Mr. Hairo took a deep breath. "We've been here a long time," he began, reflecting, "Life is simple when you're young, single, and without children. I didn't worry much or overthink things. I was skilled at creating large machines and didn't consider their consequences. I wanted to see what I could achieve, how big and powerful I could make them. I was living my dream and earning well. I would work day and night, often for several days without sleep, eager to see the finished product. I was young, naive, and had nothing to lose! Before long, I got promoted rapidly up the ladder."

Mr. Hairo paused and smiled.

"It wasn't until baby Rain was born that I noticed the small things. Her tiny hands and sticky, curious fingers reaching out with affection, her laughter, her curiosity about the world, and her liveliness. It affected me and made me see the world in vivid colors, not just metal gray or machinery black. I reflected on what I had done and wanted for the future. Not just for Rain but for all the little children in Ourania. I researched the impact of my creations on the people it affected, and it wasn't the future I wanted to support or build. It wasn't the legacy I wanted to leave behind. It wasn't the world I wanted Rain to live in. Everything started to change for the better until upper management noticed the design and directional change."

Mr. Hairo took a deep breath, his tone growing more profound and serious. "Helen and I talked for months and decided to destroy all the machines that would cause inhuman pain and suffering. The plan was for Helen to erase all the data and programs while I initiated the self-destruction of all the machinery and robots. Accessing the files and programs was easy, but she didn't expect it to take so long to delete them. I was unaware as I was focused on bypassing the security panels."

Mr. Hairo's eyes filled with tears. "Helen was supposed to take Rain far away when I activated the self-destruction process. But she was still at the command center at the top. The first two sectors to our far right, holding buildings, exploded, followed by the second and third sectors to our left. I saw the windows shatter at the top command center. I looked back at her, and she screamed to me to save our baby! I told her to forget about the programs and that we needed to leave. But she wouldn't until all the programs were deleted from the core systems. Otherwise, everything we had done would be for nothing!"

Tears rolled down his face. Viggo and Leaf were engrossed in the story, their bread untouched.

Mr. Hairo continued, "The Elite Black appeared and rushed at her. The next thing I knew, there was an explosion at the top of the command center and the center sector where I stood."

"How did you survive the explosion?" Viggo asked.

"Someone activated the telegate on me to where Rain was. That was one thing I could never figure out. We destroyed a third of the Totalist core system, but they recovered their losses within two years and rebuilt bigger and stronger. What we did was futile. Rain lost her mom, I lost the love of my life, and we've been here ever since."

Mr. Hairo wiped his tears away.

"Sorry," Leaf said softly.

"For Rain's sake, I've numbed my memories enough to move on. I started doing repairs for the folks here," Mr. Hairo said.

Viggo thought momentarily before asking, "Can you rebuild a big machine?"

"What kind of big machine?"

"A Hell Raptor?" Viggo inquired.

Leaf's eyes widened.

Mr Hairo tapped his chin thoughtfully, "Yes, yes, but where will you get the parts or the shins to buy them?"

"That's all I needed to know! Leave the rest to me; this will be our ticket out of here, Mr. Hairo! I'll take all of us to a new place!" Viggo exclaimed.

He shoved the remaining large bread into his stuffed mouth and muffled, "Luf... go..."

Leaf quickly stuffed bread into his mouth, hopped off his chair, and followed Viggo, waving goodbye to Mr. Hairo.

Viggo and Leaf ran along the building.

"Brother, where will you find a Hell Raptor?" Leaf asked, trailing behind.

"If I remember correctly, there's one crashed in Vellatine Forest years ago, and I believe it's still there. If we can find and repair it, it'll be our way out! We don't need to rely on anyone else or do their dirty jobs!"

Leaf's eyes and smile widened. "We can leave together as a family?"

"Yeah, together as a family. I like that!" Viggo said happily.

For once, he felt good, and there was real hope.

"But even if we find that Hell Raptor, how will we get the shins to fix it?"

Viggo stopped, turned around in the alleyway, and whispered to Leaf, "Arison has a few of these plates, too. If he used White String connections, we can find some buyers."

"You're so smart, brother!" Leaf exclaimed.

"Of course!" Viggo laughed as they continued their way.

"Are we going to look for Arison?"

"No. We'll find Rain and tell her the great news!" Viggo smiled.

"Oh yeah! I bet she'll be super happy!"

❖

Rain stepped into a dilapidated building, the inside dimly lit and shadowy. She approached the counter, swung her teddy bear backpack around, and pulled out a metal cylinder. A large, imposing man in a baggy hoodie crept up behind her and settled beside her, scrutinizing her closely.

"Where's Rayco?" Rain asked.

"In a hurry?" the man inquired.

"Only when you're around," Rain responded without glancing at him.

The man chuckled, his hand slowly reaching behind her. A high-pitched gear revved up in the metal cylinder.

"It will blow in ten seconds," Rain warned.

"Am I supposed to be scared?" he sneered.

"Take your gentlemen's charm elsewhere, Drak," Rayco said, emerging from behind a black curtain and taking the metal cylinder from Rain's hands.

Rayco wore a long brown cloak, a hoodie, and heavy black leather attire. As a member of the SKA Rebels, his brown eyes carefully examined the metal cylinder and then deactivated it.

"She clean?" Rayco asked.

"Clean? Since when do you check me?" Rain retorted.

Rayco glanced at Drak, who nodded.

"Four days ago, we lost all communication with Queen Bee and our other teams. Moving forward, everyone gets checked," Rayco explained.

"What happened?" Rain inquired.

"We're mostly in the dark, but it seems likely the Totalist Federation did something," Rayco replied.

"Well, I know nothing about it," Rain stated.

"You sure?" Drak leaned in and sniffed.

Rayco slid a silver shin across the counter to her.

Drak chuckled. "A businesswoman. Are you going to buy me a drink?"

Rain ignored him, picked up the silver shin, and tucked it into her back pocket. She looked at Rayco. "No wonder you have no business with this gnat hovering around."

"It's chaotic right now, and the Totalist Military is everywhere. Stay low and out of sight, Blue Rabbit," Rayco advised.

"Worry about your friend here," Rain said, walking out.

Rain exited the dark alley and saw Viggo and Leaf approaching a large crowd in the Street Market's center. She ran to them, leaped in front, and twisted their ears.

"Owww!" Viggo and Leaf screamed, pushing her hands away.

Rain laughed and smiled, "What are you two doing here? Are you trying to sell some useless things?"

"We're looking for you," Leaf said, grinning.

"Me? Why?"

Leaf looked at Viggo excitedly. "Tell her, Brother, about the family!"

Rain looked puzzled.

"I've got a plan to get us out of here!" Viggo said.

Rain twirled around laughing, hopped onto a large rock, and sat on it. "Your crazy ideas never work, Vgoo! Why should I believe this one will?"

"Well, your dad thinks it's a good idea, and it's our ticket outta here!" Viggo said.

"Don't drag my daddy into your wild and crazy ideas. We need to stay low and not draw attention. Something bad happened."

"What happened?" Leaf asked.

"Something bad!" Rain said.

"Bad?"

"Yeah, so don't do anything stupid like Vgoo," Rain smiled.

Leaf nodded.

"How do you know something bad happened?" Viggo asked.

"I have my connections," Rain winked.

"Well, we're not involved in whatever that 'bad' thing was. We're minding our own business," Viggo said.

Rain jumped off the rock and said, "Well, for the SKA to be shaken like this..."

Viggo covered Rain's mouth as strangers passed by, heading toward the growing crowd in the Street Market.

Viggo whispered, "Shhh! Don't mention SKA!"

Rain pushed his hand away. "I ain't scared!"

"Well, you should be because I'll be very sad if something happens to you," Viggo said.

Rain was momentarily speechless.

"Brother, there are a lot of Totalist over there. Should we go check it out?" Leaf asked.

"Last one there is a stinky big toe!" Viggo shouted, taking off.

"No fair!" Rain yelled.

Leaf laughed and ran with them toward the crowds.

Chapter 18

Vdin

General Crocrovich sat regally on his throne, encircled by Totalist soldiers wielding steel batons to keep the crowd at bay.

The crowd gathered around. It got larger and larger. Viggo, Rain, and Leaf squeezed their way to the front, standing next to Mr. Sill.

"What's happening, old man?" Viggo asked.

Mr. Sill never take his eyes off the scene, replied, "I've lived here my entire life and not once have I seen them step foot in Section 12. Either something bad has happened, or something terrible is about to. Nothing good comes around here. Be ready to run if something goes wrong."

"Don't worry about us, old man. Make sure your rusty legs can get moving," Viggo retorted.

"Better get out of my way when that happens. You might get trampled," Mr. Sill shot back without looking at Viggo.

"Hmph! Don't be screaming my name when you fall, old man."

Mr. Sill smacked Viggo on the head with a rolled-up newspaper. "Learn to respect your elders, Viggo!"

"Respect is earned! Not given!"

The crowd buzzed with excitement as General Crocrovich's throne rose above them. Silence fell as he stood and addressed the masses.

"Donte cronimon. Let justice serve through the actions of my power!" General Crocrovich proclaimed, tossing a bag onto the ground as gold shins to spill out. The crowds surged forward, pressing against the soldiers.

"What mortal men would not fight and die for it?" General Crocrovich taunted.

The crowds pushed harder despite the soldiers beats them back with their batons.

"What betrayal will you offer for this bag of gold shins? Which of your brothers or sisters will you sacrifice to dig your dirty, filthy fingers into the luxurious world of Venice? Come claim this bag if you have what I seek."

The crowd murmured amongst themselves.

"Wow! Is that what gold shins look like, brother?" Leaf asked with eyes wide opened.

"Yeah, and he owes me one!" Viggo replied.

"That's a lot of gold shins. They look like little yellow rocks!" Leaf observed.

"Can you imagine what our life would be like with all those gold shins? I can see it now," Viggo said dreamily.

Viggo imagined himself with one arm around a giant chicken leg and the other around Rain. He laughed on top of big muffin clouds. Leaf envisioned himself hugging a giant blueberry, running and laughing.

"Yeah... that would be nice. What do you think he's looking for, brother?" Leaf asked, snapping out of his daydream.

"Wish I knew!" Viggo replied, eyes still on the prize.

"Whatever it is, It won't be good," Rain said, her worried voice tinged.

Slitter Clyde approached the soldiers. "I like to speak with General Crocrovich," he announced.

A soldier scanned his face. "Slitter Clyde. Age sixty-seven. Exiled Majestic Royal. No Match," the Female Voice Scanner reported.

"Go ahead," the soldier permitted.

The soldiers parted, allowing Slitter Clyde to approach General Crocrovich.

"You think you have what I'm looking for?" General Crocrovich questioned, his eyes narrowing.

Slitter Clyde rubbed his hands together, eyeing the bag of gold shins on the floor and nodding. "Oh, yes, great General Crocrovich! I'm just an old gentleman and do not want much trouble. My only wish is to see the great Venice and live in its glory for the remainder of my time."

He lowered his head, glancing side to side with a sinister grin. "Do you see that big, ugly gargoyle butcher over there? I hear he wants to put your head on his chopping block for the flies to enjoy."

"Watch what saying, old man! I slice tongue and feed to rats!" the Gargoyle Butcher shouted furiously.

Slitter Clyde raised his eyebrows, still rubbing his hands. "See."

General Crocrovich snapped his fingers. A gunshot rang out, and the Gargoyle Butcher fell to the ground, dead. The crowd screamed and backed away from the body. Viggo looked around the rooftops and spotted Totalist snipers with long rifles aimed at the crowd. Slitter Clyde continued to rub his hands, smiling. Four soldiers dragged the dead body and placed it before General Crocrovich as his gold throne descended.

"O great General Crocrovich, now that I've saved your life, may I receive my rewards now?" Slitter Clyde asked eagerly.

"Is that all you have for me?" General Crocrovich asked, his tone skeptical.

"Umm..." Slitter Clyde glanced nervously at the crowd, seeing only angry faces. He walked closer to General Crocrovich and nervously asked. "If I tell you this, will you escort me to Venice with my bag of gold shins?"

"If you have what I'm looking for, I will personally escort you to Commander Bazyli for a job well done. But if you've wasted my time, the gold shin will be the last thing you'll ever see."

Slitter Clyde swallowed hard. "Umm, I know the SKA Rebels have been a thorn in your side. Rumor has it they disrupted a critical project our great Totalist Military was working on. I know someone in the crowd linked directly to the SKA Rebels' commander."

Intrigued, General Crocrovich leaned forward. "Is that so?"

Slitter Clyde scanned the crowd, his eyes narrowing. Rain ducked behind others, trying to stay hidden. A dark green hooded figure began pushing through the crowd.

"There! The one with the dark green hood," Slitter Clyde shouted, pointing excitedly.

Four soldiers moved quickly, knocking others out of the way and firing their assault rifles into the air. The crowd ducked, and the soldiers aimed their weapons at the fleeing figure. "Halt! Or we'll shoot!"

The green-hooded person stopped. The soldiers dragged the figure to General Crocrovich and threw her to the ground. A soldier pulled back the hood, revealing a bruised woman with long black hair. He yanked her head back, forcing her to look up. A soldier scanned her face.

"Ivy Black. Age twenty-six. SKA Captain. No Match," the Female Voice Scanner reported.

Slitter Clyde clapped his hands excitedly.

"A captain? What a prize. You should already know it's an automatic death sentence for you. But if you hand over the key, I will ask Commander Bazyli to spare your pitiful life," General Crocrovich said.

Ivy gritted her teeth as her head was yanked back harder, but she remained silent.

A soldier smacked the back of her head, forcing her head to bow.

She slowly raised her head, defiant. "You can crawl back to your rotten pig and tell him he failed!"

"For a ranking captain, your etiquette is lacking, but you should have anticipated what's coming," General Crocrovich replied coldly.

A soldier raised his steel baton. General Crocrovich nodded, and the soldier began beating Ivy repeatedly. The crowd murmured in distress, some pushing against the soldiers in a futile attempt to intervene.

Leaf turned to Viggo, desperation in his voice. "Brother, we have to help her."

Viggo shook his head, his expression grim. "Leaf, these are Totalist snakes. Look at what they're doing to her! If we step in, we'll be beaten too. They don't care about you or me—only their desires. So keep your voice down and your head low, like Rain."

Leaf ducked his head a bit, glancing anxiously at Ivy.

The crowd grew more agitated, rocks and trash flew passed General Crocrovich.

General Crocrovich held up the emblem and shouted over the chaos, "Quiet! I hold the Black Onyx Emblem of Vellatine here. Anyone who disrupts our proceeding will be given the Legacy Death. You will be executed on the spot, along with your entire family and friends!"

The crowd stopped and fell silent. General Crocrovich stepped down from his throne and approached Ivy Black. The soldier who had been beating her was exhausted, his baton hanging by his side. Blood ran down from Ivy's head and mouth.

General Crocrovich knelt beside her with a mockingly sympathetic expression, "It aches my big, gentle heart to see you like this. Why don't you just tell me? I will use the power within me to stop this pain."

Ivy painfully lifted her head, her right eye shut tightly from the blood. She looked up at him.

He smiled insidiously. "That's it, little sheep. Beg me, and I will help you."

Ivy spat blood onto General Crocrovich's face. His smile vanished, replaced by a look of cold fury. He rose slowly, his face dripping with her blood.

"When you try to serenade them, you get filth instead," General Crocrovich said as his steel boot cracked the side of Ivy's face, sending her crashing to the ground. The soldier resumed his assault as Ivy lay there. Another soldier quickly approached General Crocrovich, wiping the blood off his face and boot.

"This will be your last warning," General Crocrovich said. "Speak now, or you die here."

The soldier ceased his beating, and a second soldier pressed his rifle against Ivy's temple.

As Leaf touched his black magnetic belt, he felt a surge of determination and recalled Mr. Hairo's words, "Be a man who stands up for others, especially those in need."

Leaf's expression hardened with resolve. He stepped out of the crowd, moving toward the soldiers.

"Leaf!" Viggo and Rain shouted in unison.

Viggo grabbed Leaf's arm, pulling him back. "What are you doing? Are you crazy? Did you not see what just happened?"

"Brother, I don't know what to think anymore. All I know is I cannot stand by and watch anymore," Leaf said, his voice trembling but firm.

"She's an SKA Rebel! It's an automatic death sentence!" Viggo replied quickly.

"If it were me up there, brother, I'd wish someone would save me."

"But it's not you! I know what your heart is going through right now. Like everyone here, we must watch for our safety first, and we cannot risk getting involved."

Leaf pushed Viggo's hand away. Viggo quickly grabbed him again.

"Leaf! What are you going to do? How are you going to stop them from killing her?"

"I don't know."

"We are NOT heroes, Leaf!"

Leaf looked at Viggo with deep sadness. "I know, and we don't have to be, brother."

Leaf slowly pushed Viggo's hand away. He turned around and walked away from the crowd.

"LEAF! Why did you let him go!" Rain yelled in confusion.

"His heart already made up," Viggo said, not knowing what to do.

Leaf approached the soldiers. They talked, and a soldier scanned his face.

"Name Unknown. Age Unknown. Description Unknown. No Match." the Female Voice Scanner reported.

The soldier reported back to General Crocrovich, who glanced at Leaf and nodded. Another soldier escorted Leaf to him.

"Who are you, kid?" General Crocrovich asked.

"Leaf."

"Why are you not in our database? Who are your parents?"

"I don't know. But I want to make you an offer."

"An offer?" General Crocrovich raised an eyebrow, intrigued.

Ivy struggling to see through the blood and glance at Leaf.

"What could you possibly offer that's more valuable than a SKA Rebels Captain?" General Crocrovich asked.

"Me. You can do whatever you want with me. I promise I won't be difficult, sir," Leaf said, staring at General Crocrovich with unwavering conviction.

General Crocrovich's amusement faded, replaced by a grim seriousness. "Don't waste my time, street rat. Killing an abandon kid like you would be the least sinful thing I've done. Take it as a warning. Now leave!"

"Sir, can you promise not to hurt her anymore? Please!"

General Crocrovich's gaze twisted with menace. "Tic... Toc..."

"Tic?" Leaf repeated, confused.

Boom! A bullet struck Leaf's chest, sending him sprawling backward into the crowd. The crowd scrambled away from Leaf as the electricity surged through his body, causing him to convulse in pain.

"LEAF!" Viggo shouted, rushing to his side.

Viggo grabbed Leaf's shoulders, but the electricity went through his body, and Viggo yelled in great pain. The electricity shock through the black core in his chest. Irritating it as it grew larger. Viggo quickly pulled away from Leaf.

"The bullet turned into a large, electrified object on his chest! We need to remove it safely!" Rain yelled.

Viggo looked around desperately. The crowd scattered away from them.

Viggo ran to a burly man. "Mister! Can I borrow your wooden stick? Please!"

"Get you're own!"

Leaf screamed in agony and lost consciousness.

Viggo grabbed the stick, but got punched and kicked away.

Viggo scrambled back to Leaf and stared at the electricity. Without thinking, he grabbed the round object from Leaf's chest with both hands and pulled with all his strength despite the electric shocks coursing through him.

Viggo screamed in pain!

Traces of electricity burned through his skin, shocking him from head to toe. Rain leaped forward, kicking Viggo away from Leaf and into the crowd. The object fell to the ground, and the crowd smashed it with their weapons.

Rain quickly checked on Leaf.

Blackness surrounded Viggo.

The loud commotion drowned out.

Viggo opened his eyes, his body was floating on the black water, but he felt paralyzed. Small waves rippled outward from underneath him.

A faint sound echoed from under his ears, "Viggo..."

The ripples got bigger and bigger as the echo got louder and louder, "Viggo!"

Black hands emerged from the black water beside his face on each side. Each long finger wrapped around Viggo's face tilted his head back and dragged it under the black water. He choked violently, and the air bubbles escaped his mouth. He shook his head viciously and tried to pull it back up, but it remained submerged. Viggo's eyes opened to a faceless, blue flame eyes staring back, only inches away. Viggo screamed underwater. All the bubbles escaped his mouth.

The last air bubble slipped from his lips as he stared at it.

His body convulsed, movement slowing down until it ceased entirely.

Viggo, in a daze, pushed Rain away, screaming!

Rain pulled Viggo into her arms to stop him from fighting her, "Viggo! Stop!"

She hugged him tight, "Wake up!"

His bloodshot eyes opened, tears streaming down from his black, bruised eyes. He was terrified, disoriented, and strangers surrounded him. His hands were burnt, and he couldn't stop shaking.

Rain looked at Viggo, concerned etched on her face. "You okay?"

Viggo's gaze landed on Leaf lying on the ground. He instantly jumped up and scrambled over to him.

"He's unconscious but breathing," Rain said, tearing her sleeves to wrap around Viggo's burned hands.

Mr. Sill pushed through the crowd, shouting, "What monster would just walk in here and hurt our Totalist and children?"

The crowd murmured loudly, their anger building. Mr. Sill turned to General Crocrovich. "I don't know what you're looking for, but we don't have it here. All we have left is our dignity! We won't let bullies like you take that from us!"

The crowd roared, "Hooorr... Rraaa!"

A crowd member shouted, "We've had enough of your game!"

"Yeah! No More!! Rrrroooaaaa!" The crowd's chants echoed through the Street Market.

Another crowd member shouted, "And your unfair, disgusting justice!"

The crowd raised their arms and weapons, chanting, "Rrrroooaaaa! Hooorrrraaaa!"

Viggo stared at Leaf's small, fragile body, he seems lifeless.

The chants faded from his hearing as uncontrollable anger surged within him, blackness rapidly spreading through his body.

The crowd united, ready to fight!

Viggo's gaze locked onto General Crocrovich.

"Viggo, I hope you're not thinking what I'm thinking?" Rain said, looking at him with worry.

Viggo stood and walked towards the crowds.

"Viggo! We got Leaf back! Let's get out of here!" Rain yelled, but Viggo was unresponsive, continuing forward.

Mr. Sill grabbed Viggo's arm. It was ice-cold. "Don't. You said it yourself: We're not heroes!"

Viggo turned to Mr. Sill, his bloodshot eyes sending chills down the old man's spine, and he let go of him.

"What happened to you, boy?" Mr. Sill whispered, seeing the darkness within him.

Viggo turned and walked away.

Mr. Sill lifted Leaf in his arms. "We have to go now! We can wait at my store until everything is calm down!"

"What about Viggo?"

They pushed through the back of the crowd. "I don't know. Something triggered him after seeing Leaf like this. There comes a time when a boy will be tested to become a man. He will do what he must, whatever the outcome is. I just hope that boy doesn't get himself killed."

Rain looked back at Viggo, who pushed through the crowd and disappeared.

This is the first time he wasn't acting out of profit or selfishness. Leaf really does bring out the good in him. Rain thought.

Viggo approached the soldier and handed him a red coin. The soldier took it to General Crocrovich, who smirked and nodded.

Viggo stood before him.

"What do you remember now, boy?" General Crocrovich asked.

Viggo's eyes blazed with fury.

"I said..." General Crocrovich asked again.

"A shadow," Viggo said coldly.

"You can do better than that if you still want that gold shin," General Crocrovich said, producing the gold shin from his pocket.

"A murderous shadow with blue flame eyes."

General Crocrovich examined Viggo's bloodshot eyes. "Like the one I'm seeing..."

He paused, realization dawning. "A Solkin. Look into which one was hunting in Section 12 during that time."

"Yes, sir!" the soldier responded.

"What else do you have, boy?"

"Release her," Viggo demanded sternly.

General Crocrovich laughed. "Why are the little boys playing heroes while grown men cowardly stand aside, whining?"

Ivy looked at Viggo.

"What is she to you?" General Crocrovich asked.

"It's what Leaf wanted."

"The idiot boy who got himself killed?"

"You will pay for that as well."

General Crocrovich aimed his pistol at Viggo's head, "Tread carefully, boy. Leave now, or you will lie next to him."

General Crocrovich spun his pistol away, walked to his throne, and sat down as it began to rise. He tossed the gold shin to Viggo, leaned back and rested his cheek on his fist. Viggo stood there, staring at him with the gold shin in his fist.

The crowd roared in anger.

Slitter Clyde nervously stepped away from the thunderous uproar and turned to General Crocrovich. "Ahem... O great General Crocrovich, you can take me to Commander Bazyli now for the job well done I did for you?"

General Crocrovich glanced over. "You earned yourself a gold shin. Now get what you deserve and go back to your roaches."

"O great Gen—"

"Scram, roach! Before I crush you!"

Slitter Clyde scrambled to the bag of gold shins, his eyes widening at the treasure on the floor.

"Wing Destroyer Alpha," General Crocrovich called.

"What are your orders, General Crocrovich?" Wing Destroyer Alpha replied.

"Any match in the crowd?"

"Negative, General Crocrovich."

Slitter Clyde approached General Crocrovich, clutching the bag. "Here is your bag of the gold shin, commander—I mean, General Crocrovich," he stuttered.

"I see you understand your place well."

"Ooo, yes, if I may add, I still have lots of Intel about the SKA Rebels.

Maybe one of those could get you promoted to a higher rank you so deserve. O, great General Crocrovich." Slitter Clyde bowed his head.

General Crocrovich laughed and leaned close. "Not surprising that a roach like you who crawls in and out of this dump will have some intel. Very well, I'll entertain your offer. But one wrong move and my boot will crush your spineless shell!"

Slitter Clyde smiled, keeping his head down. "O, thank you, great General Crocrovich, for your wise advice."

General Crocrovich turned to Ivy. "Lucky you. We're not done yet. Unlike your fellow criminals, you'll see another brutal day."

General Crocrovich pushed a button on his throne. A transparent crimson shield enveloped him, Ivy and Slitter Clyde. Two soldiers held Ivy and secured her hands with magnetic cuffs.

General Crocrovich turned to his men. "Lock and Load."

The soldiers activated their crimson shields, stepping back from the crowd to form a tighter, circular formation as they holstered their batons.

"Look! They're scared of us!" a skinny crowd member yelled.

"Hoooorrrrraaaa!" the crowd roared.

The crimson shield glowed around each soldier as they swung their rifles over their shoulders and aimed at the crowd.

Some scattered and ran, but most held their ground, brandishing their weapons in the air.

"Don't let these snakes intimidate you! Stand strong!" a strong crowd member yelled.

"There's more of us than them!" another yelled.

The crowd roared in unison, "Hooorrrrraaaaa! Hooorrraaaaa!"

They marched forward, closing in on General Crocrovich and his ground troops.

"You came to the wrong side of town, little general!" a skinny crowd member shouted.

"Welcome to hell!" a strong crowd member added.

"Hooorrraaaa! Hooorrraaaa!" the crowd chanted with great morale and unity.

General Crocrovich gazed below and raised the Black Onyx Emblem of Vellatine. "Light them up."

Viggo stared at General Crocrovich, fearless.

Mr. Sill and Rain reached the end of the Street Market and unlocked the Metalware Shop doors.

A Wing Destroyer Alpha's sonic boom across Section 12 Street Market shattered all the windows. A Phoenix bomb exploded, blasting Mr. Sill, Leaf, and Rain through the doors.

Walls of fire consumed the street, sparing only those within the crimson shields. The condensed tin-can buildings contained the blaze like a rusty metal barrel.

Screams filled the air as many burns and died. The soldiers marched past the dead, shooting at those who was trying to fled.

No one was allowed to escape.

The soldiers in the circular formation rotated their automatic rifles around and aimed at the black, swirling fire tornado at the center. The black flame contracted, absorbing into a small, dark shadow figure.

General Crocrovich observed with a smirk. "Are you that dark shadow, Solkin?"

The shadow's eyes opened, blue flames flaring out.

Slitter Clyde stumbled backward, clutching the bag of gold shins tightly to his chest.

General Crocrovich glanced at the Totalist Sniper on the rooftop. The sniper fired, aiming a headshot at the black flaming figure. The bullet split in mid-air, killing two soldiers who were guarding Ivy. The sniper's rifle split in half, and he plummeted from the rooftop. General Crocrovich turned back to the dark shadow, now meeting its intense, blue-flamed gaze.

"Kill him!" General Crocrovich commanded.

The dark shadow vanished.

All twenty soldiers on the ground died in an instant.

Eight were hurled across the firewall with crushed chests.

Two split in half, falling to the ground.

Five burst through the burning tin-can building.

Three were flattened into the ground.

One flew towards General Crocrovich.

General Crocrovich caught the last soldier by the neck, tossing him aside effortlessly.

The remaining snipers fell from the rooftop, lifeless.

General Crocrovich landed on the ground, facing the dark shadow.

"I've never seen a Solkin move like this. Who are you?" General Crocrovich demanded.

"Vdin," the shadow replied.

He tore the magnetic cuffs off of Ivy's wrists. She looked at Vdin, astonished, before sprinting away.

"Are you here to avenge all these lost souls…?" General Crocrovich began but was cut off as a black arm shot through his left shoulder, narrowly missing his heart. Sparks flew as Vdin withdrew his arm.

His hand pierced my armor! General Crocrovich thought, clutching Vdin's arm in place with his left hand.

General Crocrovich smashed his fist into Vdin's face, then rammed his elbow into his temple. Vdin's head snapped downward from the impact, momentarily dazed. General Crocrovich pressed his pistol against Vdin's forehead.

Mr. Sill rubbed his head, disoriented. "What happened? Leaf!"

Leaf was burning on top of him. Mr. Sill quickly rolled him over, extinguishing the fire. Rain rushed over, frantic.

Rain checked Leaf's breathing. "He's still alive."

Mr. Sill stood, mesmerized by the shattered windows. The entire street was engulfed in a wall of fire. His voice shook as he spoke, "Those monsters!"

A black electrical fireball shot through the shop into the back room. Mr. Sill sprinted after it. Inside, he saw a burning body. Grabbing a dirty rag, he smothered the flame. He pulled the charred hoodie, revealing an electrical device covering the face, electricity coursing through the body. Mr. Sill wrapped the rag around a metalware fork handle, stabbed the object, and yanked it off. The burnt wound on the face healed instantly, the black pigments fading, and the blue flames around the eyes disappearing. Within seconds, everything appeared normal again. Viggo opened his eyes.

"Viggo?" Mr. Sill helped him up.

Rain entered, carrying Leaf. "Viggo! What happened?"

Viggo, still dazed, replied, "I don't know."

Mr. Sill cut in, "Now is not the time for chit-chat. Can you walk, Viggo?"

Viggo kicked his legs and squatted up and down. "I can."

"Good. You guys need to get out of here now!" Mr. Sill ordered and continued, "If they're willing to burn the Street Market, who knows what other evil intentions that monster have."

Mr. Sill walked to the lamp on the wall and pulled it down. A table and rug in the corner slid aside, revealing an underground passage.

"Go! Quickly! This will lead you to the outer edge of Section 12. It should be safer there!"

"That's close to my house. We can rest there until Leaf regain consciousness," Rain said.

Viggo hoisted Leaf onto his back and turned to Mr. Sill. "Thank you."

Mr. Sill managed a small smile. "I guess that blast knocked some manner into you. Now hurry and go!"

Viggo and Rain dashed down the tunnel. Mr. Sill watched them. Viggo noticed there wasn't any footsteps following behind him and turned around. Mr. Sill was still standing at the entranceway.

"Hurry up, old man!" Viggo called.

Mr. Sill shook his head. "I will be staying."

"What? Why?"

"This is my place."

"It doesn't matter to them. They'll kill you, and another grumpy old man will take over your place!" Viggo argued.

"You won't understand, boy. Now hurry and go!" Mr. Sill urged.

"You can start over! You can start over with us! We're getting out of Section 12—all of us!" Viggo exclaimed, his frustration evident.

"This is the only thing my old pop ever gave me. This is all I have left and memories of him. If I leave and let this place get burned down, a good part of me will die with it. It's too late for me, boy. I'm too old. Now go and make a life for the three of you. Live! "

Viggo, exasperated, responded, "Let's go, old man! I don't want to see another friend gone!"

"I told you, you won't understand. Thank you, Viggo. Thank you for caring and considering me a friend."

"Fine! I will never understand why someone would rather die than live, stubborn old bones!" Viggo snapped, turned around and chased after

Rain as tears flew by his eyes. Mr. Sill was the only father figure Viggo has known.

Mr. Sill watched as Viggo and Rain sprinted farther into the tunnel. He closed the hidden passage, covered it up, and deeply breathed.

A loud crash of metalware echoed from the front of the store. Mr. Sill stepped out, finding General Crocrovich and Slitter Clyde walking toward him.

"Where is that dark shadow, Solkin?" General Crocrovich demanded.

"I don't know what you are talking about." Mr. Sill said, his voice steady despite his fear.

"If you're hiding him, we'll burn this place to the ground," Slitter Clyde threatened.

"From the look of things, I think most of it already has," Mr. Sill replied sadly, eyeing the flames consuming the tables and other flammable materials in the Metalware Shop.

Slitter Clyde flipped the table over, sending metalware crashing to the floor. "Step aside."

"There's no one in there," Mr. Sill said defiantly.

"Then step aside," General Crocrovich ordered.

"I told you, there is no—"

General Crocrovich shot him in the head and chest. He was thrown into the back room. They stepped inside.

"I guess he was telling the truth, my General Crocrovich," Slitter Clyde said.

General Crocrovich glanced around the back room and exited, leaving Slitter Clyde alone. Slitter Clyde eagerly stuffed silver utensils into his pockets and grabbed some silver metalware. As he did, he stepped over Mr. Sill, who was being electrocuted.

A couple of knocks echoed through the old, rusty door.

Mr. Hairo opened it, his face registering surprise. "Hello..."

A Totalist Captain and his two soldiers stood at the door.

Mr. Hairo's gaze drifted past them to the street, where war vehicles and additional soldiers were visible. They dragged children and elderly Totalist from their homes, beat them, and scanned their faces before executing them on the spot.

"We're cleaning houses, as you can see," the Totalist Captain said, his tone cold.

He watched Mr. Hairo closely for any reaction.

Mr. Hair gazed back at him in a calm expression. "I'm sorry, I thought you were someone else. I don't want any trouble."

"Good. Can we come in?" the Totalist Captain asked, pushing the door wide open. The two soldiers moved to shove Mr. Hairo aside forcefully.

"I'm having dinner right now," Mr. Hairo said, glancing at the setting suns and noticing the fire and smoke in the distance.

"This early?" The Totalist Captain raised an eyebrow, observing the two suns dipping below the horizon.

"Yes. May I ask what this is regarding?"

Ignored Mr. Hairo's question, the Totalist Captain surveyed the room. "How many people are living here?"

"Just my daughter and I."

The two soldiers knocked things over and kicked aside clutter as they walked around the room. The Totalist Captain's eyes landed on some mechanical parts on the table. He walked toward it.

"Where is she now?" the Totalist Captain asked, picking up an oily part.

"She's out."

The Totalist Captain examined the mechanical part before asking. "Are you a scientist?"

"No, just an old mechanic. I repair small machinery for the folks around here." Mr. Hairo said, trying to keep his voice steady.

The Totalist Captain picked up a glass cylinder, scrutinizing it. "Do you know what happens to those who try to meddle in science?"

The Totalist Captain dropped the cylinder, shattering it on the floor.

The Totalist Captain's eyes landed on a Level Five hydro accelerator on Rain's desk. He reached for it and picked it up, "Why would a low-life mechanic need a classified level-five hydro accelerator?"

Mr. Hairo fumbled for words.

"Arrest him!" the Totalist Captain commanded.

A second soldier moved toward Mr. Hairo.

"Wait! Wait! I can explain!" Mr. Hairo pleaded as panic rose in his voice.

"Down on your knees and put your hands behind your head!" the second soldier ordered.

Mr. Hairo dropped to his knees as a magnetized cuff snapped around his wrists, securing them tightly. The soldier scanned his face.

"Dr. Marty Hairo. Age Fifty-Eight. Chief Weaponry Researcher, escaped fugitive. No Match." the Female Voice Scanner reported.

The Totalist Captain's tone shifted to surprise. "Who would have thought such a well-respected scientist would betray his country and now live as a criminal among the scum?"

"He's NOT a criminal!" Rain shouted, bursting through the door with a firm grip on a metal pipe.

She swung the pipe, landing a solid hit, cracking the second soldier's face. He flew across the room and crashed to the ground, unconscious. Rain hurled the metal pipe at the Totalist Captain, who blocked it with his arms. Drawing his silver patrol pistol, the Totalist Captain aimed at Rain's back as she ran toward the kitchen.

"No!" Mr. Hairo cried out, hurling his body into the Totalist Captain.

They collided into the work table, crashing to the ground. A few shots rang out as Mr. Hairo head-butted the Totalist Captain repeatedly until he fell unconscious.

The third soldier swung his automatic assault rifle at Rain, opening fire. Bullets ripped through the wall, destroying anything in their path. Rain leaped over the dinner table, dragging it down for cover. The table splintered under the barrage of bullets. Rain rose, brandishing her rock cannon. She fired at the third soldier.

It missed!

The soldier ducked behind a corner to reload.

Viggo, carrying Leaf securely on his back, leaped from a fallen chair and tackled the third soldier. He drove his red powder-coated palm into the soldier's face, rubbing it into his eyes. The soldier screamed in agony.

Viggo seized the rifle, swinging its butt into the soldier's temple, knocking him out cold. He then sprinted to the front door and kicked it closed.

"We gotta get outta here now! The soldiers from across the street are coming this way!" Viggo yelled, shoving large furniture in front of the door. "I'll try to hold them back!"

Rain nodded and frantically searched the second soldier, finding the demagnetizer. She used it to release her father from the cuffs.

Mr. Hairo winced in pain as he sat up. "Rain... I'm so... glad to see you're OK."

Rain leaned over, hugging her father tightly, "I'm glad to see you too, Daddy! We need to go now!"

"I don't think I'll be joining you, kids," Mr. Hairo said through gritted teeth.

"Why?"

Mr. Hairo revealed his leg and the side of his stomach.

Blood seeped through his clothes.

"O no! No! No!" Rain panicked, her eyes filling with tears.

The heavy knocking sounded from the door. Viggo pushed hard against the furniture with his legs, struggling to keep it closed as the door tried to force open.

"Captain! Are you OK?" The soldiers shouted from outside.

The glass window shattered into the house! Automatic rifles aimed through the opening. Viggo aimed at the window and fired, causing the soldiers to scatter and seek cover. Bullets pierced through the windows and door. They whizzed past, narrowly missing Viggo's head. He quickly ran to Rain's side.

"Viggo, can you please take care of Rain for me?" Mr. Hairo pleaded, his voice strained while looking at him.

Viggo tightened his jaw and nodded.

"Don't say such things! They already took Mom away from us! I'm not going to lose you too! I don't want anyone except you!" Rain cried out, her voice filled with desperation.

She pulled her father's arm over her shoulder and attempted to lift him, but he was too heavy. Tears streamed down her face as she struggled. Mr. Hairo placed a comforting hand on her shoulder. "Honey, you and I both know..."

"No! I'm not leaving you behind!" Rain shouted angrily, her determination palpable. Rain lifted him with all her might and cried, "You are all I have left!"

Her heart-wrenching plea pierced his soul. With a pained but resolute tone, Mr. Hairo said, "OK, honey!"

He grabbed the edge of a nearby table and pulled himself up. They slowly stood together. Mr. Hairo placed weight on his injured leg, which sent a jolt of pain through him. He instantly collapsed, and they both fell to the floor. Rain tried to lift him again, her determination unyielding. The Faith of One necklace slipped from her shirt as she struggled, catching the light and shimmering before Mr. Hairo.

Mr. Hairo smiled weakly. "That must be a very special necklace."

Rain, with teary eyes, nodded. He grasped the table's edge once more, pulling himself upright.

"Rain, you carry Leaf," Viggo said, "and I can help your dad."

Rain looked at Viggo with sudden relief.

Viggo quickly unknotted the cloth wrapped around him and gently laid Leaf down. Mr. Hairo put his arm around Viggo, leaning most of his weight on him. They moved as quickly as possible towards the back door. The blood covered the side of Mr. Hairo's leg, and the sheer pain etched shock into his face with each step, but he kept going for Rain's sake.

Blood soaked the bottom of Mr. Hairo's shoe, causing him to slip. They both fell to the floor, Mr. Hairo groaning in great pain. Viggo tried to help him up, but the pain had become too overwhelming for Mr. Hairo to bear, and he exhausted all his energy.

Turning to Viggo, he begged, "Viggo, please, please take Rain! Protect her from any harm!"

Rain ran to her father and embraced him, burying her face in his chest as she cried. Mr. Hairo wrapped his arms around her, tears streaming down his face.

He patted her hands and steadied his tumbling voice the best he could, "You've been such a gifted little girl ever since I can remember. Now, you're a strong-minded, beautiful young lady with a heart to be loved by many. Always look forward to the future, honey, and everything will be fine. You made your mom and I very, very proud!"

Rain sobbed uncontrollably.

Mr. Hairo composed himself, "Don't worry, Honey. They won't do anything to me."

Rain raised her tear-streaked face, "You can't trust them! They are monsters!"

"I was once their Chief Weaponry Researcher. I am still very useful to them. Rain, take the artifact with you and remember what I told you."

Rain hugged him tightly, "OK. I promise I will come back for you, Daddy! I promise! We will go to a better place far away from here!"

"I promise to take care of Rain no matter what happens, Mr. Hairo!" Viggo said.

Mr. Hairo smiled and nodded.

Viggo helped transfer Leaf from Rain's back and securely tied him to his back. Loud kicks came from the front door, and the furniture scraped against the ground.

Viggo aimed at the window and door, firing to keep the soldiers at bay.

Rain rushed to the table, grabbing the Level-Five hydro accelerator, the metal sphere, the box on the top shelf she had promised not to open until she was eighteen, and a few more items. Rain opened a wooden plank on the floor next to the table, retrieved the artifacts, and stuffed them into her backpack.

"Can you get me the small black box behind the toolbox on my table?" Mr. Hairo asked.

Rain ran to him with the box, "I will come back for you, Daddy! Wait for me! I promise! I love you!"

"I love you to the moon and beyond, honey!"

She nodded tearfully, turned away, and fled with Viggo through the back door.

Mr. Hairo opened the box. Inside was a family photo of Rain and her mother from when Rain was six. Beneath the picture was a small black button device.

Mr. Hairo lifted the photo, his voice trembling with emotion. "Helen, our daughter is all grown up now. She's just like you—clever and beautiful. I know you'd be so proud of her. It's been ten years since you left us, and not one day do I not think of you. I missed you so much."

The front door exploded inward. Soldiers stormed in, quickly securing the area. A Totalist Captain approached Mr. Hairo, noting the pool of blood beneath him.

He scanned the scene: three soldiers incapacitated, a face covered in red powder, and a missing automatic assault rifle.

The Captain whistled sharply, signaling a team of soldiers to search through the back door.

"Great, Dr. Hairo, where are they? I know you didn't take down two experienced soldiers and a captain alone. You're an educated man, not a fighter."

Mr. Hairo remained silent.

The Totalist Captain knelt beside him and saw the family photo. He snatched it from Mr. Hairo's hand and examined it. "A sweet family photo. A cute little girl. Now, where is she?"

Mr. Hairo stayed silent.

The Totalist Captain pressed his thumb into Mr. Hairo's wounded leg. He screamed in pain.

The Captain drew his pistol and pressed it against Mr. Hairo's other leg. "You can tell me now or take unnecessary pain. We'll find her either way."

Looking at the photo again, the Totalist Captain smirked. "She must be a young woman by now. I'll make sure to take good care of her, personally."

Mr. Hairo's eyes were locked on the photo. He tried to snatch the photo back as they tugged back and forth. The photo ripped in half, and Mr. Hairo fell backward. The Totalist Captain fired his pistol. Mr. Hairo screamed in agony, clutching his leg!

The Totalist Captain stood up, glanced at the ripped photo with a smirk, and slipped it into his pocket. "Take him."

Mr. Hairo looked at the torn picture of his wife. The pain was overwhelming. He closed his eyes, tears streamed down his face as his lips trembled, and thought, *I'm sorry I couldn't protect our little girl. Rain, I will always be with you!*

Mr. Hairo activated the black device in his hand.

KA-BOOM!

The small tin can building erupted in a massive explosion.

The shock wave roared across the mountainside, causing Rain and

Viggo to stumble and stop. They turned and looked down at the destruction below. The tin can building, once home, lay in ruins, flattened and engulfed in flames. Debris was scattered everywhere, and dead soldiers were strewn across the ground. The remaining soldiers, severely injured, staggered amidst the wreckage.

Rain's legs gave way, and she sank to her knees. Her eyes, filled with tears, were fixed on the flaming wreckage falling from the sky. The grief was overwhelming, and her voice cracked as she screamed into the desolate air.

"DADDY!"

Chapter 19

Ignite!

The night enveloped Rain and Viggo in a dim orange glow, their silhouettes stark against the backdrop of the fierce blaze below. Black and gray smoke billowed into the sky, and the fire burned with relentless intensity. Viggo, carrying Leaf on his back and clutching a rifle, stood silently beside Rain.

The cold wind whipped around them.

The yellow and orange glow gave a slight warmth to her tear-streaked face. Everything she knew and loved was gone. Now, she is the only one left in this world. That sudden realization made her lonely as anger gradually rose.

Viggo observed the scene below, where Totalist soldiers were regaining control amid the chaos. He gently touched Rain's shoulder, "Rain..."

No reaction.

"We should get going. They'll be swarming this place soon."

Rain remained silent, her gaze fixed on the destruction.

"Rain..." Viggo repeated, his voice tinged with urgency.

"I'm not going."

"There's nothing we can do here."

Rain became quiet.

"Rain..."

Determination hardened her features. She grabbed a rock and stood up, her fists clenched. "Daddy might still be alive."

Viggo's voice wavered with shock, "Rain, the chance of him surviving that explosion..."

"You weren't there. You don't know exactly what happened."

Viggo's frustration grew. "We both knew his leg was injured and..."

"Stop!" Rain's voice broke. "We never leave those who are in need behind! That's what he always taught me. I'm not leaving without him!"

She turned to leave, but Viggo grabbed her arm. "Where are you going?"

"I'm going back!"

"You can't!"

She yanked her arm free. "Don't tell me what I can or cannot do!"

"You're not thinking clearly right now!"

"That's my daddy down there! He's all I have!"

"You still have me!"

"I don't need you!"

Her words stabbed through his heart. He clenched his jaw.

Rain turned back toward the path.

"Don't be blinded by your emotions! Look down there! There are so many of them. What do you expect to accomplish with just a rock?"

"I promised I'd come back for him, and I am doing just that!" Rain snapped, walking away.

"Rain!"

She kept walking.

"Don't make your dad's sacrifice meaningless!"

Rain stopped, her face flushed with anger. "He's NOT dead!"

"Rain!"

"You can do whatever you want and run away!"

"I'm not running away!"

"Then don't get in my way!"

"I'm not letting you go on a suicide mission! You can't take on all the Totalist soldiers down there! Open your eyes!"

Rain stared at the blazing fire, "I don't care how many there are. I don't care if my emotions blind me. I don't care if it costs me my life. I don't care. I'm going to save my daddy!"

Viggo stepped closer, trying to reason with her. "Be realistic, Rain!"

Rain slowly turned to face him, her voice trembling. "What is real when everything you've ever known is about to be gone?"

"But what you want to do right now is not the answer. I know you're upset, and I understand—"

"You will never understand! You never had a dad!" Rain yelled, her eyes blazing with fury.

"I don't need a dad to see what you're becoming!"

Rain slapped Viggo across the face. His cheek quickly reddened, the sting sharp, but his heart ached even more.

"You will never know how it feels to lose not one but two parents!" she cried.

"What! Do you think I just fell out of the sky…?" Viggo paused, then continued, "You're right! I would never understand how it feels to lose someone so close and dear to you for so long. But what I know is none of us wanted this! None of us! Leaf is hurt, and I'm about to lose you, too! If your dad were here, he would beg you not to throw your precious life away like this."

"If it were you down there, I would do everything I could to save you. I will not stand here and give up, especially when it's my Daddy!"

"You're doing the same thing that Leaf did. I let him go because his desire to help someone in need was so strong I could feel it in his eyes! Now, look what happened!"

Rain glanced at Leaf, barely clinging to life. Her anger softened into sorrow. She looked at the rock in her hand.

"We're not in a position to do anything right now. We don't have to always fight. We can walk away for now. Rain. Please."

Viggo watched as she closed her eyes, tears streaming down her rosy cheeks.

"Who's there?" a Totalist soldier shouted.

Viggo and Rain turned to see three soldiers nearby, their flashlights shining directly at them. Rain threw the rock, hitting one of them in the head and knocking him down. The soldiers opened fire.

Viggo ducked.

Rain screamed and hit the ground.

"RAIN!" Viggo yelled, pulling up his rifle and firing back.

The soldiers scattered for cover.

Viggo ran to her, "Are you hurt?"

"Just a small graze on my arm."

Viggo helped her up, and they ran into the bushes. The soldiers fired as they chased them.

A soldier radioed in, "Squad Leader, we have three suspects in the forest near the explosion. They are armed and dangerous."

"Send your pin location to Hell Raptor," the Totalist Squad Leader ordered.

"Roger."

Inside the Hell Raptor cockpit, an infrared display showed the suspects running, projected on the windshield.

"Location received. We have three suspects confirmed."

Viggo crashed through the branches as a deep hum sound coming from the distance.

"I can fight them!" Rain shouted.

"No! Do you hear that? That's the sound of death! We might all die if you don't quickly realize what's happening! If you want to do something, survive this and fight another day!"

Bullets zipped by them. They rushed out of the bushes and ran to the wooden bridge. Rain stopped in front of it, the sound of raging water echoing from the darkness below. Memories flooded Viggo's mind, paralyzing him with fear. Rain stepped onto the bridge—it wobbled and creaked under her weight. She took a couple more steps.

The soldiers emerged from the bushes and saw her in the middle of the bridge.

"Freeze!"

Bullets zipped by, hitting parts of the bridge and rope. Bullets struck around Viggo's feet, snapping him out of his daze.

"Run!" Viggo screamed as he sprinted across the bridge.

Viggo's heavy footsteps broke through one of the old wooden steps. His chest smacked against the wooden plank, and he slid down through the hole. His hands frantically reached for anything to grab onto as he slid backward, fear gripping him. His fingers caught the edge of a wooden plank.

"Rain!" Viggo yelled, struggling to pull himself up with the weight of Leaf on his back.

Rain turned back and saw Viggo hanging, his face pale with fear. "Hold on!" she shouted, rushing towards him.

She grabbed Leaf, pulled with all her strength, and lifted him as Viggo scrambled back onto the bridge. He untied the knot that held Leaf to his back, panting heavily. Bullets continued to zip by. Viggo turned to face the soldiers with his rifle and fired. The soldiers ran for cover behind the bushes.

Inside the Hell Raptor cockpit, the windshield scanned the faces of Viggo, Rain, and Leaf.

"Squad Leader, we have one unknown suspect, but no match on all three," the Hell Raptor pilot said.

"Then, get rid of them," the Totalist Squad Leader replied.

"Roger that."

The bridge swung wildly from the incoming gust of wind.

Rain held Leaf tightly in her arms, "Why couldn't Daddy just wait for me?"

"I'm sorry. He must have his reasons," Viggo said.

"What reason is worth risking your life over?" Rain cried.

Viggo looked at Rain, his voice softening. "You."

Sparks and flares lit up behind them as the Hell Raptor launched its missiles.

Viggo saw the uncontrollable pain in her eyes, tears streaming down her face.

The bridge exploded.

They were thrown into the raging river below. The Hell Raptor's spotlight followed them as they struggled in the water.

Viggo tried to keep his head above the freezing water and saw Rain and Leaf ahead of him. "Leaf! Rain!"

Viggo swam toward them, tucking his arm under Leaf's armpit to pivot his upper body above the water.

Rain gasped for air, her arms flailing wildly as she struggled to stay afloat. The roar of the rushing water grew louder and deeper, echoing ominously in the darkness ahead.

"What's that?!" Rain shouted, her voice trembling with fear.

"I hope it's not what I think it is!" Viggo yelled back, his voice strained against the roar.

Without warning, they were swept over the edge of the waterfalls.

❖

Rays of sunlight filtered through the small opening at the top of the cave, casting a soft glow over the blue bioluminescence pond. The water trickled down the opening, creating a serene cascade. Rain lay by the pond's edge, the gentle blue light from the water caressing her left hand. The soothing sound of the continuous splashing slowly roused her from unconsciousness. She opened her intense blue eyes as the bioluminescence enhanced her hue. She gazed at the rippling water beneath the small waterfall, watching it fade away as it rippled outward.

She felt a profound sense of calm and wondered, *Am I dead?*

She lifted her hand, watching the glowing water drip off her fingers. With a groan of discomfort, she rolled onto her back. Her face jerked from the pain, and soreness stretched through her entire body. She noticed the dancing reflection of the water on the cave ceiling and long green vines hanging near the top opening and along the cave walls.

The cave was dimly lit and cold.

Rain pushed herself up with her hands pressing against the soft, moist moss beneath her. The realization hit her that her moment of anger had clouded her judgment, making their situation worse. Ignoring the persistent pain, she rotated her backpack to the front, retrieved a small cube, and carefully slid her fingers over its top surface in a coded sequence.

A blue halogen line spread from the cube's center, forming a stylish design as it transformed into a robotic squirrel. The squirrel's body outline lit up with a thin green glow, indicating its energy levels. It began to move, wandering around with a purposeful gait.

"Marshmallow, lights on to forty percent," Rain ordered.

Marshmallow's body illuminated half of the cave in white light. Rain surveyed the surroundings: wet moss covered the ground, the walls were black with jagged rocks jutting out, and a small stream flowing from the pond into the dark tunnel. She spotted Viggo lying nearby.

She helped him sat up as he coughed up water.

He grabbed her hand, concern etched on his face, "You alright?"

She stood up, and Viggo's eyes widened when he saw Marshmallow behind her with white eyes, "Watch out! There's a glowing demon behind you!"

Viggo instinctively pulled Rain behind him. Marshmallow, frightened, played dead. Its lights dimmed.

"It's OK, Marshmallow. This is Viggo. He's our friend," Rain reassured.

The green light traced around Marshmallow's body and began to glow again. The robotic squirrel opened its eyes, got back up, and ran around in a circle.

"It's not a demon?"

"No, he's one of my robotic pets."

Viggo leaned forward for a closer look. Marshmallow did a backflip.

"Wow! That's cool! Leaf would... Leaf!" he exclaimed, suddenly looking around.

Marshmallow hid behind Rain. "He's not here," Rain said softly.

Viggo quickly got up and felt great pain, "Oow!"

"Take it easy." Rain said, supporting him.

"We have to hurry and find him! Do you have any ideas where we are?" Viggo asked urgently.

"My best guess is that we fell over the waterfall, floated down the river, and fell through there," Rain said, pointing at a small opening at the top of the cave.

She walked over to the blue bioluminescence pond. "Looks like we have two options: the dark tunnel behind us or diving into the pond to see if there are any passages to lead us out."

Viggo examined the pond, the dark tunnel, and the top of the cave, "If we fell through that hole, can't we just climb back up?"

"Those sharp rocks look too slippery, especially with the rushing water. It would be nearly impossible."

Viggo turned his attention to the pond. "I'll take my chances with the dark tunnel. I'm not sure how long I can hold my breath underwater, and whatever makes this water glow might be poisonous. Marshmallows might not even survive the water."

Marshmallow jumped into the water and was doing backstrokes. The blue bioluminescence glowed vividly around its body and the splashing water.

"Wow, really?"

"All my gear is water and dust-proof. Marshmallow is programmed to be an excellent swimmer," Rain explained.

"Why don't we just send Marshmallow down there?"

"Even if he found a pathway, it doesn't mean you or I could fit through it or make it with one breath."

"Then why did you even suggest the pond?"

"To gauge your logic and judgment."

"You're testing me?"

"From here on, things will get very dangerous. Any of us making a bad decision could cost us our lives."

"I thought you were ready to give up your life?" Viggo asked.

Rain looked at the sparkling water, "I was. I could have gotten us killed, and nothing good would have come from it. I'm sorry, Viggo."

Viggo smiled, his voice full of warmth. "Me too. And if you need a strong, muscular shoulder to cry on, I'm here."

Rain poked his shoulder.

"OWW!" Viggo shouted.

"I thought so," Rain said with a smirk.

"Give it a few days. Then you can touch me again."

Rain rolled her eyes and began walking along the edge of the cave wall. "Nothing we can say or do right now will change what's happened."

She picked up a long, thick wooden stick.

"What's that for?" Viggo asked.

"If we are going to be walking around this place, I need to ensure the ground is stable and safe."

"That's a great idea!"

Viggo's eyes had adjusted to the lighting of the cave. He stretched his body up and down and side to side, making a painful face each time. "There, that should help."

"Doesn't seem like it did."

"Now my body is full of pain. I'm pretty much numbed by it."

"Your logic doesn't make sense."

"It does to my body," Viggo laughed.

He walked to a different part of the cave, picked up a hand-sized rock, and tossed it up and down, noting it was lightweight.

His eyes widened as he spotted an enormous rock. "Whoa!"

Viggo dropped the small rock and walked over to the larger one on the ground. He spread his legs wide, squatted down, and lift. His struggle and shakiness showed as he tried to walk with a giant rock between his legs.

"What's that for?" Rain asked.

"Protection. I don't know what we might run into," Viggo said, his voice straining.

"It looks cumbersome and heavy."

After five labored steps, Viggo's crab legs stopped walking, "I don't... think... I..."

He dropped the rock. Instant relief spread through his body, and he dusted himself off.

He quickly caught up to Rain as they walked toward the dark tunnel along the stream. "I think I'm much deadlier with just my two bare hands!"

"Then why are you hiding behind me?"

"I'm protecting you in case something scary attacks from behind!" Viggo said, walking closely behind her.

As they moved deeper into the tunnel, the cave grew darker. Marshmallow's light led them forward until an orange glow appeared up ahead. They emerged from the tunnel and stood at its edge. Before them, a massive rock glowing orange stretched from the ceiling to the water below.

"What is that?" Rain asked, eyes wide.

"I don't know, but I bet it's worth more shins than we could swim in!" Viggo said excitedly.

"I don't think we should touch it. It's not natural for a rock to glow."

"There's a lot of unnatural things in this world," Viggo replied. "Besides, it shouldn't be too dangerous. Look at all those beautiful things living down there."

They looked around. The area was stunning, with beautiful wildflowers blooming around the giant orange rock. Deer grazing nearby, exotic birds with long tail feathers flew about, singing melodiously, and colorful fishes swam in the clear water.

"It is a nice place," Rain said, "but best not to touch that thing until we know exactly what it is."

Giant ropes of roots dangled from the ceiling to the ground beside them.

"It doesn't look like there are any exits. How do these animals get in and out of this cave?" Viggo asked.

Rain watched the water moving up and down the cave wall. "The water."

"Water?"

"The water level drops," Rain explained. "Once it's low enough, the animals can swim out. Marshmallow, lights off."

Marshmallow turned off its light.

"You mean the water is being sucked out of the cave right now? How?" Viggo asked.

"Low tide," Rain said. "When that occurs, it opens up the cave. During high tide, the water floods back to the ground level below. It acts like a door. It looked like a long way down from here, though, about 200 feet."

Viggo tugged on a nearby root rope. "The roots seem sturdy enough. Leaf and I climb down this kind of path every morning. If you're scared, I can carry you."

"Don't worry about me."

Viggo smirked and walked off the edge, disappearing from view. Rain leaned over and saw Viggo saluting her as he fell backward. He turned mid-air and kicked the side of the root, propelling him to another. He hopped from root to root as he descended.

Rain turned to Marshmallow, "Looks like our turn."

Marshmallow jumped onto Rain's shoulder. Rain pulled her backpack around and retrieved a larger box. She slid her fingers in a coded sequence, and the blue halogen light stylishly outlined in the center transforming into a giant robotic hawk. Its metallic wings had dual rotating air engines to lift it.

"Booster, bring us down there."

Rain held the stick horizontally with both her hands. Booster swooped down, grabbed the stick with its claws, and lifted her, flying toward the ground. Rain passed Viggo on her way down.

"What the heck is that? Why didn't you tell me you have one of those? I could've ridden on it!" Viggo called out.

"You left before I could even offer," Rain replied.

Rain landed on the ground. "Thank you, Booster."

Booster perched on Rain's left shoulder and folded its wings. Viggo landed beside her, slumping against the ground with his arms spread out. He tilted his head back and looked up, exhausted. "Boy, I'd hate to leave anything up there."

Viggo felt a small rock under his hand and picked it up.

"Didn't I say not to touch it?" Rain said.

"I didn't! It touched me. But it's OK. See? Nothing happen."

Viggo held up a small piece of the orange glowing rock, marveling at it. "Can you imagine how many shins we could get for this?"

Rain glanced out of the cave, seeing the clouds reflected in the water. "Shins are the least of my worries right now. Let's go."

"Right now, we can go look for Leaf! Once we find him, we can show him this cool place and sell this giant glowing rock for zillions of shins! Then all three of us can go anywhere in Ourania!"

"There's only one place I need to go, Gear Light," Rain said.

"Gear Light? Who's there?" Viggo asked.

"Drais McCloud."

"Drais McCloud?" Viggo repeated, puzzled.

Rain raised the stick. Booster flew up, grabbed it, and headed over the water towards the cave exit.

"Wait, who is Drais McCloud?"

She flew out of the cave.

"Wait! What about me!" Viggo shouted at them.

Viggo looked at the glowing rock, sighed, and muttered, "Sometimes being a rock is less stressful."

He stowed the glowing rock in his fanny pack, jumped into the water, and swam out of the cave exit. It led out to the middle of the river, and Viggo saw Rain making her way towards land. He glanced back at the now pitch-black cave opening, which had grown wider as the water level dropped. The structure of the cave's mouth, reached to the bottom of the riverbed, looked ominously like a monstrous maw. The scary sight made him swam faster. The river was wide, with a strong current and many unknowns lurking beneath the surface.

What if there are sea monsters? I don't want to die! Viggo thought anxiously.

Onshore, Rain stood under the warm sunlight, her eyes closed and she tilted her face toward it. Marshmallow's body lit up green and blinked as it recharged from the sunlight. Viggo walked out of the water and noticed Rain's face sparkling in the sunlight.

He found her beauty enchanting.

Sensing Viggo's gaze, Rain opened her eyes.

He looked down, wringing the water from his cloak sleeves.

"Why do you have to be so perverted?" Rain asked, a hint of annoyance in her voice.

Offended, Viggo shook off the water and retorted, "Perverted? It's natural for one to be attracted to the beauty the world has to offer."

"Don't stare too long; your eyes might get poked out," Rain teased.

"Why did you head off like that? I could have been eaten by a sea monster or something!" Viggo retorted.

"It could have been worse. I could have left you here without waiting. We're at Forest Edge, where the river meets the Grand Ocean. Forest Edge is full of unknown secrets and dangers. I wouldn't be surprised if sea monsters do lurked in the water."

Viggo glanced farther down the river as it merged with the Grand Ocean. "You knew this, and you still left me? You'd be sorry if a sea monster had eaten me!"

"Well, isn't it obvious?" Rain replied.

"What is?" Viggo asked, confused.

"The sea monster doesn't want anything to do with the bottom of the food chain."

Viggo couldn't tell from her tone if she was joking or being mean. Regardless, he was relieved that her thoughts weren't focused on her father.

"So you know, this is premium ribeye quality!" Viggo said, patting his flat stomach.

"Don't try to sugarcoat yourself. It doesn't make you any tastier." Rain shot back.

"Sugarcoat? My statement is factual. I could have died."

"Well, you didn't. If you want to keep yapping, then go under a tree. Dark clouds are rolling in from the Grand Ocean."

Rain glanced at the sky, noticing the dark clouds gathering. She realized today marked the ninth day. Today was her mom's death anniversary, and her father wasn't with her at Forest Edge. She stared at the vast Grand Ocean, where large dark clouds brewed and lightning struck in the distance. Viggo noticed the sudden shift in her demeanor.

"Rain?" he asked softly.

She turned to him, her face serious but her eyes filled with sadness.

"We should hurry and look for Leaf," Viggo said.

Rain nodded, and they continued walking along the river.

The water had become rough due to the approaching storm. The birds had stopped chirping, and a family of deer had hurried upstream. Forest Edge had grown eerily quiet as the wildlife took shelter.

"Where should we look first?" Viggo asked.

"First, we need to find out where we are."

"That's easy. I can climb one of these trees and see which direction is Vellatine City or Section 12."

"No need for that. Booster, take flight, and locate Vellatine City."

Booster took off from a nearby tree and soared above the forest canopy.

"Vision on," Rain instructed.

Eyeglass piece emerged from each side of her temple and connected in the center, forming one solid sunglasses. Through Booster's eyes, Rain saw the beautiful Vellatine City perched on a mountaintop, its towering statues visible. The name "Vellatine City" appeared, indicating it was sixty-seven miles north.

"Marshmallow, return," Rain ordered.

Marshmallow leaped into Rain's palm and transformed into a small cube she stowed in her backpack.

"You. Are. So. Cool!" Viggo exclaimed.

"Vision off," Rain said.

The eyeglasses retracted back into her temple.

"Man, you've got the coolest toys! When did you get all this stuff? Can you make me something like that?" Viggo asked, eyes wide with admiration.

"No," Rain replied curtly.

"Why not?"

"It would be mistreated."

"For crime-fighting!" Viggo insisted.

Rain shot him a skeptical look.

"Fine! I don't need your fancy gadgets when I've got my trusted deadly weapons and traps!" Viggo said, swinging his fanny pack to the front, pulling out Mr. Stinky by its tail.

"You still have that skunk? Didn't you say your fanny pack is waterproof?"

"Yeah."

"So how does he breathe when no air gets in?"

Viggo shrugged, "I don't know."

"Is Mr. Stinky dead?"

Viggo leaned close to Mr. Stinky, "Mr. Stinky is probably just sleeping."

"You need to take better care of your pets. I give my unlimited warranty of love and care." Rain poked Mr. Stinky a few times on its belly. Mr. Stinky's eyes popped wide open, and he snarled at Rain! Mr. Stinky sprayed yellow liquid goo all over their faces. They gasped and screamed. Viggo dropped Mr. Stinky in shock.

Viggo's nose sniffed the yellow liquid goo by his upper lip, "O, my eyes!"

Rain continued to scream horrifically from the smell. They rushed to the river, fiercely splashing water on their faces. Viggo dunked his head in the water.

"Who in the world carries a skunk in their bag!" Rain yelled.

Viggo's head bobbed in the water, blowing bubbles. Rain yanked him out, and Viggo gasped for air, taking deep breaths, and suddenly paused.

"You stink, Rain!" Viggo shouted, jumping up and running away.

"You stink!" Rain called after him, giving chase!

Viggo laughed, "Stinky Rain! Stinky Rain!"

Rain's eyeglasses instantly transformed outward and connected. She stopped.

Her sunglasses detected six soldiers to the southeast, twelve from the east, and five across the river on the higher ground to the west.

"Booster, return! Vision off," Rain ordered.

Her sunglasses retracted into her temples. Boosters flew back to her, diving towards her with its wings closed like an arrow. Boosters transformed into a box, gently landing in her open backpack with a slight air release from the bottom.

"Viggo, we gotta get out of here! There are soldiers everywhere, and six are heading our way."

"Do you have any cool gadgets to make us invisible?"

"No, and this stinky smell isn't helping."

"Who told you to poke Mr. Stinky?"

"I thought the poor thing was dead!"

"Shhhh... I have an idea, but we'll need Mr. Stinky's help."

Rain and Viggo ducked into the bushes by the river.

Nearby, six soldiers approached and stopped near the bushes.

"What is that smell?" the Totalist Squad Leader asked, wrinkling his nose.

"It smells like rotten eggs!" the first soldier added.

The soldiers covered their noses as they edged closer to the bushes.

"It's getting stronger," the second soldier whispered.

Mr. Stinky suddenly leaped from the bush, startling the soldiers. They jumped back, drawing their patrol pistols as Mr. Stinky hissed angrily.

The soldiers and Mr. Stinky locked eyes. With a quick handstand, Mr. Stinky arced his tail back. A brown leaf fell from the tree, swirled, and landed between them. Mr. Stinky unleashed a rapid spray of yellow liquid goos in their direction.

"Run!" the Totalist Squad Leader shouted.

The goo flew past the Totalist Squad Leader's ear and splattered onto the second soldier's face, leaving him in shock with his mouth agape. The others ducked and scrambled, trying to evade the attack. Yellow goo covered most of them as Mr. Stinky continued his handstand, fumes rising from his tail. Bullets whizzed by, hitting the ground around Mr. Stinky. He bounced around, dodged the bullets, and dashed into the bushes. The bullets shred the bushes apart, leaving only a single branch.

"There, problem eliminated," the Totalist Squad Leader said.

"But you still stink, sir. But in a nice way, I mean in a good tone, not that you're fine. But I'm not saying you're not fine!" the second soldier babbled.

The Totalist Squad Leader smacked the second soldier on the back of the head, "Your breath isn't all cherry and honey, either. Let's rendezvous at the rally point and clean up, boys."

"What about our search, Sir?" the third soldier asked.

"We'll continue the search later. A storm's rolling in," the Totalist Squad Leader replied.

"Yes, Sir!"

The soldiers retreated in the direction they came from. Viggo, Rain, and Mr. Stinky emerged from the water.

"Thanks for pulling me under," Viggo said, brushing water off of him.

"I'd do it again if I had to," Rain smirked. "I didn't expect them to be so harsh on a small animal like Mr. Stinky."

"They have no heart! Thanks for saving us, Mr. Stinky!" Viggo said, kneeling to pet him.

"Thank you, Mr. Stinky!" Rain added, kissing him on his head.

"What about me? It was my idea to use Mr. Stinky," Viggo complained.

"You're right. You deserve a reward," Rain said with a grin.

Viggo's eyes sparkled with anticipation. He puckered up his lips and closed his eyes. Rain lifted Mr. Stinky, wiggled his tail, and let him lick Viggo's lips. Viggo was taken aback by the intense roughness on his lips and face. Mr. Stinky's big brown eyes met Viggo's eyes. His face was in horror! Viggo stumbled backward and dashed to the river and dunked his face in.

"Boy, Mr. Stinky sure seemed happy!" Rain laughed as she set him down.

Mr. Stinky shook himself vigorously, splashing water everywhere.

"Return!" Viggo commanded.

Mr. Stinky happily hopped back into Viggo's fanny bag, comfortably beside the little glowing rock and the rat. Viggo zipped up his fanny pack and turned to Rain.

"Look like he likes the way you smell," Rain commented with a smile.

"I hope you're satisfied," Viggo said, wiping his face.

Rain smiled, "Yeah, I am."

They continued their journey and climbed to the top of a hill.

"Earlier, Booster detected a piece of dark clothing past the waterfall, further up the riverside, and there was a faint blood trail." Rain said.

"Blood trail? I hope it's not Leaf! Let's hurry!" Viggo said with concern.

Without hesitation, they started up the path toward the waterfall.

High above the clouds on the left palm of Commander Bazyli's statue stood Lieutenant General Bradstone, Major General Vic, General Crocrovich, Colonel Steel, and Admiral Baylee before Commander Bazyli. He was focused on the Hologram Ourania World, which flickered with various data and projections.

"Now that we have lost, what would you like us to do next, Commander Bazyli?" Major General Vic asked, his voice laced with apprehension.

"Proceed with the transition of knowledge and power," Commander Bazyli ordered, his voice unwavering.

"Yes, Commander," Major General Vic responded.

"We're just going to hand it over to the Ukko Empire?" Colonel Steel asked, a note of skepticism in his tone.

"The unspoken rule of the tournament dictates that the winner gain control of the Stone of Truth, Stone Runes, along with all information, until the next nation claims victory," Major General Vic explained, his gaze fixed on the hologram.

"We were so close to unlocking the Stone of Truth's secrets and power. We had one of the Stone Runes, and X was nearly within our grasp!" General Crocrovich angrily exclaimed.

Commander Bazyli's gaze turned sharply toward General Crocrovich.

"My apologies, Commander Bazyli," General Crocrovich said softly, placing his hand over his heart and respectfully bowing.

"Regardless of the outcome, we will rise above all," Commander Bazyli declared.

A sense of ease calmed the concerned atmosphere.

"What about King Roy?" Admiral Baylee inquired.

"What about him?" Major General Vic responded.

"Do we need him?" Admiral Baylee continued. "With Commander

Bazyli leading us, we can rule Vellatine City without any complications."

General Crocrovich nodded in agreement.

Lieutenant General Bradstone listened with an amused expression.

"Is that so?" Major General Vic asked skeptically.

"He's always complaining and panicking. Overreacting…" Admiral Baylee started, but Major General Vic cut him off.

"Such a tone could land you in the deepest ocean." Major General Vic warned sharply.

Commander Bazyli turned his gaze to the Hologram Ourania World and spoke with resolve. "The Royal Family has been with us since the inception of Vellatine City. King Roy is a crucial barrier between us and the so-called elites who constantly inquired demands. He has allowed you to focus on your tasks without being bogged down by trivial issues. With the Lighting of Dreams over, Lieutenant General Bradstone, I need you to search for the two remaining Stone Runes."

"Isn't that Ukko's responsibility now?" Lieutenant General Bradstone asked.

Commander Bazyli's gaze sharpened.

Lieutenant General Bradstone bowed his head in acknowledgment and vanished.

"Admiral Baylee, you will meet Emperor Razen and process the power transfer," Commander Bazyli added.

Admiral Baylee bowed his head and vanished.

"Colonel Steel, present the Timeless Island mission and the X Chamber failure at The Lilac Garden, Section Two, tomorrow," Commander Bazyli instructed.

"Yes. Commander Bazyli," Colonel Steel replied, his head bowed and hand over his heart before disappearing.

"General Crocrovich, what is the status of X?" Commander Bazyli asked.

"We are working diligently on it, sir," General Crocrovich said, bowing his head with his hand over his heart.

"Major General Vic."

"Yes, sir."

"Assist General Crocrovich after the report tomorrow."

"Yes, sir."

❖

The roaring waterfall thundered over the cliff, churning into the rough pace of the river below, and surrendered seamlessly to its flow. Viggo and Rain gazed up at the majestic cascade from the opposite bank, feeling the mist kiss their faces.

"Leaf would have loved this. He always had a soft side for things like this," Viggo remarked.

Rain took in the waterfall's beauty. "You knew him well."

Viggo fell silent, his expression darkening as he realized they had both fallen into the river and disappeared. The haunting memories and a persistent sadness would forever linger in his heart.

They continued down the slope and along the river. Viggo noticed a small, torn piece of dark cloth clinging to a tree branch by the river, marked by a thin, diluted red trail.

"Do you think that's Leaf?" Rain asked, her voice tinged with concern.

Viggo nodded and studied the trail in silence. He unzipped his fanny pack, retrieved a bag of pepper, and led the way through the dense underbrush.

"Viggo!" Rain whispered urgently, pointing to a small dark hole behind the thick trees.

"I hope it's not a poisonous animal's hideout," Viggo said, his voice laced with anxiety. He unzipped his fanny pack again and pulled out more bags of pepper.

Thunder cracked across the sky above them, making them both flinch.

"Why don't you stay out here? If you hear me screaming, run for your life," Viggo suggested in a low voice.

"I'm not afraid," Rain replied, her blue eyes reflecting determination.

Her words and unwavering gaze left him grateful to have her by his side.

"Let's go."

They entered the dark, musky cave, with only the faint light from the entrance illuminating their path. Inside, it was pitch black, and their eyes struggled to adjust. Viggo pulled out a green glow stick from his fanny pack, and every step echoed with their nervous feet.

Viggo stopped abruptly.

Rain bumped into him with a soft yelp, "Oow..."

A small, green outline moved slowly ahead of them.

Viggo's eyes adjusted to the darkness and followed a shirtless boy who paused before them.

"Who are you?" Viggo asked.

"I'm Ignite."